STEPHEN THE MARTYR

# STEPHEN THE MARTYR
*— a novel —*

## ROGER ELWOOD

VINE
BOOKS

SERVANT PUBLICATIONS
ANN ARBOR, MICHIGAN

Vine Books is an imprint of Servant Publications especially designed to serve evangelical Christians.

Published by Servant Publications
P.O. Box 8617
Ann Arbor, Michigan 48107

Cover design: Paul Higdon

97 98 99 00 10 9 8 7 6 5 4 3 2 1

Printed in the United States of America
ISBN 0-89283-984-8

LIBRARY OF CONGRESS CATALOGING-IN-PUBLICATION DATA

Elwood, Roger.
    Stephen the martyr/ Roger Elwood
        p.   cm
    ISBN 0-89283-984-8 (alk. paper)
    1. Stephen, Saint, d. ca. 36—Fiction.   2. Bible. N.T. Acts—History of Biblical events—
Fiction.   3. Christian martyrs—Palestine—Fiction.   4. Christian saints—Palestine—Fiction.   I.
Title.
PS3555.L85S77  1998                                          97-32452
813'.54—dc21                                                 CIP

*To*

*Bill Petersen and Bert Ghezzi*
*—the rarest of friends*

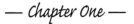

## Chapter One

*S*tephen had gone to Tarsus because he thought that was where the Lord wanted him to spend some time, talking to the religious leaders as well as trying to evangelize whatever number of citizens he could reach with the Good News.

*It was a bold step, not something a coward would have attempted. After all, Tarsus was the hometown of the man who had been seeking his death for many months.*

*Saul.*

*This acclaimed rabbi had more targets than just this one young man. In fact, his mission was to eradicate all Christians, hunting down every last one until they were wiped out, ultimately to be forgotten by history or else remembered as a strange little group with minimal impact upon the society they had sought to convert.*

*Stephen's friends had warned him not to go anywhere near Tarsus. Stepping into that lions' den, as the prophet Daniel once had, seemed a foolhardy scenario to repeat.*

*"You are needed elsewhere," one friend said. "You must take care that your time of preaching and witnessing is as long as possible, without it being cut unnecessarily short."*

*At first that remark made sense to Stephen. But then, as he considered it further, he could not get Tarsus out of his mind, could not sleep well at night, wondering if he should go to Sepphoris or Kko or Dothan instead.*

*And then a singular fact rose above all others: Saul would continue his pursuit against Christians no matter which route Stephen took. So he might as well continue on to Tarsus if by doing so he was fulfilling the will of his heavenly Father ...*

Stephen was nervous that day. And very tired.

He had been traveling throughout the Middle East, helping fellow brothers in Christ form churches in major cities and small villages alike. Isolated from the rest of the world, some lived in places so starkly backward that it seemed each was altogether forgotten by Almighty God and sinful man alike, struggling to survive as human beings and as Christians.

Not a few of these small communities were in valleys surrounded by the tallest mountain peaks of that region. To the north of Israel, the ancient city of Petra in Edom, in which the Nabateans settled, could be reached only by way of a natural but exceedingly narrow path through mountains that otherwise completely surrounded it.

Getting to these Christian communities meant undertaking the most arduous of treks, treks so daunting as to thoroughly discourage most other men, men less dedicated than Stephen.

But Stephen had decided he could not do otherwise. Now he was on a singular mission that he assumed would take the course of many years; he hoped one day he would have much to look back upon, including some miracles, because his conversion had given him the gift of healing.

"I have been sent," he would tell anyone interested in what was behind his determination never to give up, "and I shall not return until I have accomplished what my Lord wants me to do. What more needs to be said?"

As long as this remarkable young man was certain that he continued to have the support and the encouragement of his Creator, he would do whatever needed to be done to accomplish that mission, no matter what it cost him personally.

"How could it be otherwise with me?" he once told another believer. "If I were to give up, I have no doubt that would displease God. What could I hope for in that case. What, I ask you? Would my life be any the easier for it? It might well be, yes, that is true, but what of the life that is to come? Dare I covet the ease sought by men and earn instead the scorn of my heavenly Father?"

He paused, his emotions controlling him, and then he went on.

"It is not ease that concerns me, though most of my life I have known such ease to an extent that would drive most men to terrible envy. You see, I am resigned to sacrifice. I know it is at the core of what I am doing, and that will never change, not at *my* instigation. Shall I suddenly tell the blessed Father, 'No more, my God, no more. I am tired, I am weary'? How could I ever do that when He is my strength?"

The fellow believer to whom he was speaking broke into tears and hugged him.

"Stephen, Stephen, what an inspiration you are," this man, also quite young, whispered into his ear.

But Stephen pulled away from him, grabbed his shoulders, and gently shook him.

"You must never say that, my brother," he cautioned in love. "I am not an inspiration to anyone, but it is the risen Christ who inspires through me."

Stephen could have been recorded by history as another Paul, who would come later. Perhaps ironically, Paul might then have been known as another Stephen.

But it was not to be.

It was not to be for this young man. He knew somehow what it was about that one day, out of all the days and weeks and months and years since his conversion, and thus, despite his courage and his faith, he was nervous as he awakened, and thought about the next few hours ...

*The best of times, the worst of times ...*

Famous words such as these could have been applied to any number of different periods throughout the course of human history. But they were never more appropriate than when God-in-the-flesh walked the earth.

It had to be the best of times, because Jesus the Christ was alive in His incarnated form. Along with His twelve apostles, He was traveling from village to village, crowd to crowd, performing a host of miracles while dispensing the unparalleled wisdom of heaven.

*The best of times? Oh, yes, it was that, with such a Man in the flesh, in real time and space, walking among the crowds, touching and being touched ...*

Think of the enormous privilege people had, yet so few took advantage of it or knew about it, this privilege that could have changed their lives if they had embraced it with belief, instead of mere curiosity. On their way they went, with blissful indifference, leaving behind the Man unlike any other.

They could actually *see* the Son of God!

The Messiah was no longer a mere theological concept found in dust-covered old prophetic scrolls, a source of heady speculation by

scribes and others as they tried to pinpoint the exact date of the fulfill-
ment of each one.

They could *hear* His voice.

It was a rich voice, amplified somewhat mysteriously so that great
crowds could hear Him sufficiently to grasp what He was saying to
them, the voice of a Man accustomed to having an audience as the voice
reached out to them, familiar as it had been to ten thousand upon ten
thousand angels who had heard it for countless millions of years. Deep
and untroubled and completely mesmerizing that voice was for those
who actually chose to *listen* at length without turning away, those who
allowed themselves to admit He was precisely what He said He was.

The Nazarene spoke *to* crowds and *among* crowds. He came to them
as an impressive figure, tall and always well-groomed, presenting an
image that was far from the straggly wild-man look of John the Baptist.

They could reach out and touch the very hem of His garment or
feel, so very briefly, His flesh against their own. But this would mean
something only if their eyes were opened and they saw beyond the trap-
pings of an ordinary man, saw Who was wearing that garment, saw that
the flesh they touched was animated by Deity.

*Only once before ...*

Adam and Eve had been similarly privileged many thousands of years
earlier. They could walk with the eternal God, talk with Him, hear His
response as words to their ears and not simply sensed in their minds.

*God actually spoke ...*

And that was how Adam and Eve were different from those confronted by Jesus during His earthly ministry. They knew who shared
their garden with them because it was the One Who had created Eden
in the first place.

But for Jesus, instant recognition was denied Him because He was
seen as a man instead of God masked by human flesh.

Those days two thousand years ago were days of wonder and awe
and astonishing feats.

That the Nazarene attracted so many large crowds meant only one
thing ... His fame was being generated by word-of-mouth at an astonishing rate, one villager telling another, one leper passing the words to others similarly afflicted, men on horseback or riding camels or simply walking from place to place or in the case of the lame, hobbling along on

makeshift crutches, those not having even these simple instruments crawling instead, inch by inch, eating the dust of the ground beneath them but not letting that stop the journey that had to be made, the journey to tell someone else that a Man of miracles had stepped among them.

And they all wanted the same thing, to have their maladies lifted from them so they could stand without falling or hear or see or live in bodies no longer made grotesque by leprosy.

Men, women, and children were being instantly healed of blindness or lameness. Their deafness was taken away, their twisted bones were straightened, their minds were healed, and their souls were given rebirth.

One by one.

Just as salvation could not be brought about *en masse*, so it was with the precious blessing of healing.

A touch by the holy hand of God's Son.

That was what it took in that ancient time.

There could have been another way, of course, the way used by those charlatan faith healers in the centuries to follow, but it was not for Him, not something He would ever do.

His was not today's mass-produced healing that seems so indiscriminate, offered to the faithful as well as to the merely desperate.

Pretenders would come.

Those pretenders who would present themselves, either subtly or blatantly otherwise, as Christ's successors, bestowed with His healing power and now able to "touch" thousands, or hundred of thousands or, yes, even millions, and bring to many the healing they sought or what *seemed* to be that healing.

This was real, when Jesus trod the dusty roads of that ancient land, not hype, real healing in the course of three-and-a-half years on dusty roads and in ancient villages, by the sea or a lake, anywhere that He went, which meant crowds following His every step, hoping for a word, a touch, seeing the promise of lives freed from handicap of one sort or another.

Walking with the King of Kings. Brushing up against Divinity encased temporarily by mortal flesh.

*Only Adam and Eve, before they sinned, had been similarly privileged many thousands of years before ...*

But a difference existed, of course; Adam and Eve knew God was with them. The Jews of Jesus' time of incarnation, at least that great majority of them whose hearts had been hardened over the centuries of awaiting the Messiah, did not. They would eventually demand His death. Even Adam and Eve never went that far.

*The worst of times ...*

Jesus' ultimate death on a rough-hewn cross at Calvary stemmed from one root cause.

Disbelief.

At least that was what the public was told.

"He is an impostor!" one or another of the religious leaders would shout from a balcony or in the midst of a town square. "You cannot believe what He says. He is a deceiver of the worst sort! He comes from Satan. Stay away. You are fools if you allow yourselves to be taken in by Him."

Countless numbers of Jews and visiting Greeks and those from the Orient and elsewhere did not pay heed, for they chose to stand or sit and listen and respond to the Man who was far, far from ordinary.

With the Pharisees and the Sadducees, however, there may have been another, sinister reason that eclipsed anything else, the possibility that some among them actually may have *believed* the multifaceted series of messages that Jesus had been delivering for slightly over three years.

Including Caiaphas, the high priest.

Of medium height but excruciatingly thin, with tiny brown eyes that seemed perpetually bloodshot, Caiaphas was charismatic to a degree, greater of voice than of appearance, his words sounding almost like the voice of God addressing Moses atop Mount Sinai centuries before. But the man was utterly unprincipled, speaking of the need to preserve the distinctiveness of Jewish life while negotiating secret deals to save himself should Roman forces ever need to put down the insurrectionists altogether. A motley group of rebels was being stirred up by a misfit named Barabbas, and Caiaphas was taking no chances. He understood fully the position he enjoyed in the life of the nation he would betray given the slightest of provocations.

*Understood, yes, and enjoyed ...*

He liked the expensive, elaborate clothes available to anyone who became high priest. Poverty could be rampant in certain regions of Jerusalem, as it was over the centuries, joined by bouts of famine and pestilence, but the high priest always had a wardrobe that was lavish.

A robe called the *ephod* ... that was one of Caiaphas' favorites.

Worn over other clothes, it was an outer garment made from one piece of fabric and completely devoid of seams. Sky blue in color, it had an opening for his head, with a narrow collar around the edge. Sleeveless, it was just long enough to reach to below his knees. Around the bottom hem the *ephod* was embellished with a design of pomegranates alternating with bells of gold, on a background pattern of violet, purple, carmine, and white flecked with gold thread. On the shoulders two onyx stones were fastened in gold rosettes, the names of the twelve tribes of Israel engraved on them, six to each stone. Hung over the *ephod* was a breastplate containing twelve jewels in four rows of three each.

Caiaphas did not admit the truth to himself, truth represented by all the amassing of finery, truth that screamed at him the addiction he had developed for material things at the sacrifice of true spirituality.

And the Nazarene represented a danger of the most alarming sort, for Caiaphas found, in moments alone, that he had to acknowledge the likelihood that Jesus *was* the Messiah, yet he found himself looking at a Man Who was totally different from the Messiah he had been expecting all these years, different from what he had been teaching others to expect.

A Man Who could take everything away from him!

*I believe Jesus could be the Promised One, yet how can I accept Him as He is?* Caiaphas would think mournfully. *This is no vengeful champion of our land, no conqueror of our oppressors. He has not come to throw the yoke of Rome from off our shoulders. Instead He could someday tell the masses the truth about me and the others, and we would be through.*

The high priest would tremble with fear at that thought.

*If the people knew as I know, if they believed as I believe, it would surely change them, and not for the better, since it would mean more waiting, more hoping, more prayer on protesting knees. In time, and not very much time at that, they would surely give up and go another way, ending the long wait by turning their backs on the Sanhedrin and embracing Barabbas, uniting behind him as their messiah even though he would be a poor substitute against whom Rome would send its full might, causing my fellow Jews more suffering than even they could possibly imagine.*

*Father, destroy this Jesus. Brush Him aside as though He were a mere ant or flea, and send another. Please do that, Yahweh; please do it soon.*

However blasphemous, that *was* the high priest's prayer, begging Jehovah to act as the Sanhedrin wished and remove Jesus permanently. If not, he had a plan of his own, whether or not it was God's will.

If Rome had never taken control of Israel, then Caiaphas would have been very nearly as powerful as a ruling king, perhaps second only to Herod the Great and Herod Antipas.

Control.

That was the core of everything he did, every thought, every word, every deed, the reason for every action, for he was after control, wanting to dominate every aspect of the life of his nation and its people.

Caiaphas had amassed more control than any other high priest in the history of Israel. The potential for influence, for domination, always had been present with others who had been high priest, but he was the first such man in centuries to seize hold of it and bend it to his will in a calculating and astute campaign for control of the Sanhedrin and, from there, to the nation of Israel as a whole.

"I have wanted this for a long time," Caiaphas had confessed a number of years before to one of the few individuals in whom he ever had felt confident enough to divulge anything of the sort. "You know, I thought of being where I am now from my early days as a teenager."

His eyes widening, he had spoken faster.

"No one could challenge me; that was what I wanted," Caiaphas continued. "Nor could anyone truly depose me. The only way I could be stopped was by assassination or infirmity of age or injury or disease."

All of those were increasingly possible as time passed, but in truth, Caiaphas actually *feared* only assassination.

Enemies.

He knew they were present and could be plotting against him; he knew he could trust no one any longer and he had to be vigilant every moment of every day of the rest of his life.

"Power brings with it those craven souls who are unable to cope with someone such as me," Caiaphas remarked on another occasion. "They realize that they are indeed inferior to me in every way, and they are going to try to eliminate the source of their intimidation."

Certainly, Caiaphas' conduct in office was far from being acceptable to every member of the Sanhedrin, especially Nicodaemus and Joseph of Arimathea, and he found it necessary to quell what he sensed might be a rebellion, but as high priest, he had become expert at this.

He achieved his desires by having separate meetings with the conservatives and the liberals, pledging to each group what he knew they wanted to hear, for example, about their share of the temple worship revenue. When the time came to deliver on his promises, he would back off, poor-mouthing the state of the temple treasury. By now, the original matter that had stirred them was essentially forgotten, and none would register his objections with any substantial vehemence.

"I have never been opposed successfully," Caiaphas would brag to visiting dignitaries, men of wealth and position who were invariably impressed by the reservoir of power and influence the high priest had amassed.

"I usually achieve whatever it is that I intend," he would continue, relishing the expressions on the faces of his victors, even when they were not expressions of appreciation but scorn. "With each victory, gentlemen, later defeat becomes ever less likely. Would you not agree?"

He would always smirk as he spoke about such matters, and this added to an image of gathering arrogance that someday would come back to haunt Caiaphas and destroy him.

Whatever the case, the high priest, the most powerful religious leader of all the Jews of that time and that place, decided to instigate the Nazarene's death despite the horrendous potential costs, even while suspecting that to do so would put him on a collision course with the God Whom he was supposed to be worshiping—yes, worshiping and representing as well.

But Caiaphas and others among the members of the Sanhedrin had long ago ceased to be truly concerned with the will of God as it was and had shifted to the will of God as they *decided* it was.

Jesus was a persistent reminder that they were off course, that their dictums had taken precedence in their lives and in the lives of those who looked to them for spiritual guidance.

What greater sin could men be guilty of?

Knowing that the carpenter from Nazareth was truly God in the flesh, and yet they wanted Him out of the way! If nothing else, Jesus was a constant threat to their consciences, for He was capable of judging their innermost beings, and none would be able to pass His scrutiny.

"He must die," they would rant in their private chambers. "He could destroy all that we have concocted over the years."

If Jesus was not killed, then He might eventually take away their power as well as their influence over the populace, because He would know how corrupt they had become, turning His house of worship into a den of thieves and manipulating their positions of authority into figurative whips they used to force the people into submission.

*... He could destroy all that we have concocted over the years.*

They came to be obsessed by that eventuality. After a certain point, it no longer mattered to them whether Jesus was speaking the truth. Either way, He was dangerous, and He had to be stopped.

"Money ..." Caiaphas, the high priest, suggested. "His kind always responds to an offer of financial gain."

But that maneuver was never pursued, because Caiaphas and the others eventually decided that Jesus, if He were God in the flesh, would look with disdain upon any sum of money, no matter how large.

"We can have Him banished," offered another member of the Sanhedrin. "Pilatus would find no difficulty in ordering exile if we handle him properly. He owes us something for the peace we have given him."

"Peace?" Caiaphas spoke up. "With that crude and repugnant insurrectionist out there, stirring things up? It may be that Pilatus imagines that we are craftily trying to play both ends against the middle, claiming peace while secretly giving support to the troublemaker."

"Troublemaker?" Nicodaemus said. "He is much more than that, I suspect, much more. I would be lying if I said that Barabbas did not have the potential for far greater danger, you know."

The rest seldom paid much attention to Nicodaemus anymore, so he left that particular meeting feeling quite useless. If they knew he intended to contact the Nazarene under the cover of night, they would kick him out for certain.

"Good riddance ..." a Sanhedrin member muttered.

Considered next was the possibility of having Jesus sent to Patmos or some other isolated spot; that seemed the easiest choice.

"We will do it quietly," Caiaphas mused, "hopefully in the middle of the night, and soon. Yes, it *has* to be soon. The Nazarene is influencing greater and greater numbers of people, the masses and others."

Including some Romans.

Visiting dignitaries from the Eternal City had noticed Jesus speaking as they rode past Him on the outskirts of Jerusalem.

One of them was a tall, proud, utterly self-serving individual named Quintus Papirius Maxientus, rich, powerful, not an impossible choice for emperor at some point. A member of the Senate, he had more influence than most men and counted among his friends such individuals as Livia Drusilla, the wife of Emperor Tiberius, and other members of the Claudian family.

A man of passions and curiosities as varied as the opportunities to indulge them, he ultimately became curious about the Jews, and that curiosity soon fanned into a near-obsessive fascination.

"They seem so crude a people, yet they have written some works of genuine substance," he had told one of his friends after a banquet in Rome a few weeks earlier. "I must go down and see for myself."

Caiaphas, recalling what had happened to the visiting Maxientus, glanced about the room.

"Do we want that episode repeated?" he asked. "Do we truly want that sort of thing to happen again? Do we risk the wrath of those who have overrun us?"

It was too fresh in their minds for anyone to dare to say yes.


Jesus was just commencing His Sermon on the Mount, with thousands of people listening to Him.

"Blessed are the poor in spirit," He said with great authority, "for theirs is the kingdom of heaven."

He stretched out His arms as though to encompass everyone in that multitude of men, women, and children.

"Blessed are they who mourn, for they shall be comforted," He continued. "Blessed are the meek, for they shall inherit the earth."

The Nazarene was not like any speaker those listening that hot Middle Eastern afternoon had ever heard.

"Not even our religious leaders have ever spoken as He does," muttered a wealthy old man who had arrived early, beckoned by word of mouth and expecting something quite special.

Jesus was standing on the mountain, and for the most part, the listeners were sitting below Him on the mountainside, spread out over the slope.

"Blessed are they which do hunger and thirst after righteousness, for they shall be filled," the Nazarene went on. "Blessed are the merciful, for they shall obtain mercy. Blessed are the pure in heart, for they shall see God. Blessed are the peacemakers, for they shall be called the children of God."

He started to walk down the slope, carefully stepping over people or taking any openings they gave Him by moving to one side.

"Blessed are they who are persecuted for the sake of righteousness," the Nazarene told the rapt crowd, "for theirs is the kingdom of heaven. Blessed are ye, when men shall revile you, and persecute you, and shall say all manner of evil against you falsely, for My sake."

He looked out over them all.

"Rejoice, and be exceedingly glad," He spoke, the richness of His voice captivating them as much as His words, "for great is your reward in heaven, for so persecuted they the prophets who were before you."

Maxientus was spellbound. And he noticed that his companion was hardly bored by what this Jesus was saying.

"Who is that man?" he asked Pontius Pilatus. They were being driven to several points of interest on the outskirts of Jerusalem, a standard itinerary for visitors from Rome who were as influential as Maxientus had proven himself to be over the years. Seeing the crowd stretching out over a nearby hillside, Pilatus had ordered the driver closer so they could investigate.

"The tall one," the proconsul asked, "with that red-tinged beard and a majestic voice as though from the very gates of heaven?"

Maxientus chuckled as he turned to Pilatus.

"You *know* who it is that I speak of," he said admonishingly.

"Oh, *Him!*" Pilatus replied, feigning surprise.

After enjoying that little moment, the two men became considerably more serious.

"You are well aware of Him then?" Maxientus asked.

Pilatus nodded and was frowning, not pleased that his friend was showing any interest in the Nazarene.

"Exceedingly."

"Why do you frown?" Maxientus asked.

"I know all too much about this one, Quintus."

Maxientus squinted under the afternoon sun as he studied his friend's face.

"This is deep, is it not?" he asked.

"Very deep, friend, deeper than you could possibly guess."

"What does He *do?* I mean, he is a Jew after all. What could be so special about *any* Jew?"

"You hear Him as well as I do. Do those words sound as though they are coming from an *ordinary* man, Jew or otherwise?"

Maxientus evaded giving a direct answer.

"Tell me more, please."

"He preaches exclusively now, though he used to be a carpenter."

"Preaches? Nothing else?"

"I have uncovered no more."

Maxientus moved around a bit on the seat of the chariot, a twinge of discomfort touching him.

"What is the extent of His education?" he asked.

"Local only."

For the visiting Roman, education defined the worth of a man. It was a sacred duty of parents to provide the finest of teachers so that their offspring could be equipped for potential greatness during the years ahead.

*... local only.*

Maxientus was flabbergasted now that he had heard the Nazarene speak such words of power and dignity and eloquence.

*"Only that?"* he blurted out.

"You find that surprising?" Pilatus said. "He is the rule, not the exception. These Jews are in no way a cultured people. And that makes

His sophistication doubly mystifying, does it not?"

Maxientus had seen many other Jews, and in his mind they were a craven lot, both in their manner and their appearance, with noses that were large and crooked, thoroughly unpleasant-looking people who were unable to look him straight in the face without their eyes darting from side to side. And he was unconvinced even of their personal cleanliness. For Romans, bathing several times a day was both a cherished ritual and a necessity if they were to maintain any self-respect.

But not the Jews.

They seemed, on the whole, dusty and dirty and reeking of odors that were foul to any Roman.

And so he had no trouble agreeing with Pilatus' pronouncement.

"I can see that that is the case with most of them but this man—" he started to say, but felt curiously overwhelmed by words the Nazarene had said that refused to release their hold on his mind.

Maxientus became silent, trying to gather some sense out of the conflicting realities: a Man whose pronouncements bordered on the brilliant, educated only at the modest level of what most Romans would consider near-illiteracy.

Pilatus waited several minutes, trying to be patient with someone he dared not offend.

"What were you saying?" he asked politely, well aware of his visitor's vast power base in Rome.

Maxientus shook his head, then started speaking again.

"Something about His words," he recalled, "something beyond the words themselves."

Now it was Pontius Pilatus who was given to brief introspection, for he had listened to Jesus from a distance on many occasions, as had Procula, his wife, on occasions that were often more than accidental, occasions when the proconsul would arrange his schedule and his travels so that he could be near where the Nazarene was supposed to be on any given day.

"Many feel that way," he spoke honestly.

"This is my first time. You have heard Him more often undoubtedly. What do you think?"

Pilatus seldom was at a loss for words, but he had never truly analyzed the Nazarene's appeal.

"It is unfair of me to spring all this on you," Maxientus admitted. "The real purpose of my visit, you know, is to revitalize our friendship."

"And to report to the emperor how I am managing all of this," Pilatus said cynically.

"Our friendship mandates a favorable response, whatever the reality," Maxientus responded.

Pilatus acknowledged that he had become a little too cynical about everything over the past few years.

And then he added, "I have decided to ignore the Nazarene as much as possible and let His kind figure out who or what He is."

The other man nodded and said, "Yes, I see, Pontius."

"We should be going back. That banquet with the Sanhedrin starts early this evening. You have had a very long trip. I can imagine that you are quite tired right now, my dear Quintus."

Maxientus agreed heartily.

"Some fine banquet in my honor, I trust …" he said.

"Which you richly deserve," Pilatus replied diplomatically.

As the driver got the four horses pulling the chariot to start moving, the visitor from Rome turned and looked back at the Nazarene, and there was a curious longing in his heart.

## Chapter Two

A night of vague memories resurrected themselves and appeared fresh before Stephen, memories of beggars and others he had ignored over the years in displays of contempt as their hands reached out for him as he walked by, pretending they did not exist and stopping only a second to spit on the ground and then flash a look of disgust their way as he passed by...

Maxientus did not sleep well during the early part of that night, in part because he hated playing the part of a fool, and he perceived that his reaction to the Nazarene was making him act and think foolishly.

"He surely must be having someone else write those words, which He then intones well enough," he told himself out loud as he got himself ready for whatever his host had planned. "Otherwise, how is it that such eloquence comes from a carpenter from Nazareth? I passed through that village on the way to Jerusalem. It was barely noticeable."

... *He surely must be having someone else write those words.*

Maxientus could not let himself believe anything that contradicted this view, for he measured a man at least in part by heritage, and this carpenter seemed to have none that was at all worthwhile.

"No mere wanderer could be capable of saying what He did and coming up with those ideas in the first place," he added.

He knew he would have to find out more.

Doing so probably would be easy enough, under the circumstances. After all, Maxientus was staying at the residence of the proconsul and had been assured there were no limitations on him. He could get or do whatever he wanted and go anywhere he wished, including, happily, ordering any available food he might desire at the vaguest hint of hunger.

On a whim, feeling the slightest of yearnings for some beverage or delicacy within reason, Maxientus could be served at *any* hour of the day or night; and along with his meal, he could enjoy having a whole chorus of dancing maidens perform for him, since Pontius Pilatus had arranged to have a number of visiting Arabian beauties stay in Israel for as long as he wished, paying them well indeed, though he imagined they supplemented that income by providing certain "services" to wealthy visitors. Whenever that possibility was raised, Pilatus, very liberal in terms of social mores, simply shrugged his shoulders and dismissed the matter from consideration.

And then there was one of Pilatus' personal chariots as well as its driver, ready for his summons, to take him anywhere he wished.

*You are certainly trying to make a good impression,* he thought of Pilatus, *but then that was what I expected. You should not be the proconsul of a barren land such as this. Perhaps I can do something for you when I return to Rome.*

Before retiring for the night, after a day filled with activities planned to impress and amuse him, Maxientus stepped outside on the balcony adjacent to his quarters.

Minutes later, someone knocked at the door.

"Please enter," he said.

The door was opened, and Pontius Pilatus walked into the bedroom.

"I thought you might still be awake," the proconsul remarked.

Maxientus congratulated him for his astuteness.

"And I am beginning to think that you should have something better to command," he remarked, not entirely as mere flattery.

"Better than such a historic country as this?" Pilatus spoke facetiously, grimacing as he did so.

The two Romans enjoyed laughter over what both perceived as an uncouth land and nothing more than a bunch of low-life inhabitants who eventually would bore any man of substance.

"Even the rich ones seem little more than pigs pulled out of the muck and mire," Pilatus remarked, "cleaned up and rubbed with cologne, but underneath, yearning to be filthy again."

Maxientus nodded knowingly.

"Their God seems a bit misguided, does He not?" he said. "I mean, they are supposed to be His chosen people. Even Diana, in her most erotic moments, would not have made such a choice, I am sure."

Pilatus was still chuckling.

"He could have selected Romans instead," the proconsul remarked. "We have so much more breeding, charm, prestige, everything that these wanderers have lacked over the centuries. But then the Nazarene is supposed to be His only begotten Son, so who knows?"

"You are serious?" Maxientus asked disbelievingly.

"I am terribly serious, my esteemed guest."

What Pilatus was not telling the other man was that he considered the Nazarene to be several cuts above the average Jew.

*That is one of the reasons why they hate You so,* he thought. *You remind them of how very crude they are.*

Maxientus looked out over the surrounding countryside, with the Mount of Olives to his left, and beyond it—

Suddenly—

He pulled back, startled, even audibly gasping a bit.

"What is it?" asked Pilatus, concerned.

The visitor's voice trembled slightly, a lapse of self-control that he regretted in the presence of the proconsul.

"Over there, to my right," he spoke, trying to subdue nerves that had responded to the very real shock of unexpectedly seeing a ghostly skull-like figure looming in the darkness.

Pilatus strained his eyes but failed to see what had concerned otherwise unflappable Maxientus.

"Yes? What do you see?" Pilatus asked, feigning a touch of desperation.

"The moonlight on that pile of rocks yonder."

Pilatus squinted through the half-darkness.

"Over there," Maxientus told him.

"I am looking…"

"The one that looks very much like a human skull …" his guest said, sounding a bit exasperated.

Now Pilatus *knew* what Maxientus had become concerned about, and he could laugh then and there but all the while realizing that he had felt much the same way when he faced that spot the first time.

"Ah, yes, Golgotha," he said finally and with a matter-of-factness that did not sit well with his Roman visitor.

*Golgotha.*

It was a dreary place, especially at night, the combination of silvery glow and partial darkness exaggerating the look of it.

"Very strange in this light," Maxientus said. "It is as though the skull of a long-dead giant had been dropped there."

Pilatus thought that description was one of the more eloquent ones he had heard to date.

"I agree," he said, sighing. "It is not a pleasant spot at best. I prefer to look in the opposite direction."

To emphasize this, he turned 180 degrees.

"What is there, may I ask?" Maxientus asked, anxious to turn his attention from Golgotha.

A smile edged up the side of Pilatus' mouth.

"Gethsemane ... one of the loveliest spots in this wasteland," he replied, "sweet, sweet Gethsemane."

"What is this place?" Maxientus asked.

Pilatus sniffed in the chill night air, which had the hint of water in it from a *wadi* that was only a few hundred feet away, as well as the earthy scent of nearby animal dung; but above all, the fragrance of jasmine, fairly strong, was carried on a breeze from some spot nearby, to be savored in a moment of near ecstasy.

"Smell that?" he spoke.

The question was needless, the jasmine unmistakable, intruding like an unexpected but welcomed guest and greatly appreciated.

"Yes, I do," Pilatus told him. "Quite lovely. It is from Gethsemane."

"Do you ever go there, to this Gethsemane?" Maxientus asked.

The proconsul seemed wistful.

"If I can be sure that no Jews are in the vicinity," he replied.

"Why do you prize this place so much?" Maxientus asked.

"It is special because it seems to have a peace that is not of this world. Do not misunderstand me. It is a garden, but it is not brimming over with exotic blooms, though there is a fair degree of color within its confines."

*... a peace that is not of this world.*

Maxientus, curiously, was drawn to recall the Nazarene.

"Does this Jesus—?" he started to ask, then stopped himself.

Pilatus waited patiently, aware that his visitor was struggling a bit.

"Go ahead," he said, genuinely encouraging the man to speak freely. "No need to hesitate for fear that I will report you if it is something controversial that you care to unburden yourself of."

"Nor I you, Pontius."

"Then finish what you were about to say."

"Does the Nazarene ever go to Gethsemane," Maxientus asked, "that you have heard of, I mean?"

Pilatus faced him then.

"I know for a fact that He does."

"You have seen Him do so?"

"I have been there when He slipped away by Himself, not even one of that band of twelve with Him."

Maxientus' palms, strangely, had become sweaty.

"Did you speak, either of you?" he asked.

"No, I did not. He was the One to do so."

"And what was it that this Jesus said to the ruler of His nation?"

"I happened to be leaving as He was entering. We both stopped, looked at one another, and then He said, 'Is it for peace that you come here?' At first I thought that was rather presumptuous, but then, I had heard being shy and backward were not among His traits.

"I held back any irritation or offense I was feeling and pretended that He had not bothered me at all by being so forward. 'It is,' I replied simply. 'Am I a stranger to you?' He asked. 'No,' I had to tell Him in all honesty, 'no, You are not.' 'We shall become much closer, you and I,' He added. I was about to question Him as to His meaning, but before I could open my mouth, the Nazarene was gone."

It was becoming chilly. The two men grunted and went inside.

"A little cognac?" Pilatus asked. "As you know, the Gauls can do only a handful of things well. And such a superb drink is one of them. To think that it is distilled from a simple white wine!"

Maxientus' eyes widened at the thought of such a pleasant end to the evening, a perfect beverage to have before going to bed.

"You import it, of course," he said.

Pilatus nodded without hesitation.

"One of my few extravagances," he acknowledged. "I can do little to make the life I lead here more than barely tolerable."

"Does the emperor know?" Maxientus asked slyly.

"He is the one who authorized the continuing shipments and pays for them out of the empire's treasury."

"Now that is something, Pontius. I *am* impressed."

Pilatus was becoming embarrassed.

"How he must value your service," Maxientus added.

"No, he does not."

All emotion had left the proconsul's voice, and the harsh reality of where he was and what he was doing took over.

"But the cognac—" Maxientus said.

Pilatus interrupted the other man.

"It is his way of fooling me into thinking that he does."

That was enough to make Maxientus chuckle as he said, "You know our leader better than most other men do."

"It helps me to survive, if not prosper."

Maxientus knew what he meant. Pilatus' yearning to be rid of Israel and back in Rome was nearly palpable.

The image of moonlit Golgotha remained vivid for the visitor.

*It is not a pleasant spot at best …*

"Pilatus?" he asked as the two men sat in what might have been called a den in later times.

"Yes, my friend?"

"You spoke of Golgotha not being a pleasant spot at all."

"I did. And it is not. It is quite awful."

"Merely because of the way it appears, much like a human skull? I have a problem believing that."

Pilatus was moving around in his chair, abruptly acting uncomfortable.

"Something more," he said tersely.

Maxientus wondered if the proconsul was stretching matters out for some dramatic purpose.

"Tell me," he said, trying to be patient.

The subject was a grisly one for Pilatus. He was reluctant to get into it but knew he had to be courteous toward his visitor.

"Executions."

Maxientus had not anticipated that answer.

"There? On top?"

Pilatus downed the last of the cognac he had poured.

"Yes. Atop Golgotha, Maxientus. The worst criminals have had their blood shed at the Place of the Skull."

Maxientus was becoming more and more curious.

"What means of death?" he inquired. "Have they been beheaded perhaps? Or hung from a gallows?"

"None of that."

"Then what?"

"Crucifixion, Maxientus. A dozen men have been crucified during the past year alone, most of them fomenting this insipid but perplexing insurrection that someone named Barabbas has been leading."

The visitor visibly shivered.

"How ironic."

*A brow ... with two empty eye sockets, the remains of a nose and—*

"That it looks like a skull?" Pilatus asked.

"Yes," Maxientus replied. "Was the choice of that site a deliberate one for that reason?"

Pilatus shook his head as he spoke. "Oh, no, that would have been too morbid, even for brutal men."

"It is highly visible. People can see Golgotha for quite some distance from every direction."

"A warning to all!"

"No doubt."

Maxientus was quiet then, wondering if he should admit something to the other man and finally deciding the proconsul seemed to exhibit a certain degree of trustworthiness.

"I have never seen anyone die," he admitted.

Pilatus turned away from him.

"Did I say something that was offensive?" the other Roman asked, concerned that etiquette between them had suffered.

"You did not. I was reminded, Maxientus, that's all."

"Reminded? Of what?"

"The men I have killed in battle ... and here, with no war officially declared, I have had them slaughtered just the same, and all in the name of maintaining order so that my emperor will be pleased."

"Very sorry ..." Maxientus said with some sincerity since he had grown to like Pilatus during the two days they had spent together.

"Pay no heed to my old scars. It is just that I have done ghastly things to these men, my poor victims. I have sent them to *be* killed as though I were their commander. But it is here, in this untenable place, that I have gone beyond the atrocities of battle and committed a whole new category of anguish."

Veins were standing out on Pilatus' forehead.

"And right there, atop Golgotha," the proconsul continued, "I have watched men die. My order could have given them life. But I have spared no one."

"Not a single innocent individual?" Maxientus asked incredulously, then recovered. "But surely all have been guilty. You are to be admired, Pontius, for doing what a ruler must, however grisly each moment."

Pilatus looked at him, that *patricius* face, so nobly honed by what his parents believed to be a special dispensation from the gods barely masking the struggle within him, a struggle to fight the liberty he felt with this man, a liberty that might ease him into confessing too much that could return later to haunt him.

"Are you well?" Maxientus asked.

"Yes, I'm fine."

"But you seemed so—"

"I *seemed* what I was," Pilatus said, raising his voice. "I *seemed* a man who is constantly reminded by the sight of Golgotha that he has sentenced men to the agonies of the worst form of execution known to man. The barbarians are at least quick, off with their heads, you know, over with in seconds."

He pointed in the direction of the Place of the Skull.

"There it can take hours, my friend. Long, horrible hours."

"That may be regrettable," the visitor agreed, "but they were, after all, guilty, as you say."

"I *thought* them to be so, Quintus," groaned Pilatus, finally admitting what had bothered him.

This time it was Maxientus' turn to react.

"Some may not have been guilty at all?" he asked. "Is that what you are attempting to tell me?"

Though Pilatus seemed more than able to connive anything he wanted, in explaining to Maxientus he would be admitting that some "backward" Jews may have been, at least momentarily, his equal.

"A large number were crucified at the behest of the Sanhedrin," acknowledged the proconsul.

"For what reason?" Maxientus asked.

"For being false messiahs."

"Like the Nazarene is accused of being?"

"Exactly, Quintus. I wonder how long it will be until He is next."

The visitor was appalled by that possibility and blurted out, "What a sick, bloody people!"

"I agree. At least Romans slaughter those they *know* are enemies. The Jews allow themselves to succumb to the wildest suspicions, and they immediately order the death of anyone unfortunate enough to run afoul of laws and doctrines and such that are so obtuse that the whole, cumbersome lot seem incomprehensible to men such as you and me who have not grown up immersed in them."

"How often do you crucify criminals in that location?"

"Three times a year, it seems. But the longer Barabbas holds on, I am sure, the higher that figure will go, for I must put to death his kind as well as those who offend the Jews so deeply, and sometimes, my dear man, the one is the other."

"I should think the Jews would aid the insurrectionists," Maxientus speculated, "call them liberators, that sort of thing, you know."

"The Sanhedrin is very comfortable with the status quo. They have what they need because they have power and money. They are feared, Quintus."

"And Barabbas would change all that?"

"Oh, he would indeed. He has called the high priest a contemptible fraud, a lackey of the Romans."

"The fact that he is correct," Maxientus said slyly, "makes his statement all the more dangerous. Am I right in that, Pontius?"

Pilatus nodded.

"I worry ..."

Oh, how he did worry, especially when he was pressured by Procula, his much-loved but increasingly unstable wife. At least he considered her to be unstable—actually on the edge of utter madness.

"About what? Or whom?"

Maxientus was thinking more of Pilatus not just as a host doing his duty as ruler of the land but as a friend and, in fact, felt the stirrings of a rather perverse sort of jealousy, not of the comparative rigors of life in Israel but of his being able to observe the Jews close up day after day.

"The Nazarene," Pilatus replied.

That hardly surprised the visitor.

"He is a danger, I suppose." Maxientus spoke logically since logic was a god on a pedestal to be worshiped as far as he was concerned.

Pilatus shrugged his shoulders and said a bit uncertainly, "Not to the same extent as the insurrectionists but then—"

"Yet you are still apprehensive, it seems."

"I am."

Maxientus recalled that in recent years there had been a rash of charlatans claiming themselves to be God's messengers, a few going so far as to say they were Yahweh in the flesh.

"Another false messiah?" he offered.

"To the Jewish religious leaders that *is* what He appeared to be, and therefore He would be subject to the same crucifixion as all the others and Barabbas' followers as well."

Maxientus was greatly distressed.

"But this Man, from what I have observed, seems to use mere words, words that express rather gentle ideas of peace and kindness, a beguiling collection of them, I must say. Nothing I heard Him say seemed threatening as far as I can tell, Pontius, or have I missed something perhaps? I ask for some enlightenment from you."

"You have not," the other man agreed. "And, I fear, that is the problem."

Maxientus was frowning.

"I do not understand."

"The influential Jews ..."

"You mean those in the Sanhedrin?"

"Yes, I do. You know about such things?"

"I have studied."

Pilatus smiled, showing a mixture of surprise and admiration.

"What about them?" his visitor asked.

"They are coming to the conclusion that He may be as much a threat to them as Barabbas is. Yet the masses love Him whereas the other messiahs, still worthy of death in their eyes, nevertheless were far less dangerous since they were pallid in their protestations, hardly believable."

"That is why they have waited so long without approaching you about seizing the Nazarene?"

"Very good, you know. I admire your discernment."

"It has had much practice in the byzantine world of Roman politics."

"Of which I am wholly familiar," Pilatus told him.

Maxientus blushed at having to be reminded of this.

"I meant no offense," he said.

"And I felt none."

Pilatus was tired, and Maxientus decided not to tax his host's energies any more than he had already.

"Should we get some sleep now?" he asked.

"I expect so, Quintus. These are increasingly irksome and debilitating times, I fear. And I am stuck so in the midst of all this irrationality."

The two men shook hands and headed for their separate quarters. As Maxientus was opening the door to his own, he hesitated.

"I am not so tired," he whispered to himself.

And so he went back down the hallway and outside.

The chariot horseman had fallen asleep but had enough training to be able to wake up in an instant.

*Pontius was serious when he said that you would be available to me any time of the day or night,* Maxientus thought as he approached.

He awoke the man.

"Are you familiar with the Garden of Gethsemane?" he asked.

"I am, sir," the horseman, a very young man, dark-haired, round-faced, replied. "Would you like to go there in the morning?"

"Now ... I would like you to take me there right away."

Without a hint of irritation or concern the horseman told him, "As you wish," though he was obviously more interested in getting some sleep.

As he was getting into the chariot, Maxientus said, "I will make sure the proconsul allows you to sleep later in the morning."

The young man was genuinely grateful and smiled pleasantly as he said, "That is kind of you, sir."

Quintus Maxientus wondered, with some irony, how many people back in Rome ever thought of him as kind.

*Midnight ...*

The four horses pulling the chariot were stopped at the entrance to Gethsemane, which was surrounded by a low stone wall except for that one opening. Spilling just over the top was some pale green vine with light pink blossoms from which a hummingbird was getting pollen, even at night, normally not a time when it would be doing anything of the sort.

Maxientus watched this little tableau caught in the light of an overhead moon.

"See how frantic it is," Maxientus observed, "as though it has no time to spare. How curious!"

The horseman spoke up. "They seem to have the ability to sense storms, sir," he said.

"Little creatures like that?"

"And bigger ones too, cats and dogs and others. They have senses that give them a warning somehow."

Israel was a land of roving wild animals, hyenas and lions and others. It was dangerous to travel at night because if the animals did not attack, then the insurrectionists and common robbers and other criminals might.

Maxientus was dubious.

"But I understand that it has not rained in many weeks. And there is no hint of a coming storm, not that I can see."

The young man looked up at the sky.

"Not many stars tonight, sir. Clouds moving in."

"That is hardly proof."

"The worst storms, sir, are the ones that let loose without warning. There is so little preparation for that kind."

Maxientus started to walk through the entrance and began sniffing the air.

"Jasmine," he observed. "I smell jasmine. It is much closer now."

"Over to your left, sir," the horseman said as he pointed in that direction. "The clumps tinged with yellow, with multiple leaves."

Maxientus approached cautiously, almost reverently.

"So fine ..." he said, his voice showing his awe.

The visitor glanced around at the little garden, the shapes of bushes and shrubs and trees outlined in the moonlight, and he was astonished at the mixture of sparseness and beauty, represented by the curiously pale-gray stones with a hint of moss on them and the brilliant hues of groups of flowers scattered throughout, some brilliantly colored, others paste, a few dead but allowed to remain where they were because in that state, they possessed yet a different kind of pristine beauty.

"This is, after all, sir, a garden."

"Of course it is, with flowers and—"

Maxientus looked about the place, its shapes half-lit by the moon.

"A garden, set off by itself."

He looked at the horseman.

"Some sort of retreat?" he asked.

"Yes ... very much that, sir. It is a place in which to gather together your soul."

*... to gather together your soul.*

Maxientus thought about how lovely that phrase was. He was beginning to see in this young man something more than the *pro forma* warmth he projected, which he could turn on and off like an oil lamp.

"What does Gethsemane mean?" he asked.

"Oil press, sir, fragrant oils," the horseman said.

Maxientus walked about, sitting down on a flat stone then standing and examining other sections of Gethsemane.

"I no longer wonder why this spot is so favored as a retreat."

"There is something else, sir."

"Tell me, young man."

"Just behind us."

Maxientus turned around, saw a shape looming behind him.

"I see ... a hill, a mountain," he observed. "What is it called?"

"Olives ... the Mount of Olives."

"What is special about it?"

"The Messiah will speak to us from it someday when He decides it is time to come and rule."

Maxientus ignored that, for it smacked of some of the elements of sedition he had learned of in Rome before leaving for Israel, and he did not want to turn his quiet moments in the garden into anything political.

He moved to another flat rock, this one near the entrance.

"Quiet, almost serene," he whispered.

"It is, sir."

"You seem quite familiar with Gethsemane," Maxientus observed. "I gather that you have been here before."

"I have come each time with the proconsul. At first he asked that I wait outside. Later, though, he told me I could come in with him."

"You feel at peace here also?" asked Maxientus.

"We both do, the proconsul and I."

"Will you come in now and join me?"

The young man had remained just outside, not wanting to be so forward as to join the other man without being asked.

"I would be honored."

"I might need protection if I stay here far longer than I expected," Maxientus jested but with an edge of seriousness since he wondered whether or not they were courting danger, perhaps at the hands of roving insurrectionists. "If someone is tipped off that I am here, it might be dangerous."

"Not here, sir," the horseman told him. "Anyone who enters the Garden of Gethsemane is safe."

Maxientus scoffed at that.

"I see no guards," he said, looking around in an exaggerated manner.

"Local stories say it is angels that guard Gethsemane."

Maxientus started to chuckle.

"Are you a believer in angels?" he asked.

"Yes, sir, I am."

"Have you ever seen one?"

"Have you ever seen any of your Roman gods except as they are represented by statues, sir?"

Maxientus could have taken offense at that remark but found it instead a rather reasonable reply.

"You have a point, young man," he started to comment, "and I must compliment you on your—"

*Movement ...*

They both heard the sounds of movement coming from the more narrow western end of Gethsemane.

"I hardly thought anyone else would be here at this hour," the Roman said nervously, always alert to danger in lands that Rome had conquered. "Are you sure we will not be harmed, that—?"

The horseman was unperturbed, and Maxientus cut himself off.

"I suspect I know who it is," the young man replied.

"Who then?"

The horseman, Shemuel, smiled in such a manner that it seemed as though his entire handsome face was lighting up from within.

"The Nazarene, sir," he announced.

Maxientus snapped his head around and looked at the young man whose rather handsome countenance was sheathed in moonlight.

"As we speak ... here?" he asked, not certain whether to be pleased or angry because of the possibility that he was being set up.

"I did not catch a glimpse of the Nazarene, sir; it could be anyone," Shemuel said nervously. "I am just guessing."

"Of course. I am sorry to bark at you like that."

They walked slowly down the narrow path that twisted and turned through the garden. Eventually they came to an alcove, more bare than the rest of the garden, mostly configured of stones and a handful of pale green bushes but with no flowers in sight.

And then they saw Him. A figure sitting on a blank stone, His back to them.

As they quietly stepped forward, He spoke. "Quintus Maxientus and Shemuel, do not be hesitant," He said in a calm, warm voice.

The middle-aged Roman senator and the young horseman exchanged glances but continued to walk forward.

Jesus of Nazareth stood and faced them, and Maxientus had to stifle a gasp at the regal nature of His countenance.

"How could You possibly know my name?" Maxientus asked,

wondering if Pilatus was putting him at the center of some elaborate hoax. "Were You told that I was coming here?"

"And who would have told Me that?" He asked.

The Roman shrugged his shoulders.

"No one, I suppose. I am just astonished that You could call me by name without facing me first. How could You do that?"

The Nazarene did not answer directly that last question.

"I saw you pass by as I spoke outside Jerusalem," the Nazarene said obliquely.

"That may be so, and You can recognize my face easily enough, I suppose, but it does not explain how You know *who* I am."

"I know who you are and what you are."

Maxientus felt a chill down his back.

"What I am?" he repeated. "What do You mean by that?"

Maxientus could not read the expression on the Nazarene's face, which made him uneasy.

"You are a member of the Roman Senate."

The tone in the voice, however, was unmistakable.

"You speak almost with loathing," Maxientus told him. "How dare You address me as You have!"

"That is how you *thought* you heard Me."

"So there was no scorn in what You said?"

Jesus nodded solemnly.

"What then?"

"Pity."

Maxientus stiffened.

"You pity me because I am an influential member of the most powerful body of men in the world?" he asked loftily.

The pity remained, stronger than seconds before, as Jesus said, "Men who acknowledge their emperor as a god."

Maxientus was prepared to leave immediately but hesitated because of what the Nazarene said and the fact that He knew enough to say it.

"How is it that You are aware of such things?" he asked.

Jesus gave no reply.

"I asked You a question, Nazarene," Maxientus reminded Him. "Are You so foolish as to ignore me? I can have You taken prisoner in an instant if I wish it to be so. Are You willing to act so dangerously now?"

"I could give you the answer that you seek, but you would not accept it," Jesus told the visitor.

"You are playing word games. You are not as honest and straight-forward as I have heard."

"And you are seeking answers to other questions far more important but do not have the courage to offer them right away, if you ever do."

Maxientus' mouth dropped open.

"Are You capable of reading minds?" he asked.

Again the Nazarene did not deal directly with Maxientus' question.

"You are lonely," the Nazarene said.

"Yes, I am but—"

Maxientus scolded himself for admitting anything of the sort, especially under the circumstances.

But Jesus was not finished, for He added, "And you no longer believe in what the Roman Empire is doing."

Maxientus' temper was beginning to flare.

"Now, just a minute," he said defiantly, "You really are approaching a point of—"

Jesus interrupted him again, as though He had not heard the visitor's protest.

"You question the reason for its very existence," He said, "the many evils it has perpetuated."

*Countries overrun ... local despots put in power ... the might of its vast army constantly threatening if any local government tried to overthrow Rome's control ... a one-time benevolent state now given over to the appalling legacy of Caligula.*

The color drained from Maxientus' face.

"You want to resign from the Senate," Jesus continued, "and devolve yourself of all governmental responsibilities."

"I am being betrayed by an informant within my inner circle," Maxientus said. "That must be it!"

"By no one, Quintus Maxientus, by nothing except your own soul."

Abruptly, the visiting Roman felt dizzy, weak, forced to lean against young Shemuel.

A look of the sweetest, warmest compassion fell upon the Nazarene's strong-looking face.

"You have been thinking about death," Jesus told Maxientus.

The visitor managed to steady himself.

"Yes, I have!" he exclaimed. "I have thought to embrace it of my own will rather than wait for the gods to act. They have been known to take forever, but that is not what I would wish."

The Nazarene reached out and touched his shoulder.

"Wealth and power and so much else that is a part of your life no longer mean what they once did, is that not so?"

Maxientus stepped back.

"Are You a devil?" he blurted out. "Is that why You ... You—"

Shemuel, nervously, entered the conversation.

"Jesus is not a devil," he said, a tremor in his voice. "He is something else. I believe Him, and Pilatus is just beginning to do so. Jesus is many things good and holy, but He is not a devil."

"Holy?" Maxientus repeated. "You call this wanderer holy? That is heresy! No man can be holy. Is that not what your religion teaches?"

"Except your emperor?" the Nazarene interjected. "He is a man doomed to an eternity of punishment, a craven beast not fit to walk the earth that My heavenly Father created."

The visitor was flustered because what the other Man had said then was enough to have Him arrested. And yet—

"You speak about some God with authority," he declared. "How can You do that, Nazarene?"

A touch of arrogance infused Maxientus' manner.

"We all are mortals, are we not, and at the mercy of the gods? We are born, we live, we die—poor and wealthy alike share this dreary and monotonous succession of inevitabilities."

The young horseman named Shemuel was listening with great intentness, totally unlike the kind of shocked reaction that Maxientus was manifesting.

"I must leave now," the Roman said. "This is not the place I thought it would be. And You are not the man I had begun to hope You would be."

Shemuel placed his hand gently on Maxientus' shoulder.

"Sir?" he asked.

"Yes, young man, we have to leave; this Nazarene is too strange, far too—" Maxientus said.

"Sir?" Shemuel said again.

The visitor started to walk past him, toward the entrance, to the awaiting chariot and horses.

Shemuel was sweating, knowing he dared not do anything to upset Maxientus; his job and possibly his life would be at stake if Pilatus should decide to punish him by putting him in one of the truly awful Roman prisons that were being maintained throughout Israel.

But then Maxientus stopped and looked over his shoulder.

"What is it?" he asked. "Why do you linger?"

"Sir, would you wait just a little while?" Shemuel asked.

The young man's manner was so disarming and innocent and affecting that Maxientus hesitated.

"You have been with the Nazarene before, right?" he asked.

"Yes, sir, I have."

"It could be your life if you waste my time. You do know that."

"I do, sir; I truly do."

"And still you want to risk irritating me?"

"You will not regret the time, sir. And I place myself in your hands if you should feel otherwise."

Quintus Maxientus stayed.

## Chapter Three

*Morning light.*

*Neither Maxientus or the young horseman named Shemuel returned to the residence of Pilatus by sunrise nor for a long time thereafter.*

*At first Pontius Pilatus was quite oblivious to what was happening to his esteemed visitor and his best horseman.*

*It was only as dawn came that he had reason to be concerned ...*

The proconsul could not stay in bed after five that morning because Procula, his wife, awoke early, blabbering on about the Nazarene, sometimes in her sleep, sometimes while wide awake.

So, the most powerful man in all of Israel arose, ate a light breakfast, and waited for his guest from Rome to awaken, not knowing that Maxientus had decided to go to Gethsemane hours earlier.

After waiting for more than an hour, Pilatus impatiently strode down the long whitewashed hallway lined with multicolored tapestries imported from the Orient.

He tapped lightly on the door to his guest's suite.

Half a dozen other suites were scattered throughout the palace-like building. Maxientus' suite was the largest one of all. It had been planned for important visitors, to impress them—and Quintus Maxientus was someone Pilatus was most anxious to impress.

*I sense that you can get me out of this outpost,* Pilatus had thought when he learned that Maxientus soon would be arriving, a man whom he had heard about frequently over the years. *You are closer to the emperor than I am. If I asked, he would only remind me that we had an arrangement—the money, the three physicians, other bonuses—but you could do so, you could ask this of the emperor and he would be compelled to honor your request as a favor to Maxientus that he definitely did not owe me.*

There was no response to his knock.

*How odd,* Pilatus told himself. *You might be someone who can sleep through the fiercest of storms.*

He knocked a second time.

Nothing.

*Has he drunk himself into a nightlong stupor that has not as yet ended?* he wondered.

Pilatus tried yet again.

Still no response.

"Quintus ..." he said, raising his voice a bit, "I do believe it is time to get up. We have a full day ahead of us, you know."

Still no reply.

Irritated by the lack of an answer, which was something of a breach of etiquette as practiced by the Romans, for whom proper conduct in such matters was primary to their lives, Pilatus banged much more forcefully on the door.

He encountered only continuing silence.

Taller than her completely bald husband and blessed with long, soft, light brown hair that was invariably braided, Procula had heard the noise and hurried from their bedroom to where he was standing, his display of temper gathering momentum.

"How dare that—!" Pontius Pilatus nearly swore, then saw Procula looking at him. "He is an impudent one, this Quintus Maxientus."

The regret he felt was written across his face.

"I had started to think that Quintus was perhaps different from the rest," Pilatus muttered.

He was about to reach for the latch when she rested her hand gently on his and smiled.

"Stop," she said, hardly above a whisper.

Pilatus jerked his head around.

"But my guest might be ill, and I could be angry for nothing," he cautioned. "That is the only other explanation I can imagine."

Procula shook her head.

"What is going on?" Pilatus asked, puzzled by her response and a bit irritated since women were not generally regarded as having anything worthwhile to say in most matters of any substance, particularly in contradiction to their husbands.

"I know where they are," she acknowledged, her voice so low she seemed to be whispering.

"*You* know?!"

Procula nodded without any great concern because she was not a wife who feared even such a powerful husband.

"I do, my love," she added.

"But how could you? This is none of your concern. What could you possibly know that—?"

Procula bristled at his tone.

"Oh?" she interrupted, arching her eyebrows. "Suddenly your opinion of me is not so high as you have been claiming over the years?"

"It is a matter of state," Pilatus remarked, "government business."

"And nothing a wife should concern her empty little head with?"

"I have never treated you that way!"

"But then how *have* you treated me, my beloved?"

Pilatus was annoyed and disappointed that she would pose such a question at all, let alone with the intonation that she used.

"With respect."

"When you are in my presence, yes. But as soon as I am elsewhere, admit it, you ruminate with some of your visiting cronies about my state of mind."

"But Quintus Maxientus is not a crony of mine."

"That means only that you did not voice your suspicions about me to him, or perhaps you did so anyway."

"Would I unburden myself as you suggest to some mere stranger? *Think*, Procula, please."

She placed her hands on her hips.

"Oh, I have done much thinking of late. I realize that you have allowed yourself to be convinced I am losing my mind and that someday I will have to be returned to Rome and locked away from the world."

Procula narrowed her eyes as she stared at her husband.

"You talk so much about my burgeoning madness, Pontius, I begin to wonder if you dread that decision which surely must come as an apocalypse of some kind, or do you *relish* the advent of it? After all, it is a sturdy enough reason that would justify petitioning the emperor about the need for you to follow me there."

He raised a hand to slap Procula and saw her expression, a look not of anger or fear but of resignation as though she were saying, *Knock me down, ship me back to Rome, whatever it is that you feel you have to do, and then throw away the key you are given to whatever dungeon I am assigned, but realize, dear husband, that nothing will change the woman I am becoming.*

Pilatus had, after nearly twenty years of marriage, come to the point where it was as though he could read his wife's thoughts.

"Do you *see* what you are becoming?" he asked. "Do you *know* how twisted your mind is at this very moment?"

He started pacing the hallway.

"There was little wrong with you until you became infatuated with the Nazarene!" he declared.

"Infatuated?" Procula repeated. "Do you think His appeal is the kind that makes me want to get into bed with this Man?"

"Have you given me any reason to think otherwise? You can hardly stay away from Him. I know how you lie in order to be at His side, the excuses that masquerade as truth.

"How many trips to the *agora* have you made lately? Why have *you* started to buy so much of the food rather than have our hired help do it? I *trusted* you, so I never thought there was any reason to question where you went and how much time you spent doing whatever it was that you do."

She avoided her husband's gaze.

"How many dinners with other Romans living in this city have you attended? You have even led me to believe that you were willing to sit down with some *Jews* socially and eat with them."

Pilatus stopped pacing and stood within a couple of inches of her.

"Were there other lies that I missed," he demanded, "lies that seemed less obvious so I had no reason to question them?"

She clasped her hands hard against one another.

"I had to be with Jesus!" Procula exclaimed.

He was trying earnestly to understand.

"To my eye, He seems to be someone who is little more than the simplest of ordinary men and certainly not a wealthy man, nor a powerful man either. And yet this Jesus seems to satisfy you better than I have been doing of late!"

Procula slapped her husband hard across the cheek, but he did nothing in return except to drone on.

"I admit that He is quite handsome, yes, but is that all? Am I so homely in comparison? You must tell me, Procula!"

Ashamed of herself for what she had just done, Procula reached out and cupped her hands around his face.

"Will you listen?" she asked. "Will you actually listen? I could endure whatever the future holds if you would just listen to me now."

Pilatus had spent his anger. There was no rage left in him. He would accept any answers she had for him and be grateful she was still there to give them.

"The Nazarene claims that He is God incarnate, the *true* God in human form," Procula Pilatus began. "I believe Him, my dearest husband, I believe Him."


Pontius and Procula Pilatus arrived outside Gethsemane within half an hour, taking the route of a dry *wadi* that stretched from just beyond their residence to a hundred feet outside Gethsemane. The land of Palestine was littered with these dry creek beds, signs of the continual water crisis that afflicted this desert nation.

"This is absurd!" he grumbled. "I should have summoned more of the palace guards. We have so few with us, and who knows what this Nazarene may be up to!"

"You need no others," Procula told him confidently.

They saw Shemuel.

The young man was sitting on a stone near the entrance.

*Sobbing ...*

He was sobbing.

Pilatus jumped out of the chariot, which he had driven himself rather than wait for another horseman to get ready, and hurried to Shemuel's side.

Other proconsuls of other regions subscribed to the unofficial dictum that no emotion was to be shown toward those who worked for them either as freemen or slaves. As far as these Romans were concerned, any genuine *feelings* were to be reserved for members of their own families and other individuals of their "station," not lowly servants. Pilatus, though, never failed to show his care and concern for his workers.

Visiting dignitaries, exposed to Pilatus' relationship with his household staff, invariably reported what they saw to the emperor, but he was wise enough to let his proconsuls rule as long as they kept order in the conquered provinces of the Roman Empire.

Shemuel seemed beside himself.

"What happened?" Pilatus inquired, genuinely concerned about someone who seemed almost like a son to him, a relationship that was especially important since his marriage had produced no offspring, the barrenness of it haunting him. Shemuel's company helped, to some degree, to make the interminable duty in Israel a bit less irksome, the two of them going off on hunting trips while Procula stayed home and did whatever it was she did to fill her own hours of loneliness and despair.

He reached out, tapped Shemuel's shoulder.

"What terrible—?" he asked.

His young friend looked up at him, and the proconsul abruptly stepped back, startled.

A smile.

Shemuel was smiling through his tears.

"I cry, sir, not out of sorrow caused by some tragedy," he said, knowing that it would be difficult for Pilatus to grasp what was going on.

"Then why?"

Shemuel glanced past him and saw Procula approach.

"Go ahead, my brother," she said, smiling.

The proconsul spun around and faced his wife, noticing that her expression was more radiant than he had seen in some time.

"*My brother?*" he nearly shouted the words. "Listen to yourself, Procula! Have you finally lost your—?"

"Lost my mind, Pontius?" she finished his question for him. "No, I have not, my dear husband. I have gained my soul."

She stood beside Shemuel, who remained sitting.

"You can treat him like a son," she said, "but you are not able to cope with the fact that I called him 'my brother?'"

"This is too much," Pilatus said. "I am going to find Maxientus and leave this place. You can come with me or stay."

Shemuel finally stood.

"Let me take you to him," he said.

"Is he close by?"

"Yes, sir, quite close."

The young man walked slowly toward an alcove tucked into the edge of Gethsemane, a distance of less than fifty feet.

"Has anything happened to Quintus?" Pilatus asked apprehensively. "Do I need to call out the guards?"

Shemuel stopped for a moment and looked at him, the love that had settled on that handsome face astonishing.

"A great deal has happened to him, sir," he replied. "Be patient. You shall see. But it is not something for which any of the guards will be necessary."

In seconds they had reached the alcove.

Pilatus finally saw Quintus Maxientus.

*Kneeling ...*

The Roman official was kneeling before the Nazarene, Who had just reached into a tiny nearby stream and brought up some water in His tightly cupped hands to drip slowly over Maxientus' bowed head.

"Your sins are now washed away," He said, "just as this pure water now washes over you."

"But, Lord, Lord, how can that be?" Maxientus said as sobs tore through him. "I am so unclean, so ... filthy. How can *You* tell me this?"

"Because I have forgiven them," Jesus spoke. "As far as My Father is concerned, they do not exist."

Pilatus stepped forward.

"What is this nonsense?" he asked angrily. "Quintus, get out of the dirt *now!* He is but a carpenter from—"

Jesus shot a glance at him.

Suddenly Pilatus had no voice and he had to turn away, tears pouring down his own cheeks.

"Do you see, sir?" Shemuel asked. "Do you honestly see? He has power over everything, and He uses it with the greatest wisdom."

"Some kind of spell ..." Pilatus muttered, finally able to find his voice.

"No, it is—"

But the proconsul would hear none of this.

"Procula, return with me now!" he ordered.

"Are you ignoring what you see?" she demanded of her husband. "Are you trying to pretend that this is nothing?"

He glowered at Procula as he grabbed her hand and started to pull her out of the alcove and toward the entrance.

The Nazarene approached him and placed a large hand gently on top of Pilatus' hairless head.

"Let the woman go," He said gently.

"She is my wife! How dare You—?"

"How dare *you* try to thwart the will of Yahweh!"

"Do You claim to be He?" Pilatus asked, "this so-called God of the Hebrews, this impotent—?"

He began to laugh harshly until he started choking, choking so completely that he dropped to the ground and found that Gethsemane was spinning around in his vision.

Procula rushed to her husband's side.

But he brushed her away.

"Leave me alone!" the powerful man cried out. "Stay here or come with me. I no longer care."

He tried to stand, but weakness suddenly consumed him.

*His tunic!*

And then he saw the front of his tunic.

*Soaked!*

It was soaked in blood.

"You are a wizard!" he exclaimed.

The Nazarene said nothing, but His expression was mirrored by Procula and young Shemuel. The horseman was taking a chance expressing disapproval in any form; although Roman society allowed dissent, this was a privilege enjoyed only by those of a proper social station and was little tolerated from anyone else.

"I must get back!" Pilatus exclaimed. "I must summon the physicians and get them to stop this—"

Finally Jesus stepped forward and extended His hand, an expression of pure kindness on His face.

But Pilatus looked at Him with haughtiness.

"No!" he shouted. "I shall get there without *Your* help!"

Procula spoke up.

"You cannot even stand!" she told him. "Grab the Nazarene's hand, my beloved, *do it now!*"

"I shall *not* take the hand of a carpenter from a dirty little village in a misbegotten land, a land that is reeking with traitors such as Himself!" he rebuked her. "No Roman can sacrifice his dignity so blatantly and expect the gods to be happy."

"*The gods?*" Procula spoke incredulously.

"They have kept us safe until this very moment."

"But where *are* they now?"

"You ridicule *them?* And choose this Jehovah of the Jews, I suppose! Is that what you are doing?"

"It is, Pontius. And I pray that you do likewise."

"*Never!*" he shouted as he tried again to stand.

Shemuel tried to help him.

"So you too have deserted me," Pilatus rebuked him. "I need nothing from you *or* my wife!"

Procula got down on her knees.

"Please let us help!" she begged.

But he turned his head away as he struggled to get to his feet.

"It is your life at stake, not your dignity," she told him. "Do not sacrifice the one because the other seems endangered."

But Pilatus would not listen.

"Then die I shall, here and now, but I die as a Roman, not some poor soul groveling at the feet of this ... this—!"

He was on his feet but wobbly.

"I *shall* walk away," Pilatus said defiantly. "I shall reach the chariot and climb up into it, and—"

"You have no strength," Procula said. "Please listen, please—"

For an instant he saw his wife and his favored horseman and the Nazarene, and then there was nothing at all except the expanding light, light so powerful that the darkness fled without protest.

Seeing his friend kneeling before the Nazarene, hearing the nonsense that was being spoken to him that awful morning, Pilatus began to wonder if the gods of Rome *had* turned their celestial backs on him.

*"I want those physicians with me!" Pilatus demanded, modulating only his tone out of respect for the emperor. "They are learned men, and I trust them. Am I not worth this final concession?"*

*The most powerful man on earth had agreed ...*

One of Pilatus' conditions for agreeing to serve the Roman Empire by being stationed in such a disagreeable outpost as Israel was that he take with him the three physicians who had always been available to treat him in Rome. At first the emperor objected, particularly about the expense since it would be necessary to pay those learned men an extra-ordinary amount of money to accommodate Pilatus' demand, but then he had to acknowledge that no one else in all the top echelon of Roman military men would have been willing to go under *any* circumstances, though they risked supreme wrath by refusing. Also, Pilatus was in fact the best man for the task of keeping order in a region given historically to upheaval.

Those three physicians now were standing at Pilatus' bedside, relieved when he finally regained consciousness.

"Praise the gods!" the bald-headed, round-faced older one named Septimius Cornelius Mancinus said.

Procula was standing to one side.

"What happened to me?" Pilatus asked while noticing that he had been cleaned and given a fresh tunic to wear.

"We think a number of blood vessels close to the surface of your skin broke," Mancinus replied, "and the blood seeped through your pores. It is rare, this circumstance, but not completely unheard of. Some individuals experience it only in the palms of their hands."

*... only in the palms of their hands.*

Pilatus winced at that image, thinking of the many men he had ordered crucified since taking his post in Israel. At night, since his residence was relatively close to Golgotha, he could hear, carried on a passing breeze, the sounds of men moaning as they hung from their crosses, the most painful and prolonged of executions dragging out their anguish.

"What would cause this condition?" he asked.

"Something very intense, proconsul."

"Intense?"

"Yes, physical or emotional."

Pilatus had propped himself up on his elbows. Now he fell back against the soft goose down mattress.

"Are you dizzy?" Procula asked as she hurried to the edge of the bed in which they both had slept since the first day of their arrival in Israel.

"No," he told her. "I am just remembering all that has happened."

"You must not weary yourself," she cautioned. "You must rest throughout the day, Pontius."

The three physicians were mumbling agreement.

"I treated you and Shemuel so badly, and for no reason," Pilatus asked, fragments of guilt claiming their place in his thoughts. "Will you forgive me for that? *Can* you forgive me?"

"Forgiveness is part of—"

He placed a finger to his lips, and she stopped.

None of the three physicians present could be trusted to be completely loyal or, for that matter, even discreet, despite what he had done for them to help make them more comfortable while in Israel.

And so it was merely being prudent for both Procula and him to avoid making any statements that would unduly connect her with the Nazarene's doctrine of love and forgiveness, now well-known throughout the land and highly suspect at the highest levels of government in Rome.

Procula nodded, appreciating his wisdom.

*Some months after he left Jerusalem to begin his ministry, Stephen learned that Procula Pilatus had taken an interest in him. Apparently she was interested in contributing to his ministry.*

*"Why?" he asked simply of the man who had informed him of this.*

*"Because you are so much like Jesus."*

*At first Stephen could not accept that, but then he realized Procula could not have understood the implications of those words, and he stopped frowning and was about to speak when his friend interpolated, "She meant well, Stephen. And she feels guilty that she was unable to stop the crucifixion."*

*"Stop the crucifixion?"*

*The friend nodded.*

*"Thank God she was not able to do so!" Stephen exclaimed.*

*"Why do you, of all people, say that?"*

*"Because it was what God the Father had decided. Because Christ's shed blood washed away sin."*

*The other man's eyes opened wide.*

*"I see what you are saying. May I tell this dear woman?"*

*"Please, yes, tell her. And assure her that I shall do my best to return to Jerusalem as soon as possible."*

*"She will be eager to see you. And—"*

*The friend hesitated.*

*Stephen waited patiently then asked, "Is there more?"*

*"There is."*

*"Tell me then. I must be on my way."*

*"Procula Pilatus is convinced that as your fame grows you will need protection, protection from some of the same conspirators who were behind the death of the Nazarene."*

*"Tell her I shall be glad to discuss the matter. I want nothing, though, that seeks to thwart God's will for my life."*

*"That will never be her desire, Stephen."*

*The young missionary smiled as he said, "Then I shall look forward to spending some time with her. Yes, very much."*

## Chapter Four

Minutes later, the physicians left, but Pilatus asked his wife to remain.

"Where is Shemuel?" he asked.

She was biting her lower lip.

"Has anything happened to him?"

His fatherly affection for the young man was making him nervous about Shemuel's safety.

"I cannot say," Procula replied.

"You have no idea where he is?"

"He ... he—"

Pilatus saw that she was becoming distraught.

"Calm down, Procula," he told her. "Please forgive, once again, my manner as you have done so often, born as it is of despair and impatience because of being stationed in this wretched place. But, you see, I am very fond of that young man."

"He's like the son I never gave you, yes, I know of your fondness."

She had, at first, mistaken it for something else but knew in her heart that her husband had never shown any propensities of that sort.

"Then tell me more," Pilatus said. "You must do that, for surely you have more details than you are offering."

"He was informed of something about Quintus Maxientus two hours ago while you were still unconscious."

"Told *something*? Is that all you can say?"

Pilatus narrowed his eyes as he looked at her.

"Do not be concerned with my feelings. There is no need to spare them. I want to know it all."

"Yes ..." she said. "There is more."

"Then go ahead, Procula."

"Your new friend from Rome is—"

She could not finish.

"Is what?" he pressed. "Quintus is—?"

"Nearly dead," Procula said, "as well as the horseman you sent with him to the harbor where his ship has been anchored."

Pontius Pilatus blinked several times, as though not able to understand what she was saying.

"Nearly dead—?" He spoke lamely, so shocked by what she told him that the words would not rush out as usual, an unusual condition in this man who often talked far too much, boring those with whom he kept company.

Procula wished she was not the bearer of such tidings.

"Wounded," she told her husband, "gravely wounded by henchmen sent by Barabbas the insurrectionist."

"Why?" Pilatus asked, not expecting her to know the answer. "What could they have had against him? He was truly innocent of any mischief against Barabbas and his kind. No one would shed a tear for the insurrectionists, but Quintus is another story, Procula."

But she surprised him.

"Simply that he was a Roman," she declared, "nothing more than that in times such as these, my beloved."

"If he had only waited! I had a contingent of my men on their way to escort him to the harbor and give him safe passage."

"He was too anxious to get back, I suppose."

"Get back? Why?"

"To share the joy he felt."

"Joy? At meeting the Nazarene? That must be nonsense, Procula. Are you so blind that you cannot see it as such?"

"Are you not the blind one?" she retorted with equal emotion. "You cannot see Who Jesus really is because it would destroy every spiritual thought you have ever had, every thought given over to the false gods and goddesses of Rome."

Procula sighed, showing the futility she was feeling.

"You wallow in your own delusions, my husband, while accusing me of being seduced by Someone Who is so much more than any man you and I have ever met, but your own stubbornness refuses to let you open your eyes and see the truth about the Nazarene.

"But then you are hardly free of seduction yourself. Diana and Venus and the others ... you believe in *demons*, my husband, if they even exist, for that is all they can be, millions of us held in their sway over the generations of time since Rome butchered its way into control of the world!"

Pilatus let out a scream of rage and despair that brought several members of his household staff to the bedroom door, but Procula told them everything was all right, and so they left, muttering among themselves.

"What an evil land! It is destroying you and me, in separate ways, but destroying us nonetheless," he said, closer to tears than she had seen him in a very long time. "Where is Quintus now?"

Before she could answer, he continued to speak. "Being treated by my physicians, I trust? Did anyone think to summon them, or have you all lost—?

"No, they were not gotten out of their beds," Procula told him, speaking in a manner suggesting that she could guess what his reaction would be after she had told him everything.

"Why is that so? What could you have been thinking?"

"They could accomplish nothing."

"You cannot be certain. You are not a physician yourself."

"I went with Shemuel."

"You—!"

His face was a deep red.

"Are you really my wife? Or some impostor? You dared to—"

"Pontius?" she said softly.

"Quintus is with the Nazarene. We found Him, and He agreed to go with us. It happened near Gethsemane. I hurried back to be here when you awakened."

"With the Nazarene? For healing? You are surely not serious. Quintus Maxientus needs doctors, not a faith healer."

"He is nearly gone now. Doctors could never help him."

"And this Jesus can, I suppose."

"I think the help He will give is not the kind you could possibly have in mind right now."

Procula saw that her husband was rubbing his arm.

"Are you feeling what I am feeling right now?" she asked.

"Dread ..." he told her, "the awfulness of dread."

"For me, it is different."

"Why, Procula, why?"

"I know what is happening or has already happened to your new friend. I know what it is like for Quintus Maxientus."

"You met him for only minutes when he first arrived and then at dinner. How could you know much of anything?"

"Because it has been so with me."

"You? You are not close to death. How can you expect me to accept what you are saying? It is senseless blabbering as far as I am concerned."

"And evidence of my madness?" she asked pointedly.

He pretended not to have heard her.

"We must hurry," he said. "Get the physicians over here, please. Will you at least do that for me? I will have someone else from our staff summon some legionnaires. They are always looking for something to do."

And this Procula did for the only man she had loved for just over twenty years, knowing that the doctors would be going on a futile mission but not wanting to upset him any longer.

A dozen of the top Roman legionnaires stationed in Israel and under the proconsul's command were with Pilatus and Procula. The battle-hardened soldiers had been ready in less than ten minutes after a member of the household staff relayed the urgent order of their commanding officer.

The road was one that Pilatus knew well, convenient to his residence but rather private. He used the ancient *wadi* regularly to go to Gethsemane on the sly, cutting down the chance that anybody would see him. And he had had the very end of the *wadi*, which was less than a hundred feet from the garden, turned into a slope that his horses could easily climb.

*The attack must have occurred just ahead,* Pilatus reasoned to himself, *as Quintus was coming out of the wadi and onto the ground just above us.*

Ahead of him Pilatus spotted a chariot on its side, one of the wheels on the ground a few feet away. He recognized it as one of his own. Few Jews were privileged enough to have such a chariot in their possession.

Two of the four horses hitched to the chariot were dead. A third was still alive but badly wounded. The fourth was gone, perhaps back to the stable.

One of the legionnaires got off his own horse and strode forward, ready to end the animal's misery.

Pilatus' years on various battlefields had made him accustomed to the sight of dying men.

But not animals.

"So helpless ..." he muttered. "They serve their masters well all the days of their lives, and then—"

Procula rested her hand on his shoulder, and he did not pull away.

Pilatus ordered his horseman to stop.

"Are you coming with me?" he asked his wife.

She nodded.

He gave her a slight smile and then jumped out of the chariot. After helping his wife to the ground, Pilatus hurried directly forward to examine what was left of the man-made slope.

To get up to ground level, he would have to climb over half-buried rocks and timbers that had been placed across the incline.

One of the legionnaires rushed up to him.

"It looks pretty tricky, sir," he said, concerned. "Please, proconsul, let us help you."

Unreasonably, Pilatus became angry.

"I am still as strong as you are!" he bellowed. "It is something I am capable of doing myself without anybody's help!"

Instantly he regretted this display of temper.

"Help my wife instead," he spoke. "Will you do that for me?"

"Of course, sir, yes, sir!" the legionnaire assured him, accustomed to his commanding officer's outbursts.

Pilatus started to climb up the slope, which required some effort because of its present condition; sharp-edged rocks that had been buried underneath dirt now poked through the surface.

Wet. Suddenly he realized that his hands were wet.

Blood. On his fingers and palms as well as the sleeve of his tunic.

At first he thought it must have been a cut he had sustained. But he quickly glanced at his hands and found nothing.

More. So much that it started to drip down onto his forehead.

After less than a minute, he had made it to the top.

Groaning. He heard a man groaning, then saw Quintus Maxientus on the ground with Shemuel kneeling beside him on one side and the Nazarene on the other.

Behind him he heard movement and knew that Procula would be following, along with the three physicians.

Already several legionnaires were walking toward him.

Pilatus was surprised.

"How did you get here so quickly?" he asked. "There was only what was left of that one torn-up slope."

Pilatus saw that several had cuts and scrape marks, and he was not surprised at what one of the men told him. "We just climbed up the side, sir, since there is no other way out of the *wadi*."

Pilatus hurried to Quintus Maxientus' side.

"He is almost home," Shemuel whispered to him.

"Home? What—?" Pilatus asked.

Maxientus feebly reached up and grabbed the front of the proconsul's soiled tunic.

"This fine young man is right, you know," he said, his voice hardly louder than Shemuel's whisper but astonishingly firm. "This life you and I lead, this world on which we walk, there is more than this, my friend.

"We live here, you and I, and our family, our friends, yes, our enemies and countless strangers alike, and we die here, but that is not the end. We are temporary visitors at a way station, and once that visit is over, we go elsewhere, we go—"

Pilatus looked sharply at the Nazarene.

"What is this nonsense that You have been telling him?" he spoke. "Home is back in Rome, not here in this horrible land."

The Nazarene replied with a gentleness that took the proconsul aback.

"Home is neither here nor in Rome but with My Father in heaven!" He said. "That is home for those who believe."

"Believe? In You? In Your faraway God? Is that what You have done to this poor man's mind?"

Maxientus tugged at him again.

"You are the poorer, my new friend," he said, "because you have eyes but do not see and ears but do not hear."

"Whatever you say …" Pilatus told this fellow Roman, realizing that Maxientus had to be kept calm.

He glanced over his shoulder at the three physicians who shook their heads sadly, one of them wringing his hands in an unconsciously exaggerated fashion. They did not need to examine Maxientus because they could see, from a few feet away, how badly the man had been hurt. His attackers had done what they had intended.

*Their expressions!*

Speaking of no hope as much as any words could.

Doctors whose dedication to saving lives was based upon the presumption that mortal life was all that existed, and once it had ended, the dead one ceased to exist in any form.

Pilatus saw this, and abruptly felt a wave of coldness overtaking his own body.

Maxientus' hand started to drop, any last bit of strength fading. He turned to the Nazarene.

"Pontius will come around," Maxientus said rather desperately. "I will tell the Father to reserve space for this good man."

And then he was gone.

Pilatus convinced himself that he could not be seen crying.

Procula fell to her knees and sobbed.

"You hardly knew the man," he told her. "He was my friend, not yours. Why do you react so?"

"Does that mean I am to have no feeling?" she said, careful to keep her voice low and even in front of the physicians and the awaiting legionnaires. "I would shed tears now for anyone such as he who had changed the destiny of his soul."

Pilatus jumped to his feet and faced Jesus.

"What is this power You have over people?" he demanded.

"And over you in time," the Nazarene said prophetically.

"Me? You *are* stupid after all."

"You must not call Him stupid," Procula managed to say.

"I must *not*, you tell me? I *control* this desolate country. Only the emperor is greater. I send men to their deaths. I spare them. I am the ultimate judge of what happens. Never tell me what I must not do or say or how I am to act. This man is stupid. I have said it. Therefore He is!"

He glowered at the Nazarene.

"If I want one of my legionnaires to run Him through with a sharp blade this very moment, it shall be done!"

He motioned for one of the soldiers to step forward, a veteran of much combat who had been with him for a very long time.

"Present your sword!" Pilatus ordered.

There was no hesitation on the part of the legionnaire.

"Be ready to pierce Him at my command!" his commander demanded.

The battle-scarred veteran stepped in front of Jesus.

"You see!" the proconsul said with something that approached glee. "I was not exaggerating."

But there was no fear on the Nazarene's countenance. Pilatus blinked once, twice, a third time.

"Raise your weapon above His neck!" he added.

Again the legionnaire obeyed.

"Keep it there!"

The proconsul jabbed Jesus in the chest with a finger.

"Your God, if He exists at all, does not have *this* kind of power," he said mockingly. "I can cause Your death in an instant. I have no indication that Yahweh, as You call Him, is about to step in and save You."

"It is only as the Father has given you power that you have it."

Jesus smiled without a trace of scorn.

"How much better for you that you consider your own salvation," He said, a kindness to His voice that made Pilatus flinch.

"You dare say that to me now? You arrogant—"

His scorn had become stark anger.

"Execute Him now!" he ordered.

"*No!*" Procula screamed as she ran in front of the Nazarene. "You must not do this shameful—"

"Restrain my wife!" Pilatus said.

Two legionnaires grabbed her and dragged her to one side as she struggled to free herself.

"I give you one chance," the proconsul told Jesus. "Recant what You have said, and I shall free You from death."

"You have no authority to do that now, and it shall not be yours even two days from now. Life and death are no more in your hands than in the hands of the poorest deaf and blind leper beggar!"

"What do You mean by that? Why do You speak of two days from now?"

"It is as you shall see, as it has been prophesied for generations."

Pilatus, frustrated, looked from Procula to the legionnaires to the three physicians, who were spellbound.

"Enough of Your ramblings," he snorted. "Do You recant?"

"Does the morning provide no sweet dew?"

Pilatus was frowning.

"Is that a no?"

Jesus did not reply.

"Kill Him!" the proconsul said as he turned his back to the Nazarene. "And throw His remains to the jackals!"

He heard the sound of a sword cutting through the night air. He heard Procula gasp, and she was not the only one.

The three Roman physicians were reacting in the same way, one of them falling to the ground as he bowed his head and seemed to be mumbling rather desperately to himself.

"What is going on?" Pilatus said as he turned around. "What—?"

And then he saw.

The legionnaire had started to swing his sword toward the Nazarene's neck, but his arm seemed to freeze in midair.

"Do it!" Pilatus demanded.

The legionnaire tried again. But he could not lower the sword.

"Forgive me!" this physically scarred veteran said, shaking from head to foot, as he dropped the sword.

The proconsul was livid. He reached down and grabbed the heavy sword himself, turning it toward the legionnaire.

"Then you shall die in His place!" he declared.

As Pilatus started to swing the weapon toward the now unarmed soldier, several of the other legionnaires reached for their own swords.

"Do you dare to defy me as well?" he asked sternly, seeing what had happened. "Are you going to die along with this—?"

"Look at the Nazarene's eyes!" Procula spoke up. "I beg you, look into them!"

With great reluctance, Pilatus did what she had asked, saw the eyes of the Nazarene as He stood just inches away, saw the peace and the joy in them, saw the forgiveness, saw the love.

"You are a fake," he said, "one of those traveling actors who reads a script and tries to make people believe he is what someone has written him to be. Yes, that is it, that is it."

"You shall not kill me this day," the Nazarene told him.

"How can You be so confident of that?"

"Because it is not the appointed time, and it is not the way the prophets have said."

"Oh, would You prefer to be crucified?" Pilatus asked, his disdain never stronger. "I can do that, you know, right now. The wood for the crosses is kept in a special location. Assembling one will not take very long."

"Not now," Jesus said simply. "Not today."

"When?"

"You will know. And you will remember this moment."

And then Jesus just walked away, with Pontius Pilatus still holding a heavy old sword, though no longer in the air, and others standing near him, watching the Man leave their presence and disappear into the early morning haze.

## Chapter Five

Pontius Pilatus could not change the appointments he had for the day as most of them concerned matters of government and were therefore typically insensitive to mere human feelings but demanded their time regardless.

Caiaphas was the first intruder, as Pontius Pilatus called the Jews who invaded the privacy of his life, sighing as he understood that there was no way to keep the craven lot of them away.

"I am most grateful that you have taken this time to see me," the high priest said as he strode forward to take Pilatus' hand in his own.

Pilatus gave him a weak smile of greeting, for this was the Jew he despised the most.

*How foul your presence,* he thought. *From what I have seen, it would be easy to choose between the Nazarene and someone like yourself. You seem more like a rodent than a human being, bent over like an old man though you are hardly past fifty years of age.*

Caiaphas had a bone condition, probably from lack of calcium, that made him stoop slightly, and because of pain in his joints, he had to walk in jerky, ratlike steps.

*Perhaps I should feel sorry for you,* Pilatus mused. *Perhaps if you were better off physically, your conduct would change.*

But he would not allow himself to feel any more sympathy than that for someone at whose instigation so many men had been forced to bleed away their lives atop the Place of the Skull.

"Who is to die now?" he asked of the high priest.

"Does it matter?" Caiaphas asked, playing his arrogance for all it was worth.

But Pilatus was not in an overlooking mood at that moment.

"*Matter?*" he replied, nearly at a shout. "You treat human life as so disposable that we might as well, you and I, be stepping on bugs when we consort to murder those men. How many has it been, Caiaphas?"

The high priest reached into his extravagantly colored, flowing robe and brought out a tiny piece of papyrus.

"Ten altogether, since you were installed as proconsul-governor of these lands," he said, no emotion twisting a face that might as well have been carved out of some granite block and surrounded by a well-cared-for beard.

"May the gods damn you to whatever punishment exists for your kind!" Pilatus exploded. "What do you have in another pocket of that very expensive imported robe, paid for out of the accumulated donations from widows and farmers and even those poor whose single proudest achievement is being able to donate the smallest-value coin to your overstuffed treasury?

"Is that a pocket for your list of how many sheep you have slaughtered, sheep bought by the unknowing faithful you victimize day after day after day by leeching from each sale a percentage for your own enrichment?

"Or, yes, I know, it must be, in that pocket, a confidential list of how much you have kept aside for yourself, a stipend for your old age that is a secret between you and your God. If He exists, He would be well advised to snuff you out before you live another year and deceive the masses that much longer."

Caiaphas was unflustered.

"Are you through?" he asked.

Pilatus knew he could not hope to maintain control over the Jews without the support of a man who was no better than a jackal in his eyes.

"I am," he replied wearily.

"I know how you feel," Caiaphas said. "But I do what I do to survive. Is that not what you have been driven to as well? Are we not similar in that? You represent a government that massacres, then rules the remnant.

"I have had to take that remnant and keep them together through enormous upheaval or else they would commit suicide by following Barabbas or some other false messiah."

"You mention Barabbas but not Jesus. Do you not consider Him dangerous as well and want to convince me to feel as you do?"

The high priest hesitated, not having expected such an incisive comment.

"Yes ..." he admitted. "It *is* about the Nazarene that I come to you now with much urgency."

"What do you wish? That He be the next victim to add His blood to the thin, infertile layer of soil atop Golgotha?"

"I do. That is precisely what I wish."

Pilatus had not been facing the high priest when Caiaphas spoke but was looking toward the balcony and thinking of quiet little Gethsemane a few hours before and those eyes, those eyes of His, eyes that had seemed to have the power of gazing directly into his soul.

"I will do nothing of the sort," he said as he turned and confronted Caiaphas. "The Nazarene is not negotiable."

"Is the way Rome perceives your competence negotiable instead?" the high priest responded.

Pilatus narrowed his eyes.

"Are you threatening me now?" he asked coldly.

"I call it a service. I am good enough to be apprising you of certain, shall we say, realities. Having done so, I may leave this very moment and be about my business for the day."

"And your business will include getting one of your obedient scribes to draft a revelatory epistle to Quintus Maxientus, in the course of which you will inform him of certain ... oh, how to say, certain aspects of my conduct in this land that would not please the emperor."

"I have no reason to suspect that the man you mention would not cooperate," Caiaphas said cryptically.

"Wonderful choice. You have heard that he and I are friends, and that, as a result, he could never compromise his own position in the Senate or with the emperor by sitting on any such communication, because the punishment for that might involve losing his life in a very public ceremony."

Pilatus saw the high priest's smile, and he felt like taking a sword and carving it right off his face.

"Jesus of Nazareth must die," Caiaphas said.

"Better you than He!"

The high priest winced at that.

"I think He would be a better leader than you ever were. Perhaps your body is the one that should be hanging from a cross."

But Caiaphas would not be deterred.

"The Nazarene must die," he said, clinging to that idea much like a survivor of a shipwreck would cling to a piece of floating wood.

"I am not convinced of that," Pilatus retorted.

"You must pay attention to my wisdom."

"If you had any wisdom, I would."

He pointed toward the balcony.

"I see *your* answers embodied in Golgotha to the left," he said. "I see the Nazarene's in Gethsemane to the right. One way is bloodshed and death. The other is peace and contemplation."

Pilatus sighed as he added, "You judge this Man wrongly, and I shall not play a part in your unholy scheme."

"Thinking like that could be a very big mistake on your part," the high priest warned.

"So be it!" Pilatus replied. "Now leave. You are empty-handed this day."

Caiaphas pulled his robe closer about himself and prepared to leave. As he reached the door, he said over his shoulder, "Quintus Maxientus is here in Jerusalem, I understand. I have much to tell him."

Pilatus was glad he had waited to tell the high priest what had happened.

"Your information is dated," he said.

"We shall see."

"Oh, it is, Caiaphas, you can be sure of that. My friend is here, yes, but he will be leaving soon."

"I shall catch him—"

"In a finely crafted coffin ready for burial in Rome."

Caiaphas stiffened.

"He was killed by Barabbas' men. *That* is the devil you should be condemning, not this good Man from Nazareth."

The high priest left without saying anything else, slamming the heavy door behind him.

*Recalling the details of what had happened to Quintus Maxientus was hardly what Caiaphas wanted to be doing. But he did respect the man and wished he had known sooner what had happened to a powerful ally in the Roman Senate ...*

"I was careless," he muttered to himself during a break in the meeting of the various members of the Sanhedrin, "stupid and careless. Now look at what has happened, a lost opportunity."

Another priest, a little man named Daniyel, overheard him.

"Caiaphas, I fear that you are on the edge of an abyss," he said, looking sternly at the other man.

"An abyss?" the high priest answered, puzzled, the notion absolutely foreign to his thinking. "Explain yourself."

"You called the death of a fine man merely a lost opportunity."

The high priest made few miscalculations, but he realized that saying that statement out loud, rather than keeping it to himself, was one of them.

"Is that all it means, Caiaphas?" Daniyel asked. "Have you so squandered your humanity?"

Daniyel had no illusions about the high priest, though supporting his leader had been a point of honor for a very long time.

*I think you can no longer count me in your corner,* Daniyel thought silently. *I think the time has come for you to give up your leadership, which has become increasingly malevolent while parading under a more respectable guise.*

Nehemeyah, another member of the Sanhedrin, stepped into the hallway.

"What is going on here?" he asked. "The others have returned already. They are impatient."

Daniyel glared at the high priest.

"Ask that of the high priest," he said, "and then throw his answer on some rubbish heap."

Glowering, he walked past.

"Daniyel is losing his grip," Caiaphas remarked lamely. "I think he will have to be sanctioned by—"

But Nehemeyah would have none of it.

"Nonsense!" he interrupted. "The man is just voicing what others among us are convinced is inevitable, given your state of mind."

"My state of mind? You question my—"

Nehemeyah allowed a grin to curl up the sides of his lips.

"You are quite determined to have the Nazarene's head, are you not?" he interrupted the second time.

Caiaphas' reply was chilling.

"Not His head, my dear Nehemeyah, but His body on a cross atop Golgotha," he said.

The younger man's face was flushed with anger.

"Because He threatens you, is that not it?" Nehemeyah declared with scorn. "Surely you would not have me and anyone else of any intelligence believe anything to the contrary."

"You have no idea, have you?" Caiaphas said.

"No idea about what?"

"The Nazarene threatens all of us. Our whole world, one that we have meticulously constructed over the course of generations—"

Nehemeyah interrupted a third time, again without any hint of apology.

"And coming to full fruition in your guiding hands, is that it?" he asked, his cynicism naked at that moment.

"You are no longer on my side, are you?" asked Caiaphas.

Nehemeyah clapped once.

"Bravo!" he declared.

"You are digging yourself a very deep grave, young man."

"Then you had better make it wider as well as deeper, because Nicodaemus and Joseph of Arimathea and I are together on this, Caiaphas. We three will soon have others joining us. Daniyel is already wavering, as you can tell."

"It will not work."

"And why is that so, Caiaphas?"

"Because I will bring *you* down and destroy you before I allow you and the other traitors to take *anything* away from me."

"And how do you expect to do that?"

"You will find out if you oppose me in there."

Nehemeyah snorted with contempt.

"Without your puppets, you would be little more than a paper tiger, Caiaphas. You are only as strong as those you seduce into submission. Otherwise you would be rather mediocre as a leader, an emasculated tyrant."

He spat on the floor at the high priest's feet and started to walk away.

"Speaking about seduction," Caiaphas growled at him, "how is that young man you have been seeing lately?"

Nehemeyah froze.

"Feel my strings?" Caiaphas intoned behind him.

Caiaphas was determined that no one else of any significance would be lost to the Nazarene. Achieving this goal would be the mission of his life, the legacy he wanted to leave behind.

"Perhaps some of us will fall under His spell," he said, looking suspiciously at each Pharisee and Sadducee in attendance, "if we do not figure out what to do and do it immediately."

The others, by and large, laughed with appreciation of his cynicism, which was scarcely unknown in him.

But not all did.

A few seemed more glum, including Joseph of Arimathea.

"I cannot countenance these meetings any longer," Joseph spoke out.

"And why not, Joseph?" Caiaphas asked in a voice that made the question a demand not to be ignored.

"I have heard Jesus speak," he told them. "He seems not at all like what you are making Him out to be."

"Then you have not heard the comments that I have heard," Caiaphas assured him. "He is like Barabbas."

That could have been another miscalculation if he had been high priest of lesser standing and shorter time in office, for the image of Barabbas that the other members of the Sanhedrin held bore no comparison to what they knew of Jesus, even in their most unsettled and apprehensive view of Him.

Barabbas had always seemed to them a man of the most unruly passions, someone who seemed infinitely more dangerous than they could ever conceive of the Nazarene being. Barabbas was a ruffian in their eyes, a bully whose uncouth manner was just one of his offending traits.

Not so with the carpenter.

Except for the temple episode, Jesus had never been "physical."

In fact, one of the problems they had with His claiming to be the Messiah was that His message was spiritual, and what they craved was physical liberation, not some nebulous-seeming spiritual emancipation.

*You misjudged the people,* Caiaphas thought, picturing Jesus in his mind. *They needed a stronger message, one that urged rebellion. As for me, it does not matter all that much unless Barabbas is installed as king after defeating the Romans. That is what I must guard against the most.*

He had a plan.

He would somehow capture Barabbas and turn the wild man over to Pilatus. Then he would trump up charges against the Nazarene, charges to be leveled by so-called witnesses.

The proconsul would then offer both to the people, asking them to choose life for one and execution for the other.

*Unless I am greatly mistaken, they will demand that Jesus be released and that the maniacal Barabbas be executed, for the majority of the people have not been stupid enough to support the insurrectionist movement.*

Gentle.

If anything, Jesus seemed too gentle for their tastes, whereas Barabbas was so violent that he scared rather than inspired them.

"He is like Barabbas!"

The others reacted with shock at that declaration, though they did not go so far as to oppose the high priest.

With one exception.

One Sanhedrin member could not accept anything of the sort.

"Now that *is* nonsense!" Joseph of Arimathea exclaimed, a rare individual who could get away with addressing the high priest in that manner. "Your comparison is without reason or logic!"

Caiaphas tried not to appear ruffled.

"In what way?" he asked with feigned politeness.

Joseph stood and spoke calmly.

"The Nazarene, in His basic nature, is very kind, it seems to me," he said, "not at all given to violence, as far as I can tell. But Barabbas has decided that disturbance is his *only* course."

That was Joseph's miscalculation.

As soon as he had spoken, he regretted saying what he did because he knew for a certainty that wily Caiaphas would remind him of the notorious incident at the temple when Jesus threw out the men in charge of the daily transactions there.

And that was what happened.

But Joseph did not pull back.

"This Jesus simply did what I wish to God Almighty that I myself had had the nerve to do," he retorted. "You all know how strongly I oppose such practices as those that we allow in the name of our blessed Creator. They are an abomination, and the Nazarene recognized them as such."

"But those practices are what keep our treasury filled," Caiaphas reminded him. "Have you forgotten that?"

"And our souls empty!" Joseph shot back.

He glanced from member to member, fleetingly hoping for even a little support from one or more of them.

Nobody joined with him.

Only silence, a curious silence since they were, in ordinary circumstances, not backward about expressing their feelings.

"Be gone!" one of them said finally, and with rising anger. "You are no longer wanted in this great council."

Joseph recognized the one who had spoken.

Nehemeyah.

"You, too?" he asked without turning and facing the other man. "I thought you at least would—"

"I do what I must," the young priest said.

"May God forgive you."

And Joseph of Arimathea stalked from that chamber.

The night air touched his face but did little to calm him down.

As he strode forward, down the narrow, cobblestoned street in the center of Jerusalem, he saw Nicodaemus ahead, another member of the Sanhedrin who knew what had been scheduled to be discussed that evening and had avoided the meeting altogether.

Joseph told him what was happening.

"I am not surprised," Nicodaemus replied. "Caiaphas seemed obsessed by the poor Nazarene."

"Oh, he is, and that can only mean trouble for Jesus, because Caiaphas must do something or lose face."

The two men ended up spending much of the rest of the night together as they discussed the Nazarene, but the discussion was far different than the one the Sanhedrin had had earlier.

"We can no longer help Him," Nicodaemus said.

And both wept.

"If only I were the high priest," Nicodaemus speculated a bit later as they sat on comfortable leather chairs in Joseph's one-story home, which was only a short distance from where Pontius Pilatus was living while serving as proconsul. "But then it might be that even Caiaphas started out with pure motives."

Having known the high priest for so long made it difficult for Nicodaemus to think of him in any way other than what he was: scheming, near-blasphemous in the way he used his office for personal gain of one sort or another, a man whose personal grooming and attire concealed a spirit that was utterly profane.

"Not that one!" Joseph retorted. "I think he must have been starting something devious the moment he left his mother's womb!"

They laughed over the impossibility, but agreed that it still described the extent of the high priest's conspiratorial ways.

"But then, have we as a people traditionally been so conniving?" Nicodaemus asked dispiritedly.

"What do you mean?" Joseph asked. "You sound like one of our critics in and out of Rome."

"It is what we have had to do to survive."

"By any means necessary?"

"It seems that way, I am afraid, my friend."

Nicodaemus mentioned Herod the Great.

"He survived and, in many ways, remade the face of this nation, with palaces and fortresses and roads and so much else."

"But he was a political opportunist," Joseph interjected. "Is that where you are heading?"

Nicodaemus admired the young priest's astuteness.

"You read me well," he said. "Herod consorted with some of the most powerful leaders of his time, from Cleopatra to Mark Antony to Octavian, the one who was renamed Augustus Caesar. There was no end to those he would bargain with, bribe, threaten, or sleep with to achieve what he wanted."

"And our high priest follows in that tradition," Jospeh concluded. "A supposed man of God no better than a hustling politician."

"And a king prostituting himself and his people!"

Nicodaemus sighed wearily.

"It is a good thing that most of the common folk do not know him for what he is," Nicodaemus mused.

Joseph nodded in agreement.

"You are absolutely right, dear man," he said. "They would look at the man and at the fact that he is supposed to be the steward of God's house, and soon they would turn against him and God at the same time."

Nicodaemus shivered as he considered that, wishing he could give his friend a gentle rebuke but harboring convictions that were identical.

... *a good thing that most of the common people do not know him for what he is.*

Nor was the thought a new one, aided by recent revelations, which Nicodaemous now shared with Joseph.

Privately other Sanhedrin members had approached Nicodaemus over the past few months, saying they would support him in a kind of temple coup if he wanted to depose Caiaphas, whose actions were beginning to unsettle them despite their rationalizations of the past.

"We long ago tried to maintain a position of studied blindness," Nehemeyah, the youngest of the priests, had confessed to him. "And can you blame us? Caiaphas *has* been beneficent, raising our *stipipendium* periodically, introducing us to foreign visitors who were notably generous with goods such as silks, leather, and perfumes. We have allowed these material things, these calculated gestures, to blind us to what has been going on far, far too long now."

The young man could have been playing a game, and Nicodaemus had known that. He could have been sent by Caiaphas to determine the true feelings of one or more Sanhedrin members.

The high priest was accustomed to using people against one another, and such a tactic now would not have been surprising since the grumblings against the high priest were increasing, and Caiaphas could not have been ignorant of this.

"Blindness?" Nicodaemus had asked, well aware of what the other man was going to say but wanting to see if he had the courage to actually utter the words. "Blind to what, my friend? What is it you want to say?"

Nehemeyah had been frustrated and ashamed.

"Blind to our complicity!" he had blurted out. "If not, then how could Caiaphas have gained so much influence, so much control?"

Nicodaemus remained silent.

"Surely you know what I mean," Nehemeyah had said, wanting the older man to make some grand statement of agreement.

"I do," Nicodaemus finally had said.

"Then why are you acting so obtuse?"

"I need to hear you tell me. I need to know that you yourself understand what it is that you desire."

Nehemeyah had been grim but determined.

"I desire that Caiaphas be ousted immediately."

That prospect had pleased Nicodaemus, but, older as he was, he also had the benefit of experience, which tended to rein in youthful pretensions.

"How much support for this is there within the Sanhedrin?" he had asked emotionlessly.

"Among the priests, I believe, a great deal."

"And the scribes?"

"Much less, I am afraid. Caiaphas has been especially generous to them, giving them whatever they have needed for research—supplies, whatever they were asking for at any given moment."

"Pampering them?"

"Oh, yes, that, *certainly* that, shoring up support for himself, closing off another avenue of discontent."

Nicodaemus had stated the obvious.

"Then this discussion is basically pointless."

He had taken no satisfaction in saying anything of the sort. He would have preferred being as optimistic as the younger man, but there was no point in any pursuit that seemed futile from the start.

Nehemeyah's shoulders had slumped.

"I suppose it is," he had said, "but I keep hoping."

The look of complete devastation on his pale face had made Nicodaemus feel sorry for Nehemeyah.

"But there may be some slim chance."

"What? Tell me, please."

"The Nazarene."

Nehemeyah had snorted at that.

"What can He do to help?"

Nicodaemus had been surprised that the young priest had missed what he was trying to hint at as discreetly as possible.

"This Jesus can rally the people. And He has already spoken against the Sanhedrin as a bunch of hypocrites, so pure and clean-looking outside but full of bones and decay and filth inside."

Nehemeyah had been again less than convinced.

"But the Nazarene has shown no inclination for that. He talks and talks and talks, discouraging any kind of insurrection."

Nicodaemus had leaned forward, frowning, his gaze fixed on the young priest.

"Against the Romans, certainly that is true," he had said, "but I am talking about an uprising against Caiaphas!"

Nehemeyah had sucked in some air and then let it out expansively, the picture his friend was painting had been a startling one.

"After all," Nicodaemus had continued, "He threw the money-changers out of the temple. And look at His loathing for the Sanhedrin. We cannot mistake His gentility for some kind of reticence or propensity toward inaction. I think He has the courage as well as the inclination."

"You think Caiaphas will make a move against him?"

Nicodaemus had thought that question showed how naïve young Nehemeyah really was.

"You and I both have heard the rumblings," he had remarked, a hint of impatience in his voice.

"But they speak out about so much. It is hard to tell when they are serious, you know."

"Forgive me for saying so, my friend, but you are starting to sound like a hapless fool."

To call any man a fool was one of the rankest of insults, nearly as severe as telling him he was a dog, and Nicodaemus had wished he had thought of another way to express how he felt but it had been too late. The words were out, and he could do nothing but wait for the younger priest's reaction.

Surprisingly, Nehemeyah had not shown any anger, because he had realized the other man was simply being truthful.

"I accept that," he had replied contritely. "I may be thinking wistfully instead of rationally."

Nicodaemus had been even sorrier about what he had said.

"They will trump up some charges and attempt to get that good Man executed, if I may use that word," he had spoken.

Nehemeyah had seemed to be studying him for a moment.

"What are you thinking now," Nicodaemus finally had asked, "how unfortunate it is to have me as a friend?"

Nehemeyah had shaken his head emphatically.

"But you must be thinking about it in *some* way," Nicodaemus had probed. "Tell me, will you?"

"I am thinking; yes, I am."

"Are you going to enlighten me?"

"You sound as though you know something special about the Nazarene," Nehemeyah had guessed. "That is what I think. I sense that you have knowledge you have been keeping to yourself."

"You may be right."

"What happened? I can be trusted even though your instinct just now might be suggesting the opposite, since I have been asking so many questions."

Nicodaemus had known he should be more cautious in these times of duplicitous behavior on the part of religious and governmental figures, but he was hoping his trust in the young man was not misplaced.

So he had decided to be completely forthright and trust in God to keep him shielded from harm.

"I visited Him early one evening."

Nehemeyah had seemed unperturbed by that admission but asked simply, "What was He like?"

Nicodaemus' eyes had been watery as he had replayed those few minutes, which had seemed, at the time, rather perplexing.

"Very calm, very—"

He had brought the back of his hand to his lips.

"Very—?" Nehemeyah had prodded him.

Nicodaemus could not satisfactorily explain to himself, let alone the other man, why he had nearly broken into tears.

"—kind, yes, He seemed kind."

Yes, *kind* was the only word that could have been accurate, so kind that Nicodaemus had been forced to admit he had never before met anyone like the Nazarene.

"What did He say?" Nehemeyah had asked, increasingly curious, or at least that was what he had seemed to be.

"That I should be born again."

"That you should somehow re-enter your mother's womb?"

Nicodaemus' eyes had shot wide open as he understood what Nehemeyah was telling him.

"That is exactly what I said. How did you know?"

The younger man had avoided his gaze.

"I have met with Him also," Nehemeyah had said, his voice hardly above a strained whisper.

"*You—!*"

"I did. A few weeks ago. I could not believe what Caiaphas was saying. And now I know how much of a liar our high priest has become."

"How can we stop him?"

"We try to embarrass him at the next session. If he persists in this campaign against the Nazarene, we do what we can to undermine his support."

Nicodaemus had swallowed hard a couple of times.

"There is much at stake for the likes of you and me," he had pointed out. "Have we the courage, my young friend?"

"That is something we will find out," Nehemeyah had told him, "sooner rather than later, I fear."

After mulling over Nicodaemus' recollection, Joseph of Arimathea spoke. "But he said nothing in favor of Jesus during the session I just left."

"No, in fact, he asked you to leave."

"Does that not bother you?"

Nicodaemus shrugged his shoulders.

"Perhaps our young friend is simply waiting for the right moment so that his stand will have the most effect."

"If he continues to hold his peace, he may run out of moments altogether."

Caiaphas had resented Nicodaemus and Joseph of Arimathea for many months.

*They try to thwart me every step of the way,* he told himself. *It is as though they are able to see through—*

He could not allow himself to fall into that trap.

His enemies were invariably weaker than he was, far less intelligent, and much less adept at intrigue, which meant that the fact that Nicodaemus and Joseph both seemed a cut above the others must not trick him into thinking that they could ever possibly be his equals, for that was not likely.

*Only Jesus.*

The Nazarene was occupying more and more of his thoughts. He went to bed thinking about a one-time carpenter and woke up the same way.

*You try to cast some spell over me,* Caiaphas speculated, *at least You try, and I wonder if You have, in part, succeeded.*

It was clear that the high priest was terribly anxious, despite the fact that no other opponents seemed to have remained to contest him.

"Now that one of only two dissenters is gone, let us see who the intelligent ones are, those truly dedicated to Almighty God, and hasten to be about our business," he told the rest, an urgency to his tone that he was sure the others would not detect since he had little respect for the intelligence of anybody but himself, "a business that, however nasty, surely must be taken care of without delay."

*Joseph and Nicodaemus ... the one a non-priestly consultant who was present at every meeting of the Sanhedrin, the other a full-fledged priest who some privately thought should have been the high priest.*

Caiaphas hated them both.

If closing his large hands around their necks and personally squeezing the life from them had not been an obviously forbidden act, he would have felt little hesitation in doing so.

"Those two seem to delight in opposing me at every turn," he once whispered to no one but felt the need to speak out loud. "I think Nicodaemus and Joseph would be very happy if someone else became high priest."

*... if someone else became high priest.*

He entertained the possibility of hiring assassins to murder the two men as well as Jesus. As a protective measure, he kept in periodic contact with members of a certain segment of society that the general populace would have been shocked to learn he ever knew, let alone consorted with for one reason or another.

*People are desperate these days,* he thought. *Women are whoring day after day, just to get enough money to buy food and pay for a place to stay and have something more than rags to wear.*

The high priest straightened his shoulders as though to emphasize his own innate righteousness.

*Men are turning ever more frequently to purveying black market goods that are smuggled into the country and sold without Roman taxes imposed on them,* Caiaphas ruminated dourly. *And the population not only tolerates this but encourages it, considering such illegal activity not wrong at all, but a matter of honor.*

Honor.

That word did not describe Caiaphas' typical conduct. He had given up an honorable course for his reign a long time before.

Pragmatism.

That was what guided him.

Any means were acceptable, so long as the end was worth it. Bribes, kidnappings, intimidation—all these and more were deemed useful "tools" that Caiaphas had no compunction against using.

"The Father's goals must be achieved, and there can be no excuses for failures," he told a visitor from Britannia.

"Even if the means you employ would be frowned upon by Yahweh?" the bearded figure replied. "Can you serve the Creator in any way honorably by methods that could be called inappropriate?"

Caiaphas was offended.

"We cannot read the mind of God," he said.

"And we need not do so, Caiaphas, as you claim, for we have the thoughts from that very mind throughout the whole of the Scriptures. And the kind of ruthlessness you often wield cannot be condoned by any right-thinking person."

The cultured visitor, a man of some ethics, saw that the high priest was starting to react indignantly.

"Have I spoken too forcefully?" he asked. "I am truly sorry about that but the real sin is yours, I am afraid."

And with that, he stalked out of the inner chamber where the high priest held most of his meetings.

"Principles …" muttered the religious leader of the Jews. "Principles are impossible every minute of every day. That fool is blind to what reality, not idle religious fantasy, foists upon people in my position."

Caiaphas did not want the threat embodied by the Nazarene to linger any longer than necessary.

"We must be prepared for this, all of us, you know, and stop it before it spreads and then is impossible to control," he told the other members of the Sanhedrin, scribes and Pharisees and Sadducees alike. "Vigilance is what will keep all of us in power. Apathy will destroy what we have as the people are *allowed* to turn from you and me to this wanderer, this *carpenter* from Nazareth.

"How many of you here tonight—men with whom I have fellow-shiped for so many years—are *disgusted* by that prospect? Are we to let our power slip between our fingers like useless sand on the shore at the Sea of Galilee?"

*Grumbling …*

Audible grumbling arose from the group at his second use of the word *power*, but Caiaphas contemptuously and with typical arrogance brushed the muttered objections aside.

"Survival," he added, "survival is what we must pursue. If we do *not* survive, then the work that God has given us will be lost. And for how many generations, I ask? *While the poor masses go on blindly without us!*"

The expressions on their faces showed that the priests and the scribes were being hit at the area of their greatest concern. Nearly all of them were potential "Caiaphases" but, at the least, they were men who would do whatever was necessary to cling to their positions even though few could equal the force of the high priest's ego, an ego that had sustained him throughout his term.

A priest named Jephthah considered something else, though, and spoke without asking for leave to do so.

Jephthah.

He was also a physician, one of the most respected in all of Israel. The dual roles he played allowed him to deal with physical as well as spiritual concerns, and he was one of the more altruistic members of the Sanhedrin in comparison to the others.

A tall man, he looked like a human bamboo shoot, very thin, his skin stretched across bones that showed clearly beneath it, but he was not in ill health, in fact had not been ill for many years.

"Caiaphas ..." Jephthah started out.

"Yes," the high priest said, going through the motions of recognizing him. "What is it that you have to say?"

"We are religious leaders, are we not?" said the doctor-priest. "We're hardly kidnappers as you want us to be."

A fresh current of muttering swept the chamber where they were meeting, the one in which the Sanhedrin had gathered for decades, since long before Caiaphas ascended to the office of high priest.

Caiaphas seemed dumbfounded since Jephthah previously was always one of the quieter members of the group.

"And is that all you wish to say?" he asked coldly, following long-established procedure.

Caiaphas never reacted well to opposition or to any comment that seemed to compromise the wisdom he felt he possessed, but this time, he actually understood Jephthah's concerns.

"I am concerned, deeply concerned ..." Jephthah continued. "Our commission is very specific, as everyone here knows. Are we not beginning to tread on the most dangerous ground?"

"Then what *are* we to do?" Caiaphas demanded, wondering if the other members would follow suit.

The other man had no immediate answer, which he regretted, for this allowed the high priest to move into the vacuum with intimidating authority.

"You have the question but no answer, I see," Caiaphas rebuked him.

Jephthah backtracked a bit.

"I was not objecting to the Nazarene's abduction but just the possibility that *we* would do it," he added quickly.

Caiaphas sighed with relief, glad that he would not have to deal with the conscience of yet another man that evening. Having Nicodaemus refuse to attend and then having Joseph of Arimathea walk out were two matters that displeased him, and he would have been very intolerant of a third.

The high priest chuckled in relief, having thought that the other man was becoming afflicted with an inconvenient case of conscience.

"There is another course," he offered.

The members waited patiently for him to tell them what it was.

"We will hire someone then," Caiaphas responded, realizing that his hands and the hands of all the other Sanhedrin members had to be kept clean of direct participation in any act such as they were discussing.

Jephthah began to feel some relief.

"Exactly what I was thinking," he said.

But then the high priest, always a worrier by disposition, began wringing his thin little hands together rather theatrically in front of the others and frowning with just as much exaggeration as beads of perspiration conveniently appeared on his heavily lined forehead.

His less than subtle intention was to garner as much sympathy for his position as possible so that there could be no recriminations later.

"But who?" he groaned.

The idea had just come to mind, and he could think of no one at first blush.

"We have never dealt with *that* element. We have never *had* to do so. That is what this carpenter is forcing us into, you know. We are responding to Him, not the other way around."

Heads nodded, but there was no muttering this time around.

Jephthah had a suggestion.

"It should be someone who has shown himself to be wholly experienced in such matters."

Caiaphas began to brighten somewhat.

"His name, please," he insisted.

Jephthah hesitated, either to build up the expectations of that moment or because he was genuinely trepidatious.

"Out with it!" Caiaphas demanded.

"Barabbas ..." the other man almost whispered the name of someone they thought of with disdain as well as a measure of fear, fear that

Barabbas' attempts at insurrection would pay off but at a brutal cost so extreme that they could not help but shiver as they thought of it.

Caiaphas' mouth dropped open.

"Are you jesting?" he asked, incredulous, assuming that the other man was trying to lighten up the proceedings.

Jephthah shook his head.

"Then you have become possessed!" the high priest exclaimed, backing away from him a bit.

"Let me explain, please," Jephthah replied. "Barabbas is known to be a disreputable sort."

No one in any kind of authority in Israel could dispute that assessment of the man who was ruled by the most explosive passions.

"I would say so," responded Caiaphas.

The high priest assumed that normally dependable Jephthah was in the process of backtracking yet again.

"But he is also extremely resourceful; we all must remember that. Look at his record: He has escaped capture by the Romans for years now. Could it only be luck? Or is he simply smarter than those who run the Roman Empire?"

*Barabbas* ... that they were even mentioning his name was a dramatic departure.

"His good fortune is certain to run out," Caiaphas suggested.

"Does it matter?" Jephthah asked.

"Certainly it does!" the high priest exclaimed, saw the other man's expression, then started stroking his beard. "I see what you mean."

"It does not matter what happens to Barabbas *after* we have made use of him, am I right?"

The high priest nodded appreciatively.

"How very right you are," he said, "how very right indeed!"

# — Chapter Six —

Barabbas had met Jesus long before the Sanhedrin made contact with him and gave him the task of kidnapping the Nazarene.

His mother.

*She seemed to be dying. The insurrectionist's father was already dead, but the shock of watching her husband die had sent her health into a tailspin.*

*"Mother, I shall summon this Jesus ..." he told her. "I have heard that He has the power to heal."*

*She moaned, barely comprehending what he had said. Her lungs were filling with fluid, and every breath she took filled her with pain.*

*Barabbas arranged to have Jesus visit with her. And as a result of a single touch upon the pale, thin woman's forehead, her condition improved overnight, and she had been well for more than a year.*

*Barabbas wanted to do something for the Nazarene and said so, but his offer, while warmly considered, was then refused.*

*"You can do nothing for Me now," Jesus replied.*

*"You are so different from all others," Barabbas acknowledged.*

*"But this is not the extent of it for you and for Me," the Nazarene added. "There will be something else between us."*

*"I do not understand," Barabbas told Him. "I have no idea what it could be that would bring us together again."*

*"But it will happen, Barabbas."*

*"How could You know?"*

*"It is wisdom My Father has given Me."*

*"Soon? Will it happen soon?"*

*"What is soon? A day, a week, a month, longer."*

*"I want to know so that I will not pass the moment by when it comes."*

*"Oh, but you surely will not do that, Barabbas. And you will do the right thing. Be at peace knowing that you have done what Almighty God wished you would do."*

*"And there is nothing more I can do?" Barabbas asked. "No horses, no food, no clothes?"*

*"At the end, we both will be taken, but only one will be released. And you will stand at a distance, watching, and weeping."*

The passing of time turned Barabbas into a harsher man, a more violent one, a man not much given to kindness.

Still, he balked at kidnapping the Man who had made his mother whole.

And that was why, surprisingly, he did not eagerly accept Caiaphas' offer but hesitated when the high priest made it to him.

"And you will do what for me?" he asked, playing the part well, a part dictating that he not appear too anxious in any event. "In return for this act, how am I to benefit? Or is there greater danger instead?"

"Danger?" Caiaphas repeated. "What kind of danger? From His twelve regular followers? How could they present any danger to a man of your ilk? Except the big one, the fisherman called Peter."

Barabbas sensed that the high priest was playing dumb, or if he really had not guessed then he was worse than dumb.

"God," he said.

"God? What about God? Who are you to speak of God?"

"It might be that I do God's will as much as you. Perhaps more so."

"You are speaking in riddles," Caiaphas told him. "First you mention danger. Then you mention God. What are you trying to say?"

"If the Nazarene is Who He says He is, then anyone who harms Him is surely in the greatest danger."

The high priest permitted a smirk to cross his face.

"Only if he is caught," he said, "only if he is seen."

"Then what hope have I?" Barabbas added.

Caiaphas' patience was nearly gone.

"Riddles again!" he exclaimed, nearly shouting.

"God sees everything, does He not, Caiaphas?"

"Yes but—"

Finally Caiaphas, highly educated, caught the point the common man was making.

"I will provide you with a considerable amount of food, clothing, safe houses," the high priest replied.

Barabbas' expression was a blank one.

"Yet no weapons, I gather?" he asked.

Caiaphas tried to be equally impassive.

"No weapons," he replied.

Barabbas frowned while playing with his beard and sighed before he spoke again in reply to the offer from one of the most influential men in all of Israel.

"And I am to do what in return?"

Caiaphas was becoming irritated but did not allow this to show.

"Kidnap the carpenter," he said with studied patience.

"What about His followers?" Barabbas pointed out. "The twelve men who travel with Him?"

"They will disband once their leader disappears."

Barabbas shook his large, thick-skulled head in frustration.

"No, no, I mean what if they decide to resist before my mates and I have taken Him?"

Caiaphas' tone was chilling, impersonal.

"Do what you must," he said.

The two men had been sitting on the back porch of Caiaphas' residence near the Mount of Olives.

"Kill them?" Barabbas asked, wanting to make certain he understood the situation.

"If you must," the high priest responded. "It is a regrettable eventuality, but it might be the only way."

"I *must*, yes, if they try to harm me and those with me. I do not covet your approval of any such action."

"Then there should be no problem."

Barabbas sat back and examined Caiaphas for a moment.

"You treat men's lives so callously," he observed.

"And you do not?" the other man retorted. "How much blood have *you* shed over the past three years?"

"I mourn every single life that I have taken," Barabbas replied with exaggeration that bordered on being a lie.

But those words had their intended effect on Caiaphas, who could not have anticipated the image of a violent man, his hands covered by the blood of strangers, suddenly being overcome by remorse.

"Surely you are making some kind of joke," he said.

"I do not jest often, and I do not jest easily," Barabbas replied. "This is not one of those times."

"You *mourn* those you have slaughtered. Did you mourn the Romans whose heads you cut off and stuck on the edges of bamboo poles outside the garrison you overran late last year?"

"They probably had wives, children, other loved ones just as I do."

"And you actually *mourned* them?"

"It matters little to me whether you believe me or not. I must say, though, that any more of this and I shall walk out of here, leaving you to find someone else to carry out this mission of yours."

Caiaphas knew he had miscalculated.

"I meant no offense," he hastened to say.

"I shall do what you ask," Barabbas told him, "and I want to be paid by the next day after the Nazarene's disappearance, but I have to tell you that I think this Jesus is much more than you give Him credit to be."

Caiaphas stood and paced.

"I know what you are saying, and I agree, but that is why He must be kept away from here for the rest of His life. He could upset everything, for He is not the Messiah we desperately need even if He is the one that has been foretold."

Barabbas found that admission to be overwhelming.

"You accept some of what He says when He makes claims about Himself?" Barabbas asked. "You accept the fact that God sent—?"

"*Not that!*" Caiaphas blurted out.

"But most of the rest?"

"He possesses some wisdom, this One does."

"Yet still you want Him exiled or dead?"

Caiaphas could see revulsion on the other man's face.

"Now more than ever before," the high priest acknowledged.

Barabbas was still reluctant but he needed the money, and he thought of something that would drive the high priest absolutely mad.

*I can tell this Jesus that I will bring Him back into the country once my own followers and I have thrown out the Romans,* he told himself.

Before Barabbas left, he turned and asked Caiaphas, "I saw one of His followers leave just as I was arriving."

"Judas?" Caiaphas asked.

The high priest had no compunctions about admitting that he was seeing one of the Nazarene's followers.

"As you say."

"But what could that have been about, Caiaphas? Are you trying every way you can to destroy the Man?"

Caiaphas obviously wondered why a man of such rotten character as Barabbas would be at all concerned.

"We were negotiating with him," he said simply rather than start a debate that could end the insurrectionist's promised cooperation.

Barabbas suspected what was going on but preferred to have Caiaphas in the position of being the one to explain.

"For what?" he asked, playing dumb.

"What else, Barabbas? Now you tell me."

"I asked the question."

Caiaphas was inclined to humor him and held in his own growing irritation at a common criminal's disrespectful manner.

"For more information about the Nazarene."

"Was this Judas helpful?"

"He had not decided as yet whether he will cooperate."

"But you are hopeful?"

Caiaphas, his scorn closer to the surface now, smiled as he replied knowingly, "Oh, yes, money appeals to every man."

But Barabbas was prepared.

"Including you, of course, Caiaphas?"

Caiaphas' self-control was beginning to slip seriously.

"What are you saying?" he asked.

"Nothing. Pay no attention. I shall do what you wish. Then I want you to leave me and my kind alone."

"What if we could pay you well for other deeds?"

Barabbas hesitated.

"Be more specific," the insurrectionist replied, deliberately trying to frustrate the man he had never admired and was now hating with increasing fervency. "Your message is not getting through. I cannot grasp what it is."

"Deeds such as—"

But even Caiaphas was intimidated by the potential of what he was going to say, realizing that his plan could rise up and backfire on him.

"I shall not wait much longer," Barabbas remarked. "Spit it out!"

"The others," the high priest went on, "every last one tracked down and stamped out, like a disease."

"What do you mean by that?"

"The other followers. Jesus calls them His apostles."

"What about the others?"

"Dispose of them ... would you get rid of them if we ask you to do so sometime after Jesus disappears?"

"By murdering the twelve?"

"Whatever it takes, Barabbas."

Barabbas was very close to punching the high priest but decided not to do so. The money he was being paid convinced the insurrectionist of the need to keep his temper reigned in.

*And I am criticized for doing what I do,* he thought. *What hypocrites these men are! They parade around in their piety, pretending they are nearly like God Himself, and yet look at their hearts. Look at—!*

He spat on the ground in disgust and went about his business.

Caiaphas waited until Barabbas had disappeared from sight, then he started dancing up and down, happy that the Nazarene soon would no longer be a thorn in his sanctified side.

*An often unruly group ...*

The insurrectionists had no members from among the wealthy class of Israel. Every man had been poor, and while few fell so far as to have to resort to begging, they were nevertheless without places to stay most of the time. In a sense they were like the followers of Jesus in that they followed a dynamic man, and none had any idea of the direction in which their lives were going.

Control.

Barabbas had nearly total control over his group of insurrectionists, and he achieved this in a singular dynamic manner with something indispensable at the very center.

The message.

He gave them something that rang clearly with idealism, patriotism, and macho heroics, a message that stirred their unshakable desire to get the oppressors out of their nation, those who had conquered it then made every Jew subservient to the dictates of Rome, a circumstance that rankled the pride of *every* Jew. Still many were not in favor of violence, preferring a more political route.

Later, during the zealot takeover of Masada, many within the Jewish community would consider the insurrectionists to be nearly as much of an enemy as was Rome, each making their lives dangerous.

"You will bring us more grief than victory," said an old woman who once approached Barabbas boldly. "We will lose many sons because of you."

"The soul of this nation is being destroyed by these oppressors," he retorted.

"This nation has not had a soul for a very long time."

"And the Romans took it from us!"

The old woman wagged a finger at him.

"You are wrong!" she declared. "Every so often we lose it for ourselves, and that means Yahweh has to give it back to us when we are so filled with guilt and shame that we get on our knees before Him and beg His intervention."

Barabbas would have nothing to do with that idea. He considered politics a facade for weakness, cowardice.

"I would rather die a foolish hero," he would tell people again and again, "than live as a fool at the feet of Rome."

Anything he did that prevented the latter was fine with him: murder, theft, destruction of property, whatever the act of defiance might be.

Including kidnapping.

Barabbas and several of his most trusted men were just outside the camp the Nazarene and his twelve followers had made for the night, as usual, in the desert not far from Jerusalem.

"So many know Him," Barabbas said, "but so few take Him in. They want what He can offer, and then they run off and forget Who gave them what they needed so completely, sight or hearing or—"

Amnon, a longtime friend even bigger of frame than Barabbas, was crouched at his left.

"You talk as though you believe that He heals," he said. "If He heals, we should be worshiping Him instead of kidnapping Him."

Barabbas nodded at the truth of that.

"But then there would be no money ..." he muttered.

Amnon bristled at that.

"Are we after precious freedom or mere lucre?" he asked defiantly. "Can financial gain ever become any part of why Jewish blood stains the soil and the sand of our oppressed land?"

*... freedom or lucre.*

It was hardly the first time that question had arisen, for it seemed to bedevil the insurrectionists almost daily. By contrast, the occupying Roman forces had no such worries to concern them.

"The one enables the other," replied Barabbas.

"Nothing other than the spilled blood of our followers!" the other man spoke. "The money is incidental. How could you suggest otherwise?"

"My comrade, my brave and good friend, you and I could have all the brave soldiers we might ever want, but if there is not enough money to buy food to fill their bellies, to provide the weapons we cannot make for ourselves, what hope would there be? Answer me that!"

Amnon nodded slowly, with great reluctance, hating the reality Barabbas had shoved at him but having to acknowledge that it was true.

*The Nazarene ...*

He was going off by Himself.

Seeing Him, Amnon gasped at their good fortune.

"It will be so much easier now!" he exclaimed in a whisper.

The Nazarene was on the other side of a small ridge of rocks elevated from the desert floor.

Barabbas, Amnon, and the men with them climbed up the western side as their target went up the flatter eastern end.

Finally, they peered over the edge and saw Him on His knees.

"Blood!" Amnon said. "At His knees!"

Barabbas noticed this as well.

"Does He not know?" he asked. "Does He not feel the pain caused by those sharp rocks cutting His knees?"

"Listen!" Amnon said.

And they heard the voice of a Man in anguish.

"I wept over you, Jerusalem," the Nazarene was praying, "as a hen eager to gather her chicks under her wings!"

Crying.

Thick tears were streaming down His cheeks.

"Look at them!" Barabbas remarked in a low voice.

"I have never seen tears so big," Amnon said. "Surely He will have no more left. He will be as dry as a bone left out under the hot sun."

None of them moved.

"But what moves Him so?" Barabbas asked. "*Listen!*"

Jesus was now recalling verses from the book of Ezekiel with such authority that they sat and listened, enthralled, momentarily forgetting the mission that had brought them to that location in the first place.

*Early morning ...*

The insurrectionists awakened at least two hours after the morning sun first appeared.

"*We fell asleep!*" Amnon exclaimed. "And look at this!"

Placed in front of them was some bread, cheese, and two flasks of wine.

"They seem to have so little, and yet look at what they have given us," another remarked.

Barabbas was the last to open his eyes.

"They left it for us, Jesus' followers," he muttered. "They must not have known why we were here. How could they?"

Amnon nodded as hunger made him break the bread and distribute it, then the cheese, and finally the wine.

"They did this for five thousand people one afternoon a few months ago, I hear," he recalled. "It is nothing new to them."

"But why us?" Barabbas asked. "They seem to have gone out of their way to avoid spoiling our sleep."

He hesitated, his mind going back over what the Nazarene had been saying just hours earlier.

"This Jesus feels so much love for Israel," he said.

"What does that have to do with us?" Amnon asked.

"I wonder ..."

His mind returned to what he had witnessed earlier that day.

*"Oh, Israel, Israel, My Israel,"* Jesus moaned. *"When you were in the midst of your greatest abominations I continued to love you."*

Barabbas was not an educated man, but he was not stupid either. Street life had given this bearlike individual a special sort of wisdom that many scholars and scribes could not lay claim to as they isolated themselves from the world of living people and confined themselves to parchments and scrolls bearing whatever scraps of history and prophecy they could find, often in out-of-the-way places.

Barabbas knew much about the genuineness or the artificiality of other human beings. He could tell whether someone was lying about a certain matter after listening for only a few minutes.

And he could find no falsehood in the Nazarene. He would have come to that conclusion even if he had not overheard the Man's agonized beseeching, spoken in a low voice so as not to disturb his comrades, who were a sufficient distance away. Barabbas and Amnon and the other insurrectionists were closer, and they could hear every word.

But Barabbas' lack of formal education meant that he had an incomplete and inadequate knowledge of the prophecies and other teachings that had been with his people for thousands of years in some instances. He was willing to die for the nation, but he was nearly illiterate about what had made Israel so important in the Middle Eastern scheme of things.

Barabbas had picked up bits and pieces of the most rudimentary knowledge as he lived his years, crumbs from the table of learning, it might be said, and yet this gave him nothing except hints, though enough knowledge was gained to confirm in his mind that Israel did have a greater destiny than to be put under the boot of the brutal Roman Empire for all time.

*Glory...*

Barabbas was convinced that that was ahead, and he envisioned himself as the instigator of it.

So it was that the Nazarene's words could not have been more disturbing.

Jesus left no doubt what Israel had been like over the centuries and what the nation could become again if its baser instincts were given free rein.

Amnon pressed his hands over his ears.

"I cannot listen to this any longer!" he whispered.

The others turned away also.

But not Barabbas.

Rather than speak to them in an angry voice that might be heard by the Nazarene or even His followers, the insurrectionist gave them a sign with the fingers on his left hand, a sign that was unmistakable in the message it conveyed.

None of them dared to object but sat down on their blankets and waited, waited a very long time until they all had fallen asleep.

But not Barabbas. He turned back to the kneeling Nazarene.

"… you were thrown out into the open field," Jesus was saying, "for you were abhorred on the day you were born. When I passed by you and saw you squirming in your blood, I said to you while you were in your blood, 'Live!'"

He went on to speak of loving Israel so much that He allowed the nation to survive and elevated it to a status of respect and power throughout the region where it had been established for so long.

"But then you betrayed Me," He said. "You went to strange gods and goddesses and committed acts of great sin."

Barabbas felt faint, though he was not normally a man given to such "spells." And there was a feeling of sickness in his stomach.

He glanced down at his men, tempted to order them to help him immediately kidnap the Man Who could speak such awful words.

"Moreover, you took your sons and daughters whom you had borne to Me, and you sacrificed them to idols to be devoured. Were your harlotries so small a matter? You slaughtered My children by offering them up to profane idols and having them pass through the fire."

Babies had been burned to blackened husks, their pitiable cries filling the air even as their parents watched, many with seeming dispassion, all because the nation had been seduced by demonic entities that corrupted its will to resist.

*Helpless babies, squirming in agony and—*

Barabbas was married and had six children, and he loved each one. To think of them being sacrificed to heathen gods filled him with revulsion so foul that he wished he had never accepted the mission given to him by Caiaphas.

He clenched both hands into fists so tight that his nails dug into the palms and caused them to bleed.

He held them out in front of him.

*They look like the hands of a man who has just been crucified,* Barabbas thought, shivering at that image.

"You built yourself a high place at the top of every street," the Nazarene continued, "and made your beauty abominable; and you spread your legs to every passerby to multiply your harlotry."

Jesus fell forward against the rocks.

"He has collapsed!" Barabbas whispered to himself.

He almost rose to his feet and jumped over the ridge to see if he could help, but a hand had grabbed his leg.

He snapped his head around to see Amnon holding on to him.

"You must not!" the other man said. "There are some acts we must not commit, my comrade."

"But I—" Barabbas started to say, but he spoke weakly, feeling much the same way his friend did but without the courage just then to admit it.

"Yes, I know," Amnon replied.

"But you were asleep."

"I was awake enough to hear what the Nazarene was saying."

And that he had been, fighting sleep to take hold of the words that were striking by themselves but even more so when considering Who was uttering them, an ordinary man, it seemed, from a carpentry business in a tiny village.

"But how could you?" Barabbas asked. "You were farther away. I had some difficulty hearing even from where I was sitting."

Amnon had begun to frown.

"Go ahead," Barabbas told him. "You need fear nothing from me if you are being forthright."

The other man sighed with great weariness.

"You were repeating most of what He said," he finally replied.

"Repeating—?"

Barabbas felt like saying something rather unpleasant and derogatory but thought better of it.

"Yes, and you fell on the ground," Amnon added, "so hard that I thought you might have broken your nose."

"I fell? Forward? But—"

Barabbas was trembling.

"I saw the Nazarene fall! Are you saying—?"

"And you did so as well, I assure you," Amnon remarked. "You were imitating Him though you must have been in some kind of daze not to know it."

"But why? What could have made me do that? It is not how I would normally act. Do you have any ideas, dear friend?"

Amnon was older, something of a wise man among the insurrectionists, and many came to him with their questions.

"Because you and He were bonded."

"That carpenter *and me?*" Barabbas said, confused.

"He seemed to be speaking to all of us," added Amnon. "His words cut through to our hearts like a well-honed blade."

*Israel, the decadent nation ...*

"Should we have killed Him for what He said," Barabbas asked, "or now search Him out and thank Him for opening our eyes?"

"I shall find out from some scribes I know," Amnon remarked. "They know far more of history than we do. They should set us straight. If He is repeating the truth, what have we against this Man?"

Barabbas started to walk down the ridge.

Amnon headed right after him.

"We can get Him another time," Barabbas whispered when Amnon reached him at the bottom of the ridge, suddenly reminded of how much they had given up for not grabbing the Nazarene when they had been given the opportunity.

"Now is not the time to be concerned with any rewards we have lost, temporarily or otherwise, is it, my friend?" Amnon remarked.

"Thinking of money seems almost dirty right now," muttered Barabbas with a degree of guilt he had seldom felt over the years filled with acts that increasingly deadened his conscience.

*Conscience ...*

Once it had been his all-powerful guide, determining every act of his five foot-ten inch muscular body. His conscience had stirred him to insurrection in the first place. He could not endure the authoritarian rule of a heathen regime over a nation comprised of God's chosen people.

"They have come from hell itself," he told an early group of supporters. "Let us be responsible for sending them right back into those eternal flames!"

A dozen men joined him then a score; month after month the number of insurrectionists had swelled as others came to him and pledged money, weapons, clothes, and food.

And there was never any doubt that he was their leader. His passion was righteous; his vision for a free Israel was righteous; and his conscience was sheathed in righteousness.

But after a long haul, and only sporadic victories, none of these significant, but rather like mosquitoes on the hide of an elephant, Barabbas began to change. If he could not defeat the Romans by direct assault, then he could terrify the empire's collaborators, visiting his wrath on "ordinary" Jews suspected of being traitors. But, often, his information was faulty, and good Jews, loyal Jews, Jews who hated the Romans as much as he did became victims of his vengeance, vengeance heaped upon them merely because they were "suspect," this in Barabbas' mind being the only justification he needed for torturing fellow Israelites and, usually, killing them, hanging their bodies on makeshift crosses in the middle of the night.

Gradually Barabbas began to enjoy the power he had assumed, the power to terrorize, ironically a power that was rarely exercised by Rome itself because the emperor had erected a facade of tolerance and peace throughout Israel.

So the insurrectionists, led by Barabbas, came to be hated nearly as much by the people of Palestine as were the Romans.

Barabbas shivered as these recollections arose to the surface of his mind and confronted him.

His friend's voice brought him out of his momentary reverie.
*… thinking of money seems almost dirty right now.*

Amnon smiled as he said, "I agree with you. I doubt that the Nazarene will ever be touched by a single member of our group."

"I wonder about the blood."

Barabbas sounded unusually cryptic.

"What blood?"

"Back there, where the Nazarene was."

Amnon shrugged his shoulders.

"You have lost me, Barabbas," Amnon acknowledged. "What are you trying to say?"

"You are making fun of me."

"I would never do that."

"Then listen, and do not look so skeptical."

"I can hardly help that, you know. You are talking about blood in the sand, but that is all you have told me."

"Yes, I know. It was so odd. I had never seen a man bleed like that, with no wound."

"The Nazarene did this?"

"Yes ..."

"How?"

"Through His skin somehow; His clothes were soaked with blood."

And Barabbas told him the rest.

Amnon's mouth opened then closed without his uttering a word.

"I must go back to see," he remarked. "Are you—?"

"No," Barabbas told him. "I saw enough."

Amnon excused himself and hurriedly and a bit clumsily walked back up the slope until he approached the top and was able to see where Jesus had been kneeling. Transfixed for a moment and then feeling ill, he returned to where the insurrectionist leader was standing.

"Was it still there?" Barabbas asked, his voice husky. "Are you going to tell me that blood remains in puddles on those flat rocks? That I did not dream up what I saw because I was starting to fall asleep?"

"You did not," Amnon replied simply. "God knows you did not."

Barabbas turned toward where his men had spent the night, unaware of what had happened.

Asleep.

Amazingly the lot of them were still asleep, their eyes closed, nearly all of them snoring.

"They should not learn of this," Amnon said.

"Are you and I so brave?" Barabbas ventured.

Barabbas and Amnon glanced at one another, then they rested themselves on the sand and let sleep overtake their wearied bodies as well, unable to dismiss from their minds that singular sight of the Nazarene's blood, not from a cut or any kind of wound, but somehow from the very center of His soul.

After partaking of the foodstuffs that had been left for them, Barabbas, Amnon, and the other insurrectionists left that spot and returned to Bethlehem where they were staying temporarily in what came to be known as safe houses, which were provided for them by those brave and loyal Jews who believed fervently in the rebel cause. The location of each dwelling was kept in secrecy, known only to three trusted individuals since traitors could be counted on at every turn, it seemed, either those who had sold out altogether to Rome through various kinds of bribes or the many others who simply did not believe in the violent means that were being used by the insurrectionists, fearing that the wrath of the emperor would be brought down on their heads if Barabbas and his cohorts became too successful.

"You should be praying that we triumph, my brother!" Barabbas exclaimed when confronted by a midgetlike rabbi named Yoab as both men were standing after a service at the local synagogue.

"I should pray for the shedding of Jew blood, is that what you are saying?" the little man countered. "I should ask Yahweh to let me stand by as our strong young men are cut down by the advancing legions? Is that what you ask of me? What has happened to your conscience, I want to know?"

"It is time," Barabbas told the rabbi, repeating something that already had become a cliché. "The Gentiles have held sway over us long enough."

Yoab snorted at that, contemptuous of the other man's attempt at justification for all the crimes against Jews for which he had been responsible over the past few years.

"I *hunger* for freedom as much as you do," he said, dwarfed by the insurrectionist but in no way intimidated. "But I want something left of this nation when that freedom is ours."

Barabbas knew he was talking to a reluctant supporter, a member of a dwindling breed, but he refused to beat around any bush in what he said to anyone—emperor or supporter.

"You try to hide your cowardice," he said grimly.

"But *you* wallow in your impetuous and suicidal actions because you surely have a death wish, Barabbas, and do not care how many lives are taken in the meantime."

"Will you turn us over to Pilatus while we are here?"

As far as Barabbas was concerned, that was an ever-present danger when dealing with anyone outside his close-knit group of rebels.

"I may not be the brave soldier you wish I were," Yoab replied, "but then I am not the betrayer you fear."

Abruptly Barabbas extended his hand, but the little rabbi ignored it and embraced him instead.

"I wish I could stand with you, even if we were knee-deep in the blood of our countrymen," Yoab whispered into his ear, "but my conscience and my sense of duty will not allow me."

"And that is why I cannot but love you," Barabbas said. "Someday we will be on the same side, I know."

"We are on the same side now; you must know that. But we each favor a different route to get there."

The insurrectionist nodded and then kissed Yoab once on each cheek.

"There is some food waiting for you, Barabbas," the aging, white-bearded rabbi, so short and thin and frail-looking, told him.

"Food? I thought—"

"I will not put a sword in your hand," replied Yoab, "but I have nothing against giving you some wine and a few fresh-caught fish."

"I am honored."

He was also touched, sensing how awkward it was for the old man even to be in his presence since the division between them was so deep.

"The food is waiting for you at Benjamin's," Yoab added.

Barabbas, a man of honor, felt an obligation to reciprocate as best as he could manage.

"Is there anything I can do for you in return, rabbi?" he asked sincerely.

"Stay alive, Barabbas," the old rabbi told him. "And do not bring shame on this land we both love."

Barabbas smiled warmly.

"Is it not true that if the Creator is with us," he said, "who can be against my men and me?"

Yoab frowned as he spoke, "You are not the Messiah."

"I am not; I know that, but I must prepare the way for Him."

The rabbi's expression was an odd one that Barabbas had trouble reading at first but then realized what it meant.

"You do not think the Nazarene is the Messiah, do you?" he asked, certain that he had misunderstood.

Yoab was beginning to seem uncomfortable.

When no answer was given, Barabbas said, "Jesus cannot be our Deliverer. He speaks in riddles and parables and lofty visions. His words are those of a scribe or a philosopher."

"Because He carries no sword, you assume He cannot liberate anyone?" Yoab commented.

"How could it be otherwise? Rome has many tens of thousands of well-disciplined and well-armed soldiers with endless numbers of lances, horses, armor, as much oil ready for burning as they can transport, and much else in their arsenal. A few gentle words will not do what must be done."

Yoab's shoulders slumped.

"Are you ill?" the insurrectionist asked, concerned.

"Not of body, but of heart and spirit and will I am very sick, Barabbas, sick unto death, I fear."

Barabbas felt guilty, regretting that his own manner had been so stern only minutes earlier.

"Have I caused this?" he asked. "Life is harsh. I am disturbed that a man such as yourself has a little more grief in his own life because of me."

"The way I feel now? You are trying to blame yourself for that? No, it is not of your making, my friend. It is simply the cry of an old man who has seen messiahs come and go."

Yoab had been waiting and looking and praying all of his adult life. Every so often someone would come on the scene and seem promising only to prove unworthy. For a time, he toyed with the idea that John the Baptist actually had something of value to say.

*... an old man who has seen messiahs come and go.*

Yoab's words had been tinged with a kind of longing that had been steeped in desperation.

"And alas, Jesus then is no better than the rest," Barabbas muttered, "yet another disappointment."

Yoab straightened up and looked angry.

"You misread me, I am sorry to say."

Barabbas was confused.

"How is that?"

Yoab looked at him as tears formed in his old, slightly bloodshot eyes.

"I think the Nazarene may well be the very Messiah," he said, "the One we have been waiting for so long now."

Barabbas was staggered by that and had to will himself not to stumble and fall, so strong was the impact of the rabbi's words.

"You are surely not serious!" he said. "You must be jesting, to lighten the mood between us!"

"I am as serious as this moment demands."

"But this Jesus of Nazareth has no sword, as we have agreed. And He does not *demand* overthrow of Rome. In fact, He goes so far as to say that we should render unto Caesar—"

Yoab interrupted him with a wave of his hand.

"I do not jest," he said brusquely, "because I would rather have a Messiah as you are envisioning him, Barabbas, a liberator with fire in his belly and words of molten iron. That is what we want, you and I, but it may not be what our God has provided. Yahweh may want us not to be freed from the grip of Rome, at least for the moment, but *to be delivered from ourselves!*"

Barabbas had been ready for any answer but that. Trembling, he turned his back to the old rabbi but not as an insult, fighting instead to deal with his emotions.

After several moments of silence between them, Yoab rested his hand on the taller and younger man's shoulder.

"I know what you are feeling," he said. "Over the centuries, every Jew has been yearning for the Messiah. His coming is the hope that keeps us going through all the conquering hordes of our enemies, through famine and pestilence, and God's wrath poured out because of our sins."

Barabbas recalled some of the Nazarene's statements from the night before and repeated as many of them as he could remember.

Yoab did not even blink.

"Are you aware of this?" Barabbas asked. "You do not seem the slightest bit surprised."

"You observe correctly," the rabbi remarked. "I am not."

"But where could He have gotten that information? I have never before heard any of it."

"From the book of Ezekiel."

"The Scriptures?" Barabbas nearly shouted. "He was quoting from the Scriptures last night?"

Yoab was being patient with him, aware that the insurrectionist was not as well educated as he should be.

"Yes, if you have reported His words accurately."

The insinuation that he had misstated something was irritating to Barabbas, but he said nothing in rebuke.

"I have, Rabbi, I have," he replied.

"Then the Nazarene must have studied the prophet well to remember so much of what Ezekiel wrote."

"Then that means this land was once strewn with the burnt remains of helpless infants!"

His anguish was unmasked and uncontrollable.

"That it was, my dear Barabbas," Yoab told him. "Anything else I would say in contradiction would be a lie."

The blood drained from the insurrectionist's bearded face, and his legs became wobbly.

"I never knew," he moaned. "I truly never knew."

"Sometimes their mothers would be overdue," Yoab went on, "and yet a ceremony had been scheduled, so the mother's stomach was cut open and the baby wrenched from her."

The rabbi, well-bred and learned, had lived with such knowledge for well over half a century. He had managed to cope with all its depressing implications, but their tentacle-like reach was never far away, and now these tormenting images seemed to embrace him afresh.

"I think every Jew is haunted by what once was," he said.

"Every Jew who *knows!*" Barabbas shot back, disturbed at what he had not learned until then. "How could I not have heard? How could I have missed this? While I have not had your education, rabbi, it is not as though I have skipped synagogue altogether. There has been nothing; I have been told nothing."

"Yes, I know."

Yoab's comment was simple but shattering.

"*You know?*" blurted out Barabbas.

"I am afraid so. This is our country's dirty secret. The learned among us are well aware of it, but the common folk have no idea."

Barabbas had to sit down on a wooden stool.

"My God, my God!" he muttered.

"You should not take His name in vain," Yoab reminded the insurrectionist.

"It was a prayer, not something profane. I was crying out to Him in desperation, Rabbi."

"I know how you feel," the old man assured him.

"How could you?" Barabbas spoke. "Have you ever shed blood for your country? Have you ever watched your comrades die for the cause? And all the time you are ignorant of how ugly the nation's history has been! Babies sacrificed by the score, I suppose! Helpless infants—"

"More than scores!"

"More than—"

"Much more, Barabbas. Thousands of babies over a long period of time. Many of our forefathers fought against this infamy but the public as a whole accepted the practice, and nothing was done until God's judgment poured out over Israel."

"I have sworn to liberate a country that deserves whatever the Romans heap upon it!"

"I think—" Yoab started to say.

"Yes, Rabbi?"

"I think the emperor *is* aware of what happened centuries ago, and if not him then certainly Pontius Pilatus, who is as astute and knowledgeable as any man I have ever met, regardless of nationality."

"Then Rome is simply an instrument of Yahweh's retribution!"

Barabbas' hand was shaking.

"How can I go on with the cause to which I have dedicated everything, even the blood that flows through my veins?"

Yoab felt immensely sorry for the other man.

"I think that Jesus may be the answer," he said as he glanced around that part of the synagogue to make sure no one could overhear his words.

"*Jesus?*" Barabbas repeated.

Frowning, the old rabbi put two fingers to his lips, and the insurrectionist, blushing, nodded.

"Yes, Jesus," Yoab whispered. "More violence is not what our homeland needs. Our past is riddled with that, sometimes at the command of Almighty God but often because of the babies we have killed, the infidelities we have committed, the disobedience we have manifested."

"But what exactly is the Nazarene's message?"

Yoab thought for a moment, realizing how essential it was for him to be as accurate as humanly possible.

"That true liberation comes from within," he said. "A nation's course cannot be changed until a nation's people are transformed."

Barabbas mulled that over before asking, "And the Nazarene actually proposes to do this?"

Yoab had heard sermons given by Jesus and thus was familiar with His message.

"He does," he said firmly, "and I have to say that people by the thousands are listening and absorbing."

Barabbas' thoughts returned to that scene of a few hours before and remembered Jesus falling forward against the ground.

"So He really *was* in agony as He spoke during the night," he said, some admiration growing for the Nazarene.

Yoab saw no contradiction between the Jesus he had seen and heard and what the insurrectionist was describing.

"I have no difficulty picturing Him in that manner."

Barabbas' eyes darted from side to side, his pulse quickening.

"I wonder …"

"What do you wonder, young man?"

"Could it be that Jesus may be our only hope as a people?"

Yoab, who had been standing, now sat down on the stool next to him.

"Jesus, I think, *is* our only hope," he said slowly.

Barabbas jumped to what seemed the only conclusion.

"Truly, He is the Messiah then."

Yoab did not answer because he could not yet go as far as that.

"If there is even the possibility that God has sent Him as the Messiah, we must do everything we can to protect Him."

"And if He is *not* the Messiah, then He has to be a forerunner of the One for Whom we have been praying for hundreds of years."

"Caiaphas and his cohorts must be upset."

Both men had had personal experience with the high priest, and they could easily agree that Caiaphas was not a spiritual man at all, but more of a corrupt politician interested only in preserving his position of power. Compared to him, Pontius Pilatus seemed a man of inestimable integrity and decency.

His own manner almost conspiratorial, Yoab leaned toward Barabbas, grimacing as some pain born of age touched the back of his neck.

"The members of the Sanhedrin are planning a move against the Nazarene," he said in a whisper, "at least most of them are. Two have objected—Nicodaemus and Joseph of Arimathea—but they have been overruled."

"Soon?"

"I believe so."

"Do you have any idea when?"

"I think soon after this Sunday."

"What is so special about that date?"

"From what I have heard, the supporters of Jesus are planning a special demonstration in His honor."

"My men and I must protect Him."

Yoab smiled approvingly.

"I think you should try, Barabbas," he commented. "I think you should try with all your mind, body, and soul."

*And so this was the era in which Stephen lived.*

*It would come to be the most important in the history of Christianity, a turning point in every respect.*

*Nothing that followed would ever match it. Christians have faced martyrdom for centuries, but during the first century the goal of the emperors of Rome was to wipe out Christianity altogether, just as Herod had tried to prevent the survival of Jesus Himself during the first two years of the Savior's earthly life.*

*A time of gathering persecution.*

*Christians would be soaked with oil and set ablaze as they hung from hastily constructed crosses or thrown to wild beasts in a stadium spectacle of death designed to entertain the masses.*

*Yet the numbers of Christians did not drop but rather dramatically increased, day after day, week after week, the many months passing and the years as well, more and more people from every known country bravely embracing the new faith while paying no heed to the personal danger this engendered.*

# — Chapter Seven —

Three friends.

They had been close for many years, since early childhood in fact, privileged children who had matured into sometimes irresponsible teenagers and now were on the verge of becoming young men in a desert land.

Nekoh, Ahiram, and Johanan, who was later known as Stephen, were all from families of wealth and influence.

"You know," Johanan once remarked, "none of us have had to beg for anything, particularly food."

"So what is your point?" Ahiram spoke up. "That we should feel guilty about every mouthful we take?"

Ahiram seemed always to seek a reason for feeling miserable, but the two others were used to this trait after so long.

Johanan shook his head.

"I honestly am not sure what I meant," he replied. "We are what we are, and they are what they are."

"Is that your wisdom for the day?" Nekoh asked with just the right touch of sarcasm to amuse his friend but not offend him.

"Did I sound like a windbag?" Johanan wondered.

Both friends laughed at his seriousness.

Twenty-three-year-old Johanan, tall, with the frame of an athlete and a muscular body that seemed to suggest he labored hard although he did not, was sitting with two friends while enjoying a particularly fine vintage of wine and some very sharp cheese when he saw the group of thirteen men approach on the country road not a hundred feet away.

"Look at the dust they kick up behind them!" Johanan exclaimed. "They seem very determined and in a hurry."

He was an intelligent young man with an inquisitive nature, basically kindhearted, but with a rebellious streak as well. Knowing wealth from the time he was an infant, he nevertheless seldom acted spoiled and arrogant.

"They seem to be heading straight to Jerusalem," observed much shorter, thinner Ahiram. "A rather boring lot, from the look of them. Do they ever smile? It is hard to imagine, I must admit."

The other young man, Nekoh, did not speak.

While he was the least gregarious of the trio, it was seldom that he had *no* reaction to an event or a circumstance. Always a bit self-conscious about his weight—he was inches shorter than Johanan but fifty pounds heavier—he tended to stay in the shadows of the other two though he was an intimate part of the circle of friends that had begun in their childhood years.

Johanan could not let Nekoh's quietness go by without inquiry.

"Are you well?" he asked.

"I am," Nekoh replied.

"Then why have you not joined in with us this day? You are so quiet even now. It is not like you."

Nekoh pointed to the thirteen strangers who were now down the road several hundred yards.

"What about them, friend?" Johanan asked, having no idea what the connection could be.

"I have seen them before now," Nekoh replied a bit sheepishly. "I have seen them more than once."

Johanan was unprepared for that.

"You have?" he said, surprised. "You mentioned nothing to either of us. Are they as unremarkable, except for their solemnity, as they seem?"

Nekoh was silent.

"Come on," Johanan said, irritated. "You seem to be playing games. What is it? Please tell us."

"I do not know about the others, but the tallest one is—"

He broke off, biting his lower lip.

"That tough-looking character? A breeze past my nose carried with it the pungent and unmistakable scent of fish just as he passed within range. Or perhaps that came from one of the others."

Nekoh was frowning.

He was, after all, in the most awkward position of revealing knowledge that would cause his friends to wonder about him, wonder how he knew anything about anybody from an obscure group of thirteen apparent wanderers, men who were probably only a cut or two above being simple hobos, depending upon the charity of those who took pity on them.

Nevertheless, Nekoh finally answered, and with a steady voice said, "No, it was he. A fisherman. The man is a master fisherman, and his countenance shows the rugged life he has been leading."

Johanan looked at him curiously.

"What impressed you about him?"

Nekoh rubbed his chin as he thought about an answer.

"His size, his strength, all were impressive, but it was another in the group who caught my attention far more completely."

"Which one?" Johanan asked, increasingly fascinated by his friend's untypical manner.

"The other one."

"Which?"

Johanan was confused.

"You said the tallest one, or did I misunderstand?"

"You did misunderstand, I am afraid. You thought I meant the fisherman. Though he seems tall enough, there is a taller one in the group. From this distance, you cannot see the difference as well as I did when I was closer."

Johanan saw that Nekoh was hiding some very deep emotions, or at least trying to do so.

"Something *is* bothering you," he insisted.

Ahiram agreed.

"Tell us," he joined in. "Perhaps we can help."

Johanan's eyes opened wide.

"Is it your mother?" he asked with great concern. "Is she worse? Has her pain increased?"

"Yes ..." Nekoh replied simply.

"You should have said something," Johanan told him. "But what does that have to do with this stranger?"

"My mother—"

The other young man found that an answer was difficult to provide.

"Yes, she is worse, but—"

"She thought this man could heal her," Nekoh interrupted.

Johanan and Ahiram, despite their concern for their friend's feelings, could not stop themselves from bursting out laughing.

At that, Nekoh jumped to his feet and walked toward the three horses tied to nearby bushes. He stopped partway and bowed his head, and they could tell he was weeping.

Both stood up and hurried to him.

"I am so sorry," Johanan told him. "It was wrong for us to laugh like that."

"Because it sounded so preposterous, I know," Nekoh spoke.

"Even so," Ahiram said, "we were being insensitive. Will you forgive us, dear friend, truly?"

Nekoh nodded.

"Mother sees in this Man something quite special," he commented.

"But why? What makes her think as she does about Him?" Johanan asked.

"You will not laugh?"

"We surely will not."

"She thinks He was sent by God."

Johanan and Ahiram exchanged glances but restrained their amusement over the delusions of an apparently dying woman.

"Mother said if she could only touch the hem of His garment," Nekoh continued, "she would be cured."

"If He did come from God, that would not be surprising," Johanan agreed, "but how can she be so sure?"

"Mother told me that His spirit spoke to her and said, 'Come unto Me, and be healed.'"

"But if He has the power of healing, surely He would have to touch her, would he not? How could your mother be healed merely by touching His garment? I would be concerned about your mother's delusion if I were you."

"I have no answer. I only know what she says."

"How did she get close enough to catch His attention? I assume she *saw* the Man and did not just *hear* about Him somehow."

"Mother saw only the back of His head as He happened to be passing by our house last week."

"And that was when His spirit somehow—"

"You are being sarcastic," Nekoh said.

"No, I am not. Just trying to understand."

"As I am. My mother could be suffering as the dying do before they leave this world, seeing and hearing things that are little more than wishful thinking. She may be no different."

Johanan had studied language with the finest tutors, wise teachers his father could easily afford. While he was younger, he had been zealous in all the rituals that his family and the society expected of him, including preparation for morning prayer, except on the Sabbath and on festival days. He would strap a phylactery, or tefillin, to his forehead and left arm, the small leather boxes holding folded slips of parchment containing Scripture passages such as the Ten Commandments.

But he had become more and more lax about such matters over the years and now preferred to spend time with his far more liberal friends. Nekoh was one of his closest. And he could detect, in the young man's words, disbelief colliding with the hope that his mother could be helped by whatever means from any source that could be effective.

"But you sense something else here, do you not?" he asked.

Nekoh had to acknowledge that his friend was right.

"Mother sees hope in this Man," he said. "She thinks He is capable of the greatest deeds."

"But that hope of hers will be crushed, as it must, because none who are of flesh and blood can heal. You know that, don't you, Nekoh?"

"Except—"

"Yes, friend, except what?"

Nekoh's cheeks were reddening.

"If He is … is … the—" he stammered.

"Calm down," Johanan told him. "We do not need to rush anything. Let's just take everything slowly."

Nekoh swallowed hard a couple of times.

"The Messiah," he finally blurted out.

Nekoh's heart started to beat faster as he spoke, and his whole manner seemed transformed from what it had been minutes earlier.

"This stranger might be the One we all have been awaiting for so long and He might—"

Johanan interrupted him by waving his hand through the air.

"You are reading too much into your mother's words," he said firmly but with kindness and more than a little affection. "She has an excuse for saying what she did, but you have nothing of the sort."

"I do," spoke up Nekoh.

"You do what?"

"I have an excuse or reason or whatever you want to call it."

"Tell us of it," Ahiram urged.

"Worry over my mother," Nekoh replied nervously. "Not wanting to face her ... her death. With Father having died last year, she is all I have left, you know. Oh, we have a legion of servants, it seems, and we can afford anything we want, except her health. Nothing can buy—"

He stopped himself.

"What are you thinking?" Johanan asked.

"Money."

"What about money?"

"I could offer that Man a fortune, a fortune that will never be missed since we have more than we will ever need, if He will come to our house and do what He can to heal her."

"His kind undoubtedly would find that appealing."

"His kind?" Ahiram asked. "What do you mean?"

"I have heard of them over the years, often in fact ... itinerant hucksters who are very good at deluding people into draining their savings for the pursuit of some kind of miracle in their lives."

Johanan was genuinely disturbed.

"It is sad and evil, this sort of thing, and I hate it. But the deceptions go on year after year, entrapping the gullible."

"It sounds so useless," Nekoh sighed, "a charade to give my mother a fragment of hope, only to have it ripped from her grasp."

Then he stopped talking, as though trying to think through what he wanted to say.

"If I could only believe ..."

Johanan was greatly moved by his friend's plight and wondered if he had gone too far in ridiculing the supposed abilities of this stranger, the one called either Jesus, or the Nazarene.

"There is a chance, you know," he said soothingly, not really believing what he was about to say but wanting to give his friend some reassurance, "a chance that this Man *can* help."

That took Nekoh by surprise, especially coming as it did after Johanan's earlier criticisms of "His kind."

"Heal my mother?" the troubled young man spoke. "The more we talk about it, the less sensible this whole thing is starting to seem, and the sillier it is rapidly becoming."

Johanan saw that his friend was on the verge of giving up any kind of hope, and he feared that Nekoh, given to impulsive behavior, might in his ultimate grief do something disastrous.

"We can catch up with Him easily on horseback," Johanan pointed out a bit desperately. "And then you can tell Him what you have in mind. Offer money, horses, land, whatever you want."

He revealed his growing fascination with what his friend had been telling him and Ahiram.

"I am rather interested in seeing how this Man reacts," Johanan remarked, "what His true character is like."

"So am I," Ahiram chimed in. "At least it is better than sitting around, worrying and crying."

Nekoh agreed with him.

"It is settled then," he told them.

They all nodded in agreement.

And so the three friends packed up what was left of their cheese and wine and mounted the horses.

"Follow the dust," Johanan said.

And that they did.

Less than five minutes later, they were just behind the group of thirteen. But the strangers were not by themselves this time.

A small crowd had gathered.

Some of the people comprising the crowd were obviously from the most humble of circumstances, with tattered, dirt-tinged garments that were nothing more than sackcloth, but others had robes of the most precious silk specifically dyed to brilliant hues of purple and crimson. A few wore jewelry, the gold flashing in the sun.

At first these onlookers were blocking from view whatever was catching their attention.

"What in the world is going on?" Johanan asked irritably.

But then several of them shifted their position, and the three friends could catch a glimpse.

*The tall one was putting his hands on a leper!*

Johanan, Nekoh, and Ahiram dismounted, staring in shock.

Lepers were unclean. They could spread their malady and cause others to come down with it. For that reason, there was periodic talk by autocratic proconsul-governor Pontius Pilatus, speaking for Rome together with certain high-ranking members of the Sanhedrin, about isolating all known lepers, perhaps on an island off the coast of Israel or sending them even farther out into the sea where the Roman emperor had established, by royal edict, a colony for those who became afflicted with leprosy. The emperor claimed he was trying to be sensitive to them, but in truth, he was bowing to political pressure not from lepers, who had no influence in the Senate, but from wealthy senators who found the presence of the afflicted to be discomforting, both because of their appearance and the possibility of contamination.

"He is possessed," Ahiram whispered. "He has condemned himself to a miserable death by touching that creature."

Shaking his head disbelievingly, he added, "Is the man ignorant? Or a fool?"

*... by touching that creature.*

For the many years that Johanan had known him, he had never heard Ahiram speak in that manner.

"*Creature?*" Johanan repeated. "Are you not being harsh?"

"Look at him! Does he seem human to you?"

The three of them stared at the leper, who had lost all his fingers. He was without sandals or any other kind of covering for his feet, revealing that six of the toes were gone as well.

"He is so pitiful," Johanan said, rankled by his friend's comment and distressed by the poor man's condition.

*His face ...*

One eye was not visible, hidden by bone and tissue long ago mis-shapen and covering it. There were growths all over his forehead and cheeks and ugly open sores on his arms and legs as well as the bottom of his feet. These deformities were the reason why most lepers did not walk very much but stayed in one spot, begging for charity from passersby who were seldom generous but turned away in disgust, or if they gave anything at all usually threw the money at them out of contempt or fear. Yet the tall stranger spat on His palm and now cupped that grotesque face in His hands.

"See!" Ahiram said, eager to be vindicated. "He—"

And then He kissed the gnarled forehead.

Ahiram turned away, and so did Nekoh. But Johanan was fascinated, fascinated and not wanting to miss whatever happened next.

"Turn around!" he pleaded. "Look at this!"

As the two young men did just that, all three were riveted by the sight of the leper stepping back from the stranger and holding his hands in front of his face, looking at all ten fingers, now regenerated.

"*My God!*" Ahiram exclaimed.

Suddenly the stranger spun around on one heel and looked at him.

"How is it that you use the name of the heavenly Father so cheaply?" He asked, His voice a rich, light baritone.

"And what is it to you, wanderer?" Ahiram shot back.

"Only the foolish profane a Holy Creator."

Johanan gasped, staggering a bit as he saw the man who had been a leper only seconds ago. The man was no longer in that unfortunate state; his skin now appeared untroubled by lesions, his toes also in place.

*And his eye!* The growth over it was gone.

Everyone's attention had shifted from the healed man to the confrontation going on between Ahiram and the stranger. No one saw the afflicted man's astonishing transformation taking place.

"*Another* man!" Ahiram spoke, trying to control his own shock at the sight. "Another—!"

The stranger walked up to him.

"Except you have faith ..." He said.

"Faith?" Ahiram persisted stubbornly. "Faith in what, I ask? You perhaps? Just because You healed that—"

But the bravado faded a bit as he found himself glancing again at the leper made whole.

The stranger noticed this and did not let it pass without comment.

"Faith in the One who sent Me," He said.

"And who might that be?" Ahiram asked, sneering as he tried to regain control of his emotions and leave his embarrassment behind.

The stranger's expression was a sad one in response, and tears were starting to trickle down His cheeks.

"Your years seem long when you are so young and robust, but soon enough it is time for them to end," He said, "and then it will be too late for you to know and accept the truth."

Ahiram found that remark to be insulting, since it came from a wandering man, obviously homeless, not dressed in the fine clothes that would indicate someone of Ahiram's equivalent in social standing.

"I *know* about life and death and all that," Ahiram said. "You need shed none of those tears for me. When it happens, I will be ready. God surely intends to welcome *me* more readily than *You* who are without a place even to rest His head."

"I shed tears for all of My children," the stranger said before returning to His twelve companions. "But then how do you *know* that I am without a home?"

"I see you now, and your cronies over there. I know the type."

"And what type is that?"

"Bums who subsist on the generosity of those they dupe into helping them. I find you all disgusting."

Ahiram's face was reddening.

"Look at the men with you!" he exclaimed. "The one over there was once a fisherman, I am told."

The stranger turned and beckoned to the big man who ambled over to Him and Ahiram.

"Simon, tell Ahiram here how you make a living," He said, that rich voice clear, compelling.

Simon was about to answer when Ahiram stopped him.

"You know my name," he spoke, astonished, his voice unsteady. "How *could* You know my name?"

"He Who numbers the hairs on your head knows the thoughts and intents of your heart," the stranger replied.

Ahiram backed away, not accustomed to such comments from anyone of obviously humble circumstances. He would have paid attention to a learned scribe but not to someone he considered to be little better than riffraff.

"You are a devil, a deceiver," he said. "I want no part of You."

As he rejoined Johanan and Nekoh, the former leper, waiting for Ahiram to leave, now rushed over to the tall stranger and fell on his face before the man.

"I owe You everything," he cried out, "yet I have little with which to repay You, Master."

"Love, not hate. Be kind. Be faithful to Almighty God. And—"

"Yes, Master?"

"You already know the rest, do you not? Otherwise, surely you would not call Me Master."

"When I looked into Your eyes, I seemed to be gazing into the kingdom of heaven itself."

The stranger whispered into his ear.

And then the former leper kissed Him on each cheek.

"I shall do as You say," he remarked, "and I shall remember You all the remaining days of my life."

"You will have many left to you," that wonderful voice said. "Enjoy them as My Father in heaven moves you to do so."

The man hesitated.

"I feel that I do not want to leave Your presence."

"You must go, for I shall not tarry much longer before I enter His kingdom again, but you must use your remaining years here to His honor and glory."

"I shall, Master, oh, I shall!"

And the man who was no longer a grotesque and pathetic leper ran up the dusty country road offering such praises that could not have been more beautiful if they were to have come from angels.

… *My Father in heaven.*

Ahiram overheard everything, as did those in the small crowd, and grumbling started, including his own.

"He calls Jehovah His father," he said. "The wretched man stumbles into blasphemy."

And so it did seem to those who were not yet ready to believe.

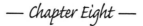

— *Chapter Eight* —

Johanan could not get the image of the Nazarene out of his mind.

He actually got himself lost after he bid good-bye to his friends who lived in another direction. Well known, he found people saying hello to him as he walked, even a *hamal* who was carrying a very large box that had been strapped to his shoulders. The exact weight of it was impossible to judge, but the young man was obviously straining as he walked, partially bent over.

Johanan also saw a man and a woman stooping over glowing ashes, baking flattened dough like a pancake, on a heated stone, the resulting bread properly unleavened according to Jewish dietary laws and best when eaten almost immediately. It was this kind of "cake baked on the coals" that was eaten by Elijah and often given to Jesus and the men with Him.

After he had returned home, he hurried to his bedroom, sat down on a bamboo chair his father had imported several years before from the Orient, and began pondering what it was that he had seen, a sight that no one could have faked. He tried to imagine the different ways such a charade could be done, and none made sense under the circumstances.

"It cannot be," he said out loud even after deciding that playacting and some fancy masquerade were not involved. "It just cannot be."

Everything he had been taught by the well-paid tutors his father had hired spoke out against what he had witnessed, not only the healing aspect of it but the capricious notion that the Nazarene was the long-awaited Messiah.

*That Man cannot be the One we await, he thought. Our great liberator will come with an army to smash the Romans.*

But as far as Jesus was concerned, Johanan saw only a Man, a tall Man, yes, rugged and rather handsome, but unlike the expected Messiah in any other way.

*What army did He have with Him today? Twelve ordinary men with no swords or other weapons in sight. They could scarcely defend themselves, let alone our nation.*

Johanan snorted as he recalled yet again that first glimpse of the Nazarene and remembered the condescension he had shared with his two friends.

And then the healing occurred, or what appeared to be a healing.

*Appeared to be ...*

Nerve ends along his neck acted strangely as he recalled the incident; he now knew more than before, when the doubts had been fresh born, that his eyes had not deceived his brain, and that he had witnessed something most remarkable.

An ordinary leper by the side of the main road leading into Jerusalem, like so many others whose weakness would not allow them to walk or stumble or crawl any further, a man once like other men presumably, but before the Nazarene touched him, a twisted *thing,* misshapen and ugly and—

Dangerous.

A leper could spread infection. He could make others what he was.

Johanan shivered, for he knew that that very act had been committed by other lepers driven mad by the pain of their malady and also by the isolation it necessarily imposed upon them.

Some had revolted against their circumstances and run amok, assaulting men, women, and children, touching them, spitting on them, screaming, "Now you will be like me, and I will no longer have your scorn!" or some variation of it. Then panic, especially in a crowd, would make people act like beasts themselves, the ones who had been assaulted pulling the leper limb from limb or throwing him over a cliff. Then they would return to their homes and await the onslaught of leprosy, which did occur with a few, but not so many as they had feared, and yet it did not occur to them that the disease could be more assuredly contracted only after prolonged contact.

But the man the Nazarene touched was not like that, not given to frustration and despair that bred a consuming revenge.

Not like that at all.

He had been in the ditch, weak and stinking, his mind clouded by pain, his tears touching the dust of that spot.

Ready to die.

Undoubtedly he was waiting for relief from suffering in the only form he assumed he would ever have.

Death would have been a friend to such a man.

But he had Another.

And he was made whole when the Nazarene touched him, banishing forever his leprosy and all its symptoms.

Even the disfigurement vanished in an instant.

"It was as though the man had *never* suffered from leprosy," Johanan said out loud. "The people were amazed."

He paused as he realized something quite stunning.

"*I* was amazed—because I too saw what had happened," Johanan continued. "I saw the twisted fingers straighten. I saw the sores disappear, the grotesque warts and all the rest of what made him appear so loathsome."

Another voice intruded.

He had not closed the door, and his mother was passing by just then.

"Then you must believe the witness of your own eyes!"

He looked up, startled.

"Mother!" he said. "You gave me a fright."

She apologized.

"I heard you talking out loud as I passed by," she told her son. "Are you all right, Johanan?"

"I am, Mother," he replied.

"But you were describing something rather odd and wonderful at the same time," his mother reminded him.

"Oh, we came in contact, from a distance, with the Nazarene today."

"I see! That One! What happened, Johanan? Some of my friends have begun to talk about Him."

"They have?" he asked. "What are they saying?"

"Gibberish, it had seemed; I was paying little heed."

"*Was* paying? That is no longer the case, Mother?"

She smiled sweetly.

"If I listen to my son, no."

Hannah sat down on the bed next to Johanan's chair.

"We have been very close, have we not, my only child?" she said, then glanced up and saw that the bedroom door was still ajar.

She took his hand in her own.

"My knees are hurting right now," Hannah told him. "Would you go and shut it for me?"

He stood immediately and walked over to the door.

"Do you have some very bad news for me, Mother?" he asked with apprehension, unsettled by his mother's manner.

"None, Johanan. It is not bad."

He could tell that she was anxious.

"Something that neither Father nor any of the servants should hear?" he asked as he hesitated pointedly.

"Yes ..."

Johanan shut the door and returned to his chair.

"Mother, what is wrong?" he asked.

"Nothing," she replied. "Nothing ... now."

"Now?"

Swallowing became difficult for him as his nerves seemed to knot up.

"What happened?"

"I ... have been very ill," she said, "with some pain that I have managed to keep hidden from you and your father."

"*Mother!*" Johanan reacted. "You—"

"Yes, very," she interrupted. "Please, my son, listen to me. Listen to what I shall tell you now."

"But you said *nothing* before now! How could you do that? How could you *not* say anything? Father does not know, either. Do you really mean that?"

"*Especially* Huram."

"Why do you say that?"

"Because of how he would react."

"To your being ill?"

Hannah, a thin, nervous woman under ordinary circumstances, seemed so calm then.

"Do you not see the difference in me?" she asked.

"You are the same," Johanan replied. "You are—"

But he could not sustain that lie. She was not the same at all.

Peace.

A peace was surrounding her, it seemed. A peace that had not been hers all the years he had known her, years of seeing her fidgeting about everything, so nervous at times that she seemed ready to collapse from the weight of real or imagined concerns.

"Yes, Mother," Johanan said, "yes, you *are* different."

"Feel my right side," she asked.

He did as she wanted. "What, Mother? What should I feel here?"

"A lump was there," Hannah said, tears starting to touch her pale cheeks.

"You are crying!" he observed. "Are you in pain?"

"No, Johanan, please listen to what I am saying. The lump is gone. Oh, the pain I felt from it!"

"I could feel nothing, as I said. What happened? How could it be removed? How could a physician attempt such a thing without Father and me finding out?"

His bemused mother merely smiled at her son and shook her head.

"But you said—"

His palms were suddenly sweaty.

"Mother ..." Johanan started to say, his eyes widening as he realized what she would say next. In that single instant, he could have uttered the words for her, one after the other.

"The Nazarene," Hannah said. "He touched me and made me whole."

Though Johanan had anticipated that, and therefore her revelation was not the shock it might have been otherwise, he still sat, speechless, for several minutes, and so did his mother.

"I saw Him touch a leper today." He finally spoke, but hesitantly, not sure of what words would tumble from his mouth.

"I know."

"You know? Were you—?"

She nodded vigorously.

"But I did not see you."

"The leper's malady was more obvious. The crowd left me as the Nazarene walked away and healed that poor man next."

"Why did you not tell me then? I am learning this only now, Mother. You did not make yourself known."

"You were with your friends. I did not want to embarrass you. They might have laughed. Who knows?"

"Embarrassed me? How could you have expected your *healing* to embarrass me? I would have rejoiced!"

She knew him better than his father did.

"Now you say that, Johanan," she remarked. "It is so much easier now, here, the two of us alone."

"Now is no different."

Hannah shook her head.

"Your aversion for the Man was obvious."

"My aversion? My—"

"Yes, it was on your face. I could see it even from that distance. I know you so well, Johanan. And, ah, those friends of yours! Both would have spat in the Nazarene's face if they had been closer."

Johanan objected.

"But, Mother, we saw what He did. We felt no disdain. We felt skepticism, yes, but nothing else."

"Are you sure?"

He was hurt that she did not accept what he was telling her.

"But it affected me deeply," Johanan protested. "That is why I was here, alone, until you entered. I was trying to sort it out, Mother."

But Hannah did not relent. She was knowingly forcing him to confront his feelings.

"Jesus is poor, Johanan," she said. "You are rich. You have never mistreated the poor, but you also have expressed your distaste for the impoverished ones you have seen over the years. You have called them foul-smelling, lazy … must I go on, Son? Must I?"

His mother was right.

Johanan' saw what she had been trying to get him to face.

"You should not be viewing the poor with such studied superciliousness," Hannah continued. "When your scorn turns to pity, and your pity drives you to help them—"

He turned his head away from her.

"Forgive me …" she said, genuinely sorry for being as aggressive as she had been, but she was acting out of emotion, not intellect, and she was beginning to have regrets that she had not been gentler, more gradual in telling him what she felt he needed to know.

"But what about the Nazarene?" Johanan muttered. "You say He healed you. How can I believe that, Mother?"

"You believed it of a leper but not your own mother?" she asked.

"I could see that poor man's plight, but I did not know there was anything at all wrong with *you*."

"I knew how you would worry."

"Am I free of worry now? What did you accomplish after all, Mother?"

"Touch my side."

"I cannot."

"Touch it, and find out for yourself."

"The lump must still be there. You just want to believe that the Nazarene did something."

"He healed me, Johanan."

"Mother, I cannot accept—"

She grabbed his hand and pressed it against her right side.

"Tell me, my son, can you find any lump?"

He swallowed hard a couple of times as he felt along his mother's side, expecting to detect the outline of some kind of lump and not knowing how he would tell her this was so, that her fantasy was nothing more than that—her imagination.

And yet—

Nothing.

Only smooth, even skin.

No lump.

"But how—?" he began.

"How do you know the lump was there in the first place?" she interrupted, anticipating him. "My son, are you so scornful of your mother that you suspect her of making up something like this?"

He avoided looking at her because he *had* been thinking that she was capable of *imagining* anything that ultimately satisfied her—in this case, being healed, a need she obviously had.

"Johanan?" she asked.

"Yes, Mother?"

"Go to see Him."

"The Nazarene?"

"Yes, please, I can arrange a private moment."

"You? You are just one of many who make such a claim. Why would you have any special influence with this Man?"

Johanan snapped his fingers.

"He knows about Father, and our position in the community, that's it, isn't it, Mother?"

Hannah knew what he was getting at, but she was there ahead of him.

"But He has refused any money!" she exclaimed.

"You *offered*? Are you not *aware* of His type? They victimize people with their lies and then move on before they can be apprehended."

"Yes, I knew all that."

"And still you offered a wandering Nazarene some of our family money, probably a sum that was quite extravagant?"

Hannah did not flinch although her son spoke the truth.

"I did."

Johanan could not help but let his astonishment show as he asked, "How could you have done that?"

"He *healed* me!"

"So He heals for money then?"

The scorn he felt seemed almost physical, born of years of absorbing his father's views in such matters and adopting them as his own.

"I told you: He would take nothing."

"No expensive clothes?"

"Nothing, Johanan, except some food and lodging."

"No gems either?"

"*I said nothing.* Will you now insult me by not believing my words? By throwing them away as though they are so much garbage?"

"You secured a place for Him to stay?"

"I put Jesus and the others up in our stables."

Johanan sprang to his feet.

"Mother, you *have* lost your mind!" he declared.

She was on her feet also and slapped him hard across the cheek.

"I am sorry ..." he told her, tears in his eyes. "Can you—?"

"Forgive?" she interrupted again. "That is at the center of what the

Nazarene teaches: forgiveness. Of course, Johanan, I can forgive you. I *do* forgive you. You are my son, and I love you."

She touched that same cheek, which was now quite red.

"Will you go to see Him?" Hannah asked. "Jesus is there now. Will you do this for me?"

And Johanan said yes.

Johanan had seldom been back to the family stables. He disliked the odors of manure and the rest. When he wanted to go riding, he would ask a servant to get a steed for him.

"And you say the Nazarene and His men are *sleeping* here?" he asked his mother incredulously as they walked together toward the barn. "Have they no shame?"

"I understand that Jesus was born in such a place," she replied, "north of here, in little Bethlehem."

"What common people they are!" Johanan exclaimed haughtily, his disdain the product of both his social class and his father's fervent ideas about separating his family from anyone "below" them. This approach to social class structure was clearly in violation of scriptural precepts, but that truth had gotten sidetracked in favor of a kind of institutionalized snobbery that was not restricted to Huram ben Sira's family, but had permeated virtually every other family of any wealth throughout Israel.

"Common?"

Hannah's reaction made her son uncomfortable because she was, after all, part of the family circle that had instilled his approach to life.

"Why are you so displeased with me for saying that?" Johanan asked.

"Your disdain."

"Disdain? It is what you and Father taught me. Were you so wrong, the two of you?"

But Hannah would not retreat.

"They are God's children, just as you and I are."

"*You* have changed, and you expect *me* to go along as easily as you seem to have done."

"The Nazarene is a wonderful Man."

"Because you *think* He healed you? I can understand that, Mother. But do not expect me to feel the same way."

"He saved your mother's life, and *that* has no impact?"

It was her turn to look disbelievingly at him.

"Mother, listen to me, please!" he asked.

She said nothing but let her son speak.

"Mother, these people are little more than beggars. We sometimes throw their kind a coin or two. Perhaps we give them a loaf of bread from time to time. But we do not invite them onto our property and let them sleep through the night."

"Is being common a sin, my son? Is being a beggar some act of condemnation posed by the God Who created us all?"

He blushed, for usually he was the most mild-mannered of sons, the most respectful. Suddenly he found himself acting toward his mother in a manner that would have been unthinkable even hours before.

"Again I am sorry for my words," Johanan told her, genuinely regretting yet another instance of what was considered gross disrespect in that time and that place, proper treatment of parents mandated by Mosaic Law.

"As you should be," Hannah agreed.

She stopped walking and stood beside him.

"Jesus saved my life," she reminded her son. "Do you expect me to treat Him as I would anyone else who is itinerant as He is?"

"You admit that He is nothing more than a wanderer then?"

"He is a wanderer with the power to heal."

"You *really* cannot be certain of that."

"What about the leper, my son? Were you under some delusion? Was it a moment of craziness on your part, a wild fantasy that had you seeing something that never took place?"

Johanan winced.

"You seem to think that I cannot say with any conviction that the Nazarene healed me. But, I suppose, if you were not imagining it altogether, *you* can be more certain that He healed the leper because you *saw* what happened?"

"Of course, Mother. The leper's fingers came back. The sores disappeared. The bones straightened."

"And you saw this with your own eyes. And those friends of yours witnessed it as well."

"Yes, Mother, yes."

"Still, you say, it could not have happened with me. A common leper, as you would call him, is worthy of immediate healing but I am not, is that what you are also saying, Johanan?"

"Mother, you know I am not saying that at all. You know—"

"I know nothing of the sort. We both are witnesses. I saw the leper healed at the same moment you did. Yet you find my eyes ill-suited, incapable of witnessing what the Nazarene did for my own body. A stranger you are willing to confirm, but your mother you dispute!"

Johanan was unprepared for the way Hannah was acting. He wanted to get past that moment, do what he had promised, forget that any of it had happened, and go back to living his life as he always had, without such turmoil.

"I do not want to go through this again," he told her, trying to assert himself. "I go now to see this Man because it seems important to you, but I will not stay longer than a few minutes and then I will be done with Him."

She smiled then.

"You find this amusing?" he asked.

"Is a smile only when some joke has been told?" she retorted. "Where is my laughter, Son? Whence the joke?"

Johanan started walking again. Less than fifty feet remained before he reached the stables.

The Nazarene!

The young man had turned his head to see if his mother was catching up to him, since his steps were quicker and he was walking in the heat of emotion.

When Johanan looked straight ahead again, he saw Jesus standing in the middle of the dirt path, as though expecting him that very moment.

"My mother—" he started to say.

The Nazarene nodded.

"—claims You healed her," Johanan spoke as he heard Hannah come up beside him. "Mother, is that not right?"

To her son's astonishment, she fell, sobbing, at the feet of the Nazarene.

Johanan's face reddened, his anger causing beads of perspiration to stand up on his forehead and trickle down the back of his neck.

"Mother, get up. If Father sees you—" he protested.

She looked up at him.

"If Huram ben Sira were here, I would *pray* that he would be on the ground next to me, at the feet of the One Who created all of us!"

Johanan's mouth dropped open.

"God?" he spoke. "You are saying that this Man is God?"

He reached out and touched the Nazarene's face.

"I can feel His flesh, Mother. I can touch the hair on His head."

He bent down and grabbed her shoulders.

"This is not God," he said. "This is a wandering charlatan, Mother, seeking those He might entrap with His wicked deceptions. You must not let Him fool you another moment. You must break away from His spell."

But Hannah would not budge.

Johanan stood again.

"You have bedeviled this poor woman!" he said, nearly yelling. "Is there no shame in You?"

He lifted one arm, intending to reach out and strike the other Man.

Jesus grabbed him at the wrist, and Johanan could not move.

"Let go!" he said lamely. "You are my guest. How dare You treat me as You are doing!"

"I am of flesh and blood, as you say," the Nazarene said. "But there is more here than you can see; there is more than you can know. Only faith will open your heart. Only faith will give sight to your eyes."

"There is nothing wrong with my heart!" Johanan protested. "And my eyes see clearly enough."

"Only what you want them to see."

Jesus let go, and Johanan backed away, rubbing his hand.

"Mother, this is not God," he declared confidently. "This is a foul beast, a crude opportunist, very strong and very clever, but scum, Mother, worse than a beggar—a criminal, yes, a criminal more than a beggar. You must get Him to leave now. If Father finds Him here along with those cronies of His, he will have them arrested and figure out the charge later."

Johanan left his mother and the Nazarene and returned to his room, where he got into bed and looked up at the timbered ceiling and pondered what had been happening.

*She has allowed herself to be duped by this stranger,* he moaned to himself. *But I know my mother so well, and I would never have thought that she would become so gullible with Someone who is obviously—*

He sat up in bed, a striking fact hitting him much like a physical blow.

"She is not stupid; Mother is *not* stupid!" he exclaimed.

He realized he had fallen into the trap of *assuming* she was under the spell of the Nazarene because she was so dumb she could not perceive what He was, that it was easy for this Jesus to entrap her.

Johanan jumped out of the large, comfortable bed and stood in the middle of the floor, trembling as images entered his mind that were so contrary to those he had entertained only minutes before.

"Since she is smarter than many other women I have seen," he acknowledged, "why is it that Mother is now like someone very foolish, utterly convinced that the Nazarene is not an impostor or a fraud?"

*… many other women.*

His parents had held a long stream of parties at their massive house over the years, and their only child enjoyed exceptional opportunities to meet people from all over the known world, men and women of assorted colors and professions, all of them wealthy by the standards of their culture and that time in history.

But the women who came were largely so subservient to the men that they seemed quite empty intellectually and very dull to be with, though there were exceptions, especially among those women from the Far East and a few he had seen from Africa.

*You outshone them all,* he thought with great pride. *Some looked down their royal noses at you, but you were so much brighter and more clever and you … you—*

Tears were starting.

*You could hold your own against anyone. You—*

He was sobbing now.

*Mother, Mother, how badly I have treated you!*

Knocking.

Someone was knocking at the bedroom door.

"Are you all right?" the familiar voice asked.

He could not answer immediately, his voice choked by the emotions that had taken hold of him.

The door was opened.

A servant entered the room, a dark-haired young man named Yiptah, just a few years older than Johanan himself.

"I heard you crying," he said sympathetically.

Johanan nodded as he swallowed a couple of times.

"I guess you have found out," Yiptah added cryptically.

"Found … out?"

"Yes? About your mother?"

Johanan felt his palms becoming sweaty as he wondered how the news about her and the Nazarene could have spread as quickly as it apparently did.

"Yiptah, please, you must keep this as quiet as possible," he said.

The young servant nodded.

"Of course I shall," he replied.

"I would be very grateful for that," Johanan told him.

"If people knew, they would treat her differently."

"Yes, exactly! We cannot allow that to happen, you know."

"That is the way I feel."

The next few seconds were spent awkwardly between them. Johanan had come to think of Yiptah with more affection than the other servants, partly because there was less difference in their ages. This was part of the bond between them, but it was hardly the sole reason. Johanan was fascinated by Yiptah's cheerfulness despite his modest circumstances and a history of illness in his parents.

*You are an only child like I am,* Johanan thought. *How would it be for either of us if we lost our parents?*

Yiptah turned to leave.

"Johanan?" he asked.

"Yes, Yiptah?"

"Because of what is going on in my own home, I have had to prepare myself for being alone."

"Yes, I know. I admire the way you have been able to deal with everything. I doubt that I would be as ... successful."

"But you should start thinking about it, especially now."

"Now?"

"Yes, your father is healthy, it seems, but now with this growth in your mother's side ..."

Johanan's blood seemed to freeze in his veins.

"You know about the growth?" he muttered. "You know it to be real?"

"Real? Of course, Johanan, I was with your mother when the physicians examined her. She did not want anyone else to know right away. She thought, with my parents' own problems, that I would understand."

Johanan's normally robust-looking face became quite pale.

"I feel faint," he said. "Will you—?"

He need not have asked. Yiptah was at his side in an instant, easing him back into the bed.

"You never knew," the young servant said.

"I did," Johanan assured him.

"But why are you so surprised now?"

"I did not believe her, Yiptah. I thought she was exaggerating."

"Exaggerating? It is supposed to be as large as a melon."

Johanan gasped at that.

"Dear God!" he exclaimed. "Dear God, forgive me for what I have put my mother through."

He leaned against Yiptah.

"How can she forgive me?" he moaned.

"She loves you," Yiptah told him.

"But you do not know what I have been saying. I have very nearly called her crazy. I have very nearly accused my mother of being blind to the intentions of the Nazarene. I told her that she risked Father's ire by bringing those people onto our property for the night."

"Jesus? What does He have to do with this? If they are here now, I will have them thrown off immediately and never allowed back. I feel as you do, Johanan, that they are leeches and deceivers, tricking the gullible into—"

"Stop! It is you who now does not know what has happened."

"She has taken a turn for the worst?"

Yiptah was alarmed.

"Is that why your mother is nowhere around?"

"She is probably still out at the stables. I doubt that she has left there since I returned to the house."

"With the Nazarene and His followers?"

"I can hardly blame her now."

"Blame her? For what? She should be here, resting, conserving her strength, not wasting her time with their kind."

Johanan grabbed the young servant's shoulders.

"Listen to me!" he said almost sternly.

"What is wrong?" Yiptah asked.

"Mother has been healed!"

"Healed? She—"

"Yes, yes, the lump or growth or whatever it was is gone."

"How could that possibly be? It was growing rapidly. The physicians held out no hope whatever, no—"

For a moment Yiptah's eyes seemed to glow.

"The Nazarene?" he spoke. "The Nazarene touched her and healed her? He made your mother whole?"

Johanan could only nod, this time with sudden great joy though not a little shame.

# — Chapter Nine —

Johanan and Yiptah waited for Hannah to return, hoping she would do so soon since her husband would return in a few hours from a business trip just a few miles inland and they would have to plan carefully how to present everything to him, if they did so at all, at least just then.

Undoubtedly he would be disturbed for more than one reason.

The fact that the truth about Hannah's condition had been kept from him would make this husband as furious as any man might be expected to be in such circumstances. And that she would seek help from someone like the Nazarene could only turn his anger into rage.

Finally, Johanan decided he could not wait any longer, so he went outside and headed toward the stable, asking Yiptah to go with him. As they approached, Johanan found a stable hand and inquired about his mother. The answer was not the one he wanted: She had left with the Nazarene and His followers!

"Where?" Johanan asked in panic. "Why did you not inform us?"

"She is the master's wife, sir," the stable boy replied succinctly but with no disrespect. "Am I to question her movements?"

"In what direction?" Yiptah asked.

"Toward Gilgal."

Johanan ordered that two horses be readied.

"Should I get some of the guard?"

This question was from Yiptah, and Johanan was momentarily amused at the level of his concern, which seemed quite genuine, not an attitude concocted merely to endear himself to the master's son.

"I wonder …" Johanan mused. "I wonder if my mother needs us at all."

The stable boy's eyes widened.

"It might be that she was kidnapped, sir," he said.

"But you said she had left with them," Johanan repeated. "That sounds as though she did so willingly."

"It appeared to be that way. But I really did see them only after they had started down the road."

"Were they on foot? Can you tell me that?"

Johanan was filled with anger and fear and not a little panic. As an only child in a society that prided itself on *large* families, he became unnerved anytime it seemed that either of his parents were in danger, for they represented the bulk of his private world.

"Yes, sir. Everyone was on foot."

"Did my mother seem to be struggling?"

"No, sir."

"Was she being handled by any of the men?"

"No, sir."

"Then why should you think she might have been kidnapped?"

Johanan was beginning to wonder if he was speaking to an alarmist.

"Because I do not trust the Nazarene."

The stable hand's expression would have said that even if his words had not.

"And why do you not trust Him?"

"He pretends to be the Messiah, but He is doing nothing to help us. He just stands and walks."

He hesitated, his eyes opening.

"What is it?" Johanan asked.

"And there have been some miracles, at least that is what some folks are claiming."

"The healing of lepers?"

The stable hand nodded as he spoke, "But others as well, sir. The feeding of five thousand people with a few loaves of bread and some fish."

"Any others?"

"It is said that He can walk on water if He wishes."

Johanan and Yiptah glanced at one another.

"And so none of that matters, right?" Johanan pressed. "As long as He has no army of liberation with Him, you suspect His intentions, is that right?" Johanan asked.

"Yes, sir."

"He talks of peace and goodwill and meekness, correct?"

"From what I understand, yes, sir."

Johanan was becoming disturbed, briefly forgoing the seeming urgency of going after his mother.

"Have you ever heard Jesus speak?" he asked.

"No, sir."

"And yet you are so convinced about the Nazarene?"

"Why else would the high priest be seeking witnesses against Him?" the youth asked. "His emissaries have even approached me."

"You? Does my father know?"

"He encouraged the contact, promising me extra benefits if I could jog my memory and think of something."

"But why? Why would he do that?"

"I think it had to do with your mother, sir."

"My mother?"

"Yes, sir."

Johanan's mouth opened, but he did not say anything for several seconds.

"Are you all right?" Yiptah asked.

"Everyone knew about this except me," Johanan muttered. "Why did *everyone* know *except* me?"

"Your mother did not want to alarm you."

"That she was seriously ill?"

"Your father found out that she was intending to go and see if the Nazarene could heal her, and he exploded when he learned of this. By coincidence, I guess, the high priest's man came by the same day, and that was when your father decided to help find a reason to bring this Jesus into custody and … and—"

"Go on," Johanan urged. "There is no need to hold anything back."

Yiptah cleared his throat nervously.

"I think the intention was to pile up such evidence as necessary to get the proconsul-governor to—"

"Crucify Him?"

"Yes …"

Though the day was proving to be a warm one, Johanan suddenly felt a chill that covered every inch of his body. He had seen just one of the public executions atop Golgotha, drawn there out of curiosity as was the case with so many other Israelites, this singularly Roman means of death unheard of before the Romans had conquered the land.

"He is such a gentle Man ..." Johanan murmured.

"Your mother," Yiptah said.

"He seems to preach joy and love and humility, not bloodshed, not violence of any kind, nor hatred, nor—"

Johanan was trembling.

"And yet they want to shed His blood. They want to put Him up on the Place of the Skull and leave Him for hours."

He had heard the moaning of other condemned men and seen people from the surrounding countryside laughing at the sight, holding their small children on their shoulders so the young ones could get a better view, women using the occasion to gossip among themselves, other men placing bets as to how long it would take for each criminal to be declared dead.

*Father, forgive them,* Johanan had told himself shortly before he left, determined never to watch such a tragic spectacle again though he could overhear some of the people bragging about how many executions they had attended.

He had stopped to grab one of these men by the collar.

"This is not a circus event," he said. "We are not barbarians thrilled by the public taking of someone's life. How can you do this? How can you teach your children to follow in your footsteps if your sandals are soaked in blood?"

"But they are criminals," the bearded man, in his early fifties, retorted. "They deserve to die."

"I can see that, and I can agree. But do your sons and your daughters deserve to see it happen? Do they deserve to get a taste of the same bloodlust to which you obviously have surrendered?"

The other man avoided his gaze.

"We condemn the games of the Romans," Johanan added. "And yet are we any different? At least *some* of those gladiators survive!"

He let go and stalked off, unable to bear that scene a moment longer.

*They found Hannah in what had been settled as a valley of lepers though it had become something quite different in recent months, something that served as an illustration of the miracles of Jesus the Nazarene ...*

Quite a distance south of Jericho, the valley was surrounded by part of Mount Guarantania, the least-known and rarely visited region near Jerusalem. That the lepers seemed to make it their own, a secluded place where they could try to come to grips with their misery, probably had something to do with the lack of visitors, except for those individuals kind enough or wealthy enough or both who saw to it that the lepers were fed and clothed. These benefactors never came in person but sent others to leave food and garments for the lepers. Fortunately a waterfall at one end of the tiny valley fed into a stream that ran across to the opposite side and through an opening beneath the mountain, presumably to end somewhere underground.

For the lepers, Mount Guarantania provided what no other location did, certainly not the Gadarene area closer to Jerusalem, to which others of their kind drifted, to live among the barrenness of that place, eating locusts and snakes and spiders and other creatures, often scratching themselves on sharp rocks and never realizing it since leprosy was essentially the deadening of a body's ability to feel pain as well as a condition that played havoc with any resistance to infection.

The valley found near the center of Mount Guarantania provided an isolated spot where the soil was rich enough to grow crops for the lepers and the waterfall and stream provided all the water they could need. Their homes were crude but reasonably effective piles of rock and dirt, though the mountain itself helped shield them from desert winds and protect them from an onslaught of predators.

"It is not any kind of heaven here," each new leper would say after arriving, "but it is far from being a preview of hell either."

*Shunted aside ...*

Beggars were allowed inside the walls of Jerusalem and other cities. So were the blind, the crippled, even those who were demonically possessed, but not lepers, for fear that they would contaminate the entire populace.

The valley was not crowded as yet, that settlement of lepers only a fairly recent phenomenon. Others found out about it only by chance since no attempt was made to spread the word. Besides, it was beyond the reach of all but the most hardy lepers, any of lesser strength who tried to make the journey inevitably becoming too tired and falling prey to roving hyenas and other creatures.

Under normal circumstances, neither Johanan or Yiptah would have been anywhere near Guarantania. Yet to get to Gilgal, they had to pass near its southernmost point. Both had heard the stories of what a sad place it was for people of misery.

"It makes me nervous that we have to be even as far away as this," Johanan acknowledged. "I wonder how long a distance the contagion spreads."

"I hear it is just by touch," Yiptah answered, "but then I feel the same as you do. We can never be too careful."

"Think of what they endure."

"I have, how I have. A friend of mine caught it."

"He became a leper?"

"He did. I spent weeks wondering if it would spread to me. I washed myself many times a day. I examined every inch of skin that I could see. And I prayed, oh, how often I prayed for the mercy of God."

"It seems that your prayers were answered," Johanan observed.

"May God gain the glory for this!" Yiptah replied.

That was when they saw the man sitting by the side of the road staring at his hands. As they approached, he jumped to his feet and waved at them as he stood directly in front of the two of them.

"Stop, strangers!" he exclaimed with obvious great excitement. "I want to show you something."

"But we are trying to reach Gilgal as quickly as possible and have no time for—" Johanan started to say.

The man, in his midthirties, was very bony and had many wrinkles on his face; he seemed not to hear what he was being told or else ignored anything but what *he* wanted to say to the two strangers.

"My hands!" he said, extending them. "Look!"

"Forgive us but we must hurry, we—" Yiptah tried this time.

"Why?"

"We have to reach Gilgal before sundown. We are hoping to find someone."

"I know a shortcut!" the man beamed.

Johanan and Yiptah were becoming tired, not used to such long rides.

"Will you tell us about it?" Johanan asked.

The man nodded.

"But first you have to look at these hands of mine," the man insisted. "You see them, do you not?"

"I do. Finely formed hands."

"That *is* right, you know, like the hands of a newborn baby but much bigger and perfectly made."

"Hands to be proud of," Johanan humored him, though quickly losing patience under the circumstances. "We really must continue on. Are you going to show us this shortcut of yours or not?"

Again the man seemed not to know or listen to what Johanan was saying. So Johanan decided not to waste any more time with him; he pulled on his horse's reins, signaling the animal to continue.

The stranger shouted after them, "Can you imagine someone like me having hands like that? Just a short while ago, they were twisted and missing two fingers on the left hand and one on the right."

In an instant, Johanan stopped his horse, and Yiptah followed suit.

"I thought I would die a leper," the man was saying as they dismounted a few feet away and walked up to him. "My parents were lepers as well. For a while, it seemed that I would not be visited with their curse. Then it started, the splotches, the sores that never healed but always got worse, the numbness all over my body."

"What changed you?" Johanan asked, pretending not to know anything about what must have happened.

"He did!"

"He?"

"The Nazarene!"

"He *healed* you?"

"He healed all of us, the entire village, one by one, going among us, touching men, women, and children."

Johanan asked the man a question that seemed to burn in his mouth as he spoke it.

"Was ... there a woman among them?" he asked.

"Several women! I told you: He healed everyone. Lepers are not only men!"

"Yes, I know, I mean among the Nazarene's followers, was there a—"

"A woman with all those men?"

The man scratched the top of his head.

"Oh, yes, I saw her. She spoke so kindly to me. Love shone in her eyes. A wonderful woman, that one!"

Johanan started to cry.

"She ... she is my mother!" he declared, startled, but with growing appreciation for what had happened.

"Son," the man told him, "she is a mother unlike so many others. Instead of being home, safe, she is out here, she—"

Johanan glanced at Yiptah, who also had begun to cry; the two hugged one another, feeling the pride of a son and a devoted servant.

"May I take you both to where she is?" the stranger asked, his voice whispery, as though feeling what the two young men were experiencing.

Johanan hesitated, asked, "Inside the lepers' village?"

"Yes, that is where she can be found."

Johanan's expression betrayed his apprehension.

"I will ask her to come out to see you," the man said. "You can stand at the entrance. You will be quite safe."

Johanan and Yiptah secured their horses under an outcropping of rock hidden from the road, then followed the stranger as he started walking toward the mountain ridges about half a mile away, enjoying the ability to move without pain.

But for Johanan, there was pain of a different sort as he thought of his mother, his emotions having gone from pride to fear, fear for what she might become after mingling with the lepers and touching what they had touched.

Shame.

That was also part of what he felt, shame that he would be unable to do that which apparently had not bothered Hannah at all, shame that he was worried, in that moment, as much about himself as about her.

And Johanan knew he would have to confess all this quite openly to her and ask her to forgive him.

The valley could be reached only by a very narrow pass through that section of Mount Guarantania. It reminded Johanan of what he had heard about Petra, a community similarly isolated from the outside world.

"Be careful!" the man cautioned them. "Some of the rocks have sharp edges. Some of the people now living in the valley had ugly cuts and scrapes after they entered."

"What is your name?" Johanan finally asked.

"Yaddua."

"I have not heard that name before."

The man chuckled.

"What is funny?" Johanan asked.

"It means 'well known,' even though I am unknown."

"Ironic ... why did your parents give you that name?"

"They had great plans for me, they did. They wanted me to be justly famous; oh, how my parents wanted that. My mind used to be filled with visions of palaces and travel and people in far lands uttering my name."

"What was to be the reason for your fame? What were you supposed to become, to achieve?"

"I never knew," Yaddua told him. "They died before I could gain from them any direction in life."

"And what have you been doing since then?"

"Shuttled from relative to relative until there was no one left; then I had to take to the streets to beg or steal food and clothes and lodgings. Sometimes I sold myself."

"Prostitution?"

"Yes ... I was good-looking before the leprosy took hold of me. Now, though I am healed of the malady, my face *has* changed in other ways, and I have aged greatly. I no longer have the same handsome features I once enjoyed."

"And yet now you seem happy."

Yaddua stopped walking for a moment and carefully turned around to face Johanan, who was just behind him.

"I was frighteningly ugly," he said. "You have no idea how twisted I was, bent over, emaciated, enough to send impressionable children back to their homes for sleepless nights until they recovered from the shock of seeing a creature such as I was."

"And all of that changed?" Johanan asked politely, with no trace of sarcasm or skepticism.

"In an instant. Have you never seen a leper healed by Jesus?"

"I have. Just today. But he seemed not nearly as extreme as you say you were."

"I think that parents use images of the way I looked as weapons to threaten their children into behaving."

Johanan did not doubt that that had been the case.

"I am happy, yes, I am," Yaddua continued. "Though I am still poor, though there are times when I know hunger, though I wear only rags, I am now part of a community of men, women, and children reborn, and not just from leprosy."

"What do you mean?"

Voices ahead.

"We will talk later," Yaddua told him. "I am anxious to tell you everything."

They were only about twenty feet from emerging out of the mountain pass and into the village.

Laughter.

Not just something casual, not the polite laughter of the dinner parties that Johanan's parents had put together from time to time; rather it was the laughter of people filled with joy so deep, so pure and unrestrained that it could scarcely be expressed in any other way.

The joy of being whole.

"Listen to them!" Yaddua exclaimed. "And know why we feel as we do. For many of us, leprosy has been with us throughout our adult lives. Can you understand how it feels to be *released* from that at last?"

Johanan was about to respond when he caught his breath.

A woman's laughter, for him distinct from the rest.

"*Mother!*" he cried out.

"Then we must quicken our steps," Yaddua acknowledged.

He did just that, as fast as the narrow confines of that mountain pass, with its jutting rocks and prickly vegetation, would allow. And, less expertly, Johanan and Yiptah followed, adding several more scratches to their bare arms.

Finally they reached the end of the pass and emerged into a clearing.

More than a score of men, women, and children were sitting in a circle around the Nazarene, not including His twelve followers who were scattered among the former lepers.

"Have they no fear of contamination?" Johanan whispered to Yaddua.

"What do you fear?" the other man asked. "They are no longer what they were."

"But the disease could be—"

"In the air? Is that what you think? If the Nazarene can heal them in the first place, can He not prevent them from becoming diseased again?"

Johanan searched for his mother and found her in the circle, joining hands with a former leper on her right and one of Jesus' followers on her left.

Singing.

After the laughter, they now had begun to sing one of the psalms written by the beloved King David.

"Then was our mouth filled with laughter, and our tongue with singing." Their voices rose and then echoed back from the mountainsides surrounding them.

Johanan was familiar with that one. He joined in with the rest as he walked up to his mother, with Yiptah directly behind him.

"The Lord hath done great things for us," he sang, "whereof we are glad."

Hannah turned her head as she heard her son, and smiled.

"And they that sow in tears shall reap joy ..." she continued.

Those in the crowd made room for Johanan and Yiptah as well as Yaddua, who had needed to break away for a time to talk to God privately and thus was outside the village when Johanan and Yiptah approached. At least that was what he thought he'd been doing out on the road, but now he realized Yahweh had wanted him there at the precise moment the two newcomers approached.

A few minutes later, the singing stopped, and everyone's attention was on the Nazarene.

"There are some who will reject you even now," He spoke, "but God is no respecter of persons. If they turn from you, My Father shall not."

Johanan had heard Jesus speak in that manner just after He had healed the other leper.

*But how can You can say that?* he thought. *You claim Yahweh as Your—*

It was then that Jesus turned and seemed to be staring right at Johanan.

"It is as I say," He went on, "for God sent His only begotten Son, that whoever believes in Him shall have eternal life."

Hannah had been holding her son's hand and now tightened her grip on it, whispering to him, "No barriers, Johanan. Just give in to Jesus. Just believe."

Johanan wanted to do that, wanted to surrender that last part of himself that was holding back, but it was not to be. Not yet, not there.

Johanan and Yiptah spent several hours at the village but then had to leave because traveling the road back home at night was not prudent since robbers were common and insurrectionists could be just as dangerous, as the death of Quintus Maxientus had proven. And that attack had happened within the city limits of Jerusalem itself, not out in the uncivilized countryside where animal predators were a threat as well as the human ones.

Johanan persuaded his mother to join them. But at first she did resist the idea of returning to an environment that she had sought to put behind her, at least for a while.

"My place is here," she protested. "I feel peace here, or anywhere with Jesus. It is a peace that passes my understanding, but I know I am experiencing it, Johanan. Please believe that, my son!"

"Your place is with your family!" he told her. "These people are remarkable, yes, Mother, who can disagree with that? But I am your son, and your husband will soon be returning home. You should be with us, not a village full of strangers."

"But Jesus says otherwise, Johanan. He tells me, and others, that unless we are prepared to leave family and friends, giving up everything and everyone for His sake, then we are not worthy of Him."

Johanan had not heard that before.

"Has He been saying *that?*" he asked, afraid his mother would take it too seriously. "Are you certain?"

The concept unnerved Johanan, and he wondered if he understood what his mother had said.

"He has, and I am," she told him firmly. "Wealth should mean nothing in the end. The old ties—"

Johanan could not let her go on with such talk.

"Enough, Mother," he pleaded, not wanting to be disrespectful but alarmed by what she seemed to be implying.

"You cannot stand the truth!" Hannah retorted.

"What truth, I ask?"

"The truth that says—"

They were standing by Johanan's horse. Yiptah had already mounted.

"I am going to confront this Man," Johanan told her. "I have never stopped thinking that He *uses* His power of healing to gain some sort of control over people, and then He openly runs their lives."

Hannah started to protest a second time, but he turned his back toward her as he felt his temples pounding. Then he saw that the Nazarene had decided also to leave the little colony of former lepers and was heading toward the mountain pass, His dozen followers faithfully at His side.

Johanan approached Him.

"You have confused my mother," he said angrily. "What gives You the right to do that to anyone? You saved her from death, it seems, and yet do You assume You can use that as an excuse to go on and take her from—?"

He stopped himself.

*… You saved her from death.*

For a little while that singular fact had become buried in the rush of events since he had learned of it.

*I would have no mother with me now,* he thought, *if You had not done that, if You had not somehow removed that growth from her body.*

"I would not have her at all if it were not for You," he muttered aloud.

The Nazarene smiled but said nothing.

"But does that mean You are to take my mother from me now?" Johanan moaned, hoping it did not.

Still Jesus avoided a reply but stood, listening rather intently.

*Suddenly a hand!*

Johanan jumped when a hand touched his back, and he turned to see who it was.

Hannah.

"My son, my son," she spoke, smiling happily, "I would never leave you and your father permanently."

"But you told me—" he said.

"I told you I had to be *prepared* to do so. But Jesus does not expect that of me, not now, anyway. He travels too many miles. Few women could undergo all that He and His followers must face."

Hannah was not exaggerating. Miles of basically desert travel, the hardest sort of travel, tested the endurance of even rugged men; how much more a middle-aged woman barely over five feet tall who had been accustomed only to being waited on by household servants, including Yiptah himself?

"I am now here, but when He leaves to go to Galilee or Caesarea Philippi or Capernaum, I cannot join Him. I do not have the strength, son."

"If you had only told me a few minutes ago!"

"Did you really give me a chance, Johanan? You heard what I said, but you did not let me tell you what I *meant*."

Johanan sank to his knees.

"I do not know what is happening to us," the young man cried out. "When Father finds out, he will be very angry. Oh, Mother, you know his rages. You have seen him rant about the Romans and the insurrectionists both. I am afraid of that anger. I am afraid of what he could do to you and to me."

"What is the worst outcome, my son; tell me, will you?" Hannah asked. "That we are thrown out of our home?"

"Yes," Johanan agreed. "To lose everything! Is that not bad enough?"

"Jesus and His apostles have no one to call their own, you know. They have been wanderers for three years, depending upon the generosity of—"

"Beggars then?" he interrupted. "They are just like beggars. How could we endure that, Mother? After all that we have known every day of our lives?"

"But that is the *worst* that could happen. Your father may not resort to that after all, you know. We are not giving him credit for any compassion."

"Compassion? It is not a word he understands at all, Mother. When his rules are violated, that is the end."

"For outsiders, I agree. But we are his—"

"The difference matters little to my father. He is capable of raising false witnesses against us, to accuse us of anything he pays them to say."

Johanan turned and looked at Jesus.

"Can you help us?" he asked.

For another moment the Nazarene continued to be silent, then He replied, "I will see your father and talk with him. But it is important that he learn from you first."

Johanan nodded in agreement.

"What about you?" Hannah asked of her son.

"Me? What do you mean, Mother?"

"Huram will be angry at me, but *you* tried to stop me. You have not accepted Jesus as the Son of God."

That was the first time Johanan had heard anything of the sort.

"Son of God?" he puzzled. "You believe that of this Man? You are so sure He is the Messiah?"

"With all my soul, yes!"

Hannah's entire countenance seemed lit up by some strange light within her.

For a short while, moments that seemed far longer than they actually were, Huram ben Sira felt it was entirely possible he had gone quite mad during that initial moment when he could think of nothing but getting his hands, with their long fingers, around the muscular neck of a certain former carpenter from the village of Nazareth. It was one privilege he would *not* delegate to his guards, driven as he was to a rare moment of physical violence. Usually, all he had to do was threaten, for he had developed a tone of voice and a positioning of his body that sent the message he intended, and few dared to stand against him, though that did happen occasionally but only because the men he confronted proved to be as mean and intimidating as Huram himself.

As he ran through the large house where he and his wife had lived for more than twenty years, he found himself screaming, "Where have you gone, Hannah? How dare you do this? Have I not provided everything you have ever needed?"

A loyal servant, an older man who had been with the household for many years, had told Huram about the Nazarene and His followers spending the night in the stables, with Hannah joining them when they departed.

"My wife?" Huram yelled upon hearing of that. "She has taken up with strangers, and common wanderers at that? Are you certain of this?"

He spoke more slowly, his voice sterner in tone.

"I will not tolerate you being wrong about such a matter. I will not tolerate it for a second!"

The servant had seen that rage before and knew he could say nothing that would seem to oppose or disagree with his master.

"Yes, sir, that seems to be what happened," he said, sweating. "And … there was your son, too."

"He joined that group as well?"

"No, Johanan seemed most upset with his mother for what she was doing. He and Yiptah took off after them."

"In what direction?"

"Toward Jericho, sir."

That was when Huram had vented his feelings, flailing his arms high in the air as he went from room to room, some twenty of them, hoping that Hannah had somehow slipped back into the house without anyone's notice.

"Do you realize what will happen when people find out about this?" he shouted to no one. "The shame this will bring upon our family name!"

Hannah's action had considerable potential of doing just that. Money and power separated the classes in Israel.

And Huram ben Sira had both.

The wealth he possessed was in part inherited, but the increase since his father's death was entirely of his own doing. He had effectively doubled the size of the original estate as a result of successful business dealings with the Romans as well as fellow Jews and the many silk dealers, leather-goods providers, and others who visited the Jerusalem area often during an average year. He also dealt in livestock, but this part of his enterprise was taken care of largely within Israel itself.

One of the dirty little secrets he had kept to himself was the fact that part of his expanding wealth could be traced to his success in getting favorable tax treatment. He had bribed visiting members of the Senate and others who returned to Rome and persuaded the emperor to make a special case for him.

Huram himself never knew what arguments the appeals were based upon, but that did not concern him nearly as much as the results, for there were some years when he never paid taxes at all and others when the amount was moderate, the latter only to keep up appearances. It was true that some middle-class families and even a few poor families frequently paid more taxes than he did.

Ultimately Hannah had found out and confronted him.

"You are shamefully greedy!" she exclaimed.

"And you have been enjoying the fruits of that greed for an awfully long time," Huram retorted.

"If I had known—"

Huram interrupted his wife.

"Easy words to utter now," he told her. "Are you willing to give up your leather goods and your artwork and your fine furniture? Your embroidered clothes and your imported foods? They were all bought with what greed provided us, enough money to enable you and me and our son to live like the relatives of some king. Herod the Great could have been pleased with just a little of what we have."

Hannah had turned away in disgust then and would not talk with him the rest of the day. But, soon, that night in fact, they made love as though she had never found out anything about one of the reasons behind the family's wealth.

Her husband was right. The *things* in Hannah's life were terribly important to her, and she could not let go of them, since that lavish environment was all she had known throughout her adult life.

Huram realized all this well enough, and he was counting on it. But he would not stop at that. There was something else he intended to do, though he wished it could be avoided, desperately wished it could be avoided.

He would turn to the proconsul-governor as the next step.

And he would do so before his loved ones returned home.

## — Chapter Ten —

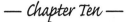

W*eary* ...

Pontius Pilatus was still weary after making arrangements to have Quintus Maxientus embalmed and sent back to Rome with all the documentation that was required. Procula wrote a letter to the man's widow and packed up a gift of mourning, one of the tapestries her husband treasured the most, one of the customs of the time mandating this, though not all Romans were as honest about it, keeping a stock of inexpensive "treasured" items ready for the next death.

Pilatus had hoped to have a cleared schedule that day, with nothing to do but finalize arrangements for his friend and then sit back and contemplate the meaning of what had happened, if any meaning could be found.

It was not to be.

The urgent entreaty, through one of the proconsul's servants, had come from an awaiting Huram ben Sira, a prosperous Jew who came to him periodically, but according to strict protocol, by asking for any such meetings at least a few days in advance, seldom any less than a week or two. This time was different. As soon as he had awakened, Pilatus had been given a message from the man begging urgently for a meeting as soon as possible.

Now Pontius Pilatus' first visitor after lunch was an especially distraught Huram ben Sira.

"My son ..." the Jewish businessman said, obviously troubled and hoping that the proconsul could help him.

"What about Johanan?" Pilatus asked, displaying his remarkable recollective gift while trying to rise above the trivialities of the moment, his mind being pulled back to what had happened just a few hours earlier. "I see the young man from time to time. He seems robust enough."

"Oh, he is healthy," the elder, thin-faced, hawkish-looking man quickly added, concealing for the moment his more immediate concern. "But he seems without any kind of direction."

"I am sorry to hear that. But I must ask you, why have you come to me about this? It seems hardly a governmental matter, Huram. And it's difficult to see the urgency."

"I know. I do not state this well. Forgive my awkwardness."

*... the trivialities of the moment.*

Pilatus sighed with a boredom he hoped the birdlike little Jew could not detect. There was no sense antagonizing anyone in the midst of such a politically tremulous period in Roman history.

"Could you arrange, I mean, could you send my son to Rome for a season?" Huram asked, requesting of the other man what he had decided was the least severe method of eliminating any further contact between Johanan and the Nazarene, even though Johanan may have been guilty of nothing more than going after his mother to bring her back home.

*If I get you out of the way,* he thought, *I can deal more freely with your mother. She is the one for whom there may be no hope.*

Pilatus frowned at the seeming presumptuousness of that request.

"But why?"

"I am afraid my boy is developing the wrong interests."

The proconsul took entirely another inference from that statement.

"Men? Is that what you are saying, Huram?" he mused. "I must tell you that sending young Johanan to Rome would do nothing to stop him in *that* regard."

That was one reason why Pilatus was glad to have left Rome. Members of the Senate openly solicited young male "assistants" but not for any legislative business. That sort of open tolerance of and participation in corruption was anathema to a man of principle, as he had been over the years.

"Heavens no! It has nothing to do with men."

Huram was becoming more nervous.

"It has to do with just one Man," he pointed out hesitantly.

Pilatus rubbed his forehead with the tips of his fingers.

"Let me guess—the Nazarene," he said. "Am I right?"

"How did you know?"

"I seem to be acquiring more than a few insights about that One!"

"I am afraid that my son is quite bored, you see, proconsul, and I worry that this Jesus of Nazareth will feed him some terrible nonsense as it seems He has done with so many others, and Johanan will leave home to follow after Him."

"What would He say that could be so objectionable in your case?" Pilatus asked of his visitor.

"The Nazarene has demanded that young people leave everything behind and follow Him or else they are not worthy enough to be called His followers!"

Pilatus nodded knowingly.

"And Johanan would take a chunk of your wealth with him, wouldn't he?" he offered. "Why not just disown the boy? Then he would receive nothing."

"He is my flesh and blood, my only child," Huram reminded him. "I could never be as angry with him as that, never!"

"You are fortunate. I have no children, and no idea of what this true bond between father and son is like."

"It is as strong as a bull, as tough and hard as Mount Sinai itself."

Pilatus chuckled at that analogy, but his visitor took offense that he would treat it so lightly.

"I am very serious, you know," the Jew said. "This is my only son. I care what happens to him."

Pilatus nodded, appreciating the elder man's anguish and softening his tone as a result.

"And you figure that if Johanan is far, far away from the Nazarene, that would eliminate the possibility of any bond developing between them? Or have I missed something that you wanted to convey?"

The visitor's eyes widened.

"Yes, proconsul!" he exclaimed. "That is what I suspect. This is an important time for him. I want him to have the right influences."

Pilatus pondered whether he should get involved but withheld his momentary indecisiveness from the other man.

"I will see what I can do," he said. "I assume you will be paying the expenses, should I decide to do this."

"You assume correctly."

"And may I also assume that you are going to send to me some more wonderful tapestries?"

Huram resisted letting a smirk cross his face.

"They will be waiting at your doorstep in a few weeks," he said nonchalantly.

Pilatus' mind was made up rather quickly then.

"You need not worry," he said. "I have some ideas about how best to accomplish this. I will get back to you."

The two men shook hands, and then Huram ben Sira left.

Pilatus watched the door being shut, then he walked out to his balcony, glancing in the direction of Gethsemane while thinking of the arrangements he had had to make for the body of Quintus Maxientus and feeling even more hatred for Barabbas, who was surely behind his friend's death.

After the meeting with the Roman proconsul-governor, Huram ben Sira felt some relief by the time he arrived back at his residence, for it was now likely that, in the near future, Johanan would be kept out of the reach of the Nazarene, though the situation regarding his wife was not nearly as clear-cut.

Of course, he could go out looking for the two of them, plus the young servant Yiptah, but since he doubted that they would stay away permanently, Huram decided to wait at home, using the time to get his thoughts together and be completely ready for any confrontation that might come.

"Jesus ..." Huram spoke in a whisper, disliking even the sound of that name as it left his lips.

Then he remembered that his friend, Saul of Tarsus, had been aware of the Nazarene for at least a year, and the two of them had discussed the matter months before. But Jesus then had seemed of little consequence, and since the controversy surrounding the Nazarene did not involve him or his family on any intimate basis, he had let the conversation slip from his mind.

"Saul, you were becoming very alarmed," he said out loud again as he sat in the large room that served as his den and recalled the talk they had had. On shelves against each of the walls except one he could see piles of parchments, each one chronicling a major business deal he had consummated during the past two decades.

Saul was perhaps the most learned scholar in all of Israel, a man whose intellect made the Sanhedrin's high priest seem rather stupid by comparison.

"It is a pity that you do not have Caiaphas's position in the Sanhedrin," Huram speculated. "I wonder how different life in this country would be then."

For one thing, he was convinced that Saul could outfox the Romans at every turn, but not simply to ensure the lining of his own pockets.

However, Caiaphas was another story.

The high priest had been interested only in what would fatten the temple's treasury, not in what would ultimately benefit his native Israel though he had been successful for so long in getting the bulk of the naïve masses to believe the opposite.

"Saul ... Saul ..." Huram muttered, "how I wish you were here now, here to talk with and then to enlist my son, to take him by the hand and lead him away from the Nazarene. He respects you. He would listen, I am certain."

But Saul was not there.

He had gone off somewhere to cleanse his spirit and had not yet returned. Before he left, he had stopped to talk briefly with Huram.

"I do not expect to be back for perhaps a week," Saul remarked.

"But where are you going, my friend?" Huram asked.

"To the Sinai."

"For a week? I see only that little leather knapsack of yours."

"It is all I will need."

"Even if you *stuffed* it with cheese and bread and some dried venison and a skin of wine, it would hold enough only for three days. Four at the most."

"The angels will sustain me after that."

Huram did not believe in such beings. And he only grudgingly accepted the existence of God Himself. So, he ignored the subject altogether, sidestepping an intensive debate with the other man.

"But why, friend? You are going to spend a week alone in the wilderness. What could justify any course of action as extreme as endangering yourself by—"

Saul interrupted him a bit impatiently.

"I need a cleansing," he said.

No emotion had crossed Saul's face.

"A cleansing?" asked Huram. "You have never seemed less than a most sanitary man to me. Why in the world would you of all people need a cleansing?"

Saul snickered at the other man's reaction.

"It has nothing whatsoever to do with my body, Huram," he replied with raw condescension.

"Then what? Riddles do not become you."

Saul's manner softened somewhat.

"My mind is clouded," he replied without a hint of irritation. "My very soul is in confusion."

"You seemed as clearheaded as always just last week."

"I may have been," Saul acknowledged.

"Then what has happened since?" Huram asked sympathetically, immediately curious as well as uneasy.

"There is going to be blood on my hands," Saul had replied cryptically as he held them out in front of him, "and I must prepare myself. I must strengthen my resolve."

"Blood, my friend? Whose? Are you talking about Barabbas? Please, tell me more. I want to know."

"The Nazarene and His followers. I have been helping Caiaphas gather information and giving him some theological insights."

Coming from any other man, the latter part of that statement would have seemed especially preposterous, but Saul was the learned individual the Sanhedrin most often consulted about one matter or another. No one else had the training that he had pursued, and gotten, all of his adult life.

"Ignorant men they are," Huram pointed out. "Foolish and, I think, self-destructive. Why would you find yourself in a position to shed *their* blood? Why would you *allow* that to transpire, my friend?"

He was genuinely distressed that Saul's time was being wasted but, more importantly, that there was danger involved that the other man had not fully reckoned with as he committed to this so-called mission.

"You talk of blood," Huram added. "Have you considered that the blood spilled might be your own?"

He had never interfered in Saul's life before then, because a long time ago, as the two men were growing up, it became *very* obvious to Huram that his slightly younger friend was set apart from most other boys, quieter, more at home with scrolls and parchments than the roughhousing games of the young, a boy who understood obscure points of theology better than men several times his age.

*I remember your going into the temple one day and confounding the scribes who were there,* Huram thought. Suddenly he rubbed his left arm as all feeling seemed to flow from it and a total numbness gripped every inch of it, only to become normal again a few seconds later.

A thought, new and startling, pierced his mind.

*The same situation occurred when the Nazarene, younger than you were, also entered the temple and—*

Huram had realized then that he was staring at the other man, just staring while saying absolutely nothing.

"Are you ill?" Saul had asked.

"No, I am ..." Huram had muttered in reply but knew he was not very convincing, causing his friend to persist.

"You look ill."

"I was just—"

A moment passed.

"Just what?" Saul prodded, not willing to accept what Huram was saying when his own intuition told him otherwise.

"Thinking."

But that was not good enough for Saul. He wanted to know where his friend was heading with such ponderings.

"Thinking, yes, but about what? I would hate to think you are playing some casual game with me."

"Remembering, actually."

"Remembering what, Huram? Come on, my dear Huram, this is becoming rather annoying, I must say."

"You."

"What about me?"

"In the temple when you were so young."

Saul's frequently somber-looking face broke out into a broad grin this time as he understood immediately what his friend was recalling.

"Oh, yes, that startled you."

"I was amazed."

"At how smart I was?"

"Yes, and how very brash."

Saul chuckled as he shared in that recollection.

"I seemed even more like a midget in those days, an undersized child with a squeaky voice. And, yet, there I was, standing up before a dozen men who were old enough to be my grandfathers."

"Telling them about prophecy and the Egyptian captivity and so much more, and doing so with the greatest insight, it seemed."

"And then they tried to rebuke me."

"But you would not give."

Saul slapped his leg with the palm of his hand, laughing.

"I held my own, did I not?" he said, grateful to Huram for reviving a recollection of an incident that surely had been a turning point in his life but one that had been lost in the mists of early childhood.

"That you did, Saul. That you did," he said.

Huram hesitated before saying anything else, choosing his words with more than usual care.

"Saul?" he asked.

"Yes, my friend?"

"Jesus of Nazareth …"

"What about Him?"

"He did much the same thing, I hear."

"Yes, I know."

"It seems that the two of you might have been suited as friends instead of enemies, however bizarre that sounds now."

The notion was distasteful to Saul.

"No man can be a friend who wallows in blasphemy."

Huram closed his eyes, his forehead suddenly throbbing for some unknown reason.

"You *are* ill!" Saul insisted.

Huram shook his head.

"No, friend, I am not, just momentarily wondering, a bit of intro-spection, nothing more than that."

"If the Nazarene could be what He says He is? I gather that that is what you are contemplating?"

"Yes, and, I wonder, foolishly perhaps, but I wonder ... what if this Jesus should happen to be the—?"

Saul did not let him finish.

"Dismiss any possibility of that from your mind."

"But—"

"Listen, Huram! He is very good at what He does, but someday He will be condemned and we will see Him hanging from a cross atop Golgotha. God would never allow that to happen to the Messiah, you know."

"This mission of yours? Will you not reconsider? So few of Jesus' followers exist. How can they be worth your attention? You are this nation's greatest scribe, its finest religious and historical scholar. Why not concentrate on something that is worth your abilities?"

"It is as you say ... now. At this moment they are few in number. But later, ah, that is what concerns me. The heresies they are capable of spreading have come to my attention for the past year or so, Huram."

"Heresies? What heresies? I thought He was a political problem, not a religious one."

"He has said He is the light of the world. He also has told listeners that except men come to God through Him, they would be damned."

Huram gasped.

"Surely you are jesting."

"I do not jest. That is but one of many statements. I have the others committed to papyrus."

"You must have heard Jesus of Nazareth speak, I assume. Surely you cannot be accusing someone of heresy through mere gossip or less than impeccable witnesses apart from yourself."

"Oh, yes, I *have* heard Him, more than once, out in the countryside as well as within Jerusalem."

"And what do *you* think of Him?"

"I have to admit that the Nazarene is impressive. He addresses His listeners with seeming *authority;* that is what concerns me. I was only too happy to see John the Baptist out of the way."

"Did you have something to do with that?" Huram asked.

Saul pointedly refused to answer directly but simply said, "John was a minor nuisance. Jesus is far, far worse."

Saul was a short man, not more than an inch over five feet in height, but he seemed strong, his features muscular, and the intensity of his gaze was similar to that of an animal on the prowl, ready to strike without warning.

"Something must be done about Him," Saul continued.

"Get Salome to dance for Him," Huram offered jokingly.

The other man had grabbed his arm as they sat next to each other on the front porch area of Huram ben Sira's residence.

"John was a creature of the flesh," he said, "but Jesus is not, it seems. He lives, He breathes, He eats, He sleeps but, as far as I can tell, He has never had sex, He has never been ill, He has never cut Himself and bled, He—"

"How extraordinary, if you are correct," Huram observed.

"The longer Jesus lives, the more He will infect our people—our young people in particular. Yet even if the Nazarene were eliminated *tomorrow*, those who are indoctrinated with His teachings would still be alive, and they are capable, I believe, of spreading like rabbits if *I* do not stop them."

"You, Saul? Why are *you* at the center of this?"

"Because I am convinced that Yahweh has appointed me for the task. And I shall *not* swerve from it. I am a vessel, and the Creator is using me as He sees fit."

Saul of Tarsus narrowed his eyes.

"On that you can wager your soul," he said firmly.

Huram ben Sira felt the grip of something dark and cold as he listened.

## Chapter Eleven

I *am a vessel and the Creator is using me as He sees fit ...*

Huram ben Sira could not get those words out of his mind after his friend had left, words that would stay with him during the months to follow, like insinuating demons haunting the hours of each day.

Saul's activities were becoming more and more intense since that meeting. As an explanation, he would tell Huram and others later, "I am a vessel, yes, but also an avenging angel, and because God is with me, no one can stand against me."

Before his own family's involvement with Jesus of Nazareth, Huram's dislike of the Messiah was rather casual and did not claim much of his time or his energies.

*No longer ...*

Now everything had changed, and as he waited for his wife and son to return, he was making plans, with his visit to Pontius Pilatus only one of the actions he would take. The next step took him to a meeting with Caiaphas, whose loathing of the Nazarene had been more intense than his own.

"No longer," Huram said. "Now I hate Him as much as you do."

"I am glad to hear that you are being sensible about this," the high priest replied. "And I have some ideas about how you can help."

Huram was delighted to hear that.

"Tell me," he said anxiously, having stopped at the temple after his meeting with Pilatus in the hope he would find that Caiaphas was available.

Caiaphas did not hold anything back.

"Get your wife and your son to say that they were kidnapped," he said, speaking distinctly and with great confidence.

"But they were not," Huram objected. "I cannot force them to lie, Caiaphas; you should realize that.

"My good fellow," the high priest went on, "how important is a bit of false witness at a time like this?"

Huram hesitated because he considered himself a moral man, and the idea of getting his family to fabricate anything was upsetting, regardless of the purpose.

"But that would be thoroughly dishonest," he said. "Surely there is some other way."

"A lie in the service of good comes as a benediction from God Himself," Caiaphas said, barely hiding his cynicism.

"But ours is a God of truth," Huram reminded him.

"Leave the theology to me, my friend."

"It is not purely theology I say but also a matter of decency."

"Have you never lied?" the high priest asked pointedly.

"Yes …"

"To consummate an essential business arrangement of one sort or another? Or whatever else you told yourself at the time?"

Huram was not comfortable admitting that sort of thing, particularly to a man who had such questionable ethics, raising the chance of blackmail later.

"Yes, Caiaphas, yes, I have."

"Some lies, a bit of distortion and exaggeration here and there?"

"I admitted that I have. Let that be the end of it!"

"So, then, with your family at stake, you are not willing to support lies? Am I to believe that, Huram, *truly* to believe that? It is fine to salvage a business deal by lying, yes, you have said that, but not your loved ones?"

Huram ben Sira was not a man who could be talked to like that.

"You cannot say such things to me!" he spoke, nearly screaming.

"I already have, and I shall continue to do so until my point gets through that thick skull of yours!"

They had been sitting on thick, tasseled cushions, the cloth a fine-spun silk donated to the temple by a visiting merchant from the Orient. Abruptly, Huram got to his feet and stalked toward the doorway.

"Leave now," Caiaphas said behind him, "and you can expect your loved ones to go the same way, through a doorway as you are doing, but from your own home this time and never returning, not your wife, not your son."

Huram stopped and said, "You have insulted me, but to find them under the spell of this foul *thing* would be a greater insult."

"Follow your heart," Caiaphas told him. "Conspire with me to be rid of Jesus, to see Him soon atop the Place of the Skull, spilling His blood."

Huram swung around and faced the high priest.

"Crucifixion?" he asked, incredulous that he was being asked to participate in such a scheme.

"He is killing what you enjoy as a family. Killing Him in return is your only action."

"I was thinking of having the Nazarene banished, perhaps to Patmos, exiled there for the rest of his life."

Caiaphas actually paused, considering that possibility, which seemed momentarily rather appealing.

"It would certainly eliminate some hurdles," he mused. "*Banishing* a man is something Pilatus would not resist as much as crucifying him. No blood, no mess!"

Seconds passed in silence between the two men. Then, the next instant, Caiaphas' manner changed.

"He would still be alive, alive to inspire His followers from afar," he spoke. "And even exile could never mean total isolation. Is it not obvious, once you think about it? An island can be reached by boats and under the cover of night. Jesus could receive visitors from time to time, especially if the commander of the Roman garrison on Patmos were paid a bag of coins whenever this happened."

Huram looked down.

"I see," he acknowledged. "If I want Him gone, it has to be from this world, not just from this country."

"I will seek His death whatever you might wish," Caiaphas said. "Please, join with me, and seal His doom."

Huram agreed.

"I will do whatever it takes to be rid of the ex-carpenter from Nazareth," he replied. "Now I must go back home. I must be ready when they return to me."

"Do you want help?" Caiaphas asked.

"I need nothing further as a result of this meeting. I truly thank you for what you are doing."

The high priest smiled.

"Now that I have *your* cooperation," he told his departing visitor, "it will be easier … and sooner."

Huram shook hands with Caiaphas and then left, walking about a block before he stopped and glanced slightly to his left.

Golgotha could be seen in the distance, no crosses on top just then.

Huram ben Sira shivered as he turned away, surprised that he felt no sense of triumph that morning.

*No activity …*

At first Hannah, Johanan, and Yiptah thought the house was deserted as they approached it along the flower-bordered, winding walkway that led to the front door.

Silence.

No one came to greet them. They could hear no voices or any other kind of sounds from within.

"Listen!" Hannah said. "Absolute quiet."

"I wonder what has happened," Johanan commented. "Yiptah, will you go back to the stables and see if there is any activity there?"

The young servant nodded and hurried around the left side of a house that was simple in design but exceptionally large in size, a sprawling, one-story, block-type structure that dwarfed all but the houses of Pilatus, Caiaphas, and a few others who either had greater wealth or position or both.

"Has my husband moved out and left everything behind?" Hannah speculated. "He has enough money to buy three other homes anytime he wants. He may have just abandoned us and our home, having no desire for a confrontation."

*… having no desire for a confrontation.*

Johanan shook his head as he repeated those words to himself.

"But that sounds not at all like Father," he suggested. "He would want to stand right up to us and settle the whole matter—in blood if necessary."

The front door was slightly ajar, and they walked cautiously inside, standing for a moment in what would pass for a vestibule in those ancient days.

"In blood, Johanan?" his mother asked. "Are you so sure? I have known him for longer than you have and—"

He interrupted her as he said, "Father would decide that spilling some blood was necessary to preserve our family bloodline."

"I have never seen anything like that in him," Hannah protested.

"But he has shown me a different side, Mother, a side he was careful to keep hidden from you. It was something to show to another man but never a woman because women always would prove terribly frightened."

No one else was in the house.

The two of them went quickly from room to room only to discover that it was completely empty.

"Could he have done something even more drastic?" Hannah asked, trembling as she considered the consequences.

"More drastic than this?" Johanan countered. "What in the world could that be? It looks as though, in his anger, Father has fired everyone, demanding that they leave immediately."

Yiptah picked that moment to return to them, saying that no one was in the stable area, either.

Hannah continued to tremble.

"What have we done by following a stranger against Huram's wishes?" she asked, frightened.

"I am afraid to think of the answer," Johanan said as he pondered the disturbing but unavoidable image of Huram ben Sira, lifeless, at the end of a rope after a self-inflicted hanging.

Yet there was no body. They searched every room, every closet, but could find nothing—no blood, no rope, no—

Johanan threw his head back in despair. He was standing outside with his mother and Yiptah, for they had been searching the grounds as well. The tension made his neck feel like a crossbeam, suddenly giving him not inconsiderable pain.

Their home was considerably closer to the Place of the Skull than were Caiaphas' and Pontius Pilatus' residences. As Johanan looked in its direction for a moment, he noticed that someone was on top.

"It is usually deserted, especially at this time of day, but not now," he observed. "I see someone kneeling down and—"

Perspiration suddenly beading his forehead, Johanan staggered for a moment, leaning for support against the wall of the balcony.

Hannah and Yiptah rushed to his side.

"Johanan, what is happening to you?" she asked in panic. "Do you want something to drink, my son?"

He told her no, that he had become faint because of what he had seen at Golgotha.

"Father ..." he muttered. "Might it be father?"

"Huram? Where?" Hannah asked.

"I think I see him there," he said, pointing in the direction of what had become a dreary place of execution since the Roman conquest.

"Where?" she asked, excited. "Golgotha?"

He raised one arm and pointed toward it.

"Look, Mother," he urged. "See for yourself."

Hannah squinted under the harsh afternoon sun, trying to see what Johanan wanted to show her.

A shape, tiny from that distance, but discernible.

The shape of a man, just one man.

She reacted first in silence, then disbelief.

"What could he be doing if that is my husband?" she wondered. "It looks as though he is kneeling."

"And why there of all places? Why would he pick that location as a place of prayer?" Johanan asked out loud. "Father *praying* there? Before now, he showed next to no interest in such matters."

Yiptah took the liberty of speaking up.

"Or he is hurt!" the young man ventured.

Johanan and his mother looked at one another.

"Beaten up by insurrectionists ..." Yiptah added. "He might have been attacked by men loyal to Barabbas."

"Get a chariot ready," Johanan ordered. "We must hurry either way."

"Either way, son?" Hannah asked. "What do you mean?"

"I was thinking that there might be a second possibility, Mother," he said, wondering if he should voice his concern at all.

"A second—?"

She saw her son's expression and seemed to know what he meant without anything being spoken.

"Suicide?" she said. "Is that what you—"

Hannah brought her hand to her mouth to stifle a scream that nearly broke past her lips. Johanan put his arms around her and held her until Yiptah had brought the horses and a chariot around to the front of the house.

As they hurried on to Golgotha, the man on its top fell forward into a puddle of his own blood.

*A light enveloping him, blocking out the whole world ...*

Huram ben Sira was on the way home after his meeting with Caiaphas at the temple, but he walked right past it as though having forgotten his destination, and he was looking straight ahead, his pace a slow, steady one.

An elderly male servant named Asael noticed him on the dirt road outside and hurried from the house to see what was wrong, since his master seemed to be walking in a rather dazed manner.

"Sir, sir!" he exclaimed, realizing that Huram had not acted in such a manner during all the years Asael had been with the family.

No reaction.

Huram paid the old man no attention.

"Sir! Where are you going?" Asael persisted, intending to call for help if necessary, summoning other servants younger and stronger than himself.

Huram looked at him oddly.

"To the Place of the Skull," he replied. "I must go to Golgotha, Asael. I must go there now."

Asael shook his head.

"No, sir," he said, "you must not walk alone. Let me have a carriage brought out for you. You should allow yourself to be driven to Golgotha, sir. These are dangerous days. Look at what happened to that visiting Roman senator, Quintus Maxientus. You could be in great danger, sir, you—"

Huram stood still and started sobbing.

"What is wrong, sir?" the old servant asked, concerned that his master was in the midst of some sort of collapse.

"I have spoken of terrible things this day," replied Huram, his mind recoiling from the images of what he and Caiaphas had discussed. "Yet I have been allowed to see—"

"What terrible things?" Asael interrupted, driven by concern.

Huram turned toward Golgotha.

There was no fog obscuring the mount that day, its ominous outline could be seen clearly for more than a mile.

"Crucifixion, Asael," Huram spoke, the word bitter on his tongue whereas just an hour earlier it had seemed as sweet as pure honey. "Caiaphas tried to enlist my cooperation. And I pledged it to him."

The old man stiffened.

"Of the Nazarene, sir?" he asked, dreading the inevitable answer. "Are you talking about the high priest seeking to have the Nazarene crucified by order of the proconsul-governor?"

"Yes, crucifying the—"

Huram looked at Asael.

"How could you know that?"

He had taken the old man for granted over the years, as was the case with most of the other servants, except Yiptah, for whom he had developed a special fondness.

Asael cleared his throat self-consciously.

"We hear things in the marketplace, sir. None of us makes any effort to listen to idle gossip, of course, but when it is being spoken all around us, not picking up some information now and then is impossible."

"And, somehow, this planned crucifixion of the Nazarene is already a topic of discussion?"

That something so tragic could be reduced to the level of marketplace gossip seemed, to Huram, gross and reprehensible, strangers learning of it presumably before the Nazarene or any of His followers.

"Yes, sir."

The old servant had not sought such talk but could not shut his ears as he had purchased loaves of bread or the light food items he could carry back to his master's home.

"People surely must be up in arms," Huram commented, coming out of his seeming near-stupor.

Asael almost choked on the words that honesty forced him to speak.

"No, sir, they are *demanding it!*" he said.

Huram seemed to be hit by a physical blow as he felt numb, uncomprehending for several seconds.

"Demanding—?"

Huram's tears were clearing, and his self-control was returning.

"How can that be true?" he asked, his voice breaking. "What has Jesus done that would merit their support of His death?"

Asael could provide nothing, though he thought intently about the matter for a few seconds.

"I cannot say, sir. He seems innocent of the simplest of transgressions. Anything worthy of execution is far from the Nazarene."

"But why then are they demanding this?"

The old man's distaste for the high priest showed on his face.

"Caiaphas ..." he said.

"And nothing or no one else?"

Huram shivered, realizing that perhaps an hour or so earlier he could have been part of any answer to that question.

"Only the high priest, sir," Asael told him.

"But what is Caiaphas doing to get the people to go along with him? After all, they were throwing palm leaves at the Nazarene's feet two days ago."

Asael held out his left hand and pretended to be dropping a number of coins into it with the other.

"Bribes?" Huram asked.

"Yes, sir."

"And they could be swayed so easily?"

Huram had never had any experience with poverty. His wealth started out as inherited, then he worked almost maniacally to build up the family business even more. He had quickly reached a point when he had enough wealth in every conceivable form—land, livestock, money—that he could buy anything any time he wanted to do so.

"When their families are hungry, sir, it does not take very much," Asael added. "Caiaphas is offering far more than a loaf of bread to each man."

Huram felt sick as he directed Asael, "Get all the servants together, and also the stable workers."

"What shall I tell them?" the old man asked.

"That their master expects them to go out and try to find the Nazarene and warn Him and His band of followers."

Asael seemed relieved.

"Do you want the guards to go as well?" he asked. "Or should they stay for your protection now that you are opposing the high priest?"

Huram had no concern for his personal safety.

"Yes!" he directed. "Everyone."

Asael obviously wanted to say something else, and Huram gave him leave.

"Right now there are traitors everywhere, sir. Caiaphas is spending the temple's money lavishly. We may not have any success. They could take what we say and keep it to themselves so as not to displease the high priest."

Huram snapped his fingers.

"You are right," he said, grateful for such wisdom.

"You would have to pay them," Asael offered. "You would have to stop Caiaphas in the area of his greatest power."

Huram reached out and gently hugged the old man.

"Perhaps you should be more than my servant after all these years," he spoke appreciatively.

Asael blushed and said, "I am not worthy of being more than what I am."

Huram felt great sorrow.

"That will change," he said.

"I am too old, sir. I cannot change. And I am not unhappy, you know."

"But sometimes I have been so awful."

"You are not awful now, sir. It gives me joy, sir, to see you like this."

Huram put his hands on Asael's shoulders.

"Do you know where some of my money is kept?" he asked.

"Yes, sir, your wife has always trusted me. She has given me the duty of counting the household funds every so often to make sure no coins have been stolen."

"Then use whatever it takes. Spend every last one if necessary. I have deposits elsewhere."

"Caiaphas has a rich treasury, sir."

"I know. Much of it is there because of me. I wish I could reclaim every coin, every animal, every deed, but that is not possible."

His face flushed a soft red as he thought of the challenge ahead.

"I *will* pay people to support Jesus, if that is what it takes, or at least pay them not to be against Him. And I want to pay them also to direct you to Barabbas. He will help if he is given enough coins. His movement needs what he can beg, borrow, or steal. I can give him livestock and whatever else he might need."

Asael bowed his head.

"Sir?" he spoke, his voice scarcely above a whisper.

"Yes?"

The old servant hesitated, biting his lower lip.

"I know where Barabbas is," he replied.

"You do?" Huram asked, surprised. "Get to him then."

Seeing that as the only course of action to take, he went on, talking faster, with great anxiety.

"Tell Barabbas what is being planned. Mention that I sent you. I cannot believe that a man such as he will stand by and allow this mindless atrocity to occur at the hands of those hated Roman executioners—yes, at their hands but precipitated by the spiritual leaders of *our* people."

Asael could not look Huram in the eye.

"I cannot, sir," he said slowly.

"Is Barabbas so inaccessible?"

"Yes, sir."

Huram found that difficult to accept.

"Where?" he asked. "Surely he can be reached if enough people are paid enough money to let you through."

"No, sir. None of that will do any good in the case of Barabbas."

"But why? Is he on top of a mountain somewhere, cut off from everyone, even his supposedly loyal followers?"

Asael raised his head, and it was easy to see that tears were forming in his eyes.

"Sir?"

Huram's never unlimited patience was being tested by the old man's seeming reluctance to tell him about the insurrectionist.

"Yes, Asael, spit it out," he declared.

And that was pretty much what the devoted servant had to do, the news bitter to his tongue.

"Barabbas has been imprisoned," he said.

"By Pontius Pilatus?"

"Yes, sir, he is awaiting his own crucifixion."

*As they hurried on to Golgotha, the man on its top fell forward into a puddle of his own blood …*

"*Huram!*" Hannah exclaimed after she, her son, and the young servant, Yiptah, had climbed up the Place of the Skull.

Johanan raced to Huram ben Sira's side.

"Father, Father!" he said. "All this blood!"

"My blood shed before His …" Huram said ironically, moaning, before more of it gurgled up his throat, through his mouth, and down his chin. "Our God is a God of irony, my son. I have been screaming out to Him so long that—"

"And your hands, sir," Yiptah said, kneeling next to him, looking at them in shock. "They are nearly raw!"

*… nearly raw.*

They were more than that: bruised, ruptured flesh, bone showing through at the knuckles.

Huram was covered with perspiration, and he was shaking as his son sat down next to him and gently lifted his head up from the hard rock.

"Banging my fists against stone, screaming, begging God to forgive me, begging Him to listen to my cries," Huram said as he leaned again.

Sitting down on his other side, Hannah put her arms around the man she had loved for more than two decades.

"You've done nothing—" she started to tell him.

"You are wrong, my dear wife. I committed to something evil. I—"

And there he was, stricken by the knowledge of that evil, beating himself bloody as he faced what he had told the high priest.

"I thought I had done the right thing, agreeing with what Caiaphas was planning" he said sobbing, "until—"

Yiptah had taken off the top of his garment, torn it into strips, and wrapped two of them around Huram's hands.

"I had nearly reached home when it seemed that I was *thrown* to the ground," he said, "and I heard a voice calling to me."

He straightened himself and pulled away from Johanan and Hannah.

"*So much light!*" he exclaimed. "It was brighter than the sun. And that voice was so strong, yet kind."

He glanced from his wife to his son.

"You cannot know what it sounded like ..." he said. "I ... I could do nothing but sit and weep."

Huram started shivering, and Johanan reached out to hold him again.

"Your heart is beating so fast, Father," he started to say. "You must calm down or you will—"

"Or I will die? I saw what kind of man I was, and I *wanted* to die. How could I live with the shame? How could I face myself or you or your mother or anyone else ever again? *I had pledged to work with Caiaphas toward the crucifixion of the Nazarene!*"

Hannah gasped, covering her mouth with her left hand.

"But why?" Johanan asked. "Why would you do that?"

"Because I was told that you had gone off with Him, that you had left me to become His followers, that He required those with Him to be prepared to do this."

"Father, Father, we would never leave you," Johanan replied. "Jesus is a wonderful Man. He calls some but not others. We just wanted to spend some time with Him. We—"

Huram grabbed the front of his son's tunic.

"Man?" he repeated. "Johanan, Johanan, you must never say that again. Jesus is more than a Man."

Momentarily he seemed to be choking on saliva, cleared his throat, struggled to speak, and then finally added, "I think He is Someone far greater."

"But I see only a Man, a remarkable Man. How can you—?"

"That voice I heard."

"What did it say to you, Father?"

"The voice told me, 'Jesus is My beloved Son in whom I am well pleased.' Then I asked, 'But who are You?'"

Hannah, Johanan, and Yiptah were sitting as though hypnotized, intrigued by the experience Huram had had.

"This is what I heard: 'I am the Alpha and the Omega.' 'You are God then?' I asked. 'It is as you say,' it replied."

Huram's eyes were wide open; excitement filled his voice.

"God spoke to *me!*" he told them. "I am not sure why except that He did not want me to have the blood of Jesus on my hands."

He smiled as he added, "And now I have a mission."

"To stop this murder?" Johanan asked.

"Or else I fear a curse upon this nation," Huram said, "a curse that will hang over us for centuries to come."

This was a remarkable proclamation for a stern and forbidding man who had felt so differently only hours before, but it was spewed forth from deep inside him, not as a few words that meant little to him.

*… a curse that will hang over us for centuries to come.*

Again the weeping, every muscle in his body trembling from the emotions that had seized hold.

"The Messiah?" Hannah spoke. "You think Jesus is truly the promised One? Is that what you are saying?"

Abruptly, by an act of sheer will, Huram calmed himself down.

"I must continue," he said. "I must tell you the rest."

"First we should get you home," Johanan told him. "There will be plenty of time later to let us know everything."

"No!" his father insisted. "This place where they plan to crucify Jesus is where I must tell you the rest."

Both mother and son gasped.

"That will not happen, Father!" Johanan exclaimed. "We can stop it, you and I and others. My friends have fathers who can speak up for Jesus. What about Nicodaemus and Joseph? You know them both. They are influential men. And Pilatus. You have as much pull with him as any other man."

"To do it would mean subjecting Caiaphas to loss of face," Huram pointed out. "He will fight like an enraged lion to stop that from happening."

"But we cannot give up; we must not give up. Mother and I have seen the Nazarene close up, you know. There is nothing evil about

Him. People will realize the truth in time if we can just get them to listen."

"I hope so, my son. I had hoped to send our entire staff of servants to go and try to locate Barabbas."

Johanan became excited over the possibility of that happening.

"He could hide Jesus away as he has hidden himself so well. That is a wonderful idea, Father."

"It is not. Barabbas cannot help at all."

"But why not?"

"Barabbas has been captured by the Romans and is right now awaiting his own death sentence."

Though the sun was nearly overhead, and a typically hot Middle Eastern day had begun, they all felt cold, a cold born of despair in that bleak place of death named Golgotha.

They managed to persuade Huram ben Sira to return home. But when they arrived he refused to go to his bedroom and get some rest.

"That is what your physician would demand," Johanan told him.

"I pay the man to do what I want, my son," his father asserted sternly, "not the other way around."

They had managed to bind his wounds, get him into a change of clothes, and have him drink some wine to calm him down and settle his system. Yet he was still anxious to tell the three of them about the rest of his experience.

"I had a sign just before it happened," he recalled.

"What sign, my husband?" asked Hannah.

"A gazelle. It was extraordinary," he said.

"A gazelle?" Johanan repeated.

"I saw one walking down the center of the street. I could scarcely believe the testimony of my own eyes."

A gazelle was much admired in Palestine but virtually never seen in or around Jerusalem. In the book of Samuel, the animal was described as "light of foot as a wild roe." Even the Song of Solomon contained a passage expressing the great king's admiration for the animal's gracefulness. While the gazelle could be hunted as food it was never to be used as a sacrifice.

"It was so beautiful," Huram continued. "I could not stop gazing at it."

And then it was gone.

"Fast as a bolt of lightning. One moment it was walking slowly; the next it bounded away and was out of sight."

He stood, amazed, as though seeing the memory again.

The gazelle had preceded his encounter with a holy God.

*Brighter than the sun. And that voice was so strong, yet kind …*

"The light was so powerful," he said as the others listened, transfixed. "While I listened to the voice, with the light all around me, I felt as though I was someplace else, not on a very familiar road. I seemed to be separated from everything and everyone in the world that I knew intimately."

"Were you scared, Huram?" asked Hannah.

"Only at the outset. In a very short while, I knew some real peace."

He smiled as he recalled the sensation.

"It was as though I was being protected from everything," he told them. "But that did not last."

"What happened next, Father?" Johanan inquired.

"Shame."

"Shame? Why shame?"

"Because of what I was conspiring to do with Caiaphas. But not only that. I saw before me all the men and women who turned their backs on God as a result of the callous way I had treated them. I am, after all, one of His chosen people! And yet I acted with such selfishness, such dedication to wealth, that acquiring more money, more property, more of anything replaced Yahweh."

Hannah knew the truth of that, for she had seen her husband go from regular attendance at synagogue services and at the Jerusalem temple, to only those times of special occasion and then to none at all. While she and Johanan worshiped, Huram spent the Sabbath negotiating business deals or arranging special concessions from the proconsul-governor or any of a myriad number of related activities, his manner becoming meaner and meaner in the process. He seemed compelled to acquire whatever parcel of land he spied, whatever new stallion caught his attention, whatever piece of furniture, tapestry from the Orient, or a thousand other items that would eventually become owned by Huram ben Sira, the richest man in the centuries-long history of the land of Judah.

Just then, one by one, servants began to return to the house, and Huram focused his attention on what they had found out.

Their answers were frustrating and discouraging.

"Some would accept payment," he was told, "but others would not."

"Why would they refuse money?"

"Because Caiaphas convinced them that the death of Jesus would be good for the country in the long run until the *real* Messiah comes."

Each man or woman returned to Huram with virtually the same story.

"Even my wealth cannot help the Nazarene!" Huram exclaimed after they all had left the inner sanctum that he and his family usually kept off-limits to everyone except themselves."

Blood started dripping from his nose again.

"Yiptah!" commanded Hannah. "Get the physician. And hurry!"

"Yes, ma'am," he told her, rushing off.

Huram was too weak to protest.

He had been sitting comfortably on a sofa-like piece of furniture with a bamboo frame and down-stuffed red leather cushions. All of a sudden, he could not hold himself up but fell back against it.

Hannah rushed to his side, but he assured her that he was not dizzy or ready to pass out, nor was he in physical pain.

"I am sick, yes, dear woman, but it is a sickness of my very soul," he told her. "My support may have encouraged Caiaphas. What if he had been wavering? What if, without me, his plan would have meant nothing?"

"You can do no more," Hannah replied. "You must not give up your life, but that is surely what will happen if you worry yourself into some sort of attack. Can you not see that, my husband?"

Johanan was listening intently.

"Why not, Mother?" he asked. "If Jesus is the Messiah, should we now act as cowards before Him? You are alive from His healing. He gave you back your life. Should you not be willing to sacrifice whatever it takes to keep Him from Golgotha?"

She could not look at him, could not admit the truth he had stated as though it had been an arrow shot by an expert archer.

"Father, you heard the voice of God," Johanan reminded him.

"I ... I think that that was what it was. But how can I be sure? I have tried everything, son. Is there something else? Tell me, and I shall do it. But should I risk the ire of Caiaphas to the extent that he puts me—"

Huram stopped while thinking of the crucifixions he had witnessed, each one grisly and disgusting.

"—on a cross next to the Nazarene's?"

The images that gripped Johanan's mind were terrifying as he envisioned his father crying out in pain as onlookers stood and laughed and gossiped, some while holding the hands of their little children.

"Surely he would not," he said, more as a profound hope than a statement.

"He is capable of the worst infamy. And Pilatus is so dedicated to *political* stability that he hands the high priest whatever is demanded, though I predict that, one day, Caiaphas will push even Pilatus too far."

Hannah had been quiet for several minutes but finally spoke up.

"I have an idea," she told them. "I know someone who might be willing to help."

"Who is that?" Huram asked, but not sounding very hopeful.

"Procula Pilatus."

"His wife? What could she do? And why would she do *anything*, Hannah?" Huram said, perplexed.

Hannah smiled as she replied, "Because the lady has become a secret follower of the Nazarene."

"*What?*"

For Huram, that was both startling as well as exhilarating news. If anyone could get through to the proconsul-governor, it was Procula Pilatus. But he wondered if he dared to hope this was the answer they needed.

"Are you quite certain, my dearest?" Huram ben Sira asked, needing to be absolutely convinced.

Hannah took no offense.

"I am," she answered. "She wanted me to convert some weeks ago, but I refused at that point."

"You never told me. I would have registered a complaint with her husband."

"That is *why* I never did."

Huram chuckled a bit as he said, "And look at us now!"

His son had been listening with a feeling of intensity that, from the beginning, had not stopped growing. He was seeing his father change before his eyes, a change so pervasive that he could almost have convinced himself that an impostor had somehow taken Huram ben Sira's place.

"Father?" he asked.

"Yes, Johanan?"

"While Mother is going to see the proconsul-governor's wife, would you object if I looked for Jesus?"

"But, son, all my servants could not find Him. Would you hope ever to do so?"

Johanan did not want to be judged as insolent, so he spoke with some care. "Father, is it possible that they just did not know where to look?" he asked quietly.

Huram saw that his son was serious.

"Do *you* know?"

"I may, Father. I may."

Huram was aware that the times in which they lived were dangerous, filled with roadside robberies and midnight murders.

"How can I let you go?" he asked. "Anything could happen to you."

"But how can you wait until the guards return?" Johanan replied.

"Yes, I know, and yet most of the servants *have* returned. Take several of them. You cannot be reckless these days."

"We must move quickly. The spot I have in mind is small. If the Nazarene is there, we can get Him away quickly."

"Go ahead, but please, at least take Yiptah with you."

Johanan nodded, anxious to make his father feel less apprehensive.

Then he turned to his mother.

"Gethsemane," he told her knowingly. "They may not have suspected that He will be there. But I must go now, Mother."

Hannah was fighting tears.

"Oh, my son, my son, surely it will not come to this," she said. "Surely some members of the Sanhedrin will stand up to Caiaphas and make him back down."

Johanan shook his head.

"It seems to have gone too far," he said.

And his father added, "The high priest has hated Jesus from the beginning. For the first time in years, someone is here to compete for the attention of the people. He cannot endure anything like that."

They were silent, feeling the awful melancholy of that moment.

"If I can do something about it," Johanan persisted, "if I can alert Him and get the Nazarene to flee to safety somewhere, I will do so."

Hannah cupped her son's face in her hands.

"I do not want to lose you," she said. "Your father is right. There is danger in this, Johanan. You must know that."

"I have avoided danger all my life until now," he told her. "Is it not time for me to risk myself for some reason?"

Johanan spoke then to Yiptah.

"You do not have to go with me," he said. "Nothing requires you to be at my side if it means great risk."

"I have known no other family," the young servant replied. "Never have I been hungry, never have I needed clothing, never have I been treated harshly. Your father has offered me freedom many times."

Surprised by this, Johanan shot a glance at his father, who seemed embarrassed by the sudden airing of his generosity.

"It is right that I should go with you," Yiptah concluded. "This Man they seek to murder deserves only life."

The young servant expressed a noble truth, and Hannah's face drained of color.

The spoiled young man, submerged in wealth all his life, who had never known any adversity or danger, kissed his mother first then his father, embracing each one while never admitting to either of them that he felt a touch of fear, knowing what might happen during the next few hours.

*... this Man they seek to murder deserves only life.*

That was all he could consider with any clarity. It was, after all, Jesus who had saved his mother's life. And it was this same Man who spoke only of kindness and joy and forgiveness and blessed eternal life.

*I have no choice,* he told himself. *How I wish I did, but there is none.*

As he and Yiptah hurried to the front door, intent on reaching Gethsemane without delay, Johanan thought that his parents had immediately dropped to their knees, for he heard both start to pray with great intensity.

Someone was waiting outside.

Saul of Tarsus.

The little man proceeded to brush past him without smiling or otherwise acknowledging his presence.

"Huram! Huram!" he said excitedly. "I have the most wonderful news for you. By tomorrow morning, the carpenter will be in custody. Pilatus is already having His cross and two others built!"

Johanan turned and shouted back at Saul.

"Wonderful news, you say?" he spoke. "Why is the death of an innocent Man as wonderful as you say?"

Saul swung around and faced him.

"It matters not whether He is innocent. If He gets the people to believe Him, there will be trouble."

"What if Jesus *is* the Messiah?" Johanan asked.

"He cannot be."

Johanan started to say something, but Saul interrupted the young man with a wave of his hand.

"Besides, we want a Messiah who stands up to the Romans. According to the Nazarene, we should render unto Caesar everything that is rightfully Caesar's. *Nothing* in this nation rightfully belongs in Roman hands!"

"Or else *you* would *know* it, right?"

Johanan snickered.

"How much of your behavior is righteous, and how much is the fact that Someone may know more about the Scriptures than you do?"

Saul interrupted him.

"Your arrogance is like a gnat on an elephant's hide," he said with contempt so naked it seemed to seep like saliva from the corners of his mouth.

"If *you* are the elephant, then I would agree in part with what you say," Johanan retorted, enjoying that moment.

Huram was now on his feet.

"Do you sanction your son's impudence?" spoke Saul.

"Considerably more than I would ever sanction what you are encouraging!" Huram shot back.

"I thought you would be pleased."

"A short while ago, I might have been, but no longer."

"What has happened to transform you?"

"I was walking home ..." Huram started to say as Johanan closed the front door behind him and Yiptah. They left with regret that they would not be able to witness the battle of words that would instantly commence between two old friends who would split apart only a very few minutes later, not speaking again until another time, another place.

## Chapter Twelve

D*usk ...*

*Just beginning, the first hint of stars.*

*So much time had passed without the family of Huram ben Sira being aware of it, as they had talked and prayed and worried about the immediate future.*

*It seemed so illogical for any of them to be caught up personally in the drama that involved the carpenter from Nazareth. It had seemed, at the beginning, none of their concern, Jesus just another itinerant blowhard, trying to convince people of His sincerity even though He might not have been sincere at all.*

*"They are, these traveling preachers, very good thespians," someone had commented. "But just as an actor convinces you that he is someone else while he is on stage, so their kind can do the same with gullible multitudes."*

*And yet Huram, Hannah, and Johanan were now at the center of that very drama, with a young servant joining them, four people drawn to Jesus of Nazareth as the continual crowds had been drawn all along ...*

Johanan and Yiptah hurried on to the Garden of Gethsemane, riding their horses bareback, not taking the time to harness them to a chariot.

"I am very scared," Yiptah acknowledged. "I hope you do not think less of me for saying that."

"So am I," Johanan agreed. "Just three days ago—"

A safe, predictable world.

That was all he had known, and he had assumed it was all he would continue to know until the day he died.

"I shall inherit much wealth someday," he continued. "But my father and I could spend it all right now and still it would accomplish nothing."

"The love of money? Is that something to think about now?"

Johanan considered what his young servant friend had said.

"If I think I cannot do without it, with what it can accomplish," he mused out loud, "is that love of money?"

"It might be worse," Yiptah offered wisely.

Johanan agreed.

"I think so," he said. "I wonder if God is testing this family right now?"

"Jesus said it would be easier for a rich man to get through the eye of a needle than for him to enter heaven."

"So much wisdom," Johanan pointed out, "and yet so many people who are blind to its wonders."

"As you and I and your parents were until a short while ago."

Gethsemane was but a short distance ahead. Already they could tell that something was very wrong.

Soldiers.

A dozen Roman soldiers in battle gear were heading toward the garden by another route a short distance to their left.

And someone else was with them, not a Roman officer or anyone of that sort but a man who seemed not much taller and broader than Saul of Tarsus, a beard covering much of the lower part of his face.

Yiptah snapped his fingers.

"I have seen him somewhere, I think," he said, his vision hampered by the accelerating darkness.

"Me, too," Johanan spoke, squinting his eyes. "I wonder if he—"

"We must hurry," Yiptah interrupted. "They are on foot. We have horses. We can make it."

As they forced the animals to run faster, the riders became careless, not paying attention to the twists and turns of a dirt trail that represented a shortcut but had several obstacles, sudden turns, jutting rocks, and tree branches that were young and narrow and could act like the most punishing of whips.

Yiptah rode the lead horse, which was traditional in that servants and slaves rode ahead of their masters so they were first to encounter or perceive danger and could issue, under the best of circumstances, a warning that might stave off harm to those who were following.

Yiptah was hit around the bridge of his nose by a low, supple branch and knocked off his horse, blood surging over his lips and off his chin.

"*Johanan, watch out!*" he was able to say as he tumbled to the ground.

At that moment, Johanan's horse lost its footing on some loose stones, tripped and fell, throwing him off.

*Pain.*

Immediately it surged through his body.

Johanan tried to stand but could not.

He saw Yiptah, unmoving, on the ground just a few yards away and yelled to the young servant, but there was no response.

Unable to get to his feet, Johanan pulled himself forward a few inches at a time, trying to ignore the sharp stones and exposed undergrowth that pressed hard against him, sometimes cutting, sometimes—

He was only a foot away from that motionless body when his right hand touched something wet.

Red.

He could see that it was red as he raised his hands and looked at the fingertips. Seconds later, he was slapping Yiptah's cheeks that already had begun to turn cold.

*Strange ...*

The young servant's eyes were wide open, and his lips were curled into the suggestion of a smile.

"How can you be—?" Johanan said. "The pain you must have felt, and the darkness ... darkness covering you."

He sat there, quietly, for several minutes, stunned and hurting and confused. To his right he heard the approaching sound of the Roman soldiers on their short march to Gethsemane.

One horse.

The other had fled, presumably back toward the family's stables, which was generally the way with those animals.

But the horse Yiptah had ridden was standing next to his body. Johanan remembered that the young servant had grown close to a particular stallion, the two of them spending much of Yiptah's spare time together.

"Will you let me mount you?" Johanan whispered as he managed to stand, leaning for a moment against the horse's strong shoulder.

No reaction.

"Does that mean you will not throw me once I am on your back?" Johanan spoke again very softly.

He felt wobbly, and sickness threatened his stomach. He had to stand still, not moving until the nausea eased.

The sounds from Roman soldiers were fading, which meant they could not be very far from Gethsemane.

Johanan mounted the stallion without a hint of protest from the animal and steered it in the direction of that little garden, knowing he might have as little as a minute or two to warn the Nazarene, so brief a span of time yet one that could mean the difference between life and death.

"If I can only make it in time," he said out loud, thinking of Jesus. "You could hide somewhere outside Gethsemane. They will think You have left and have no idea where You are headed."

Ahead was a left turn in the road. Just beyond that was the garden.

But Johanan never made it, not according to his own timing, for he was plunged into the hands of Another, and no longer would his life be as it once was.

*"It was brighter than the sun. And that voice was so strong, yet kind."*

His father's words became Johanan's own as he seemed frozen, his horse trembling under him, the two of them seemingly as hard and immobile as a block of granite that had been carved by a master sculptor.

Johanan could not even feel his heart beating, though he knew it must be pounding so fast that a seizure could come at any moment.

"I must get to the garden!" he was able to cry out. "There must be no delay. This is too important!"

*You will not ...*

The voice seemed to come from everywhere yet from nowhere, sudden and powerful, freezing his attention.

"I must try to warn Jesus before it is too late for Him," Johanan persisted. "Surely that is not wrong, to save the life of—"

*He must die for the sins of the world ...*

"The Nazarene *is* the Messiah?" Johanan said, trying to cope with the very idea. "He has never lied about this?"

*It is as you say ...*

"All the more reason to save this Man!" Johanan exclaimed, perspiration drenching his body.

*My Son is not as you think Him to be ...*

"The Messiah is to come and liberate us from the yoke of a foreign conqueror," Johanan protested. "We will fight at His neck, and the plains of Megiddo will be drenched with blood, the last great battle."

*My Son is come to liberate those who believe, to free them from no earthly oppression except that of sin ...*

Johanan faced the onrush of panic as the seconds passed and he could do nothing but remain unmoving, listening to a voice out of nowhere.

"Then let me save Him from capture," he pleaded.

*Jesus must die before others can be given eternal life ...*

"But that means He is going to be crucified!" Johanan protested. "He will endure the agony of hell itself."

*Yes, He will ...*

Johanan felt some anger.

"And You do nothing?" he cried out.

*It is written that this should happen ...*

"Are You our Father in heaven?" Johanan asked tremulously. "If You are, then You *must* act to save our nation!"

His answer was a clap of thunder so loud that it seemed to deaden his eardrums and a sudden bolt of lightning across the evening sky.

Johanan flinched, wondering if God was going to visit upon him some terrible judgment now.

Only that one warning.

"What can I do?" the rich young man begged, relieved.

*Be prepared to give up everything, even your life, Stephen ...*

"But my name is Johanan," he said.

*No longer ... You shall be known as Stephen throughout history ...*

"Throughout history?" Johanan asked, puzzled and very confused, and more scared than he had ever before been. "I am nothing. I matter little to anyone."

*You will matter much to countless millions who will look to you as an example long after you are gone from this world ...*

Johanan was cold then, colder than the presence of darkness would normally mean, a cold that seemed to come from within him.

"I am not brave," he said, speaking a fact that could not have been more evident at that very moment.

*You shall be ...*

"Father God," Johanan called out for the first time, "You are wrong about me. Surely there is someone better."

*You call Me Lord, yet you again dispute what I say?*

Johanan realized what he had done.

"I meant no disrespect," he said quickly, "but—"

*You will do as you have been commanded ...*

He had no idea what God wanted of him.

"Lord, I am confused. I need help. I do not know where You want me to be now or a day from now or next year."

The voice softened.

*What you now seek shall be given to you soon enough, young Stephen ...*

Johanan felt even more uneasy.

"Lord, I ... I am called Johanan," he pointed out, his voice unsteady, his heart beating faster. "I do not know about Stephen. Why must my name be changed? Cannot things remain as they are?"

*No longer ...*

But he persisted.

"Why, Lord? What is so important about names?"

The voice was quick to answer.

*You will no longer live as you once did. That is past. It shall not be brought back. Countless millions will come to know you as someone most remarkable, a young man named Stephen. Johanan will be forgotten ...*

Stephen started to weep.

"There is too much!" he exclaimed. "I am not capable. You do not know all that goes on in my head."

The voice replied with great simplicity.

*I created you. From the beginning, I fashioned your destiny ...*

"I have lied," Stephen confessed.

*So has every man ...*

"I have stolen apples and pears and even bread," he went on. "I am hardly worthy of *any* honor."

*But you are here, nevertheless. As a result of your example, the other apostles soon will be able to spread the reality of what has happened and what will happen, spread it because they are emboldened by you.*

Stephen wondered if he had heard properly.

"Soon, Lord?" he asked. "Did you say soon?"

*I did ...*

Knowing that did not comfort him much.

"But they do not know that I exist," Stephen said. "How could I ever inspire them, as you say?"

*A year ...*

Not much time.

"Only a year, Lord?"

*On the anniversary of My Son's death ...*

Jesus dead!

Then it *would* happen; His crucifixion was unstoppable.

"But I wanted to try to prevent the death of the Nazarene," Stephen remarked. "Crucifixion is so terrible a thing to inflict upon such a Man. Surely You can help me stop what's happening. Surely You will!"

Silence.

As Johanan, he had never realized how few times he had experienced real silence during the course of his life. Usually he was with his friends, and they were decidedly not inclined to silence. Or he would be at home where the often intermixing sounds of servants and slaves, the conversations of visitors and his parents, the neighing of horses and others filled the air without letup. Even at night, as he was going to sleep, he heard crickets, and dogs barking, and chariots racing by.

Never this silence, never this silence as it descended in Gethsemane, more like the silence of an ancient tomb.

*You shall not succeed, but you may try ...*

Stephen disregarded the "not succeed" part.

"So You will let me try?" he asked.

*Yes ...*

"In the garden?" he continued. "Should I hurry on to the garden?"

Suddenly, the light was gone.

Stephen made the horse move ahead as quickly as the narrow path would allow.

Around the turn was the Garden of Gethsemane.

Despite the absolute portended reality of failure from God Himself, Stephen knew he could not give up.

*A voice ...*

He sucked in his breath.

*The Romans!* he told himself. *They must have reached the Garden of Gethsemane ahead of me.*

He tied the horse's reins to a nearby bush and walked around the northern edge of the garden.

No Roman soldiers.

Stephen gasped so loudly that one of the apostles—sleeping, as were the others—stirred grumpily but did not awaken.

The soldiers had not arrived as yet, and eleven of the Nazarene's followers were dozing unconcernedly, but Stephen could not find Jesus Himself.

*Where are the soldiers?* he asked himself. *They could not have been more than a few minutes behind me at best, but then that light ... How much time did I spend talking with—?*

God.

He shivered as the truth of that encounter presented itself again with even greater impact. Every part of his mind wanted to shout, *No! No! It could not be. I am going mad. I am not yet thirty years old, and yet I am imagining—*

But he knew he had not imagined it.

*It was God!*

Stephen felt weak as he grappled with that truth, feeling it take hold of every inch of his body.

*And Jesus is the Messiah!*

His hands starting to shake, he stepped over the low stone wall that bordered Gethsemane.

Stephen listened.

Still no soldiers.

*Now they surely are near the very entrance of Gethsemane,* he thought. *They should be entering it in another—*

Sobbing.

Not soldiers. Not the sound of their metal breastplates. Not the sound of their heavy marching feet.

Someone sobbing.

Stephen saw the Nazarene in an alcove separated from the apostles, on His knees, His face covered with—

Blood.

*He has been hurt,* Stephen assumed. *I must do something.*

As he started to walk into the alcove, the young man saw Jesus take a cloth and wipe His forehead and cheeks. Then He stood.

Sounds.

Sounds just outside the garden.

Finally the Roman soldiers were approaching.

"Leave now!" Stephen shouted as he entered. "I can show You where to hide for the time being. You must hurry. It is a cave. Only some friends and I know about it. Then my father can get You a boat—"

The Nazarene shook His head.

"It is the time that My Father has appointed," He replied. "Should I dispute the will of Almighty God?"

Stephen grabbed His wrist and tried to pull Him, but Jesus would not budge.

"Leave this place now," the Nazarene said with such kindness that Stephen momentarily fell silent, awed by the warmth of that voice, the peace in it.

Jesus placed a hand upon the young man's shoulder.

"You have a year," He spoke. "Use every minute of it, Stephen, to spread the Good News."

The young man fell at His feet, grabbing His legs, clinging to them like a child not wanting his father to leave.

"They will kill You, Jesus!" he sobbed. "How can I leave and do nothing?"

"You will tell of it, and what is to follow, with such power that thousands will flock to you, wanting what you can offer them."

Stephen had a dilemma. He could leave as Jesus had directed and send Him to certain death atop Golgotha, or He could somehow drag the Man from that spot, against His wishes, and incur the possibility of divine wrath.

It seemed that Jesus could read his thoughts.

"You must go now, young Stephen, and you must study for the next three months, then be on your way," He said.

"Be on my way to where?" Stephen asked.

"The Holy Spirit will show you."

He had never heard of the Holy Spirit, and his expression betrayed his puzzlement.

"When?" Stephen repeated.

"On the Day of Pentecost, and for many days after that. All shall be revealed."

Stephen tried to stand but could not. His muscles were beginning to show their rebellion. When he was thrown from his horse, he must have been more injured than seemed the case at first.

"Pain ..." he said, his voice hoarse. "I feel some pain."

He nearly blacked out, that little alcove spinning around in his vision as he tried to keep himself steady but failed.

*The soldiers!*

*Very close.*

*A voice.*

*"Show us the One we seek, Judas!" barked a centurion.*

"Go, Stephen!" Jesus urged. "It is not My Father's will that you suffer along with Me, not now."

He paused, and then He said, with a curious mixture of sorrow and triumph, "That will come later."

"But I cannot stand," Stephen said. "My legs ... I cannot—"

Jesus placed the palm of His hand on the young man's forehead.

"I go now to the destiny that was written before the beginning of all things," He said. "We shall meet again, Stephen. Good-bye until then."

Then the Nazarene was gone, walking away to meet those armed with swords and spears, a single kiss betraying Him into their hands.

Long after Jesus and the Roman soldiers had left and the apostles had fled, Stephen was still huddling in the little alcove at the eastern end of Gethsemane.

Afraid.

He was afraid to stand, afraid that his legs would not support him, but then it was more than that, a fear that went in two opposite directions. On the one hand, he feared that he would stand and find his legs completely healed, and yet he had been so useless to the One Whose touch had been responsible, allowing Him to be captured by Romans, without trying a final time to get Jesus to flee; and another fear, as strange and unreasoning as the first but there it was, almost like something that had been lurking in the darkness and it finally had sprung and swallowed him whole, suffocating him, a fear that offered nothing more than despair, despair that would shatter any hope he harbored that the Nazarene was what He had proclaimed, that the voice Stephen had heard was right, and this was truly the Messiah, not just a man with a captivating voice and fine words, but the One promised from centuries ago by the most illustrious of the nation's prophets, a fear that all this was for nought, and he would have to leave little Gethsemane with no hope, carried by anyone who would happen to befriend him because, after all, his legs had not been healed, and it may have been that they would remain crippled for the rest of his life.

He could wait no longer.

Stephen had to try, for the sake of his parents, if for no other reason. They would have no idea where he had gone, and it might be some time before he could be found.

*But what can I lean against?* he asked himself. *There are only small shrubs and a few rose bushes here.*

Abruptly he heard that voice again, but this time it was not in the midst of blinding light.

"Dear God!" he exclaimed but not in vain, more like a prayer as his fear assumed yet another face.

Inside him.

But the voice was not completely in his mind, not something born of his imagination.

It was as though he could actually hear the voice, its power sweeping over him from his head to his feet.

*Stand, Stephen ...*

He protested, saying, "But I have nothing to hold on to, Lord!"

*You have Me. Stand ...*

And he did.

He did something that once was so ordinary, so commonplace a part of his life, that it deserved no special notice.

He stood.

And as he did, the most profound tears of joy of his young life flooded from his eyes and down his cheeks.

Instinctively he reached out as he cried, "Lord, Lord! I *can* stand!"

*And I shall never leave you, my beloved Stephen ...*

He could barely speak.

"I know, Lord!" he muttered. "I shall fear nothing from now on."

The voice spoke a final time in Gethsemane.

*Not even death, Stephen?*

The answer burst out of the young man's mouth.

"Not even death!" he exclaimed.

A gust of chill wind swept through the little garden, and then the voice was gone, an overhead moon reflecting light so pale yet so beautiful that it seemed Gethsemane had been turned into an exquisite mother-of-pearl rendering, intricately carved by a master craftsman to preserve every detail.

Stephen wiped his eyes with the back of his hand.

"Lord ..." he said. "I know not what the morning will bring. How is it that I now feel such peace that floods my very being?"

Young Stephen received no answer except that joy, that peace, and this was enough; this was enough.

The three members of Huram ben Sira's family were gathered together by dawn. They chose to meet in the banquet hall, which often had been where a hundred or more guests gathered during a special feast, men and women from Jewish society as well as Romans and other visitors. Traditional Jewish food was served along with other dishes that would especially appeal to guests from other lands.

"Only one young man is missing," Hannah muttered, "but how empty it seems, knowing that."

*Yiptah ...*

Three members of the family's personal guards had been dispatched to bring back his body. When alerted that the flat carriage was returning, the father, mother, and son hurried to the front entrance of their house and stood outside.

*"My God, my God!"* lamented Huram ben Sira but in a prayerful manner, one of sorrow so strong that it seemed like a hand wrenching his insides. In a short span of time, the young man's flesh-and-blood form had been set upon by scavenging beasts and was badly torn.

"So perfect a body!" Huram sobbed. "Now look at it!"

"What shall we do?" one of the guards asked. "Dispose of it at Gehenna?"

*Gehenna ...*

*A ghastly, putrid place of burial, or rather disposal, just outside Jerusalem, pits with fires at the bottom where bodies were tossed, sliding down the sides until the flames reached them. Only the poor were treated like this. When the practice was originally started, it had been for the purpose of keeping disease from spreading in times of one epidemic or another, but no one had thought to stop the practice even after these periods of disease had ended ...*

Stephen did not give his father an opportunity to respond.

"*No!*" he exclaimed. "He is to be buried among the family plots."

Not long before, Huram would have stepped in and stopped any such breaking of tradition. But he said nothing to object while his son made the arrangements.

"I will see to it that he is treated—" Johanan's father said, but he could not continue, turning away from the sight of that ravaged body.

The guard nodded, and he and another took the remains to the stable until the body could be prepared for burial.

When Stephen saw how distraught his father was, he hesitated to say anything about the night's encounter with Yahweh and what had been mandated, and yet delaying seemed to offer nothing worthwhile. In fact, he decided that getting the elder man's mind off Yiptah might be wise.

And so they sat on pillows on the floor of the banquet hall.

"What is it, my son?" Huram asked, looking apprehensive and hoping he was not to learn of any other tragedy so soon after Yiptah's death.

"I have something most wonderful to tell you," Stephen said.

"Yes, Johanan?"

Stephen swallowed hard.

"Father …"

And then he spoke to both parents about his encounter the night before. Neither interrupted him; both were stunned by his words.

"After that, I heard nothing else," Stephen concluded, and then waited for his father and his mother to respond.

Hannah was the one to break the brief silence.

"If God has ordained this," she said, "how could *we* stand in the way?"

They both turned to Huram.

He was still sitting, though both his wife and his son were now on their feet.

"I just lost a young lad for whom I felt some affection," he told them, "and now you are asking me to encourage my own son to start a direction in life that could lead to a similar tragedy."

Huram knew in greater detail the state of crime and violence and such in and around Israel than either his son or his wife did. He had learned of reports dealing with Barabbas and other insurrectionists and the acts they committed, acts that were no more noble than those of common robbers and other criminals.

"I think they will bring unspeakable harm," he had told a business associate just a few weeks earlier, "because their actions will bring the wrath of Rome upon us to a greater degree than it has already. The emperor is trying to act in a restrained manner, but each time a Roman garrison is attacked, his determination weakens.

"Can you imagine what that will mean? If Barabbas keeps on, soon we will have their iron-covered fists in our faces. What if they truly Romanize Israel? Our heritage will be as garbage. Jews will be scattered across the world. We will have nothing left, including our homeland."

Now that Barabbas had been captured and was scheduled for execution, Huram initially had felt less troubled, but then he saw that it meant the insurrectionist, a man of dubious character, and the Nazarene would be crucified together, on side-by-side crosses, as gawking crowds indulged their bloodlust.

And Huram ben Sira knew that he could not allow this to happen if he could do *anything* to prevent it.

Stephen managed to fall asleep but only for three hours. When he awoke, he was covered with perspiration because he had been in the midst of a nightmare. He had seen himself being crucified instead of the Nazarene, his mother and father standing at the base of the cross as he cried out in agony.

"I could not let the Messiah die instead!" he had moaned in the dream. "How could I allow the only begotten Son of the living God to shed His blood as I am doing?"

Hannah had reached out in her son's dream, wrapped her arms around his bloody feet, and begged God to do something.

"Get Pilatus to change his mind!" she had pleaded. "Father God, work a miracle in that man's heart. This, my son, is innocent."

Suddenly a bright light had covered the top of Golgotha, and a voice had spoken to them from heaven itself.

"So is My Son innocent of sin ..." the voice had said with clarity. "Should He have hung instead from the cross?"

"But You seemed willing to sacrifice Him," Hannah sobbed. *"You* made that terrible choice."

"And your son made his own."

"But I have only one."

"And so do I."

"But You are God. And I do not have Your strength. I *need* my son. I do not want to go on living without him."

The voice seemed to be hesitating.

"It is as you say," came the final words from heaven. "Pontius Pilatus has just sent a Roman soldier with orders to release your son. Jesus shall be slain instead. My sacrifice instead of yours."

And so the young man was taken down, and the Nazarene nailed to the cross in his stead, and at the first cry of pain from Him, Stephen awoke, glad that the dream was over but fearing what reality would have waiting for him.

# — Chapter Thirteen —

T he normally chaotic morning scene behind the walls of Jerusalem the next morning had gone a step closer to bedlam, but it was not the rhythm of craftsmen and other goods providers setting up shop in the marketplace that caused the mayhem. This was something different, something that had the edge of madness to it.

"We must go the long way around," Huram ben Sira told Hannah as they faced the swirling, shouting, ill-tempered crowd whose behavior seemed ready at any moment to explode into a riot generated by an unhinged mob.

"Yes ..." she said nervously. "There is no shortcut today."

So they pressed back along the street, quickly heading toward the main gate area of the ancient walled city.

A variety of scents filled the air, ranging from those of animals and their droppings to that of bread being baked.

And sweeter ones.

Perfume.

They saw the women, middle class and rich alike, all behaving as though disturbed. It was easy to tell the difference between the rich and the poor. All wore black eyeliner and mascara, which they made by mixing ground antimony with water or gum, to highlight their eyes as well as to protect them from the glare of the sun. But the wealthy women had one distinguishing feature to their makeup: rouge. Made from mulberry juice or red ocher, it colored their cheeks, sometimes to an extreme degree.

Seeing the other women, Hannah realized she had rushed out of their house without any thought of enhancing her appearance and was momentarily embarrassed.

"I must look so pale and—" she started to say.

"You are not going to see the wife of the proconsul-governor; we're not going to some social function, my dear," Huram interrupted her.

Hannah blushed and nodded.

"This was a bad idea," Huram said. "I should have known."

Both husband and wife wondered what was happening, why the people seemed to be gripped by such increasing frenzy, as though aware that something extraordinary was about to happen but not knowing exactly what it was, and this uncertainty made the people uneasy, close to the edge of panic.

Their son was on the way to see Saul of Tarsus, who apparently was remaining in that area. This family friend had been particularly kind toward Stephen over the years, bringing him gifts from various regions where he had been traveling.

"I may never have a son," Saul had told the boy's father.

"Why is that?" Huram asked.

"I am too stern for most women."

"You are a scribe, a philosopher. You know well the existence of good and evil. How can you be otherwise?"

"But it does not help with the loneliness. I look at your son and know that I likely shall never be blessed as you are."

"Is that why you do what you have been doing all this time?"

Saul was silent, uncomfortable with being reminded of his generosity.

"Toys from the Orient," Huram said, "leather goods from Europe, even a monkey from Africa."

"Who else do I have in my life? Apart from God?"

"You have us as friends, and you have whatever mission attracts your attention. You are a man of passions whose feelings threaten to spill over. I remember how you once reacted to the treatment of lambs and goats before they were offered as sacrifices. You told me, 'They die for the sake of heaven. I cannot endure the thought that they are in a living hell before that.'"

But that was often the case, atrocities perpetuated by those in charge of livestock for the temple administrators.

Including Caiaphas.

The two men had clashed often during that period when the animals had been the center of Saul's mission. That Caiaphas and Saul would later become allies determined to rid the land of Jesus was ironic and unfortunate, because Saul could have effectively stymied the high priest's ignominious and dictatorial rule.

*It could have happened....*

But Saul instead became obsessed by the Nazarene.

Initially he proved somewhat of an admirer, but when Jesus made the first of many "controversial" statements about His relationship with God, about His mission on earth, about the power available to Him if He wished to use it, Saul turned against Him.

"The arrogance of this carpenter!" Saul shouted, stamping his feet as he did so. "He tries to make people believe that He knows more than I do, that He is more learned, more—"

He soon became obsessed by the implications of those growing numbers of people who chose to follow the Nazarene. His normally insular personality became even more so, and he stopped over to visit the Ben Sira family less and less often, because he was more interested in finding out the names of those who looked up to Jesus and either trying to talk them out of their acceptance of Him as Who He said He was, or having it beaten out of them by all-too-willing Roman centurions while Pontius Pilatus looked the other way.

It was Saul that Stephen would have to face while his mother confronted Procula Pilatus and Huram himself petitioned proconsul-governor Pontius Pilatus.

Ironically, the two Romans would agree to help but the Jew would not—not Saul of Tarsus.

Stephen managed to find Saul just as the scholar was leaving a small synagogue near the center of Jerusalem, walking with the aid of his stout walking stick.

"Johanan!" Saul spoke rather cheerfully.

Stephen winced at the use of his old name.

"Sir ..." he started to say, wanting to get his appeal over with but knowing what kind of reaction would come from a man as zealous as Saul of Tarsus.

"Now let me guess: You are here to tell me that the Nazarene is in custody?" Saul said. "Thank you, my boy, but I knew that already. And the news is spreading rapidly. People are rejoicing everywhere."

"Everywhere?"

The other man was amused by Stephen's nakedly shocked expression.

"Of course," Saul said, grinning. "The great impostor is going to be sentenced to death."

"How can you be so sure?"

Despite having seen what had occurred the night before, Saul's celebratory confidence was nonetheless bloodcurdling.

"It has been arranged," he announced, rubbing his hands together. "All we need now is for Pilatus to make it official."

Saul's exultant manner made Stephen feel quite ill, but he forced himself to say nothing for the moment.

"With the head of the beast gone," the Hebrew scholar went on, "the body will shrivel up soon enough."

Still Stephen kept silent.

"No reaction to this marvelous news?" Saul prodded.

Finally the young man shook his head.

"I cannot understand you," he said.

"What is so difficult, Johanan?"

"The sort of event that makes you as happy as you obviously are."

"That it does. And why not? You act a bit befuddled, I must say. As for me, I am delighted, because my job will be so much easier after He is gone."

Saul's hands were trembling with the excitement he was feeling.

"Sir?" Stephen began.

"Yes, Johanan …"

His vocal chords seemed on the verge of freezing, but Stephen would not allow this to happen.

"My name has been changed," he proclaimed at last.

"Your name?" repeated Saul.

"Yes."

"But why did you do that? Your father cannot be pleased. Surely you know that."

"He does not know as yet."

"When are you going to tell him what you have done?"

"I did not do it."

"But you said—"

Stephen interrupted him.

"—that it had been changed, sir," he corrected the older man, a breach of etiquette in itself, "not that I had done it myself."

"Your father did this then? How odd of him. I would never have pictured Huram ben Sira doing anything of the sort."

Stephen was trying to remain calm but was sensing that he could not do so for very much longer.

"He was not the one to change it either," he added.

Saul's eyes narrowed suspiciously, a gaze that seemed to cut through to the young man's soul.

"You are playing some sort of joke then, right?" he asked, obviously not the sort of man capable of tolerating anything of the kind.

"No, sir, it is not a game."

"Then what is going on?" Saul asked, his impatience increasing.

Strangely, Stephen was finding the words he needed to have.

"God, sir," he went on. "It has a great deal to do with Almighty God."

"What about God?" Saul asked pointedly. "Are *you* going to tell me something I do not already know about God, after I have studied all of the ancient texts and fasted regularly and prayed several hours each day?"

He was, and not subtly, trying to put someone much younger on the defensive, a tactic he usually found successful.

"I do not mean to be presumptuous," Stephen said with absolute sincerity, "or in any way arrogant."

"Then what is it you are fumbling with as you try so lamely to tell me what is going on here?"

Saul's approach seemed to be working, for Stephen nearly decided to let it drop then in favor of another time and place.

"Go on ..." Saul persisted. "Or are you prepared to admit—?"

"God did it, sir," Stephen spoke. "He was the One. I can claim no other."

"God?"

"Yes ..."

"Changed your name?"

"Yes, sir."

Saul spat on the cobblestones just inches from the young man's feet.

"And when did Yahweh do this?" he demanded, all the studied sarcasm at his disposal soaking every word of his question.

Stephen told him.

"You had a direct revelation?" Saul summarized. "Along with Moses and Elijah and Isaiah and others? God somehow chose a feckless boy while ignoring someone such as myself who has been serving Him for twenty years?"

Saul threw his head back in contempt.

"No wonder you have not told your father. He would think you disrespectful or mad or perhaps both, though the latter would be preferable. At least then it might be said that you could not help yourself."

*... while ignoring someone such as myself.*

Stephen felt an unaccustomed boldness grip him.

"Of what are you accusing me? Blasphemy? Stupidity? Or are you showing only vile pride over the fact that you have never been chosen for such a moment that I, your inferior, have experienced?"

"You are no better than—!"

Stephen interrupted his elder.

"The Nazarene? Are you comparing me with Him?"

It was Stephen's chance to smile now.

"Thank you for the honor," he said, suspecting that the other man could not tolerate this.

"Honor, you say?" Saul shot back. "A common carpenter who claims to be the Son of God? You find *that* comparison an honor?"

"Your father was a tentmaker, sir. Are you also belittling that profession? Carpenter or tentmaker, are they so far apart?"

"My father never claimed to be God incarnate!"

"Would your father have demanded the death of someone who was innocent of any real crime worthy of such punishment?"

"The crime is heresy."

"And your rejoicing over Jesus' impending death is somehow more acceptable to our heavenly Father?"

Saul needed a walking stick to help him because of a leg injury from his own youth. It was not a smooth piece of wood but had an uneven surface, except for the polished handle he was gripping; the walking stick was very strong.

Abruptly he raised his walking stick and hit Stephen across the cheek with it, sending the young man tumbling over on his back.

Someone passing by stopped, rushed over, and grabbed the stick away from Saul.

"You could have broken that lad's jaw," the tall black man said.

"He *adores* the Nazarene!" Saul told him. "If his jaw is broken, he can say nothing that will confuse others."

"Are you his father?" the stranger demanded.

Saul shook his head.

"Then whoever you might be, you are a fool or worse for taking the duty of a father upon your own inappropriate shoulders."

"Are you his guardian?" Saul shot back.

"If I am not, then that young man must fear for his life in *your* presence, for you seem quite mad, mister, and capable of anything."

The black man was tall, broad-shouldered, and exceptionally muscular. Few men would have been a match for him.

"I shall take him to his father's house right now, and then you shall see what true punishment is all about," Saul remarked.

"If I were that father, and saw that someone outside the family had done this to *my* son, it is not that child who would be quaking in fear of retribution."

Stephen managed to get to his feet.

"You … are … vengeful," he said painfully. "My family … will … have nothing to do with you … after this … day."

Saul glowered with smugness.

"Obviously your jaw is intact, Johanan," he said. "Good! There can be no delay when your father *demands* an explanation."

"I am no longer known by that name."

"Oh, yes, I forgot. You now go by the name *God* bestowed upon you," he said sarcastically.

Saul left no chance for Stephen to provide an answer but spat in his face and started to walk away.

The black stranger grabbed him by the shoulders and lifted him several inches off the ground.

"Why do you not spit in *my* face?" he demanded. "Are you purely a coward who victimizes young men and others who are not quite up to any 'battling' with you?"

Saul's face was turning completely red.

"Let me go now!" he demanded, then gulped a couple of times, gasping for breath.

Now it was the stranger who spat at Saul just before releasing his hold on the other man's shoulders.

"You *dare* to—!" Saul sputtered.

"Hit me then. Kick me, little man. Show me that you are not a coward after all. I will not strike back at you."

He stood there, arms folded, waiting.

Saul merely grumbled and started to walk down the ancient street but stopped midway, turned, and shouted at Stephen, "You may not have a home after this day, young man!"

Stephen shot back, "But I *will* have a Savior."

Saul stood for a moment, glowering at the two of them, and then seemed to be swept away with the constantly moving throng.

The stranger introduced himself as Skeyas.

"But that is a Hebrew name," young Stephen observed.

"I was adopted into such a family many, many years ago," the other man replied. "During a famine in Africa, my parents both died, and I could do nothing but sit by the side of the road and wait to die. I was passed by again and again. But this one couple stopped and took pity on me, and I was with them for twenty years until I struck out on my own."

"Are they both living?" Stephen asked.

"Oh, yes, and living in the very fine home that I was able to provide for them, along with my wife and four children."

"It must be *very* large then—or very crowded."

Skeyas chuckled.

"It is both at times."

"What is your profession?"

"I am a chief of a very large tribe; I have judicial and other powers. My parents and I provide leather goods for many customers, using the hides of animals we trap and kill ourselves. Each one of us is considered a craftsman, with our wares going near and far. We even get some business from the Orient."

He stretched expansively.

"Since we raise our own crops, eat our own kills, make many of our own clothes, we can use the earnings of our craft for other purposes."

Skeyas was proud as he spoke, describing his family's success.

"And what would some of those purposes be?" asked Stephen, his interest captured by what the man was telling him.

It was then that Skeyas' pride became something else, humility mixed with a certain joy.

"Helping the disciples of Jesus," he replied.

Stephen was taken completely by surprise, having no idea that the Nazarene's influence had spread so far.

"Into the jungles of Africa?" he asked naïvely.

"Oh, yes, my young friend," Skeyas told him. "By the way, I do not know your name. What are you called?"

"Johan … er, Stephen."

"You were starting to give me another name. Why is that?"

"Something happened just last night."

Skeyas was intrigued.

"Would you tell me?" he requested.

Stephen said he would be happy to do so. That clearly pleased the big man.

"Then we shall go to the quarters I have rented at an inn nearby," he stated, "and there you shall tell me everything. But first, I suspect you should not use your jaw more than necessary. I have some ointment that might help. It is very cold when applied. I thought I would bring some with me on this trip, anticipating the possibility that I might be hurt myself."

"You have quarters already?" Stephen asked, his jaw now throbbing.

Skeyas chuckled and added, "Actually I have rented the whole inn!"

Stephen decided he liked this tall, muscular, outgoing black man and would accept his invitation.

"I look forward to telling you," he said forlornly. "It's just such a pity that we have met on such a sad, terrible day."

The other man was concerned.

"What do you mean, my friend?"

"You have not heard?"

"I just arrived yesterday, you know, and have been sound asleep until just a short time ago. The Romans could have been overturned and I still would not know."

Now Stephen understood and said, "We shall go to your quarters then, and I will tell you everything."

"You act as though it is some awful tragedy."

"It is, Skeyas. You will think of it in no other way."

When they reached the inn where the visitor was staying and were sitting down inside, Stephen told him everything.

"My Lord, hanging from a cross?" Skeyas moaned.

"Unless something can be done."

"If only I had known I could have brought my security forces, and we might have been able to wrest Jesus from their control!"

"My mother and my father might be able to do something."

"Are they well connected, Stephen?"

"Exceedingly."

"Is there anything I can do?"

"I know of nothing."

Skeyas' shoulders slumped.

"How sad!" he said.

*Later ...*

Skeyas and Stephen were interrupted by the sound of a shouting mob outside the little inn on a side street in ancient Jerusalem. Skeyas hurried to a window overlooking the scene below.

"What is going on?" he shouted with a strong voice that was not difficult to hear.

One of the women, who must have weighed well over two hundred pounds, looked up at him and replied, "The Nazarene may soon be sentenced to death."

"Where?"

"On Golgotha."

"It will be quite a show. I am bringing all my children to watch."

"You want your young ones to witness someone dying in agony?"

"This Jesus means nothing to me. Who cares?"

Skeyas would have liked to say something quite angry and obscene to her, but that kind of response belonged to the days before he became a follower of the Nazarene who eschewed all coarseness, all vulgar speaking.

"I came here to see this Man," he said after stepping back from the window. "I never imagined I would witness His death."

"When Jesus spoke to me yesterday in Gethsemane," Stephen recalled, "I saw no fear in Him, yet He seemed to sense the future, not just any future but *this* one. Even so, well, it was not just bravery as such, a courageousness, but, rather, I saw instead a kind of inevitability."

"How sad. To be certain that you are going to be executed unjustly and not be able to do anything about it."

"He could have left. A minute or two might have made a difference. I know this whole area. I could have kept Him hidden."

"Hidden, and then have to be on the run for the rest of His life? Would that have been very good?"

"Better than death."

"I wonder …"

"But why? Is it not clear? Life on the run instead of the most painful death imaginable?"

"Oh, no, hardly that. I mean, from what you tell me, this Caiaphas and my new adversary, Saul, seem to feel that a dead Jesus will mean that His followers will eventually scatter in every direction since He will no longer be alive to inspire them. In their fear they may die in the same manner as their leader."

"You do not agree?"

"Let me tell you a story, Stephen."

Skeyas told him of a time a century earlier when various tribes were at war with one another. Finally, through mounting savage and bloody victories, only two tribes were left, the others having given up and retreated to their territories.

"The ruling council of one of the tribes convened a meeting and tried to figure out the secret behind the opposition's successes on the battlefield. There were no greater numbers of them. They had no larger stock of weapons. They were not tougher, it seemed. Then why had they kept on winning?"

"Their leader?" Stephen said, aware of where the other man was leading him.

"Yes!" Skeyas exclaimed. "You see what I am getting at! So they decided to assassinate him, certain that no one else could take his place and that they could move in for the kill after he was gone. So this leader was murdered in an ambush, and his killers rejoiced, anticipating a victory at last."

"But they were to face quite a surprise, right?"

"Right you are, Stephen. Killing him meant that he immediately became a martyr. Killing him did not end his influence but only made it more intense after his death."

"And you think that might happen after Jesus dies?"

"Let me say this: Caiaphas and his lackeys may regret what they are setting in motion."

Then he pounded his fist on the small table in front of him.

"You are forgetting something!" he declared.

"My parents!"

"Yes ... they may have returned by now. Should you not be going back to see if they have been successful in their righteous mission?"

"Yes, of course," Stephen agreed, more than a little embarrassed that so much time had passed. "Will you come with me?"

"I think I shall remain behind. You never know how I might be able to help here."

Stephen kissed him once on each cheek, as was the custom of the times.

"May God be with you," he said.

"Right now, I think, it is more important that God be with *you*."

Stephen hurried down the steps to the first floor and then outside, running as fast as the noisy crowd would allow him.

When the young man arrived home, he found that his parents had already returned, and that Saul of Tarsus was with them or, rather, that their longtime friend was being thrown out of the house.

Huram and Hannah had gained the cooperation of Pontius and Procula Pilatus. That fact overrode the significance of their bitter confrontation with Saul.

"He is obsessed!" Hannah said afterward. "There is a madness in those small eyes of his; surely you noticed it as well."

"I know …" Stephen remarked, cupping a hand around his jaw, the swelling down, but a gruesome-looking bruise from his ear to his chin marking the spot where Saul had hit him with the walking stick.

"Is he the one who caused that?" Huram asked, fury starting to build, his hands clenching in fists.

"Yes …"

Huram's instinct was to run after Saul, drag him back to the house, and "properly" punish him.

"You should have told me straightaway," he said, his voice tense and perspiration dripping down his forehead.

Stephen was prepared for that reaction, since he knew his father's emotions all too well, and he said, "You might have done something terrible, Father."

"But the man *deserved* just that!"

According to ancient Hebrew laws, only a father had the right to do what Saul had done. Taking that kind of extreme "punishment" away from Huram ben Sira represented a significant transgression.

"My jaw is better now," Stephen said, trying to defuse the situation.

"How could it be, my son?" asked Huram. "Your jaw might have been broken. Look at the pain you would be experiencing *then*."

Stephen told him about Skeyas.

Huram had never been comfortable around black people. They were, in his view, Gentiles of the worst sort, given as they were to rituals and other practices dedicated to heathen gods, more so than the Romans who gathered together in worship more for political than for spiritual purposes, at least among the wealthy class.

Many Jews treated blacks with coldness and contempt while others went several steps further and tried to get them kicked out of towns or cities like Jerusalem until they realized that many of the blacks they saw had plenty of money to spend on Jewish products, and held their emotions in check for the sake of commerce.

*... it is better now.*

"Just like that?" Huram probed.

"No questions asked. He saw that I needed help, and he gave it. There was no selfishness in him."

His father pondered that for a moment before observing, "It must be that he also is a follower of the Nazarene's."

Stephen stifled a gasp before asking, "Father?"

"What is it, son?"

"You said *also*."

Huram nodded a bit reluctantly.

"I did; that is right. I suppose I must resign myself to the direction you have chosen for your life."

The three of them were sitting on pillows rather than chairs.

"When I see what Saul has become," Huram said, "and begin to see what you are becoming, I have to decide which is better, and I must admit that you make that decision very easy, Johanan."

Huram ben Sira stood and motioned for his son to do likewise, then he reached out and embraced the one he knew as Johanan.

"Father?" the young man asked again.

"Johanan, my son, say whatever it is you want, or should I call you Stephen from now on?"

For a second or two, while Stephen heard what his father said, it did not register, and then he stepped back, his eyes wide, his mouth open, but no words coming from it, amazement freezing his reactions.

"You look as though you have seen Abraham's ghost," Huram said, using a favorite expression of those days.

Stephen's voice quivered.

"You know!" the young man blurted out. "Somehow, I think, miraculously ... you actually do, Father."

Huram was amused by his son's reaction though it was hardly unanticipated.

"I must know, must I not, to call you what I did?"

Stephen was flustered.

"Saul must have told you. I'm sorry, Father. I was trying to get up the courage to tell you myself, and I am relieved that that is no longer necessary but—"

He had difficulty with his speech, and this embarrassed him as he tried to show his father how mature he was.

"When you calm down, do you want to hear from your father how I really came to know," Huram asked, adopting a mock-severe tone, "or are you intent only on engaging in your own speculation?"

All the young man could do was nod rather lamely.

"After visiting with the proconsul-governor and his wife," Huram recalled, "we were being taken home and suddenly—"

"A vision, Father, you had a vision?"

It was the elder man's turn to nod.

"Not completely like the one you experienced. There was no sudden light, just a voice. And it told me that you would become someone special."

"Me? But I—"

"That was the way I reacted … Stephen. To me and to your mother you always have been special."

Father and son were fumbling for those words that they should speak next. Hannah wanted to say something to them too, but for her, the mother, it was an especially discomforting idea for what it implied, formless possibilities that seemed only dark and with an edge of vague terror about them.

Stephen broke the silence.

"I do not know what is going on, Father," he acknowledged. "I look forward, and I fear what is in store. How could I be capable of anything that—"

"Nor I, but the voice gave your mother and me some clues."

Huram, a man for whom any kind of outward emotion had been awkward over the years, now started sobbing.

"Father, Father!" Stephen exclaimed as he reached out for Huram.

Hannah got to her feet. She too was crying.

"You will do wonderful things," she said. "You will reach many, many people with a message none of us has ever heard before."

"So why are you crying?" Stephen asked.

"And then you will be gone from us," his mother said.

"On a trip, a long trip perhaps?"

Her lower lip was trembling.

"Your father and I cannot say," she told him. "We just know that the tone of the voice we were hearing seemed so sad then, so very sad."

"Could you be mistaken about that?" Stephen asked.

They both would have liked to say yes, would have liked to humor their son but were determined not to be dishonest, regardless of the reaction he had.

"I doubt it," Huram told him. "The voice was trying very hard to prepare your mother and me, trying to—"

Suddenly Stephen hugged himself nervously, and his face became as pale as a cloud.

Both parents were alarmed.

"Are you going to faint?" his mother asked.

He shook his head.

"It is not that," he reassured her.

She wanted to believe him, but his skin looked so pasty, with a coating of perspiration over it.

Then Hannah touched her son's cheek and pulled her hand back in an instant.

"You are cold!" she exclaimed, her eyes widening. "Your skin, your skin ... it ... it feels almost—"

Hannah had to sit down on a nearby chair.

Nor had Stephen improved in the few seconds that had passed. A moment later, he tottered and nearly fell, his father hurrying to his side to steady him.

"I will send one of the servants for a physician," Huram said. "You both may need treatment."

"No ..." Stephen pleaded. "It is not—"

"But I insist," his father interrupted. "You are a Jew, not a Stoic."

"My health is not what caused my dizziness. You must believe me. No physician can help me now."

"I am not convinced, Stephen."

"The Nazarene ..."

"What about Him?"

"He is going before the people very shortly," Stephen whispered, convinced that he had not slipped into some fit of unfettered imagination. "They are to be given a choice this day, Father."

"A choice? What kind of choice?"

"Between Jesus and Barabbas."

"How do you know that?" Hannah inquired, some strength returning to her own body so that she was able to stand once again.

"I *feel* it, Mother; I feel it all over my body. There is a link between me and Jesus now. Our spirits are connected, I think."

Huram and Hannah ordinarily would have scoffed at any such possibility, but what they had experienced silenced any skepticism.

"But Pilatus is going to stop it," Huram told him. "I believed the man when he told me that."

"He may *try*, Father, but he will not succeed."

"But you cannot be sure."

"I can only tell you what is inside me, Father. I know nothing but sorrow. When I think of the Nazarene, it is as though I am feeling His own pain."

"We must hurry then," Huram said. "If you are right, then it will happen outside the proconsul-governor's headquarters. There is no time to waste. We must loudly add our voices of dissent."

Stephen accompanied his parents but felt no sense of anticipation, no hope of victory. While he told them nothing, remaining silent as a long-time servant commanded the horses pulling their chariot to run faster, he thought he heard briefly, but only in his mind somehow, a sound like that of thunder. Then there was a vision of lightning from a pitch-dark sky, the heavens being torn asunder, and what he assumed was the rage of a holy God visited upon those who would conspire with the prince of lies to murder His only begotten Son.

# — Chapter Fourteen —

Pontius Pilatus was standing on the balcony of his headquarters that overlooked an area called, ironically, the Place of Justice, essentially a cobblestoned section where people could come and plead for the lives of family members or friends who had been apprehended and were about to be sentenced by the proconsul-governor.

*Surely you will demand that Barabbas be crucified,* he thought, so secure in this assumption that a certain smugness crept into his outlook. *The insurrectionist crossed the line, he and his henchmen terrorizing you as much as you think Roman rule has. Support for his stand has slipped, and you will surely demand that Jesus be released while Barabbas is crucified.*

This plan was what Pilatus had devised after Huram ben Sira had appealed to him so eloquently to save the life of the Nazarene. That such words had come from a man who had previously been involved in plotting the very death that he now wanted to abrogate was a large part of why he had consented to do what he could.

"But you are the master of this domain!" Huram had exclaimed. "Your word is law, and you can do what you want. If you wish Jesus to be released, all you have to do is release Him. Or have I missed something?"

"You indeed have."

"But what? Enlighten me."

"There are certain political realities. The rule of law is a distinctly Roman concept, you know, and I can hardly violate what I have sworn to uphold in the lives of others. I would be accused of hypocrisy or worse."

Huram nodded with a heavy degree of reluctance at the logic of what the other man told him.

"So what can you do?" he asked.

"I can give the crowd such a choice so black and white, a choice so stark, that their answer becomes inevitable," the proconsul-governor told him. "I ask the whole mass of them: Jesus or Barabbas?"

Huram liked the simple genius of that.

"Barabbas has become so loathsome, so hated that—" he mused.

"Jesus is the obvious choice for freedom," Pilatus interrupted. "After all, He has released, for three years now, so many from the shackles of blindness, deafness, leprosy, whatever else, that if just those who owe Him such a debt were to fill the Place of Justice, there could be no room for anybody else!"

Huram could offer no rebuttal.

"I compliment you, sir," he said.

"You have been remarkably persuasive, but it is my wife who has been, if you will, your John the Baptist."

"My wife is seeing—"

"Yes, I know. But there was no need for that. She required no persuasion of her own. I have heard little else since we have learned of Caiaphas' intentions."

"What can be done about this devil?"

"We must learn with him. We must grit our teeth and realize that no other choice exists until he is incapacitated or dead."

"God's high priest now Satan's servant ..."

"I do not share your beliefs, of course, but I would agree with that description in principle."

In the meantime, Hannah and Procula Pilatus had spent their time together in prayer—and in tears.

"Surely God will strike dead those who oppose His Son," Hannah speculated, speaking freely in the other woman's presence.

"I am not sure of that," the wife of the Roman proconsul-governor confessed, not from cynicism but, rather, from a conviction that neither of them knew fully what God had in mind.

"What else could happen?"

Procula reached for a six-inch-square piece of parchment on the marble-topped table beside her.

"I have a copy of a portion of the prophecies of Isaiah," she said, looking at the yellow-tinged sheet with some awe.

"That is rare and revered!" Hannah remarked. "How did you get it?"

"You ask a Roman official's wife such a question?"

Hannah blushed and dropped the subject.

"Sorry," she said. "I meant no offense."

Procula smiled and patted her gently on the shoulder, adding, "I understand your feelings, you know. And I truly understand that seeing Gentile hands touching something as revered as this can be upsetting."

As she handed the sheet to Hannah, she said, "It seems to suggest that the Messiah will actually die."

"Can you be sure?"

"See for yourself."

Hannah read those ancient words quickly, her eyes widening as she came to the same conclusion.

"So we can do nothing," she said.

"I gather by this prophecy that whatever *our* efforts, *God's* will shall be done, dear Hannah," Procula said.

"But we must not give up trying," Hannah spoke urgently. "God knows we must not do that!"

"I agree, but we should be prepared for an outcome that seems to have been ordained centuries ago."

*... ordained centuries ago.*

Suddenly both were quiet.

Thunder.

"Strange," Hannah observed after waiting a few seconds.

"What is strange?" Procula asked.

"We have heard the thunder, but the sky is clear."

It had not come. And there were no other claps of thunder immediately following that first one, which had been so strong it shook the earth beneath them for a moment.

"God's warning us," Hannah said. "He is trying to get our attention."

"Could He be—?" Procula started to say.

"Go ahead. Speak what is on your mind."

"Could this God, this heavenly Father in Whom I have come so recently to believe, be telling us, you and me and ten thousand upon ten thousand others, that He *is* doing what He has promised for so long but woe unto those who have made it necessary, especially the servants of darkness who are *doing* it?"

Gasping, she said, "If the Nazarene is crucified this day, my husband would be among them!"

Abruptly weak, Procula seemed ready to fall, but Hannah reached out for her and kept her standing.

"Do you want to sit down?" she asked the other woman.

"Thank you but no," the wife of the proconsul-governor replied shakily. "If I do so now, I fear that I shall never rise again."

*Eyes filled with hatred, mock or otherwise, saliva spilling from their mouths as their rage seemed to erupt like a volcano's sudden outpouring of red-hot lava ...*

Stephen saw the crowd gathered in front of the balcony where Pontius Pilatus stood.

*They seem so angry,* he thought. *Why are they as angry as that? How could they feel as they do about Jesus?*

He glanced over at the Nazarene, on Pilatus' left.

*So calm,* he observed. *It seems almost as though You have accepted Your death and are unwilling to do anything to deter it. Are You not eager to stay alive, to heal the bodies of the many Who come to You regularly? Is that not a reason to go on living?*

People in the multitude were raising their fists and shaking them.

"Crucify Him!" they shouted. "Crucify the charlatan!"

Stephen's parents were standing next to him. He could see that his mother was crying, and he thought he knew why.

*Several days ago, they had been putting palm leaves in front of Him and shouting "Hosanna!"* Stephen recalled. *Now this crowd, with many of the same people in it, is demanding His death!*

He wondered how they could change so quickly, and in another respect as well. Their reaction had flip-flopped on Barabbas, who had been losing support among everyday Jews for months, with only the *intelligentsia* still tolerating him to any degree, though it was an odd alliance because the insurrectionist, a man of no great intellectual aspirations or abilities, was hardly their type. Barabbas was someone who would rather destroy an opponent instead of reason with him, but then the *intelligentsia* were always dreaming of an Israel free of *any* foreign domination, free to pursue *Jewish* thought and only that. Except for some Latin influence, Jews of that day were extraordinarily provincial, which meant that the influx of Romans, along with their mores, architecture, customs, and whatever else, was anathema to this section of the population of Israel, and Barabbas seemed to be their only hope, however pallid that hope was, of achieving the kind of freedom for which they had never stopped yearning.

Barabbas ... standing to Pontius Pilatus' right.

He seemed a different man then, certain that he would be spending the last hours of his life on a cross atop Golgotha; his cockiness was gone, his face was quite pale-looking, and his knees were shaking as though they were threatening to collapse any moment.

*... how they could change so quickly.*

As though on cue, he found out.

Three suspicious-looking men, bearded, well dressed, but acting as though they were doing something that was more the work of criminals than they seemed to be, stood at the back of the Place of Justice, directly opposite the balcony. Every so often someone would approach them and hold his hand out in an inconspicuous manner, and something would be slipped into it by one of the three.

Then the three left.

"Father, I am going to follow—" he started to tell Huram ben Sira.

"Go, my son," his father interrupted. "I have seen what you have seen, and I want to find out, as you do, what is going on."

In the crowd Stephen was careful to seem nondescript. Eventually the men arrived at the temple where Jesus had cast out the money-changers. Never once had they looked behind themselves, for they must have assumed that no one suspected them of doing anything special, or perhaps their demeanor was sheer arrogance since they were about the business of the ever-powerful high priest and no one could stand against them.

Stephen saw one of Caiaphas' minions come out and hand each of them some coins and then retreat to an inner sanctum.

Then someone else entered the scene who obviously had not been expected.

The follower of Jesus named Judas, who had betrayed Him in Gethsemane.

"You too were paid?" he asked.

"As were you," one of the men replied.

"What was your task?"

"To stir up the crowd into a frenzy, to make sure they would demand the death of Jesus."

Judas looked horrified.

"We are no worse than you," another of the men said. "We have no connection with this Man, but you were His friend. We owed Jesus no loyalty. You, however—"

"*No! No! No!*" Judas exclaimed.

He backed away from the three as they started to laugh at him.

"We are going to spend our filthy lucre on an evening to remember," the third man added. "Where are you headed?"

"*To hell!*" the former apostle shouted. "I will get there before you, but someday I shall welcome you among the flames."

And then he was gone from that spot.

Stephen felt some compulsion to follow Judas, to corner the man and demand to know what had caused him to betray a friend, especially a friend of the caliber of Jesus.

"How could you do this?" he muttered to himself. "How could you listen to all that He had been saying for three years and then just simply turn Him in?"

Judas fled down a side street then wound his way through some alleys until he emerged at the northern edge of Jerusalem.

Suddenly Stephen realized where the former apostle was heading.

Gehenna, next to the potter's field, a place of burial for the poor and the disgraced.

The diseased who had died were also taken care of in that isolated location, not by being disposed of in a crude grave, either by themselves or their bodies joining others until no more room was left but, rather, into one of half a dozen pits.

Stephen saw it for the first time, for it was not a place that anyone visited even out of curiosity. Its existence cast a stench, a literal stench over that section of Jerusalem and the adjoining countryside, a stench as well as a visible pall from dark clouds of smoke that seemed perpetual because people were dying day after day and being thrown into the pits.

Gehenna.

It had been the singular point of reference when prophets over the centuries groped for an image they could use to describe what God had revealed to them of hell. The difference was that the hell ruled by Satan was a place of punishment whereas this Gehenna was nothing more than a dumping ground for human bodies.

Judas stood not far from the end of one of the pits, sobbing, his body hunched, his chest torn with pain, alternately spouting obscenities and cries of shame and stricken conscience.

Even during that short time, men in black hooded garments came with carts or wagons and emptied these of bedraggled and wretched bone and flesh that tumbled down into the inferno at the bottom, a fiery mass of wood and oil and anything else that would burn, and keep on burning if replenished periodically.

*Sometimes there were screams ...*

Stephen was abruptly drenched in cold sweat as he heard them.

*Screams, the cries of men and women and not a few hapless children, homeless beggars depending upon the oft-nonexistent kindness of strangers, human beings from the youngest of ages to the very old who were not dead after all....*

Stephen had been aware of the rumors that had surfaced periodically over the years of his youth, sometimes gross and always discomforting stories of sloppy, uncaring pronouncements offered callously by those assigned the task of determining where death had come or not. These men, for whom dead bodies, emaciated bodies, bodies beaten and torn and bruised by robbers or insurrectionists or both, were often all too casual about the breath of life, assuming that a beggar who was thought dead yet lived might as well die in the pit of Gehenna because his value was doubtful anyway, and that he would but hit the streets again if he should recover by some miracle, annoying those who passed by him since he seldom bathed, and his odors were appalling.

Weakened by hunger or disease or both, many would regain consciousness only as their bodies hit the side of whatever pit had been chosen, and they would feel and hear and, yes, see the gold-red flames and start screaming, their fingers digging frantically into the side of the pit. But still they would slip downward, crying out, "I am alive! You must help me!"

But no help was ever given.

To the contrary.

When some of the stronger ones made it close to the rim of a pit, they would be pushed back, offered up as perverse sacrifices to flames that would embrace them and melt the flesh from their bodies and keep on crackling, ready for the next batch, whether alive or dead.

"I give myself to you!" Judas shouted. "I pass from this inferno to another, for it is all I deserve. How cheap the price of my soul!"

He had been clutching an empty leather purse, which had once contained the thirty pieces of silver he had cast at the feet of those who had paid him to betray Jesus. Now he flung this last vestige of shame away from him.

"I longed only for truth. I grasped so pitiably after it, thinking that mercy or grace would bestow it upon my miserable self," Judas whispered so softly that Stephen had to strain to hear him. "And now I die where the poor and the deranged and the lepers are shoved, nameless, into oblivion."

Stephen knew he had to act or lose any further opportunity since he noticed that Judas was loosening the rope around his waist as he headed toward a tall tree at one end of Potter's Field.

Judas turned and saw Stephen standing now not far from him, a pit of fire on either side of him.

"Leave me alone, stranger," he demanded. "I have done the worst act of all. I have condemned the Son of God to death."

"You have done that, yes, you have," Stephen said. "And I ask you to tell me why if you know who He is and have always known it."

"I wanted to push Him into doing something. I heard the grumbling. I knew people desperately wanted to believe that He was what He told them."

"The Messiah?"

"Yes, our liberator, the One Who would vanquish the Romans and hold them at bay until their empire floundered and fell. All He cared to do was talk—talk and heal, and nothing more. The Romans cannot be charmed or scorned out of our land."

Judas could not look at Stephen directly.

"I wanted Him to do what I knew He was capable of doing but which He seemed too reluctant to do on His own without some crisis erupting. I set about to provide that crisis. That was what I wanted to do."

"And it did not matter what Yahweh wanted?"

"I was *tired* of waiting ... so many dusty roads, so much dirt ... so many nights when we did not have enough to eat but fell asleep with the sounds of our stomachs in the background. If Jesus was God's Son, why was the Father treating Him and us so badly?"

"So you thought that betrayal was the answer?"

"Not betrayal, you fool, *liberation!*"

Judas' eyes narrowed.

"And who are you to accuse me without confronting the sin in your own life?" he asked defiantly.

"I am Johan ... I am Stephen."

"*You* are he?"

"Yes, I—"

The expression on Judas Iscariot's face was odd, and Stephen did not know what to make of it.

"Get away from me!" the former apostle demanded.

"But you should not die now. Whatever you have done, you should not take your life before God is ready."

"I took His Son's life, now why not my own?"

"Jesus spoke of forgiveness. Do you reject that as well?"

Judas hesitated, his manner changing.

"God help me!" he cried. "I have no choice. I can see them right here, waiting, and I have no courage to pull away from them, to send them running."

"Whom do you see, Judas?"

"Creatures ... awful creatures ... waiting like vultures for my soul ... ready to carry it away to their master ... my master!"

"But I see nothing."

"You are not evil. You are but good. I know about you, Stephen. Jesus told us of you."

"Told you of *me?*" Stephen asked, incredulous.

"Told us of your old name then your new one and said that you would become known like the rest of His disciples though you would have so little time."

"But I am a young man!"

"And you will never reach middle age!"

Despite the heat from the flames to his left and his right and in back of him, Stephen felt unutterably cold.

"I have lived longer than you by ten years," Judas added, "and I envy you. I envy the kind of death you will have as angels sing their welcome."

He glanced toward the towering shape of the tree, green and thriving and strong, spreading its leaves wide and whispering in the breezes of that open spot.

"As for me, beasts of perdition scream for my soul, and I shall hand it to them without further delay."

Judas sprinted for the tree.

One end of the rope already had been fashioned into a noose, and he slipped it around his neck.

"Give redemption a chance!" Stephen screamed as he ran after Judas.

But Judas was too fast. He scrambled up to a high limb, tied the end of the rope to it securely, then jumped to his death, his neck broken within seconds.

Stephen fell to his knees, nearly surrounded by pits of flame. He saw the eyes of Judas Iscariot seemingly staring in his direction, a look of pain and terror on the lifeless face. Stephen knew he had to leave that place immediately, imagining that he could somehow see through those now sightless eyes of the man who had betrayed his Master and beyond, deep into the dark and ghastly corridors of hell, as Judas' soul descended into damnation forever.

*The mood of the crowd in ancient Jerusalem was changing into something darker, meaner, more vicious . . .*

As Stephen hurried back to the Place of Justice, he noticed the changing character of the crowd through which he had to plow.

*Frantic . . .*

The people around him seemed just short of frenzied as they pushed in one direction only.

*They seem to be no more than scrambling beasts lured by the promise of shed blood,* Stephen thought, surveying with growing distaste the angry faces of those around him in every direction.

Stephen brought his hand to his mouth to stifle a scream.

Hurrying so frantically toward Golgotha, like maddened lemmings toward the edge of an abyss.

*Oh, God,* he thought, not profanely. *Oh, God, it already has been decided. What are we to do?*

And then he saw Barabbas ahead, standing on the second floor of a building on the eastern side of the street, looking in his direction but *behind* him.

At that point, the narrow street widened just a bit as steps led down to another level. Stephen turned quickly and was able to see what had caught the insurrectionist's eye.

Jesus.

Just a few feet away.

Stephen had to press himself up against the building behind him, sucking in his breath so people could pass by without sweeping him along with them.

The Nazarene was carrying a cross, and around His forehead was what only could be called a crown of thorns pressed so hard against His skin that drops of blood were trickling down His face.

"My Lord!" Stephen cried out, tears starting to flow.

Jesus turned for a moment and looked at him, whispering, "Weep not for Me, Stephen, but for those who would cause this infamy."

Stephen's instinct was to push through the people, cast off that cross, and take Jesus with him, but he knew the Roman soldiers with Jesus could stop a well-built but untrained young man without even sweating.

He took out a handkerchief from his pocket and tried to wipe the Nazarene's brow but could not get close enough.

A few feet farther along, Jesus stumbled and fell, the cross breaking away from His grasp and landing next to Him. Stephen saw a chance to do something finally, and he hurried to where Jesus was trying to gather the strength to stand and take up the cross once again.

*Someone else ...*

Ahead of him. Someone he recognized in an instant.

A tall, muscular black man.

Skeyas.

"I have many friends right here," he was saying into the Nazarene's ear. "I can pay many more. We can spirit You away from the grasp of Rome."

"It is not to be," Jesus told him.

"But I must do something."

One of the soldiers, overhearing that part, grunted to another; they grabbed Skeyas, and said, "Then you take the cross He is carrying and help Him."

Skeyas resisted.

"*No!*" he said, ignoring the danger. "I want to liberate Him, not help Him to His death!"

"Take the cross *now!*" the soldier demanded. "I compel you to do this."

Jesus was already weakened and could barely stand even though He no longer had to carry the cross, and it seemed that perhaps He might die in that very spot. The same soldier prodded Him, demanding that He stand and act like a man.

"What sort of king are You?" the Roman asked with scorn that seemed almost a living thing in itself, foul and wretched.

Jesus looked up, not with anger or pain but with compassion.

"May My Father in heaven have the mercy on you that you are unable to show others ..." He muttered.

The soldier was about to strike His cheek with a leather thong but stopped midway, hesitating, then backing off.

"Put Your hand on my shoulder, my Lord," Skeyas told the Nazarene.

"But you already have so great a burden," Jesus said.

"If it means less for You, then it is not a burden for me at all."

The Nazarene leaned on Skeyas' broad, strong shoulder and managed to get Himself to a standing position.

"If I could die for you, Lord, I would nail myself to this cross," the black man told him.

"You are not to die for Me," Jesus responded lovingly, "but I for you and the whole world besides."

Skeyas' eyes widened.

"Is that what must be?" he asked.

"And more besides as My Father casts down His anger from heaven."

Skeyas touched the brow of his Lord.

"I hope I shall not long tarry," he whispered.

"You will live, faithful one, for long years in which many will know Me because of you."

And then they continued on to Golgotha.

*Minutes later ...*

Not a long period of time, just what was needed for Stephen to climb up the side of Golgotha and reach the top, stand briefly and look at the horror just before him, three men on crosses, the timbers stained with their blood, groans coming from each of them, and a large crowd gathered, watching the spectacle.

Stephen approached Mary and the apostle John, who were standing at the foot of Jesus' cross.

"I am Stephen," he told them.

The youngest of the apostles turned and looked at him, the expression of recognition on his handsome face unnerving.

"Jesus spoke of you," he said simply, "more than once, and with the greatest sense of appreciation. The first time was a year ago."

*A year ago! Stephen was still named Johanan then and had had no interest whatsoever in the Nazarene!*

"But I did not know Him then," Stephen managed to say in the midst of his shock. "How could He tell you *anything* about me?"

"He knew about all of us before we were ever born," John continued. "In the beginning was the Word ..."

Stephen was ignorant of such a description.

"The Word?" he asked.

"There, above you," John added, pointing to the agony-wracked body. "God and the Word are one and the same, eternal."

Stephen had not been able to look directly up at the countenance of the Nazarene but now he forced himself to do so, forced himself to examine that body, once so vibrant, those hands that had touched the sick and the dead and raised up everyone who came to Him in supplication.

*Now stuck through with nails, now covered with blood that continued to flow in trickles and hit the rocky ground of Golgotha ...*

Stephen stepped forward a few inches. A drop of precious red touched his forehead, and he left it there.

"Jesus, my Lord ..." he whispered.

The Nazarene's eyes had been closed briefly but now opened. He looked down at Stephen, and a tender smile crossed His face.

Jesus then turned His eyes toward His mother and John.

Stephen stepped back.

He had accepted the reality of Jesus, the divinity of Jesus, only the day before. But now Jesus seemed to recognize him from the cross. Perhaps the Nazarene was delirious, overwhelming pain and coming death robbing Him of coherence.

Another drop of blood, this time on Stephen's cheek.

Stephen touched it with the fingers of his left hand.

"My Lord, my Lord ..." he said, but Jesus had passed out.

Stephen turned and looked at the crowd that was gathered atop the Place of the Skull. Only a few seemed reverential. Some were laughing and pointing or spitting in contempt on the ground. One man had taken a swatch of cloth, hurried to the base of the cross, dabbed it in some of Jesus' blood, and brought it back to his young son.

"Look," he said excitedly, "this is a fine souvenir."

"Yes, Father, I shall show it to all my friends," the child answered.

Apparently others had seen this, and several tore off sections of their clothing, ran up to the cross, and soaked these pieces of cloth with blood, then hurried away before the Roman soldiers could decide to stop them.

At first Stephen was touched, then horrified, because he overheard plans to *sell* the bloodstained pieces of material in the market area of

Jerusalem, and talk of how much pure profit was involved.

He felt sick.

"Lord, how can You ever forgive them?" Stephen asked, the dirt on his cheeks now streaked with tears.

Slowly, with obvious agony, Jesus opened His eyes, turning His gaze toward the heavens.

"Father, forgive them, for they know not what they do," He said, His voice hoarse, His words barely discernible.

But there were more enterprises like that one. Another man was selling crudely drawn maps showing where Jesus had been born. A third, a man who had been healed, was regaling people with stories about his "relationship" with the Nazarene as long as they continued to slip him coins. And a group of soldiers had taken Jesus' robe and were casting lots for it.

Then Stephen saw Caiaphas and Saul of Tarsus, as did his parents, who had joined him as he stood before the cross.

"I must go to them and say something," he told the two of them.

"Do you want me to stand with you ... Stephen?" Huram ben Sira asked.

"Stay here with Mother, please."

His father nodded, smiling just a little.

"I am proud of you, my son," Huram said. "Yahweh will give you the wisdom you need."

They embraced, and then Stephen hurried on over to the two other men.

Saul stiffened as he saw the young man approach, but Caiaphas, noticing that the very influential parents were not far away, smiled a bit.

"You must be rejoicing, Johanan," the high priest spoke.

"Over what?" Stephen asked.

"That imbecile dying before our eyes."

"You think this is cause for celebration?"

"Oh yes, indeed it is. You should see what I plan later. Perhaps your entire family can come."

Stephen shook his head.

"We do not celebrate ignominy," he said.

"You think this event is shameful, young man?"

"Not only that, but surely it is blasphemy."

Caiaphas chuckled as he replied, "Surely you are jesting, you the son of a man who agreed to join with me in seeking the death of the Nazarene."

"That was before my father saw a vision sent from God. That was before *I* met Him."

"Have you both fallen under His spell?"

"And my mother as well. Are you calling us fools because this is so?"

Caiaphas restrained himself, knowing how influential Huram ben Sira was at more than one level. He was about to speak again when Saul interrupted him.

"The high priest may not call you fools, but I am doing just that," he said.

"Who is the greater fool," Stephen remarked, "the man who accepts the Son of God or the one who rejects Him without even listening to those portions of Scripture that can only be pointing directly to Jesus?"

"You lecture *me* about Scripture?" Saul asked.

"Is it better for me to do that or for God Himself to stand before you and condemn that bloodthirsty soul of yours?"

Saul raised his hand, and Stephen winced, preparing for another blow, but there was no walking stick this time, and he grasped the older man's wrist and held it tightly.

"You do that to me just once," he said. "The second time I separate your hand from your arm, and shove it down your throat, fingers first."

Stephen regretted letting his anger show with such words, but once having spoken them, he knew he could not retreat or he would lose face.

"Saul, did you strike this young man?" Caiaphas asked.

"I did, yes, and I am proud that I can say so," Saul replied. "I am only sorry that I was not able to break his jaw."

The high priest, ever a politician, reprimanded him.

"Your dislike of the Nazarene should not be directed against such a young man as this. He comes from a family that has—"

Saul interrupted him.

"Do you truly know what is going on?" he demanded.

"Has it *ever* been otherwise?" Caiaphas spoke indignantly.

"Your pride is showing."

"And you are a model of humility, I suppose, Saul?"

Saul knew that the other man was a match for him, unlike young Johanan, for whom he had little or no respect.

"Are you aware that this entire family has become followers of the Nazarene?" Saul asked with loathing.

"Your jesting does not become you," Caiaphas remarked, brushing aside the other man's pronouncement.

"Am I jesting? Can you be so sure?"

"I can."

As far as Caiaphas was concerned, that was the end of the matter, but Saul would not let it rest.

"Ask Stephen!" he demanded.

"Who is Stephen?"

Saul pointed to the one they had known as Johanan for many years.

Caiaphas was certain that the man from Tarsus was losing his mind.

"Tell this … this lunatic that he is very wrong," he remarked, trying to be as nonchalant as possible.

Stephen said nothing.

"Go ahead, please," Caiaphas insisted sternly, not at all happy with the implications of the young man's silence.

This time, standing straight, his wide shoulders pulled back, Stephen declared unashamedly, "What Saul says is true."

Blinking once, then twice, the high priest instantly showed by his manner that he was stunned.

"You *accept* the Nazarene's heresy?" he asked, still not convinced that he was the object of anything but a misguided and irritating practical joke, and a ghoulish one at that, considering where they were.

"It is not heresy," Stephen replied. "God has spoken both to my father and to me."

"God has spoken—"

Caiaphas was nearly choking with a mixture of disbelief and rage.

"I am tired of hearing about people to whom God has spoken. If He were to speak to anyone, it would be to *me!*"

A slight change of tone briefly crept into his voice.

"And He has not done that for many years."

Then Caiaphas turned to Saul.

"I am sorry that I doubted you," he acknowledged.

"I can understand why. If things go well, you will not have to be concerned with the escapades of Huram ben Sira's family much longer."

For Saul, that was not so much a propitious revelation as an attempt to unhinge the youngest member of that family.

"What do you mean?" Stephen asked. "You do not have any power to hurt us."

Saul nodded mischievously as he said, "You are right, Johanan. *I* do not!"

He looked toward the cross from which Jesus was hanging and spat on the ground, then he roughly grabbed Caiaphas' arm.

"Let us return to the temple," he said. "You and I have much to discuss even this late in the day."

Caiaphas wrenched his arm away from Saul's grasp.

"You must stop this demonstration of foolishness," Caiaphas said to both of them. "I might be convinced to give you a chance, Johanan, after all, but I need time to think and—"

"Pray?" Stephen finished the sentence for him. "Why do you even *bother?* You are interested only in your will, not God's. When His will conflicts with your own, you find some excuse to ignore whatever He expects of you."

"Listen well, Caiaphas," prodded Saul. "See how much he has been corrupted, and think what it would mean if that corruption is allowed to spread."

Stephen grabbed the smaller man and started dragging him the short distance to Jesus' cross.

"You look at Him from a distance. Why not up close?"

Stephen flung Saul's head back so hard his neck seemed close to breaking.

*"Look at Him!"* he demanded. "Look into the eyes of the One Whose death you have sought, you and that other monster, Caiaphas."

The Roman soldiers seemed ready to act but held back for a moment.

At the base of the cross, Stephen flung Saul down into the dirt, slamming his head into a pool of blood.

*"No, son!"* Huram ben Sira's voice broke into the haze that clouded his son's mind, a haze born of rage and disgust.

Stephen let go and staggered backward, holding his hands out in front of him, seeing the blood on them.

"Forgive me, Lord!" he cried out just before running to the edge of a rocky outcropping on the side of Golgotha. For a moment he considered the possibility of throwing himself over the edge because of the shame his actions had caused his family, but then he felt a hand again gently touch his back and saw that it was his mother, who whispered, "Come home with your father and me. The Lord would not want it to end like this." And he could not disagree, could not at all, so the three of them left the Place of the Skull as the crowd returned their momentarily distracted attention to the Nazarene, who was soon to die.

And that, they thought, would be the end of it.

## Chapter Fifteen

I *am disgraced!*

Saul's mind shouted words that he would never allow from his lips so that others could hear him.

Saul heard the tittering laughter, for common people harbored a desire to see great men cheapened, and he considered himself a target for their repressed derision, but then he could endure the ridicule of the lesser, while it was those whose respect he craved that bothered him should they join in and laugh as well, which was what they were doing that afternoon on Golgotha, Caiaphas and others from the Sanhedrin, showing the contempt he had suspected they were harboring all along for an outsider such as himself.

As he raised himself up, he saw, for a moment, the Nazarene staring down at him, and he thought he heard, in his head, but without his ears being involved, as though the voice originated *inside* him instead, he thought he heard Someone say, "Saul, Saul, why persecutest thou Me?"

And he knew, in an instant, that it was Jesus speaking to him, mind to mind, infinite to finite, though he would not acknowledge the latter at all.

Saul folded his hand into a fist and shook it at that now frail-looking Figure above him, spewing an ancient curse at God-in-the-flesh, while pretending to himself that Jesus was little more than a charlatan.

As he thought that thought, as it settled in and took hold of him, Saul felt curiously ashamed, and this magnified the laughter around him though that laughter in reality was already dying away, the ridicule he suffered not nearly enough to sustain the attention of anyone anymore.

Saul stumbled back, and beyond his ability to control, words ripped past his lips, "I am sorry. I am so sorry. Please forgive me for—"

*You are forgiven, Saul. Now run from this place and try to hide, if you can. But you will not succeed, Saul, because you do not know the end of it.*

That fleeting instant of vulnerability was gone.

"I need nothing from You," he said defiantly, "because You are nothing to me. You are little more than the dirt under my feet."

*... now run from this place.*

And run the man from Tarsus did, brushing past the members of the Sanhedrin, and down the side of Golgotha where, at the bottom, he stopped, and saw a tomb in the side of the mount, and the round stone rolled to one side. He reached one hand out toward it briefly, then pulled it back.

And he commenced running again, through a *wadi* a short distance away, then above ground. He ran on and on—ducking into alleys and skirting stone walls. He felt pursued and did not know who chased him. After hours of aimless escape, senseless hiding, he collapsed in exhaustion and misery, unaware of his surroundings. After a while he managed to revive himself. And when he looked around he saw that he was near the home of Huram ben Sira. He stopped, looking at it with a hatred hot and vicious and frightening.

"Years of building respect!" he shouted to the air and the trees and whatever animals lurked out of sight. "And you have ripped that from me today. I shall not forget what has happened. I shall take vengeance just as surely as the sun rises and sets. God will bless me for doing this."

To his surprise, Hannah opened the front door. She stood there, listening to his rage and watching him sadly. Then her husband and her son joined her.

"How happy you three look this moment!" Saul exclaimed, mistaking their manner. "How you gloat!"

Huram ben Sira tried to talk to him, tried to reason with the man, but Saul would not be dissuaded from his anger.

"I have never had money or power!" he screamed. "I am paid very little from the temple treasury for my research. Tentmaking! That is how I earn enough to buy clothes and food. But I have no servants. I live in a humble house, not a grand one such as you have."

"But you have been serving God far longer than we have," Huram said. "Where was our dedication until yesterday?"

"And you are going to tell me the Nazarene changed all that?"

"He did, my dear Saul. Do you not see that? Do you not understand that He is guilty of nothing but being what He is?"

"A blasphemer, yes! I believe *that*."

"No, no! He is what He says."

"The Son of God would not die on a crude wooden cross as a common man. He and the two criminals with Him are—"

Saul was interrupted.

Thunder.

The sound of thunder rolling across the land, so strong that the ground shook underneath them.

And lightning, one bolt after another, more in the passage of a few seconds than any of them had ever seen.

Trees were set aflame, crude thatched huts and people also.

"Oh my—!" Huram exclaimed.

He saw, in the multiple flashes of light, creatures unlike any he had ever imagined, radiant and iridescent, shimmering with a vast array of colors beyond what he could count.

*Pointing* ....

They were pointing, not at him, not at Hannah or Saul.

At his son.

The creatures, with one accord, were pointing at Stephen.

Huram glanced over at his son, and he did not know whether to laugh or to cry, to celebrate or to—

Just as the lightning ceased, so did those beings blink out of sight, and he felt saddened for the loss of their beauty.

But something else was to happen that would shake them all.

*"Look!"* Saul heard Stephen cry out. "Step aside ... now!"

Just behind Saul, a man was stumbling toward him, clothes ablaze, arms outstretched, mouth moving but no words coming. He fell inches away, his body soon looking like a large log in a fireplace, blackened and shriveled.

Saul was stunned, every nerve in his body feeling the strain of what he had just seen, and he was again close to collapsing, fighting for strength to remain standing.

Seeing this, Stephen ran to his side and held him.

"Let go!" Saul demanded. "I am all right. I—"

But he was not all right. He was weak from shock, and his legs were trembling as they threatened to give way.

"Come inside," Stephen urged him. "Come inside and rest."

"Why are you doing this?" Saul asked. "I nearly broke your jaw. Why are you showing such kindness toward me?"

"Because Jesus spoke of mercy and humility and kindness."

Saul pulled away from him.

"Jesus again!" he muttered. "Always this Jesus. I see in Him a devil; you talk as though He is—"

Stephen smiled serenely, aware of exactly what Saul had been about to say.

"God?" he spoke. "But He is that, Saul. The Nazarene truly is—was—God in the flesh. And He loved you. He did not want you to perish. He—"

"Perish? Me? You insolent—"

Saul raised his hand to hit Stephen again and slapped him across the cheek. Huram started toward Saul, yelling at him.

"No, Father!" Stephen said. "I will do what Jesus wanted."

The cheek that had been hit was red now, and it hurt. Stephen turned the other one toward Saul.

"Strike this one too, if you want," he said with no trace of contempt.

Saul seemed ready to do just that but stopped his left hand about an inch from Stephen's face.

*... and he thought he heard—in his head, without his ears being involved, as though the voice originated* inside *him instead—the words,* "Saul, Saul, why persecutest thou Me?"

He let out a scream of rage and fear.

"Because You are *not* the Son of God!" he yelled.

Stephen and his parents could see that Saul was near the point of a complete breakdown.

"Come inside!" Stephen said as soothingly as he could manage.

*"I will see you perish first!"* Saul replied with mounting hysteria, and then he ran again, ran away from the three of them, ran away from their emerging pity. But he tripped and fell as another round of thunder, worse than the initial one, made the ground shaky as though it were in the grip of an earthquake.

*Golgotha ...*

Saul could see Golgotha from there, could see tiny figures scattering, leaving three dying men remaining on crosses.

"You are going to be dead soon!" he shouted defiantly as he turned and faced them. "And then I am going to hunt down Your followers one by one until their blood runs thick in the streets."

And then Saul of Tarsus was gone, disappearing into the premature night.

*A hurricane ...*

That was what it must have been, perhaps the most severe storm, outside of the Flood, that that region had ever known.

Continuing for hours, it was so severe that part of the Jerusalem temple was destroyed. More damage occurred elsewhere. Homes were reduced to rubble. People were killed as they tried to flee. Caiaphas himself had not made it back to his quarters before the worst of it began. Lightning seemed to be *aiming* for him, hitting trees and bushes on every side of him. He was surrounded by flame, his skin feeling the nearby heat.

And he too saw creatures.

But they were not the same as the radiant creatures Huram ben Sira had glimpsed. These vile monsters seemed to rise up from the ground beneath him, horrible manifestations of evil, loathsome in their festering countenances, with talon-like hands that reached for his robe, and tiny, blood-red eyes that terrified him with their sheer malevolence.

"I am a man of God!" he cried out. "You cannot have me."

The demonic beings seemed to nod their foul heads before speaking in words that bypassed his ears and went directly to his brain.

*"Yes, you are a man of God!"* they hissed. *"But which god?"*

Caiaphas shivered as he looked at the wreckage of his chariot and the body of his driver, whose death would not be easily forgotten for he had been struck by lightning, and every part of him had seemed to glow for an instant before he had tumbled to the ground.

Nor had the horses been willing to cooperate. Terrified, out of control, they galloped blindly into a *wadi*, pulling the chariot into it with them. Briefly Caiaphas was knocked unconscious. But the heavy rain of the storm hitting his face revived him, and he groggily awoke from the momentary blackness.

With no way to escape except by running, he climbed out of the *wadi* and found his way to the main road that led back into Jerusalem.

Bodies everywhere.

Once he glanced back at Golgotha and saw only one cross still standing, and the Nazarene yet hanging from it.

*I refuse to believe that You are behind this,* Caiaphas thought, *or that Yahweh is showing any displeasure over what I have done.*

Minutes later, the most powerful high priest in the nation's history approached the ancient and familiar walls of the city in which he had spent all of his adult life as well as a large percentage of his boyhood years.

*Just before the rain stopped …*

The storm had abruptly ended, and he slowed his pace as the danger seemed to pass.

*Just before the hailstones suddenly commenced …*

Large ones, many the size of oranges, the rest as big as fat grapes.

Caiaphas was being pummeled.

In panic the high priest started running again. The main gates were not more than a few hundred yards ahead.

One of the bigger hailstones hit the back of his left shoulder, causing pain so intense he thought he might pass out again.

His body was becoming sore in half a dozen places.

For a few seconds, Caiaphas feared that he might die. But just as he felt he could not go on, just as he thought he was falling for the last time, he saw in a vague haze brought on by pain and weakness someone familiar running toward him.

Nicodaemus.

"Not you!" Caiaphas exclaimed. "Why you?"

"An angel came to me and said that I should make all haste to the gates," Nicodaemus told him, "that someone there would need my help."

"You tried to warn me."

"Yes, I did. Joseph and I both did. But not only about this, Caiaphas."

"Much else, I know, for years now."

They reached the temple and hurried inside through a private side entrance to avoid contact with anyone since both men were exhausted and neither relished the task of explaining just then what had happened.

After stripping themselves of their wet clothing and slipping into dry robes, Caiaphas collapsed onto a large pillow on the floor of his inner quarters, motioning to Nicodaemus to do the same. Both rested for several minutes before saying anything.

The high priest was the first to speak.

"Jesus is dead now, is He not?" he asked.

"I do not see how it could be otherwise," Nicodaemus replied, squirming a bit in the robe that had been given him since it was much too big for someone of his far slighter frame. "It has been hours. Even—"

"What were you about to say?"

"You would not like it, Caiaphas."

A typical smirk settled on the high priest's face as he asked, "Has that stopped you before now?"

"Even for God in the flesh, a physical body can hold out only so long," Nicodaemus replied.

"But He has said that He will rise up again. Has that changed now that death has come? Was it only an idle boast to entice the masses?"

Nicodaemus hesitated.

"Speak up," Caiaphas told him.

"I have heard that Pilatus has ordered—"

Caiaphas knew what the other man was going to say, and he responded, "I *demanded* that he do so."

"Soldiers? To guard the entrance to wherever the body is to be buried? So my information is correct, then!"

"Very much so."

Nicodaemus sighed with a resignation acknowledging that God had answered his prayers but not in the way he had hoped.

"Joseph and I will be taking Him to a tomb as soon as the storm lets up."

"Where is it?"

Nicodaemus told him.

Caiaphas nodded as he replied, "Very good choice."

Strangely, the high priest's manner then softened even more.

"Out there ..." he started to say.

"You almost died."

"Almost...."

"You never came so close to death before, did you?"

Nicodaemus was sensing a vulnerability within Caiaphas, and he did not want to squander the potential for some fledgling change of attitude in a man who had seemed unreachable only the day before.

"I have not, Nicodaemus. I imagined ... I imagined—"

Stuttering was not something the high priest had done since he was a very young child, when it had made him an object of ridicule for other youngsters who cruelly gave him little peace throughout his childhood, embittering him even so many years later as an adult.

"I imagined what ... what it was like for the Nazarene."

He could not bring himself even to turn in the direction of the Place of the Skull.

"My death would have been instant, and yet for Him, there was incomparable agony ... agony for these long, long hours."

Caiaphas' hands were shaking, but he did not seem to care.

Nicodaemus noticed this and decided to say nothing.

"How many have I conspired to send to such a death?" the high priest continued morosely. "Yet I am the one who has escaped while they did not."

Caiaphas became more intent.

"Many widows live lonely lives because of me," he went on. "Do I pass by them on the street without ever knowing it? How much hatred do they have toward me?"

"Perhaps as much hatred as you had toward Jesus," Nicodaemus offered.

Caiaphas seemed on the verge of shedding tears at being reminded of that.

"You *truly* hated the Nazarene," Nicodaemus added.

"I did," the high priest acknowledged.

"Are you honest enough to admit why?"

Caiaphas did not hesitate.

"Because He was a blasphemer," he said.

Nicodaemus was determined not to let Caiaphas get away with so simplistic an answer.

"Has being so near death left you with your hypocrisy intact?" he asked with cynicism unusual for him.

"That *is* why, Nicodaemus," Caiaphas stressed, struggling to keep his temper under control.

"It may be *a* reason but it is not the paramount one."

"Then tell me what that is."

"Do you really want to hear it? And if you do, will you then throw me out and add me to your list of enemies to be disposed of at the most opportune moment?"

"I will do nothing of the sort. You have my word."

"You sought Jesus' death because you considered Him a threat. If He reigned ultimately, you would suddenly be subservient to another, and that was too much for you to contemplate, to accept."

In fact, Caiaphas did not become enraged but simply sat there, remembering, delving back into his state of mind during the days when he had first started receiving reports about Jesus, reports that told only of exemplary behavior by Him and every other member of the group of thirteen.

"I approached Him at the beginning, you know."

"I was unaware of that."

"I admired what He was telling people, until He began to give the impression that He was God."

"And that bothered you?"

"It seemed heretical at best."

"But still you were supportive?"

"At first, because I thought I might have misunderstood. That was when I arranged a meeting between us."

It had lasted only a short while, Caiaphas explained, because Jesus had reiterated what He had said previously and then added something else.

"When I return, all earthly institutions will be abolished," the Nazarene had said. "There will be a new heaven and a new earth."

*... all earthly institutions will be abolished.*

Those few words changed Caiaphas for the worst. All he could see was the elimination of his position as well as the Sanhedrin itself.

"I began to see how artificial He was, how manipulative," he told Nicodaemus. "He knew the power He had over people, and He took advantage of them, got them to believe whatever He said, no matter how ridiculous."

"Did you see that truly?" Nicodaemus asked. "Or did you merely talk yourself into such an absurd position?"

Just then one of the rabbis knocked on the door, and when given leave to enter, asked if he could pour them some wine. Both men welcomed the refreshment.

"Jesus repeatedly used the symbol of a vineyard," Caiaphas recalled. "'I am the vine,' He would say."

"I remember that," agreed Nicodaemus. "And you sought to use His drinking of wine against Him, accusing Him of being a drunkard."

Caiaphas waved his hand through the air.

"No more ..." he said.

"Does it hurt to be reminded of the lengths you will go to in order to guarantee the success of whatever twisted plan you might have hatched at any given moment?"

Caiaphas sighed.

"I am no longer the one the followers of Jesus will have to fear the most," he said cryptically.

Nicodaemus' palms became sweaty.

"What are you saying?" he asked.

"Saul."

"Of Tarsus? The noted scholar?"

"The very one."

"I had heard that he was—"

"You have heard *nothing* that tells the full truth!" declared Caiaphas with a solemnity that was frightening in itself.

"What about Saul?"

"I will seem no more than a mere fly on an elephant when compared with what *he* plans to do."

"What *can* he do?" Nicodaemus asked.

Caiaphas looked at the other man with disbelief.

"You are nearly as old as I am," he said, "and yet you sound so naïve! Do you not realize that?"

"I do not think as *you* seem quite accustomed to doing. Tell me now, please, what *will* Saul be attempting?"

"He wants young Johanan dead, for one thing."

Nicodaemus' eyes widened.

"I know the family," he said. "They are too rich, too powerful, even for a man of Saul's stature. They would surely be beyond his reach."

Caiaphas shook his head gravely.

"You are very wrong, my dear man," he said. "Saul is the most remarkable human being I have ever met. If he wants Johanan dead, then that young man had better savor whatever time he has left."

"I will tell Huram, and he will hire guards to keep Johanan safe."

"It won't be enough."

"But Saul is not superhuman, Caiaphas. He can only accomplish so much. In this case he will fail."

"What happens when Johanan travels?"

"The guards will go with him."

"I think such a young man would manage to evade them whenever he wanted to do so, regardless of any danger, if he saw an opportunity to continue with his mission. After what happened today, I wonder if anyone can keep him reined in for very long."

"Today? At Golgotha? I could not bear to go. I should have been there, yes, but I might have gone berserk and done something very foolish."

"As Johanan did."

And then the high priest told him what had happened.

Nicodaemus was shaken but not surprised.

"Now I understand why you think Saul would be dedicated to destroying Johanan," he said.

The two men talked for a few more minutes, and then Nicodaemus, some pain in his joints, stood with difficulty as he prepared to leave.

An odd expression on his face, Caiaphas reached out and gently folded his fingers around the other man's bony arm.

"I do wish you would stay," he said, a plaintiveness in his tone that greatly surprised Nicodaemus.

"But I need to warn the family."

"I am sure they suspect the danger already."

"But I—"

Caiaphas became more intense, a sudden edge of desperation about him as he said, "Nicodaemus, I need to talk with you."

"You experienced more than you have told me, did you not?"

Caiaphas could do nothing but admit that he was right.

"So dark, so awful …" he said, his nerves still frayed as he thought of the pure evil he had encountered.

"Then I shall stay, as you ask."

They continued on for the rest of the day and well into the night, a different Caiaphas emerging than Nicodaemus had ever known before.

tephen was allowed to stay in the vicinity of the Place of the Skull for as long as he wanted after the storm had passed, and everyone seemed to forget about the latest victims of Rome's power of life and death, returning to their homes, their businesses, lives that needed to be lived as usual.

*Those no longer lame ... the blind given sight ... the lepers made clean again ... they all left, some even laughing for whatever perverse reason ... left without looking back ... only one did that, a harlot with tears.*

But not Stephen.

He felt that he could not stay away.

First, he climbed to the top of Golgotha. The crosses were no longer there but splotches of blood were, and items the crowd had left behind, including little pieces of papyrus. He bent over and picked up several, tossing all but one back on the ground.

A note.

It read: "This day mankind committed its most shameful act."

But who had written it?

He probably would never know, though he guessed it might have been the youngest apostle, the only one of the twelve atop Golgotha, the others having fled to places of safety, their cowardice glaring.

Stephen approached the spot where the crosses had been set into permanent holes about a foot deep in the hard, ancient rock of that place.

*How many lives have been wiped out here?* he mused. *But none as precious as His.*

He knelt there, bowing his head.

"Father God, help me make my life count for Thee," he said. "Drain from it any waste, any frivolity. Help me to understand what You need me to know, and send me from Golgotha with a clear understanding of whatever mission You want me to pursue for Your honor and glory."

Voices.

Stephen heard voices below, and he stood, walking to the edge. Harsh voices.

Soldiers.

The Roman guards were engaging in idle conversation, trying to break the monotony of that particular assignment.

"What glorious service we have been given!" one exclaimed sarcastically. "All for the sake of mighty Rome."

"Yeah, I know … guarding the tomb of some Jew," another added cynically, "a wonderful use of manpower."

The third yawned.

"You two be on alert," he remarked. "I am going to get some sleep."

The others laughed.

Stephen waited for a moment, getting his emotions in order before he climbed back down the side of the hill.

A moment later he came to the tomb, a large, round stone rolled over the entrance. He started to approach the soldiers.

They both commanded him to stop.

If Pontius Pilatus had not done a favor for Huram ben Sira, Stephen would never have been allowed to get as close as he did, especially since it had been necessary to station several soldiers at the tomb to make sure Jesus' followers did not steal His body and pretend He had risen up as He claimed He would do.

"That is my greatest concern," the proconsul-governor had said. "At this point, I must decide not to trust anyone."

But Huram had been persuasive, and he had gotten a decree from the reluctant Pilatus, which Huram had given to his son.

"No one is allowed here!" one of the guards exclaimed, brandishing his lance in a way that left no doubt about whether he was prepared to use it. "Now get away!"

"But I—!" Stephen protested.

"*Go or else!*" the soldier told him. "Or did you not hear me?"

"I heard you."

"Then do what I say, or else you—"

At that point he started to walk toward Stephen and would not have hesitated to do him some harm.

"I have permission from the proconsul-governor," Stephen interrupted, not without some satisfaction.

"Where is it?" the Roman asked skeptically.

Stephen had been carrying the rolled piece of parchment under his right arm.

"Here!" he said.

The soldier was an older man, undoubtedly a veteran of combat all over the Roman world, and he tried to appear disinterested.

"Everything *is* in order," he acknowledged.

"Thank you. I will not get in the way."

"Oh, you can be very sure of that, young man."

For some reason, Stephen felt led to speak further with the centurion.

"What is your name?" he asked.

The other man found that curious but responded anyway, saying, "Decimus Paetus. Why do you ask?"

"I was just curious, sir, nothing more. Why is it that so many Roman names, first and last, end in 'us'?"

"Have no idea," the man grunted before walking away.

Stephen stood quietly and stared at the large stone, visualizing the lifeless body behind it.

*The evil that men do*, he thought.

He could have walked away, could have returned to his home, but he chose to remain at that spot. All through the night and the following day he waited, not knowing why.

Until midnight of the second night.

Stephen had dozed off and might have remained in that state for some time, but then the ground started to rumble.

An earthquake!

He jumped to his feet, assuming the Roman soldiers would be preparing to leave that spot if rocks were starting to fall.

Asleep.

"How could you be sleeping *now?*" Stephen asked. "How—?"

Light.

That remarkable light again, the one into which he had been submerged just before he reached the Garden of Gethsemane, apparently the same light his father had encountered.

And a voice again, *the voice*.

"Stand back, My young servant," it asked of him.

And Stephen obeyed immediately.

The round stone covering the entrance to the tomb seemed to roll back of its own accord, not slowly either, but as though it was a piece of cotton and someone had blown against it. It moved instantly.

And then something rushed *out* of the tomb!

Something quite horrible. A loathsome presence that made Stephen recoil, barely able to witness it.

"The law of sin and death does not apply to My Son," the voice told him, "and the creatures of sin and death and darkness *must* flee."

And flee they did, along with others like the first one and some more horrible, vague shapes in the midst of the all-encompassing light reduced to skittering fear and panic as they tried to evade it, blinded by its intensity and its purity.

*Screaming!*

How these creatures screamed, no less in anguish than if they had been of flesh and blood and were having their skin stripped from them layer by layer.

One stood before Stephen and seemed to be reaching out for him, seemed to look him over as future prey and—

"No!" that wondrous voice declared. "You shall not take My servant with you to the pit of damnation, not this night or any other."

*A roar ...*

So heinous, so cruel and terrifying that it seemed to be born of all the evil that ever was or would be, and it was flung at Stephen, ten thousand demons venting their fury.

But then Jesus appeared.

In that instant, the Son of God stood at the entrance to the tomb, His countenance more brilliant than the light itself.

And evil fled, hissing and growling and defiant, but powerless to stand firm before heaven's Son. Even so, evil turned for a moment before hell sucked it back in, glanced at Stephen and declared, "Another time, another place, for it is not over. We *shall* have you."

Stephen heard a sound in the background, then it surrounded them, drowning out all else, a sound like the beating of ten thousand upon ten thousand wings. Wobbly, fighting to remain standing, he collapsed suddenly, hitting the hard ground with a thud. Just before Stephen lost consciousness, he saw Jesus standing over him. Then the Savior bent down and whispered into his ear, "Do not fear light or darkness or anything else of this world or another, for I shall be with you always."

## Chapter Seventeen

S tephen and the soldiers returned to consciousness a few minutes later, astonished to see the giant round stone rolled to one side and the entrance unobstructed.

*Empty.*

*Each of the soldiers went inside the tomb then stumbled out, their faces pale white. Men of combat they were, but they were frightened just then, afraid of judgment from Pontius Pilatus for what he surely would perceive as negligence on their part.*

*It was Stephen's turn now to enter and look at the vacant slab. He half-expected to hear the voice again, but that was not to be just then. That encounter was to happen a short while later as he hurried back to the home where he had spent all of his twenty-three years of life but would stay for only another day....*

When Stephen returned to his home, his parents wanted an explanation of his arrival at such an hour, when he had been missing for more than thirty-six hours.

He stood without answering at first.

After bowing his head for a moment, he looked at them and said, "I have something to tell you."

They all sat down on the leather-covered chairs.

"I was at the tomb," Stephen started to say with some hesitancy.

"I know," Huram ben Sira assured him. "Remember, I was the one who secured permission for you."

"Father ..."

"Yes, son?"

"Jesus is—!"

Stephen started to sob, but from the joy he felt, for there was no sorrow in him, only the reality of what he had witnessed.

"What about Jesus?" Huram asked, unaccustomed to the sort of behavior his son was manifesting.

"Gone," Stephen muttered, still struck with the awe of it.

"His body has been *stolen?*"

Shaking his head vigorously, Stephen jumped to his feet.

"*Risen!*" he exclaimed, too excited to elaborate beyond that single word, which he practically shouted.

Both Huram and Hannah looked at their son dumbly.

"Risen?" his mother repeated.

"I saw Him in the tomb's entrance," Stephen went on. "He was standing there, looking at me with love beyond anything I ever thought was possible."

"He was *standing*—!" Huram spoke disbelievingly.

"*Yes! Yes! Yes!*" Stephen assured them, knowing he was close to babbling. "He knew my name. Jesus was alive and calling my name. He was so radiant, as though He had been to heaven and back, still surrounded by its glory."

Hannah glanced at her husband and he at her, and then they too were on their feet, laughing ecstatically.

"I was so weak from what I saw that I fell," Stephen said. "Just before I passed out, I looked up and there He was beside me, speaking to me."

"You heard Him?" Huram remarked. "What did He say? You must tell us! Tell your parents everything."

*Do not fear light or darkness or anything else of this world or another, for I shall be with you always....*

Even as Stephen repeated those words, his manner changed, both joy and solemnity in it at the same time.

"How wonderful!" Huram exclaimed. "You were with God, son. *You were in the presence of Yahweh!*"

But then the serious side that the young man was manifesting took over, and the joy disappeared.

"You seem so sad...." Huram observed, wondering how this could be so in view of what had happened. "First you are smiling from ear to ear, and now you seem more like someone at a funeral, my son. Tell me, please, what is wrong?"

"It happened again," Stephen told him.

"What happened?" his father asked.

"A short while later, I experienced His presence again, after I left Golgotha."

"Another visitation, is that what you are telling your mother and me?"

"Yes, a second time."

"On the way home?"

"Just a very few minutes from here."

"Tell us about it, son."

Stephen seemed all the more forlorn as he spoke to his parents. "I have to leave, Father and Mother."

"For how long?"

Stephen was struggling to convey to them what he knew he could not avoid, the truth as the Son of God had given it to him.

"For the rest of my life," he said, each word a burden for him. "After tomorrow morning, you will never see me again."

Huram and Hannah said nothing for a moment, stunned.

No words came to either of them because they could not quite grasp what they had just heard.

"I must go on a mission," Stephen told them, breaking the silence. "It will take me into the surrounding provinces and beyond."

"Beyond?" Huram repeated. "Where?"

"To Petra and other places."

"That's all the way—"

Hannah gasped when she realized just how far away their son would be going.

"What sort of mission?" Huram asked nervously.

Stephen kept his voice as calm as possible when he replied, "To start colonies of believers."

Huram's tone was changing, and Stephen saw this clearly but knew it was inevitable, given what he was telling his parents.

"Believers? Believers? What are you talking about?" his father asked, puzzled and alarmed and more than a little frightened.

"The Nazarene's."

"But Jesus is dead," Huram ben Sira declared, as though he were talking to a rather backward child, not someone who had passed through his teenage years and was now supposed to be a man.

"I saw Him rise."

Huram brushed that aside with something resembling contempt and remarked, "So you say!"

"You were just dancing in joy!" Stephen reminded him. "You thought it was worth an instant celebration!"

"That was before you told me that this Jesus is going to steal my son, somehow reaching beyond the grave and into my home. How can I allow that, my son? How can I allow a misplaced Nazarene to wreck my family?"

"He is not stealing me. I go willingly, Father."

"He has cast a spell on you. And you call that willing?"

"Jesus has shown me the gates of heaven!"

"And angels, that sound was coming from angels?"

"I believe it was. I could hear their wings, Father, thousands at the same time. You have no idea how beautiful that sounded, so peaceful and sweet, a sound almost inconceivable to anyone who has never heard it before."

Huram seemed to be chewing on something as he waited a few seconds before speaking again.

"You will no longer *be* my son if you leave your mother and me without ever returning," Huram told him. "Get anyone you want to become a follower, ten of them, a hundred, a thousand or more, but you are always to return to *this* house, *is that clear?*"

Stephen wanted to reach out and hug his father and not let go until *forcing* into him some understanding of what was happening in the life of his son.

"But I cannot, Father," he said.

"You cannot, or you will not, Johanan?"

"It is both."

"Both? Jesus is now a prophet and telling you everything in your future, and that is how you know about—"

"Yes ..." Stephen interrupted him. "Until my mission is over."

Hannah spoke up then.

"Over?" she said. "What do you mean, *over*? What are you saying?"

"My death, Mother," he told her. "In a year or less, I will be dead."

"And you want to leave while *knowing* this?"

"I will be the first of many."

"But none of *them* is my son. Only you are. I lose you, and I have no more family in this world."

Stephen wondered whether it was his own life or his family's continuing bloodline that most concerned his father. Not wanting to upset the man that he loved, he held his tongue for a moment.

"Father, is it me you love or—?" he started to say at last, then stopped.

"What were you going to say, my son?" Huram asked.

"I was just thinking—"

Still the son of Huram ben Sira could not continue. But, as it turned out, he need not have done so.

"It has worried me, too," Huram told him.

"What has, Father?"

"What you tried to ask."

"But you cannot read my thoughts."

"You are right. I cannot do that. But I can *feel* what you feel. I can do this, yes, I can, because I have asked myself the questions that must have occurred to you."

"Are you so sure, Father?" Stephen posed, not convinced as yet.

"*Family blood!*" Huram blurted out.

That was important to every Jew, one reason why genealogies were so extensive in Scripture.

"It is why we *exist* at all," he continued. "A family line dies, and there is nothing but dust, words etched on grave markers."

His eyes were bloodshot.

"For centuries my family has existed. If you die without a family of your own, all that is over, that heritage—"

Stephen reached out and embraced his father.

"You are right," he said. "All that you say has been on my mind as well."

"But you never thought about death before now," Huram protested.

"I have not, but the pressure to start a family of my own has been part of my thoughts ever since I knew enough about such matters."

"You never said anything to me, my son," Huram replied.

"I did not want to distress you, Father," Stephen told him honestly. "You might have wondered about me."

"About whether you liked women or not?"

"Yes …"

"I could never have thought you guilty of what you are suggesting, *never!*"

"But I am still a virgin, Father. I have had no one."

"Obeying the laws of God makes you more a man—not less!" Huram stated what needed to be said then.

Stephen hugged his father more tightly, enjoying the man's warmth.

"I think now—" he started to say.

Huram drew away from him a bit.

"Go ahead," he urged. "Nothing you say could shame you in front of me."

"I think now that God knew what was going to happen before I was ever born," Stephen remarked.

Hannah let out a muted cry, and both men turned to her, thinking she was in the midst of an attack of some sort.

She extended her arms full in front of her.

"Come to me," she said, "come to me, my only son, my beloved child."

And he did what she asked, letting her arms fold around him.

"I have had dreams over the years," she said, tears flowing from her eyes and touching his cheeks as well as her own. "I have seen you walk away from here. I cried out for you, begging you to return to me, but you could not. It was as though someone was pulling you in another direction."

Stephen pressed closer to his mother.

"It is so hard," he said barely above a whisper. "I feel as if I can never go, yet I know I must or I will grieve my Lord."

He started sobbing as he and his mother held each other. And then he felt another hand touch his right shoulder, resting there ever so gently, and a voice whispered to him, "You will always be my son, no matter what you do, no matter where you go. God has just spoken to me, and I know that He will be by your side even if your mother and I cannot."

Stephen was surprised that not only his parents gathered to bid him farewell the next morning. Many friends gathered as well.

"How did you all find out?" he asked as he turned from kissing his mother and father good-bye and saw the crowd forming on the street in front of the only home he had known all his life, more than a score of young men and women altogether.

Including Nekoh and Ahiram.

"Your father sent servants to alert everyone," Nekoh said.

"Hoping to dissuade me from leaving, no doubt," Stephen replied.

Huram ben Sira left the front doorway to stand in front of his son and the others.

"To *encourage* you!" he exclaimed with some indignation. "I would *never* oppose the will of Yahweh!"

Ahiram walked up to his friend, looked into his eyes, and asked, "But why *are* you doing this? You are giving up everything."

Stephen closed his eyes briefly, praying for the right words to reach Ahiram's very soul, and then he opened them again, a hint of tears showing.

"Would you give your life for me?" he asked simply.

Ahiram pretended to hesitate to consider that possibility then smiled as he said, "Of course I would."

Nekoh stepped forward this time.

"So would I!" he exclaimed.

And those words arose in a common shout from most of the others.

Stephen's voice trembled as he told them all, "And I would die for you! That is what friendship means. That is what *we* mean to one another."

A young woman who seemed to be ignored by the others broke away from the crowd and walked slowly up to him. No one spoke, most of the young men holding their breath because they easily recognized her as a former prostitute with whom not a few had slept since entering their teenage years, considering this a necessary part of "growing up" while ignoring the moral implication of what they were doing.

"I am Rebekkah," she said, sounding awkward and yet happy at the same time.

"Yes, I know," Stephen assured her, remembering a previous encounter between them not so very long ago.

"I first saw you last year," she said, half-smiling.

Stephen was not nervous like his friends but expectant, wondering just why this woman had joined the others.

"Not far from the market," he said, returning her smile.

She was pleased by his recollection and also by his lack of shame over it, sensing all too well the apprehension being felt by other young men behind her.

"You remember!" she exclaimed. "I could not be sure you would."

"I remember it well, Rebekkah."

"Two of your friends tried to get you to go with me, but you would not no matter how much they urged you. I could see what your heart was like, your soul. But, still, you are so fine looking that I tried to persuade you also."

"You need not—" Stephen interrupted, intending to tell her she need not shame herself in front of so many witnesses.

"I must do this," she said. "You may not understand, but let me do as I feel God has convicted me."

There was no way Stephen could argue with that, so he kept silent and listened to Rebekkah.

"Temptation is not sin," she told him with a convincing wisdom that startled everyone who heard her. "Giving in to it is where sin begins. And you would have nothing of what I could offer that day."

She paused, her heart beating faster, and then asked, "Do you remember what you told me?"

He honestly did not, and told her so.

"I am not surprised," Rebekkah said.

"Why is that?" Stephen asked.

"You told me nothing. You just turned and walked away, which no one your age had ever done. But God spoke to me instead. I heard Him so clearly that I thought you would stop and wonder whose voice it was, so magnificent and pure and strong."

She closed her eyes, remembering.

*You shall not touch this one, Rebekkah. He is to serve Me. He is to give up his very life in witness to My glory.*

Rebekkah fell to her knees.

"I felt so unclean," she said, "so aware of every filthy act I had ever committed, every young man I had ever caused to lose his virginity and sin in the presence of Almighty God. I wanted to die."

She was looking at Stephen now with an intensity that made him uncomfortable.

"I thought of you, of what we had almost done, and I fell on my face, begging God to forgive me."

No one was moving.

There were no sounds of any kind, as though even the birds were resting as Rebekkah spoke.

"I felt a hand wrap around each arm," she went on, "and I thought you had come back, either to change your mind or out of pity, and I looked up. I looked up into a brilliant light, so strong that I should have been blinded by it, but I was not."

Both Huram and Stephen stopped breathing for a moment, their own encounters with the light as strong as ever in their minds.

"Suddenly I was being lifted up. And I knew I stood before my God, oh, how I knew it was Him; there was no doubt—His voice, His—"

She saw the expressions on the faces of those gathered nearby, disbelief becoming something else, touched with awe.

"I confessed my sins, and I felt them fall away from me as though they were heavy pieces of metal weighing me down."

Rebekkah smiled as she continued.

"I started dancing," she said. "I could not stop. I felt as light as an ostrich feather and twice as white. All of a sudden, the light disappeared, and I saw the Nazarene standing in front of me."

"'Remember always what has happened to you,'" He told me, "'and never return to the sin that ensnared you. Do this, and you will one day find your reward in heaven.'"

Rebekkah stopped talking and stepped closer to Stephen, kissing him lightly on the cheek, then told him, "You were the Lord's instrument that day, bringing me face to face with what once was but would never be again. May God bless you and keep you; may He make His light shine upon you."

Hannah had waited for Rebekkah to finish, and now she spoke up.

"I give up my son this day to Yahweh," she said. "And I know he shall never return to me alive. As a mother I know I could never do this. As someone who embraces her Creator, I know I must."

Stephen hugged her for the last time, and he did the same with his father. Then he walked toward Nekoh and Ahiram.

"It is so hard," he acknowledged.

"How can we let you go?" Ahiram told him. "Yet how can we keep you here?"

"I do not want you to die," Nekoh added. "None of us may ever know when ... when—"

He started sobbing, not caring what anyone thought of him, and rested his head against Stephen's chest.

"I shall think of you every day for the rest of my life," he said.

And then Stephen left them behind as he walked up the dirt road, heading toward Emmaus, where he felt the Lord wanted him to go. He dared not turn around, dared not see his mother and his father and all those others in tears, for he had to stay on the course set long ago, set before the foundation of the world by the God who would soon usher him past the gates of heaven, ten thousand angels bringing him the welcome of eternity.

# — Chapter Eighteen —

*S*o the last year of his life was to begin that mist-shrouded morning as he left his home. It would be a year, short a few days, during which Stephen's natural intelligence and a special anointing given him by Almighty God would carry this young man from country to country, those surrounding Israel. He was received first with suspicion, but then his personality, youthfully zestful, concerned and loving as well, helped break down the barriers, and people were naturally drawn to him. The women especially responded to his dark-haired good looks, and even when he showed them, discreetly, that he would have no relationship with any of them they stayed, listening to the words that passed his lips. They were words of extraordinary wisdom, and with such power that the rumor started in some places that Stephen was the Nazarene reincarnated, forcing the young man to squelch that notion, telling one and all how such a belief pleased Satan, not God, that it was a heresy from the pit of hell ...

Sometimes Stephen was hungry and had no immediate source for food.

That in itself required a considerable amount of adjustment for him. At home he could count on hunger pangs being satisfied with a simple call to a servant for whatever he wanted. Instantly, it would be set before him, at a table or in bed a short time later, even if his hunger struck in the middle of the night.

*All I had to do was ask,* he thought as he sat by the side of a dirt road and looked at the stretch of land ahead of him. *Nothing was refused unless it was not available at all, and then a substitute was suggested.*

Those days were gone.

He had left everything behind him.

Sometimes he had doubts about the wisdom of what he had done. Might it have been better for him to remain where he was and witness for Jesus among the household staff, the neighbors, and even his father's business associates and his vast network of customers spread throughout the land of Israel?

Loneliness.

That was another hazard of the new life he had chosen. He would meet, from that first day and beyond, only strangers unless by some coincidence somehow he chanced upon someone he had met through his father on business trips outside of Jerusalem. Otherwise all were strangers with whom he would spend minutes or a day at most and then leave them to journey to another location.

*Is this truly what You want me to do, Lord?* Stephen asked during such times of doubt and frustration. *How do I know that I am going in the direction You wish? I do not hear Your voice reassuring me.*

But he continued in prayer and did the best he could, although sometimes his dedication showed some cracks when the hunger or the loneliness or the memories hit him. Such moments generally came in the midst of long stretches between villages, one dirt road after another, dust billowing behind him as he walked, the overhead sun bringing temperatures to more than one hundred degrees. More than once, the heat overcame him, and he collapsed.

But he survived, because God was not yet prepared to call him home. He survived because other travelers would see him and stop and help, some sharing a portion of their own provision of water, some offering a little wine, while a few took him into their chariots and brought him to a place of refreshment many miles up whatever road he happened to be on. And since they, too, were usually tired and thirsty and hungry, they stopped along with him and listened as he spoke of the Nazarene.

Stephen did not collapse often, but there were many times when he just had to rest, and this surprised him at first since he had assumed he was of stronger stock. But then he realized that each time someone approached him to offer help, this was a new opportunity to spread the Good News. So he ceased being concerned about his physical capabilities, understanding that his concern had been touched with a bit of pride and thus the experience of *needing* help served the additional purpose of humbling him.

He was taken into the homes of rich and poor alike, eating on a hand-carved cherrywood table one day with servants attending him, and the next, sitting on the bare ground inside a mud hut, eating the most basic of meals with a family wearing rags seated around him.

"We have few of the good things the rich enjoy," a little, somewhat bent over, but kindly man named Machir told him. "But I have managed to avoid hunger for my loved ones and myself. Our clothes are what you see. This is the only house we have, and there is my old, old camel, but our stomachs are never empty. I am a proud man, you see, and will do what I must to make sure that food—"

He started to weep.

"What is it, my good man?" Stephen asked him, deeply concerned.

"You have spoken of heaven," his host remarked, recalling a conversation of a few minutes ago.

Stephen nodded silently, allowing the other man to say what he wanted without interruption.

"Will there be hunger in heaven?" Machir asked, his concern centered on an area that had been part of his life since his birth nearly forty years before.

Stephen was touched by the simple honesty of that question.

"No, there will be no hunger, Machir," he answered honestly, his wide lips curling upward into a smile.

"I sometimes cannot sleep at night, worrying about tomorrow, wondering what I will have to do to keep my family alive."

"All of that will have vanished."

"Will there be tears in heaven?"

"No tears, because no one will have to cry."

Stephen glanced from Machir to the man's wife and then to his six children.

"Any kind of worry and fear and hunger and pain will have no place in God's kingdom," he told them.

"And death?" Rachel, the wife, spoke hesitantly. "Will death be a part of this heaven you teach?"

"Only eternal life … no more tears, no more sorrow, no more parting."

Machir clapped his hands together.

"Then you and I shall talk further about such matters," he declared. "You will stay with us tonight, yes?"

"I *will* stay, my friend, and I am happy to do so."

Which he was.

Companionship.

He would not be alone that night. Though he was staying with strangers, that was far better than being utterly isolated, seeing only the darkness and hearing only creatures of the night call out unexpectedly.

Machir and his loved ones, his wife and the three smallest children, slept outside that night. At first Stephen protested, but his host insisted that their guest be treated properly.

"They will get used to it," he said. "We have been poor for generations. Once I am gone, they will have to fend for themselves."

"You are not well?" asked Stephen.

"I think I shall die not of any disease but of weariness that sweeps over me. My heart feels weaker as each day passes."

Stephen's concern was immediate.

"Do you have any trade?" he asked.

Stephen was unintentionally condescending, but Machir let this pass without giving him a retort.

"Like your Jesus," he said simply, "I am but a carpenter—that is, when I can find any work at all."

Stephen's face lit up as he told the other man, "Let me send you to my father, then. He may have good news for you."

"Where is your father?"

"Near Jerusalem."

Machir's manner changed.

"That is very far," he replied, a disappointed tone to his voice. "Where would my family and I stay if we went where you are suggesting?"

Stephen was given money sometimes by those to whom he witnessed, or he did odd jobs from time to time. It so happened that he had some coins now. These he gave freely to Machir.

"I cannot take what you have," the man protested, "since it is obvious that you are giving me everything you have."

"I have little, but I choose to live as I do," Stephen told him. "For you, there has been no choice. My father is wealthy, Machir, and he will use your carpentry skills at home or in his business if you tell him that I sent you."

"But how will he know my claim is genuine?"

Stephen thought for a moment then added, "Tell my father that I still remember fondly the day he started to teach me how to swim in the Sea of Galilee. He was expecting me to be quite awkward, but I was so much better than that. After just a short while, I was swimming well, and he seemed so proud of me."

Machir nodded.

"If I were your father, that would convince me," he agreed.

Just as they were ready to go to sleep for the night, Machir asked, "Will I ever see you again?"

"Only in heaven," replied Stephen, wincing a bit as he always did when he told someone that, because he had become adjusted to leaving home but the thought of saying good-bye to mortal life altogether still had a slight edge of dread.

"But you may return home one day," Machir pointed out.

This new friend of Stephen's had touched upon the center of that dread, the realization that Stephen would die before his parents, that they would be the ones to bury him, not the other way around.

"No, I will not," Stephen told him, "for it is apparently God's will that I die soon."

Machir was startled.

"How could you know that?" he asked.

"It is what I have said since before I began this journey."

"And your parents are aware?"

"Yes. I concealed nothing from them."

Machir was tired but found what Stephen had told him to be fascinating.

"If you stayed home, you might live a long and full life," he said.

Stephen considered that briefly and replied, "I suppose that that might be the case; yes, it might."

"So you willingly go to your doom?"

"It is not my doom. It will be my death, but the two need not be the same, Machir."

"How your parents must worry!"

Stephen was silent, for thinking about the impact upon his loved ones was perhaps the worst burden he carried, more than his own hunger and the loneliness.

"Yes ..." he said after a few more moments. "But I have to believe that if God is going to take care of me, then when I am gone He will not forget that they will need His sustenance—perhaps even more than I do."

"When you go to the heaven that you have described," Machir spoke, "they must cope with the world you leave behind."

The two men soon drifted off to sleep after that, the older one thinking of a journey that would send him to Jerusalem, the younger one pondering the continuance of one that would take him ever further away.

*Six months later ...*

Stephen had reached countless numbers of people with the Good News, though he never kept any records so he could not even guess the total. But piling up a long list of converts was not his goal.

"I never want to be after mere numbers," he told a rabbi named Hilqiyahu who put him up for two nights in the man's modest home near the village of Achzib, which was located on the coast.

His host, tall and broad-shouldered, looked more like an athlete or a soldier than a rabbi. Hilqiyahu nodded appreciatively.

"I feel good hearing you say that," he replied warmly. "But what *are* you after, if I may ask?"

There was no hint of any cynicism whatsoever in that question, just a healthy and friendly curiosity.

"Salvation," Stephen told him.

"But I am already one of God's people," Hilqiyahu pointed out. "How can I be more saved than that? Are you able to tell me this, my young friend?"

A fraction of the other man's age and not quite at the halfway point in his odyssey, Stephen was more than a little intimidated in such a situation, but he was gradually losing this last bit of insecurity.

"May I ask you something?" he asked with some caution, trying to keep his voice from wavering.

"You may indeed," Hilqiyahu agreed as they sat on a rug outdoors, toward the rear of the rabbi's property.

"How can one be assured of eternal life in heaven? Is it only necessary to be born a Jew?" Stephen asked respectfully.

Hilqiyahu nodded appreciatively and replied, "To be born a Jew and to lead a good life, yes."

"So, just being a Jew is not enough, then?"

"Certainly that is the case."

"What constitutes a good life?"

Hilqiyahu hesitated, grunting a bit, as he eyed someone half his age who was displaying an uncommon amount of wisdom.

"I see where you are heading," he acknowledged perceptively.

"Am I impertinent?" Stephen asked.

"No," Hilqiyahu said, "but I am afraid I was unprepared a moment ago for how astute you are."

"Someone as young as I am?"

"Precisely."

Hilqiyahu was not offended by Stephen's forthrightness but was caught off guard by someone so young.

"Let me think on this for a moment," he said.

And so neither man talked for the next several minutes until the rabbi said, "When I was very young, younger than you are now, I developed an interest in matters of the spirit—Scripture and such. I saw all around me those who were Jews, some of them quite wealthy, who would live according to a doctrine that seemed to suggest they could help others, could give much money to the poor, could help their local synagogue in every conceivable way. And yet, these same men treated their wives and children poorly, shouting at them, slapping them, showing little or no respect for those they were supposed to love unstintingly."

"And it troubled you greatly, I am sure," Stephen chose to interject.

"That it did, young man, that it did. All I had learned from those who taught me the doctrines and precepts—first as a child, later as a man—seemed only to reinforce the idea that God accepted *any* Jew who did certain charitable acts.

"Oh, of course, such a man obviously could not be a murderer or a homosexual or an adulterer or anything as despicable and of a transparently ungodly nature as that, but basically the Jewish birthright plus good acts were supposed to be sufficient to guarantee life in heaven for eternity."

Stephen was beginning to understand the other man's outlook.

"And as someone of principle," he offered, "you have never been able to put your concerns to rest."

"I have not."

Stephen sighed and was about to speak again when Hilqiyahu interrupted him.

"You are going to tell me, I suppose, that Jesus is the answer," he said.

"I am," Stephen admitted.

"Though it may surprise you, rest assured that I am inclined to agree that this is a possibility."

"What you say *does* surprise me."

"You see, my dear young friend, God gave me a mind that is blessed—though I sometimes think it can be something of a curse—to search out the truth, to seek what is behind things that do not seem altogether right and proper."

Stephen studied the other man, pleased that the conversation had taken the turn it had but sensing that something was being withheld.

"You have heard of Jesus before now," he ventured.

"I have," Hilqiyahu confessed. "I was hoping that God would send someone to me, someone who would state ideas that were more than mere platitudes, specious answers to troubling and profound questions."

Abruptly, the rabbi's manner changed to an extent that startled Stephen.

"I am grateful that He sent you to me," he remarked, "but you must be careful."

"Careful?" Stephen mused. "Of what?'

"Of *whom!* I speak of a man."

"I do not understand."

"Saul of Tarsus was here less than a week ago."

At first, Stephen did not find that revelation to be a foreshadowing of any kind of danger. He had thought about Saul often over the past months, praying that the man would change, that his hatred of anyone who followed the Nazarene would cease.

"And did he speak of me or my loved ones?" he asked.

"He did, and with much loathing," Hilqiyahu recalled.

"He has felt that way all this time?"

"My impression is that he has. Do you have any idea why?"

Actually Stephen had considered just that question more than once since he left home. Though he had no answer, he had some suspicion.

"Pride," he said.

"What sort of pride?" Hilqiyahu asked. "Over what?"

"That Jesus had made certain claims and achieved the fame He did without ever once consulting with Saul."

"Saul felt he was being ignored?"

"I can come up with nothing else."

Hilqiyahu grunted a couple of times.

"Perhaps he thought that he was the one people should be seeking, not Jesus," Stephen observed. "All Saul could see was an itinerant individual who spoke with apparent wisdom. Someone who seemed totally without the training Saul possessed, for which Saul had studied most diligently since his youth. Someone claiming not just that He was a great teacher—that would have been hard enough for Saul to tolerate—but Who presented Himself as the Son of God, the Messiah so longed for by every Jew over the past several thousand years.

"No other reason seems as clear as that," Stephen concluded. "Saul convinced himself that his mission was a righteous one because of his dedication to wiping out all heresies and punishing all heretics."

"So he could go out and persecute Jesus' followers without an inconvenient attack of conscience!" Hilqiyahu completed Stephen's summary of the disturbing situation.

Hilqiyahu solemnly faced his young guest.

"You are in danger," he said.

"I know. I have known that since I first took the path God laid out for me."

"And you will do nothing to protect yourself?"

"If God's intention is that I go to be with Him soon, is not this protection you mention the same as trying to thwart His will?"

"Interesting *dikhotomia*," Hilqiyahu admitted. "I have always considered prudent behavior one of the ways we serve Yahweh."

"Which is the most prudent way," Stephen posed, "following our will—or God's?"

"Then we must be certain that what we perceive as His will is not our own will in disguise."

Though Stephen had learned much over the months of his odyssey, he was constantly reminded that others had wisdom that he would do well to listen to with great care.

"But if I gave up all this, if I returned to my home and resumed some measure of my old life, what good would that do? It would not placate Saul, and abandoning my mission certainly would not help others come to know Jesus. Christians will be imprisoned, and many will die, regardless of my actions."

"If I cannot persuade you to return, let me send some men along with you," Hilqiyahu suggested, "at least for the next few months. Consider this my contribution."

"Contribution?"

"Yes, to the work you are doing. I want to be a part of it."

"But that means Jesus must be a part of you."

"So be it, good Stephen, so be it!"

And so this middle-aged benefactor knelt under the stars that night and accepted Jesus Christ as his Savior and Lord. But no guard accompanied young Stephen the next morning. Instead his host awakened to find a note that read, "If God be for me, who can be against me? If God wants me to enter His kingdom today or tomorrow or next week or a month from now, who are we to tell Him no? Who are we to stand in the way? I am as safe as the blessed Lord wishes me to be, dear Hilqiyahu. Bless you, my friend. It comforts me to know that we shall meet again one day at heaven's gates."

Despite the humiliation he had suffered at the hands of Stephen, Saul of Tarsus had during the ensuing months been willing to give up his pursuit of the young man, having convinced himself that, in this single instance, he could let simple friendship, however frayed, override the need to stamp out every *vestigium* of the Nazarene's influence.

*After all,* he thought, *I have known Johanan throughout his young life, and I cannot picture him as a terribly effective evangelist, certainly not as successful as the others seem to have been recently.*

The others: Mattiyah, Petros, and the rest of the remaining eleven apostles.

That none of these men as yet were dead, or had even remained in prison for long, bothered Saul, especially since he had heard that their influence had reached as far as the household of Caesar.

*I could not believe, at first, what I was hearing,* he recalled. *How dangerous this new group is, like a spreading epidemic.*

Screams interrupted his thoughts.

They came from the dungeon below the level where he was standing.

"Renounce him!" a loud voice called out from below.

Saul could not hear the response, but then the screaming continued, indicating that the prisoner had not rejected the Nazarene after all.

A Roman dungeon.

Saul had looked at the sign over the entrance.

*The Mamertine …*

Chiseled into stone, it was a symbol to anyone who might think even casually about opposing Rome in any significant way. It was reserved primarily for traitors, including insurrectionists such as Barabbas and, before him, Spartacus in 72 B.C. Saul had been able to prevail upon his contacts in the Roman Senate to allow the dungeon to be used, when not otherwise occupied, for Christian prisoners; Saul had persuaded them that certain followers of the Nazarene were more dangerous than others—the leaders who had the ability to incite mobs, not the simple Christians who were more like sheep than shepherds. Emperor Tiberius would have balked at a general persecution, so Saul craftily chose a less comprehensive approach, securing permission to deal with Christians on a "local" basis, whereby many were confined or whipped or stoned to death.

"Renounce the One called Jesus!" the demand was heard again from within the bowels of the Mamertine.

And a weak voice cried out, "Never! I say again, never!"

Something about that voice seemed like a javelin aimed directly at Saul's heart, and he jumped as he heard it.

*This one sounds like a mere child!* he thought.

He assumed he was mistaken and did nothing at first, but then he heard the voice again.

Saul had walked back inside the Mamertine and was standing in the upper room, a large chamber hewn out of rock. It was hardly opulent, but it was not cramped like the one directly below it, which could be reached only through a round hole in the floor.

"What is going on down there?" Saul called out.

Silence.

"I asked you a question!" he said more sternly this time.

"And I answer a *Jew* when I please!" a baritone voice replied.

"I shall tell the emperor of your manner."

"And he shall tell me of a little pest he must placate for political reasons but who otherwise turns his stomach."

Saul was enraged but knew that his influence went only so far, and it would be unwise to spend it all at once.

"The Christian down there," Saul went on, his tone less accusatory, "I must say that he sounds quite young."

The Roman soldier's answer was terse, unfriendly.

"He is."

"But I have never wanted *children* imprisoned," Saul protested. "They are hardly responsible for—"

"According to my orders," the centurion interrupted, "you have asked that all *dangerous* Christians be detained."

"A mere child was never on my list."

"This is a special one."

"What makes him special, centurion?"

"He happens to be the son of a member of that band of twelve original followers."

"The son of one of Jesus' apostles?"

"As you say."

"The *families* have been targeted? Are you telling me that?"

"I am."

"But they *are* innocent. I can never sanction imprisoning and torturing women and children."

"This one is different."

"I asked you a moment ago, and you did not answer: What *is* so special about him?"

"Get on down here and find out."

"There is no room."

"I shall come up. Call my comrade and have him put the rope down."

Saul turned and saw another centurion sitting nearby, this one asleep and snoring. But he awakened quickly when called and lowered the rope that was the only way of entrance or exit to the tiny space below. The centurion below climbed up the rope.

A moment later, Saul was being lowered through the hole.

Cold ... colder for some reason than even the larger room.

Saul, not a tall man by any standard, stood and banged his head painfully against the uneven rock ceiling.

"Child ..." he called. "Child, where are you?"

Groaning. Inches away.

Saul waited until his eyes had adjusted somewhat to the darkness, the only light coming through that small round opening through which he had just come.

A boy huddled just ahead of him. Saul knelt by his side, trying to see his features in the gloom.

"What is your name?" he asked.

Initially no response came, only more groaning.

"Please tell me your name," Saul asked again.

"Yabin ..." a young voice finally replied tremulously.

"How old are you, Yabin?"

"Fifteen."

"You seem younger."

The boy said nothing.

"Who is your father?" Saul asked. "I understand he is one of Jesus' original group of followers."

The boy's silence continued briefly, then he said, "Mattiyah. His name is Mattiyah, and I am very proud of him."

"The tax collector?" Saul asked, recalling that name.

"My father hurt no one," Yabin said defensively. "He is honest. It was just a job with him. He put in his time, and that was it."

"An honest tax collector who does not keep a little for himself? Then he was one of the few of his kind who worked like that!"

The boy was not looking at him but in another direction.

"Why do you not face me?" Saul asked, wondering if the teenager was going to try to hide something from him.

The groaning stopped briefly, then continued.

"I want to see you," Saul told him. "Let me see you."

Yabin turned, revealing a face littered with cuts and a large gash across his forehead.

"Why are you here?" Saul asked.

"You know why."

"I know about some cases, but not yours."

"My father. You are after my father."

"Mattiyah?"

"I already told you who he was."

Under other circumstances, Saul would have struck the boy across the cheek for his insolence, but this time he restrained himself out of pity.

"You are but his son," he said.

"And a Christian. You are trying to get to him through me. But it will not work. Our faith cannot be shaken."

"You admit that to me so freely."

"I am unable to deny my Lord."

"Even though I could leave right now and that soldier would come back down and continue his 'persuasion'?"

Saul thought he could detect a slight smile on the boy's rather handsome young face.

"God or man ... My father told me I would always have to make a choice, and I see how correct he was."

"But you have chosen the Nazarene. What does *He* have to do with God?"

"He *is* God."

"But I thought He was called the *Son* of God."

The smile disappeared, another expression taking its place, one that seemed oddly peaceful despite the circumstances.

"The same."

"He can be God and the Son of God at the same time?"

Saul considered such a possibility to be inconceivable.

"You are quite serious," he said, his sarcasm apparent.

"That is what my father taught me," Yabin said, his own voice assuming an unmistakable note of pride.

"Is there more you want to tell me?" Saul probed.

"Jesus is the Messiah."

"You say *is*. But I must remind you that the Nazarene was crucified and buried. You surely mean *was*."

Yabin shook his head with great vigor as he added, "Jesus was crucified and buried but arose."

Saul scoffed.

"From the grave?" he asked.

Yabin seemed uncommonly at peace.

"As He promised."

Saul already knew most of what was being said, having heard it in various forms from other Christians, but he wanted to see how well versed Yabin was.

"Where is the Nazarene now?" he asked.

"In heaven."

"Which means that you and the others have been left alone, is that it, essentially you've been deserted?"

"We are *not* alone!" Yabin protested.

"I do not understand. By your own words, you just admitted to me that Jesus is no longer here."

Surprisingly the teenager was not becoming flustered but explained quite calmly, "Jesus sent another to take His place."

"I know of no such person," Saul acknowledged suspiciously. "Who is it?"

"The Holy Spirit," Yabin told him.

"Who is the Holy Spirit?"

"God's Spirit within us."

Saul was becoming frustrated, not sure if young Yabin was telling him the truth or making up nonsense.

"You are very good at repeating what your father must have told you," he said, "but it would be better if you were able to think on your own. After all, he seems to have abandoned you here, a mere boy of fifteen."

Yabin continued to be in pain but managed to straighten himself as he leaned against the rock wall.

"I did what my Lord wanted," he replied.

"As interpreted by your father, no doubt," Saul said.

"He appeared to me one night."

Saul had lost patience with this teenager and was getting to his feet.

"No more of this for me," he remarked. "I have no more time to waste with deluded children."

Yabin reached up and closed his fingers around Saul's wrist.

"The light ..." he said.

"What light?"

"So white and pure."

Saul stood without moving.

*The light ...*

He remembered what Huram ben Sira and his son, Johanan, had told him.

*It was brighter than the sun. And that voice was so strong, yet kind.*

Both of them had had a similar experience. And now a teenager was describing the same thing.

"It was so bright!" Yabin told him.

"I know, I know!" Saul interrupted. "I have heard this before, young man. I want nothing more of it."

"Then surely you will believe."

"Surely I will *not*, because I see now what is going on, a conspiracy that seems so obvious. I am a fool only for not having guessed this earlier. You all have gotten together and rehearsed, trying to fool those who are more gullible than I."

Yabin tried to protest, but Saul would not listen. He called up to the guards and demanded that he be lifted up.

When he was in the larger room above, he told the one centurion, "I do see now what you mean. He is very convincing."

"Shall I beat it out of him?"

"Do whatever you wish. I am washing my hands of this clever child."

Saul left the Mamertine and stood outside, glancing to his right.

The Forum was more jammed with people that day than usual. One after the other, speakers got up before little groups willing to listen to whatever philosophy was being expounded.

Then Saul glanced in the other direction, toward what would become known as Nero's Circus.

"Whoever is imprisoned here deserves his punishment," he said out loud. "I must concentrate my efforts on Israel and the countries that border it. Coming up this far was a mistake, one I shall not make again."

Saul of Tarsus strode across the street toward an awaiting chariot. He did not hear the last screams of the dying teenage boy as the Roman centurion broke several of Yabin's ribs, one of these puncturing his heart.

## Chapter Nineteen

*The synagogue of the Libertines and the Cyrenians and the Alexandrians and of Cilicia and of Asia ...*

The irony of where Stephen found himself at what was to be the end of his journey was not lost on him.

*Tarsus ...*

As he stood in the center of the road entering the city that was the capital of the region of Cilicia, Stephen was apprehensive.

*I have nothing to fear from this man,* he thought. *He is probably many miles away. I have heard nothing about him for some weeks now. Yet, Lord, why is it that I feel as I do?*

Suddenly ashamed of himself for such tremulous feelings, he picked up the leather satchel that had been a birthday present from his parents two years before and strode into Tarsus, hoping that he could be an instrument of redemption for a jaded populace that was more interested in Greek philosophy than matters of the spirit.

Someone greeted him almost immediately.

"You are Stephen, I trust?" the red-haired, well-dressed, exquisitely beautiful young woman asked.

"Yes, I am," he said, already put at ease by her beguiling smile. "What is your name?"

"Lea," she replied. "You are as I thought you would be."

"As bad as that?"

"No, not bad! It is very good, Stephen. I was told to expect someone carrying a tan-colored leather satchel."

He wondered at the efficiency of getting information from one point to another as fast as Lea had hinted. She must have had a host of contacts along the way, well-organized and primed to give her whatever details she wanted.

"Ah, I see," he said lamely.

Lea's eyes were twinkling.

"And who is exceedingly handsome," she observed. "I see now that that description was not in the least exaggerated."

Stephen blushed, uncomfortable with any recognition of the way he looked, and turned away to comment awkwardly about how busy Tarsus seemed, tradesmen at their stands, a steady flow of human and animal traffic.

"A man who is unconceited," Lea observed appreciatively, "how refreshing!"

He returned his attention to her.

"You are a very beautiful woman," he acknowledged. "I have never seen hair so long as yours. With the sun hitting it, well, your hair looks rather like flame rolling down your back."

Lea did not blush since she was used to compliments of that sort.

"A group of Tarsusites is eager to hear you speak at dinner," she said, "but I can imagine that you must be quite tired by now. My husband and I have a residence at the western edge of town. A room has been prepared for you. Please come now, will you? Transportation is right over there."

He thanked her, and they walked across the wide street to a colorful chariot, shining in the sun as its rays bounced off red and orange and other shades applied by a skilled craftsman.

"One man did it all," Stephen said as he admired the details of the chariot.

"How did you know that?" Lea asked.

"It was one of the pastimes I had before leaving home. I enjoy studying color, paints, dyes, that sort of thing. I thought perhaps that one day I might become an artist. I always had images of one sort or another floating around in my mind."

A touch of regret made him sound wistful.

"Why would you stop now? You are hardly past your prime. And there is nothing sinful about such a dream."

He looked at her, smiling sadly.

"I have only a short while left," he told her.

On their way through the center of Tarsus, Lea questioned Stephen about what he had said.

"Why do you feel this way?" she asked.

"It is what the Lord has told me, Lea, not once or twice but a number of times. I must listen and believe."

"Yes, I know that, but why would He give you the gifts that you have, the compelling presence about which I have heard so much, and yet cut that off after just a short while? Can you be sure you are not mistaken?"

Lea was already a Christian, having been converted during a visit by another disciple the year before. She, like Stephen, had learned certain truths rapidly, finding the study of old parchments fascinating.

"How can I answer that?" he remarked. "I do not have the mind of God. I can only depend upon my perceptions, however misguided they may or may not be."

"But only our heavenly Father gave you the mind you obviously have. Must we stop reasoning and analyzing when we follow Jesus? I could never accept that, you know, never."

"But when He has laid out a path before us, should we be questioning Him every step of the way? Is that not when faith comes in and tells us, 'Know, believe, accept'? That allows none of what you are suggesting."

Stephen began to chuckle.

"What is funny?" asked Lea.

"I must be living up to my reputation," he said, "so serious that I turn any comment into a debate."

"Yes ... I *have* heard that about you," she admitted, "though it was more a compliment than anything critical."

"Forgive me, please," Stephen said. "It seems that I am not starting out as a very good guest."

She touched the back of his hand.

"I think, Stephen, that you will be the best guest we have ever had."

To have such a stunningly beautiful woman's fingers pressing lightly on his hand was difficult for Stephen. He had had to rein in his emotions several times over the past months at a time in his life when his sexual desires could hardly be stronger. And now, Lea's fingers moving animatedly as she talked, he found his self-control not without its limitations.

After arriving at Lea's home and meeting her husband, a gregarious fellow named Yirmeyahu, Stephen was shown to his room for a short nap before dinner. He had been on the road that day from just after sunrise to near dusk, and he needed to sleep as soundly as he could before meeting with Lea and Yirmeyahu's friends.

But he did not drop off as quickly as he might have wished since images of flame-haired Lea stayed insinuatingly in his mind and would not soon let him rest, but he did manage to subdue these thoughts after some struggle, and sleep finally came.

The dinner that Lea had organized for the evening of Stephen's arrival had gone well from the beginning. Each of the guests seemed to be charmed by this charismatic young man who was possessed both of good looks and a keen mind, not the usual combination as far as they were concerned.

And a strong spirit.

Stephen told them of several of his experiences during the past months, including one where he had been bitten by a desert viper.

"I thought I would die in only a short while," he said, "the pain was so unrelieved that I assumed I would not last the night. I prayed that the Lord's will be done."

He hesitated then concluded, "But when I awakened at dawn's light, it was as though I had not been bitten at all. I was completely back to normal and actually feeling better than before the viper attacked!"

Not since he had left his own home had Stephen found himself in the midst of the kind of manifestation of wealth that was being spread around him that night, and he felt a touch of the allure of living that way again, comparing it with what he had been experiencing for nearly a year.

In the society of that time and place, it was seldom that more than nine guests gathered at the dinner table, and Lea and her husband made the affair in Stephen's honor no exception. She was, again typically, the only woman present. As everyone sat on pillows—chairs were never used at the table—the food was served on fine, red *terra sigillata* plates. Wine sweetened with honey was poured into goblets of blown glass, the making of which had been out of fashion for some time but was then returning to favor. No forks or knives were used; guests plucked at their food with their fingers, and sopped up juices with bits of wheat bread. Between courses, a steady flow of servants circulated bowls of water and towels so the guests could wash their hands.

Stephen enjoyed the fellowship. Most of the people were Christians, and they enjoyed being part of a group where real spiritual harmony was present.

"That we are meeting where we are seems rather remarkable," commented a heavyset man named Hopni, "you might say, almost incomprehensible."

The others murmured agreement.

"And, Stephen, that *you* are here is surely the most incredible aspect of all," he went on, his tiny eyes sparkling though they were nearly lost behind layers of fat. "I am amazed that one so young could be doing so well and could stir up so resoundly a certain Tarsus-born individual we all know and loathe."

"You are aware of Saul's loathing of me?" asked Stephen naïvely, unsure of how widespread that knowledge was.

"We know about it, yes," Hopni told him, "and we know why. I daresay that any one of us would have gladly taken your place for the pleasure of burying that man's face in all that mud and—"

Suddenly his face reddened, and he stopped himself, bringing his oversized hand to his mouth.

"Very sorry ... may God forgive me," he said, wheezing a bit. "That dirt was made mud because of the sweat and the blood of our blessed Savior."

Another man who was sitting next to him wrapped an arm around his neck and whispered, "I am sure the Lord forgives you, my dear brother."

"For my feelings of vengeance?" Hopni asked pitiably, hearing what he needed to know but not quite able to accept it.

"Even those."

"And treating the place of His death as—?"

Hopni could not continue and started to sob, his mountain of flesh vibrating like a bowl of soup.

Stephen stood at the opposite end of the group and said, "This is a man in which the Lord is well pleased."

Instantly Hopni's head shot up.

"You are a wonderful young man," he said, "but I know you are just trying to make me feel better."

Stephen's sympathy for this overweight but kindly individual was increasing by the minute.

"I am trying very hard not to do *just* that," he continued, "but to show everybody here that anyone who has the courage to recognize sin in himself and confess it publicly then finds himself driven to tears over it is surely a man who will be welcomed someday by the very hosts of heaven with a special chorus."

Stephen glanced around at the others.

"How many of us sin and forget to ask the Lord's forgiveness?" he asked of them. "How many have become blind to the fact that moments of anger, intemperate speech, selfishness, and so much more are as much the products of our sinful nature, and therefore are sin, as theft, murder, and lying."

It was now Stephen who shed tears.

"I have never *repented* of doing what I did to Saul that day," he admitted, "I mean, *truly* repented."

Realizing this was a shock to Stephen.

"I feel as though I stand naked before you all," he told the other dinner guests as well as his hosts.

Stephen fell to his knees and prayed to God as a sinner abruptly made aware of the depth of sin in his life.

Seconds later, his eyes closed, he heard the labored steps of someone who was approaching him, breathing in a labored way from the sheer weight of his body and then kneeling next to him.

Stephen continued to pray with a fervency that seemed to come from the center of his soul. After he had finished, Hopni began to speak a prayer of his own, one so filled with anguish over sin that several of the remaining dinner guests, tough, hardened men most of them, shed their own tears.

Harmony even greater than before would now bond everyone during the remainder of that evening until, just before midnight, the outside world intruded.

The knocking was fierce.

They were in the midst of a closing prayer when the sound disturbed them. A servant rushed to the front door then hurried back to the banquet hall, telling them of the urgency stressed by the man who had insisted upon seeing them.

His name was Hadad-ezer, and he was a successful leather-goods merchant who had become a Christian not long before Jesus was crucified. Tall, thin, given to nervous gestures, he was out of breath as he entered the room.

"Saul!" he told them. "Saul is back!"

Yirmeyahu jumped to his feet.

"I know how this news must frighten you," he said, "but if we stick together, what can he do to us? We here have far more power and influence collectively than he does."

Hadad-ezer agreed with that but said, "Yes, yes, I know, but I think what he will do is single out just one individual, not the whole lot of us."

"He assumes we will not come to the defense of whoever it is," Yirmeyahu concluded, "is that what you are suggesting?"

"I think so, my brother. I am convinced Saul will do that again and again, whittling us down one by one until—" the other man said, his voice quavering so badly that he could not continue.

Lea spoke up.

"I see some sense to what Hadad-ezer has said," she told her guests. "But there is also a chance that by not letting him divide us we can destroy whatever credibility he has here and elsewhere."

Lea's pulse quickened.

"People should be able to see those who have God's unction," she said. "By contrast, Saul will seem to be working against Him!"

Others raised their hands or spoke to indicate their agreement.

"One other matter," Yirmeyahu said.

They waited for him to continue.

"We should pledge to rise to the defense of anyone who is targeted by Saul," he went on. "No one must be left alone. We are part of a body of believers, and we must function with that in mind."

Elazar, the oldest of the men, with a flowing white beard and a mane of hair that the younger ones could have envied, broke into the discussion.

"If I know Saul at all, I can guess who his first target likely will be," he declared confidently.

"How can you point out someone in particular?" Yirmeyahu asked. "It could be any of us. Or it might be someone else in the area. After all, we do not comprise the sum total of all Christians."

Elazar waved his hand impatiently through the air.

"Yes, of course, what you say could be true enough, but ask yourself this, dear friend: Why *now?* Why not a month ago? Or six months earlier? Or a few weeks from now? What is special about *today?*"

No one could see where he was heading.

"Because something *is* different as we speak," Elazar continued.

"It is the same as it has been since the resurrection," Yirmeyahu reminded him. "There are just more of us now."

"Forgive me for my contrariness, but you are wrong. We have a special guest here tonight."

He turned and faced Stephen.

"I think Saul is going after you, dear brother," he said with clear regret. "I think he wants you dead."

"But I defied him, I ridiculed him, nearly a year ago," Stephen commented. "Why did he wait so long?"

"A year, yes, a year *tomorrow!*"

Stephen swallowed a couple of times.

"I can see what you mean," he said. "But has he really waited so long for that reason? Could he have controlled his thirst for vengeance all this time?"

"You are in the town where he was born," Elazar quickly pointed out. "Saul's roots are here."

"And Gamaliel!" another guest added.

Elazar thanked him and went on, "His most influential teacher, the great Gamaliel, was here until a few years ago when he moved to Jerusalem to be closer to a great number of other teachers, scribes, and the like. The graves of Saul's mother and father are less than a mile from where we now stand. Your presence *here* is an act of near-blasphemy as far as Saul is concerned."

"Near-blasphemy?" Yirmeyahu interjected. "Is that not a bit strong, friend?"

"Hardly!" Elazar exclaimed. "I suspect that Saul feels he was miraculously anointed by God twice in Tarsus: first to become a prophet and a teacher, and years later, a second time when he convinced himself that his mission was to eradicate Christians from the face of the earth."

"Where is he staying?" Yirmeyahu asked.

"In the house where he was born," Hadad-ezer replied matter-of-factly.

"But the family has not lived there for many years."

"He apparently prevailed upon the current owner."

"You must leave tonight," Lea said as she faced Stephen.

"No," he told her. "I want to go to the synagogue as I planned in the morning. I want to talk to the rabbis as I have in every town where I have been over the past twelve months. If I let fear rule me, then Saul has gained the victory."

"Discretion can be considered the better part of valor," Yirmeyahu said. "Or do you not agree with that?"

"I do, but not when I am forced to say to the Lord, 'I have more concern for my own safety than for following Your will as You have directed me to do.' How could He be expected to honor anything of the sort?"

"Nothing will change your mind?" Lea asked.

"I would alter my course only if God did it for me."

Hopni had been sitting quietly during this exchange. Straining with all that weight, he stood, and approached Stephen.

"Perhaps you should stay with me while you are in Tarsus. I have a bigger staff than anyone else here. Some of them will become your bodyguards."

"Saul would never hire thugs."

"Indulge me this, please, young man."

With Lea and Yirmeyahu's encouragement, Stephen acquiesced and told Hopni he would be happy to accept his kind offer.

"It is not so kind or selfless," the other man admitted. "I will sleep better at least tonight as a result."

The others exchanged kisses on each cheek, and Stephen thanked his hosts. Then he and Hopni left, to be taken to the most opulent residence in all of Tarsus.

"You will sleep in my rather shamelessly excessive guest quarters," the big man told him as the chariot approached the front gate. "Pontius Pilatus was there for several nights early on while renovations were completed at his official residence. He almost persuaded me that we should switch homes, for he was impressed with the level of luxury at mine."

After they had gone inside and Hopni had shown Stephen to the guest quarters, he placed both pudgy hands on the young man's shoulder and said, "This idea of yours that you do not have long to live …"

He paused, finding the next words difficult to say.

"My men will be useless, will they not?" he asked.

"I am set to die," Stephen replied. "An army would not contain enough men."

"Have you no fear about this?"

"No longer. I have lived with the knowledge all these months."

"When it happens—" Hopni said.

"Yes …"

"Will you tell the Lord that I hope I have enough time of my own left to serve Him better? I worry about that, you know, being thought unworthy at the last minute."

"You have been thinking about death as well?"

Hopni nodded, and his whole frame seemed to shake.

"My weight," he said. "I gain no matter how little I eat. I cannot go on this way much longer, Stephen. I am looking forward to the new body He promised me."

The two men embraced, and then Stephen went inside, washed, and started his private time of soul-wrenching prayer while Hopni walked to the other end of his house and into his own room, where his bedclothes had been laid out before him.

"If only I could take his place," he whispered out loud, "if only he had the next fifty years to change this world."

Hopni was tempted to go back to Stephen and have some strong, able men bind him so he could be hidden away until Saul left.

"My God, my God!" he cried out. "What should I do?"

A few seconds later, Hopni felt shaky and sat down on a nearby chair in front of the large window in his bedroom. His servants found him still there in the morning, his eyes wide open, his head tilted toward the heavens, an expression of peace on that puffy, lifeless face.

## Chapter Twenty

Before Stephen left Hopni's residence in the morning, he asked a servant if he could say good-bye to his benefactor but was told that the master was still sleeping.

"Is it usual for him to stay in bed as late as this?" Stephen asked, concerned.

"No, sir," the young male servant told him. "But he was so happy last night when I saw him heading toward his room and yet he seemed awfully tired at the same time."

"Is he not usually happy?"

Stephen had had only a glimpse of his benefactor's dark side and had no way of knowing how frequently it showed through.

"The master is often unhappy, sir," the servant responded, apparently grieved at having to say this.

"Why?" asked Stephen, though he was quite sure he already knew what the answer was.

"His weight, all that awful weight. It has gotten considerably worse over the past two years."

"Can he do nothing about it?"

The servant was distressed, obviously concerned about his master.

"He tries, sir, but he has no control, I am afraid, when it comes to food. He cannot seem to stop himself."

The young man hesitated then added, "Sir?"

"Yes?" Stephen said.

Speaking critically or negatively in such circumstances was not acceptable behavior unless specific permission was given.

"May I speak freely?" the servant asked for the requisite approval without being certain he would receive it.

Stephen surprised him by saying, "You may."

"He has some pain that is not of his physical body."

"Tell me what you mean."

"Guilt, sir. He has much guilt."

"Over what?"

Abruptly the servant's manner changed, as though he thought better of what he had been about to say.

"I should not speak anything more about this."

"But I told you that you could speak freely."

"Yes, sir, you did, but I just cannot tell you."

Stephen's natural curiosity was being stirred, but he knew he had to be tactful, so he said, "I do not want to cause you any discomfort, but it may be that I could help your master if I just knew a bit more."

" *No!*" the servant said emphatically. "He would be very upset."

But Stephen was not about to give up.

"Is it his weight?" he asked. "Can you tell me that much?"

"Only a small part of it, sir. There is more. The master is trying so hard to fight feelings that—"

The young man blushed and excused himself.

Stephen was tempted to stay longer, to be available when his benefactor awakened, but then he decided he had to be at the local synagogue as early as possible, because it was the practice of rabbis to arrive early, do some studying, have an hour or two of conversation among themselves, and then be ready for the people who would come to them with various needs ranging from the physical to the spiritual as well as the emotional.

Three rabbis were entering the synagogue at the same time he arrived there.

"Hello," he said cheerfully.

They glanced at him, grumbled, and said nothing in return, not an untypical reaction for someone none of them knew.

Stephen followed the three.

One of the men, the oldest, thin-faced, with cheeks that showed the remnants of youthful years of virulent skin problems, parted from the others and approached Stephen.

"Are you a rabbi?" he asked suspiciously, even antagonistically. "You do not look like a rabbi."

"I am not," Stephen replied.

"What is your business here?"

"I am hoping to have the privilege of engaging in conversation with you when the time is right."

"About what, young man?"

"Life, death."

The rabbi snorted as he replied, an edge of contempt in his voice, "So what else is new? These are hardly new topics."

"You have discussed them before?"

"Of course. We are not here to chat about the weather or what we might be having for dinner, you know."

"What answers have you touched upon?"

The rabbi played with his beard as he narrowed his eyes, studying this young stranger.

"There are no answers," he said, "or, rather, *we* do not have them. Only Yahweh does. And He does not confide in us as much as we would like."

Another rabbi, not much younger than the first one, seemed quite curious about what he had overheard, and he joined in.

"Are you proposing, young man, that *you* have been able to unravel some of the mysteries of this life," he asked, "with answers to questions that could destroy our beliefs if we allowed them to do so?"

"Are you saying, Rabbi, that the questions could destroy your beliefs or the answers themselves?"

"A little of each, I suppose. To think 'Why, why, why?' is often terrible in itself when we see what we do in the lives of those who come to us for wisdom. But what of the answers? We fall into a rut with the men and women who are part of our congregations, providing easy answers that frequently have little relationship to reality but sound good, sound reassuring, and have the virtue of being handy because we have repeated them so often as the years have passed."

Stephen looked around at the assembly hall, one of moderate size, then asked, "This is called the Synagogue of the Freedmen, am I correct?"

"You are," the first rabbi told him cautiously because, though this young man looked respectable enough, the hour was early, and thieves could disguise themselves in order to gain entrance with a goal of looting the synagogue's treasury.

Stephen saw an opening and did not let it slip by him.

"But how free are you?" he asked, making sure he spoke in a consoling and not a judgmental manner.

"Free from what?"

"Free from the doubts you seek to quell in others?"

The man's shoulders slumped.

"I suppose it is obvious then," he acknowledged.

"You believe in God, but you are not certain what kind of God He is."

That first rabbi's mouth dropped open, and he asked, "How could you know that, you a stranger and a very young man?"

The second rabbi spoke up, "What is your purpose here?"

Stephen did not hold back.

"To help you realize *your* purpose," he said straightforwardly, having learned that even some controversy could prove to be the open door to a man's soul.

"Our purpose?" they both repeated at the same time.

By then, the third rabbi had returned, asking, "What is this I'm overhearing? Will someone let me know?"

The two recounted basically what had been discussed thus far.

He turned to Stephen and said, "I am Elipaz."

"It means 'God is victorious,'" Stephen told him instinctively, not with any intention of currying favor with the man.

"How could you know that?" the rabbi asked, genuinely taken aback and unprepared for someone like Stephen.

"It is not *my* wisdom."

Elipaz assumed that this young stranger was simply donning a mask of humility and asked somewhat cynically, "Not your wisdom? Then whose?"

"From above."

Elipaz placed his hands on his hips and asked, "And that means, I gather, you are some new prophet?"

Stephen shook his head.

"No, I am not," he replied.

Elipaz cut him no slack.

"Then what and who are you, young man?" the rabbi asked, stopping short of outright contempt.

"I am Stephen ... a Christian."

The three of them backed away slightly.

"And you dare to come into God's house?" Elipaz asked.

In the remarkably short span of time that he had been on his odyssey, Stephen had learned how to be artful rather than abrasively confrontational.

"I dare only to talk with you and the two rabbis with you," he said. "I seek nothing but understanding at the feet of learned men."

Elipaz was not altogether convinced.

"But you as a Christian also want to teach us?" he surmised. "Is that not what you people do?"

Stephen knew the rabbi was attempting to get him to forgo his civility, but he would not be trapped into doing so.

Instead he grinned beneficently and asked, "Tell me this, please: Is learning always in a single direction?

"I give it, and I receive it. If I am not prepared to receive, I will not have much to give as the years pass by.

"You can give me much. If I can have you receive even a little from me, I could ask little else."

Elipaz and the other two rabbis relaxed somewhat, even allowing themselves the possibility that this young man was not like other Christians they had encountered.

"Saul may be wrong about you," Elipaz said.

"You have seen him already?" asked Stephen.

"He tried to recruit me to participate in seeking your death, frankly. But I told him I could go that course only if I became convinced that you *had* to die."

Unexpectedly, Elipaz kissed Stephen on each cheek.

"You are welcome to stay," he said. "We will listen to whatever you want to tell us *if* you allow us the privilege of a response."

"And we will teach one another," Stephen stressed.

"Have you had breakfast?" Elipaz asked, changing the subject and making no secret of his own hunger.

"I have not," Stephen replied.

The rabbi was glad that someone fresh and interesting was able to partake of his hospitality.

"Please join us then," he said.

And so the four of them settled down to a breakfast, the extent of which Stephen had not anticipated.

"We eat well," Elipaz said.

"I can see that."

"Is this wrong while people—beggars and the like—are starving to death not far from this synagogue?"

"I would like to know how you feel about this," Stephen said while realizing he was showing what might be viewed as timidity instead of politeness.

"Is your tongue tempered so quickly?" Elipaz suggested. "I would find that rather disappointing, young man."

Elipaz enjoyed backing Stephen into a rhetorical corner.

"I have an opinion, Rabbi, but I will express it only if you wish."

"I would be most eager to know what it is."

Stephen cleared his throat.

"Are you ministering to the poor?" he asked.

"Regularly!" Elipaz declared. "I could not live with my conscience if I neglected that duty of mine. My comrades here feel as I do. We always go out into the street and the countryside together."

"How do you serve beggars and other homeless people and the rest?"

"By taking food to them, by giving some a few coins whenever we can, by talking to them of Yahweh."

"You feed the body and nourish the spirit?"

"There is no other way."

Stephen saw the emotions play across Elipaz's face and concluded that the rabbi was wholly sincere.

"Does Caiaphas do the same thing?" he asked.

"That scoundrel!" Elipaz exploded, the veins in his forehead starting to bulge. "He is a disgrace to all of us."

He spat out the small piece of bread he had been chewing while he talked.

"Forgive me for such anger," he said. "I loathe what that man has done. This Jesus of yours was right to throw out the money changers. And He spoke correctly when He confronted the Sanhedrin as nothing more than a collection of hypocrites, so pure and clean on the outside but full of decay and death inside."

Stephen was pleased that Elipaz was aware of those acts that had been at the center of encouraging Caiaphas' wrath.

"I feel as you do," he admitted. "That is why I will not give up."

"You feel that Jesus is the answer, do you not?" the rabbi spoke.

"I do. I truly do."

"And you believe that He was the Messiah?"

"Is the Messiah, Rabbi."

"Will He come again? I have heard this said more than once."

"He will, though no one can say when. It might be tomorrow or a thousand years from tomorrow."

"Must Jews cease being Jews in order to become Christians?"

"No, no," Stephen emphasized. "Do not believe the lies. A man can still be a Jew *after* converting to Christianity."

"I do not understand. It makes no sense. A man is a Jew or a Christian. He is one or the other, not both."

"But such a man is both, Rabbi."

"How can I accept that? It goes against logic."

"So does the parting of the Red Sea. But you accept that as a miracle from God."

"Yes, I know but—"

"And what about the three young men who survived a raging furnace, emerging from it to stun a heathen king? What about Daniel and his night in a lions' den?"

Elipaz was nodding slowly.

"When you think about it, there is no mystery to what I have told you about a man being a Jew and a Christian at the same time."

Stephen was now more intent than he had planned to be but felt what he believed was the Lord's leading.

"You are a father, Rabbi?" he asked.

"I am. I have a fine wife and three beautiful children."

"You are a father *and* a rabbi, right?"

"As you say."

"How can that be?" Stephen asked.

"Are you trying to compare being a Jew and a Christian with being a husband and a father?"

"In this way ..."

"Go ahead. Tell me. I have to admit that I find all this extraordinarily fascinating, young man."

And so the bonding between them continued minute by minute until just before the noon hour ... while outside, a short distance away, Saul of Tarsus was busy trying to convince the civic officials and some of the other rabbis that the young man from Jerusalem should not be allowed another day of life.

## Chapter Twenty-One

Stephen was about to leave at noon when Elipaz said, "No! Please, young man. I have an idea. Why not stay here?"

"But I want to go among the people," the young man told him. "That is my mission field."

"To spread the Good News, as you call it?"

"Yes, exactly that, Rabbi."

"Then stay here, and we shall go out for you. I am willing to declare that this synagogue, which is rather renowned, you know, has been opened to the general public, whether members or not."

"And I could speak from here?"

"Indeed you can."

"But why are you willing to do this?" Stephen asked. "You have chosen not to accept anything I have said about the Good News."

"That may be true, but you *have* accomplished something quite remarkable, my young friend."

"What is that, Rabbi?" Stephen asked respectfully.

"I have committed myself to opening this house of worship for others to hear you, instead of having you run out of Tarsus and barred forever from returning."

Stephen was moved by the rabbi's words, which he could not have predicted even a day before; he had, in fact, anticipated the most severe resistance.

"I do not have sufficient words to express just how grateful I am, Rabbi," he told the other man.

Elipaz leaned forward.

"Will you do a favor for me then?" he asked.

"Anything you wish," Stephen assured him.

"After you confront the crowd in a short while, can you spend a little more time with my comrades and myself, Stephen? Frankly, I need to talk with you further. Am I asking too much of a young stranger?"

"My days are set by the people I meet."

"As instruments of Yahweh, I am sure."

"Exactly that, Rabbi."

Elipaz arose, but with some difficulty. The other men jumped to their feet.

"Are you all right?" Stephen asked as he stood and helped to steady the older man.

"A bit dizzy," he said. "But whatever it was has passed already. Thank you for your concern."

Elipaz sent his two friends to spread the word about Stephen. After they had left, he said, "They are very good at this. They tell a few key people, persuading *them* to alert others. And on it goes."

They were sitting in the main hall.

"Did you ever meet Jesus?" Stephen asked.

"I only saw Him from a distance after going down to Jerusalem out of curiosity. It was the day when He supposedly fed five thousand people with just a basketful of fish and a few loaves of bread."

Elipaz would not admit it to his young visitor, but he had found the Nazarene fascinating. Ordinarily he would have scoffed at the notion that so little food had been stretched so far, but he had, after all, *seen* the basket before the fish and loaves had been handed out to a crowd, that had been so spellbound by the Speaker, many had become weak before they realized that the time to eat had passed.

*You knew this!* Elipaz exclaimed to himself. *Yet it seemed that You were ill-prepared to feed more than a small number.*

Yet the pieces of fish—St. Peter's fish, as they came to be called—and the chunks of bread just kept coming.

"When did a new supply come along?" Elipaz had asked someone.

"I have seen no one come to this area nor leave it, Rabbi," the other man had answered respectfully.

"But that is impossible!"

"Are miracles impossible, Rabbi? If you do not believe in them, of course they are. But then we limit Yahweh, do we not? We reduce Him to our size."

The one who was speaking was young, like Stephen, and Elipaz could not help but be impressed by his intelligence and his forthrightness.

"You are quite astute, young man," he had said.

"Wisdom is precious, Rabbi," the other replied. "I have never sought it blithely nor used it callously."

"And you find the Nazarene to be genuine?"

"I have found that, compared to Him, all else in this life is meaningless and phony."

And so it had been that day, a day to which Elipaz retreated in memory periodically.

"Rabbi?" a now familiar voice brought Elipaz back to the present.

"Yes ..." he said a bit distantly.

Stephen was asking him, "What was your opinion of Jesus?"

"A remarkable Man. I can understand why you choose to follow Him."

"But you cannot take that step yourself."

"Not now, perhaps never, Stephen. You see, my whole adult life has been built upon a foundation that in itself rests on generations of theological thought, perfected, I might say, by the very passage of time."

"You are a captive of tradition then?"

Elipaz winced as he replied, "Your directness should offend me, yet it does not. I suppose this is because I see the unflinching honesty behind it, the absolute lack of hypocrisy."

"Hypocrisy killed my Lord," Stephen stated simply.

"And hypocrisy is killing the Jewish people," Elipaz added. "We claim to be God's chosen, but we have come to the awful point where we now treat Him like some kind of talisman."

The rabbi was grieved by what his integrity forced him to acknowledge.

"Our worldliness will be our undoing, shaming the Jewish people for generations to come," he went on. "That is why the Nazarene attracted so many to Himself. He offered something more vital. Instead of doing in our competitors for the sake of a better business deal, He urged that we do unto others as we would have them do unto us. We were to forsake revenge and turn the other cheek."

"You know something about His teachings then!"

"But still I cannot accept Him as you do, Stephen. Allow me that, please. My whole heritage goes against doing that."

"Yet that heritage points so clearly in His direction."

"We have been promised a Messiah to free us from bondage, not one Who allowed Himself to be crucified."

"Buried and risen, Rabbi!" Stephen quickly emphasized. "If all Jesus had been was a martyr, then my faith is vain. But He is alive today, risen, witnessed, and ascended to the heavenly Father."

Elipaz would not join with this young man in any more debate.

"I am unable to believe that," he said. "But I defend your right to do so. And I declare most emphatically that you are hardly a traitor to Rome or Israel for believing as you do."

## Chapter Twenty-Two

$A$nd *I declare most emphatically that you are hardly a traitor to Rome or Israel for believing as you do....*

Whether or not Stephen was what his accusers claimed became a question that rippled throughout the crowd gathered in the courtyard adjacent to the Synagogue of the Freedmen. Evidently Saul had achieved considerable success in spreading damaging reports about the young visitor.

The mood of the people who had gathered before Stephen and Elipaz was hostile, bordering on violent.

"You claim a great deal about this Nazarene," shouted one man. "What good could ever come out of such a place as *Nazareth*? Our Messiah could never have any beginnings as you would like us to believe. How could you possibly think that God would *permit* anything of the sort?"

"But Jesus was not originally from Nazareth," Stephen retorted. "He was born in Bethlehem."

Elipaz decided to wade in at that point.

"I have spent much time with this young man," he said. "and I must tell you that I am not able to find a single reason to doubt his sincerity."

"But do you believe his *message?*" the same man shouted back.

"I find it fascinating. I find it possible. I find no reason for taking his life. In this nation of ours we have professed freedom over the centuries, and paid for it by the blood of our fathers, who we know defended it to the death."

"Do you *accept* what he says?"

Elipaz shook his head.

"I do not," he spoke.

"Then his words may be little better than lies, right, Rabbi?"

"I have already said—"

"You must be under some sort of spell, Rabbi."

Elipaz was standing beside Stephen on the columned *porticus* and becoming angry, particularly since he did not tolerate such talk from someone off the street, as this man appeared to be.

"You are the one under a spell," the rabbi shot back. "Have you forgotten the respect to which I am entitled?"

"We also are admonished to test the spirits, Rabbi," the man said, "and right now, this Stephen's conduct is failing the test."

"*His* conduct? Have you lost touch with reality? I see only one here whose conduct is objectionable in any way."

But then others started speaking up.

"This man is not alone," one said.

"I, too, have heard this Stephen make certain statements that were blasphemous or seditious!" another added.

"He is a devil posing as a saint!" a third added.

Elipaz raised both hands and spoke in his most authoritarian manner.

"Look at you all!" he said. "How shameful your very words are!"

"These men surely speak the truth!" somebody shouted. "Why should they not be heard, Rabbi?"

And then another man stepped out of the crowd and looked up at Stephen and Elipaz. He was middle-aged with a fine-looking beard instead of the ill-kempt ones sported by others present, especially those who seemed to be calling out in the loudest possible voices.

Yarobam.

Elipaz had no trouble recognizing him, though the others who seemed so determined to stir up the rest of the gathered throng were strangers.

"I am pleased to see you here," the rabbi stated, hoping that the other man would have a calming effect on those around him. "Your gifts to the synagogue have been welcome over the years."

"And you know me as a reasonable man not given to the excesses of others."

"I certainly do."

"Then I have a suggestion, Rabbi."

"Please, tell me; tell all of us what that is."

"Let the young man named Stephen speak as long as he wants without interruption from *anyone* here. And we will judge him by his words, not by mindless hearsay spouted by rabble-rousers."

As he spoke, Yarobam turned and cast a scornful glance at the three men who had spoken so accusingly, not to mention disrespectfully.

"This *is* what we *shall* do, correct?" he said with a sternness that chilled even the hot tempers that had flared up.

A murmur of assent arose from the crowd.

Yarobam turned and faced Stephen.

"You may speak as you wish, as long as you wish," he said.

Stephen had seldom had such an opportunity. He had been accepted in some villages and towns and thrown out of others, but never had he been allowed enough time to change the minds of those who wanted to harm him, no opportunity to face his accusers, because he usually was sentenced and punished by banishment or whipping or whatever else without being allowed to speak in his own defense.

*Lord,* he prayed within his soul, *if ever I needed Your wisdom ...*

Then he cleared his throat and began recounting the life of Abraham and telling them of Isaac, Jacob, and the twelve patriarchs. From there he continued on with Joseph, finally reminding them of the rebellion of the people while Moses was at the summit of Mount Sinai receiving the Ten Commandments.

Stephen paused, looking from face to face, and concluded, "Remember their sin! As Moses was receiving the Holy Law from Yahweh, the people were engaging in idolatry, sensuality, and profanity. *Even then!*"

His cheeks were flaring red.

"How could this have been?" he asked, gesturing with his arms in sudden rapid motions. "How could they be so near the presence of Almighty God and yet act with such foul abandon, *as though there was no God at all?*"

None of the people wanted to be reminded of the actions of their ancestors.

"That was thousands of years ago!" somebody exclaimed. "What is it to us today? You are just trying to turn our minds from—"

"You stiff-necked and uncircumcised and hard of heart and ears!" Stephen interrupted. "You always resist the Holy Spirit. As did your fathers, so do you!"

In spite of himself, Elipaz could not have agreed more.

"We Jews never seem to learn," he told them. "Listen to this young man. He speaks with God's *únctus.*"

Stephen felt even more emboldened.

"Which of the prophets did your fathers *not* persecute?" he asked searingly of every member of that crowd. "They killed those who foretold the coming of the Just One, Whom you now have murdered and betrayed."

He pointed his finger here and there, indicating one, two, three, and more among the men in front of him.

"You have received the law by the direction of angels from around the throne of a holy God and not kept it, not honored it, not bowed before Him in humble adoration," he went on. "Instead you have looked for any excuse to ignore His commandments, even defile them by your wanton acts. And Yahweh turns His back on you because you have committed blasphemy!"

"Enough, Stephen!" Elipaz whispered in his ear. "You need *not* march yourself to your own doom.... Let me intercede here, please!"

Stephen looked at him with some affection, extraordinary in itself considering that they had not known one another the day before.

"You will be needed when persecution comes," he said.

"Persecution?" Elipaz repeated. "I am going to save the lives of Christians?"

"Oh, yes, my friend, you will; you surely will."

The crowd was uncontrollable by then, and Stephen was pulled from the *porticus.*

"You cannot write my *epitaphium!*" he told them as he closed his eyes and fell to the ground.

"He is dead!" the cry arose from those nearest his body. "He is dead *already!*"

But Stephen instead was being given the privilege of gazing into heaven, and he saw the glory of God as well as Jesus, standing at the right hand of the One Who had sent Him to die and rise again to obtain the forgiveness of sins.

"I see the heavens opened," he told those who could hear, "and the Son of Man, Jesus the living Christ, standing at the right hand of God."

Some of those in the crowd had been in Jerusalem at the time of the crucifixion. One man had operated a concession in which he sold mugs of wine and pieces of bread for those who became thirsty or hungry as they stood and watched the Nazarene's agony. Another had encouraged his son to have a swatch of light cloth and run up to the base of the center cross, and dab up some blood as a souvenir of what was happening. Others were among the throng earlier, paid some coins for raising their voices and demanding that Barabbas be released, and Jesus be the One who would die atop Golgotha.

"Woe to the child who has such a father," Stephen said as he was being dragged past those same individuals.

"Spoken by someone who will never *be* a father," one of the men laughed coarsely and spat in Stephen's face.

Elipaz had tried to stop what was happening but had been knocked down and was forced to struggle painfully to his feet, no one nearby interested at all in helping him, though he had been an answer to prayer for the greater of them during innumerable times of great need. By that time Stephen was well past him; in fact, he had already been pushed and dragged to the gates of Tarsus.

"For the love of our Father in heaven," Elipaz cried out as he saw Stephen, dazed, on the ground and dozens of men picking up stones. "You cannot do this!"

Another voice arose.

"If you can tell me now that you *accept* as true what this young man has been saying," the voice said, "I will order them to leave him alone. Surely someone as learned as you could never be easily deceived."

Elipaz recognized the voice as soon as the first few words were spoken.

"*Saul!*" he cried out in desperation. "Stop this before the infamy is sealed by the blood of an innocent man."

Saul spoke with mocking slowness, "Do ... you ... accept ... what ... Stephen ... says ... as ... true?"

Frustrated, Saul then added in a normal voice, "Is Jesus the Son of God and the Messiah our very souls have been longing for?"

Saul grabbed Elipaz's shoulders.

"*Answer me!*" he demanded.

But the rabbi could not, because he was unable to accept as true any allusion to Christ's flesh-encased divinity.

"Then Stephen dies!" Saul said.

He had expected no one to speak out for Stephen because he had carefully assembled the crowd to include as many detractors and paid informants as possible.

Assuming no opposition, he was ready to order Stephen's stoning.

"This shall *not* happen!" an authoritative voice rang out.

Everyone turned in the direction from which it had come.

A Roman centurion and six of his men. A Roman garrison was less than a mile away, and apparently word had spread quickly of what was in progress. The scene had been so intense that no one had noticed the seven men approach on horseback.

"You shall not interfere!" Saul demanded.

"Are you suddenly a ruler given special authority from Rome?" the centurion asked sternly.

"This is a civil matter."

"I am making it otherwise."

"You do not—"

"I do whatever I wish. And I wish not to see a young man murdered, a young man who has committed no crime."

'Blasphemy is—"

"I have heard him speak before now, and found no such transgression from his lips."

"You did not hear enough."

"I hear what I consider sufficient. Let him go or the whole lot of you shall be arrested and imprisoned."

"Pontius Pilatus shall hear of this."

"So he shall. But for the moment not one stone will strike the body of this young man."

Saul and the crowd had no choice. To resist would have meant their blood being spilled, not Stephen's.

"This matter does not end here," Saul growled.

The centurion ordered his men to bring young Stephen with them. The young man was set astride one of the horses, and the group of men rode off to the nearby garrison.

## Chapter Twenty-Three

Stephen was especially treated well by the Romans, with no hint of disdain from any of them.

"My own people try to kill me," he lamented as he ate some food in the centurion's private dining quarters, a bare room with whitewashed walls, a few leather-slung chairs and a modest table in the center.

He looked up at his benefactor.

"What do I call you?" he asked.

"Diodorus," the other man replied.

"I think that Jesus would have been alive today if—" Stephen started to say, then stopped himself.

"If Pilatus had not caved in to the crowd and those who were inciting it," Diodorus finished the thought for him.

Stephen grinned a bit, amused at the other man's astuteness.

"Yes, that was what I was going to say," he replied.

"It was an obvious thought, I am afraid. Under Roman law, Jesus should have been imprisoned, but nothing more."

"Imprisoned? For being a so-called traitor?"

"For that, He would have died, my young friend. The difference is that we would have asked for more proof, and not relied on just statements vaguely hinting that something was going on."

"Being objective was not how anyone could describe Caiaphas."

"There are some words that give a more accurate picture of that beast but you undoubtedly would find these offensive."

Stephen actually blushed.

Diodorus normally would have teased him about this but ignored the young man's reddening cheeks.

"I have seen and heard Jesus," he acknowledged with just a touch of reluctance, "and found Him to be harmless."

Stephen bristled at that last word.

"Only harmless?" he ventured.

Diodorus nodded as he added, "What I meant was harmless as far as the law was concerned."

"What did you think of Him otherwise?"

Stephen anticipated sarcasm or cynicism, and was surprised when the centurion's response showed none of that.

"At first I could not be certain. But, later, I decided that He was genuine, that there was no deceit in Him."

"His ideas...did any appeal to you?"

"Yes..."

"Care to tell me which ones?"

Centurion Diodorus, who had been looking directly at Stephen, turned his attention away briefly.

"He spoke of humility and meekness, of loving our enemies. I cannot relate to that. How could I *ever* do so?"

"You, the conquering man of war."

"Yes, that, very much that."

"To think the way Jesus did, to live in the manner He exhorted, you would never be able to kill another human being."

Diodorus blushed this time.

"So young, yet so *astútus*," he observed. "You should be destined for a fate other than what the crowd had in mind."

"I will submit to whatever God wants," replied Stephen.

"Does your God want you dead?"

"I cannot say."

"Then why not be thinking of rescue rather than death?"

"How would I know?"

"So God must do it all? Self-preservation is forbidden?"

Stephen had not anticipated such questions from, after all, a Roman *soldier,* and he was unprepared, looking a bit flustered.

"I am very sorry," Diodorus told him. "I am just trying to understand. Nor am I as unsympathetic as I might sound."

The two of them continued their discussion well past midnight, and Stephen slept well afterward, his mind and his spirit challenged but, he felt, he was able to plant some seeds on receptive soil for a man who had saved his life, and, now, perhaps whose soul was on the verge of being saved.

*Late the next morning, Stephen left with only some food that Diodorus gave him, and an armed guard for some miles beyond Tarsus until it was certain that no one was waiting to do him harm....*

## Chapter Twenty-Four

Stephen was met in Jerusalem by Peter and the other apostles, and was congratulated about his accomplishments for Christ.

"You have been a light in the darkness!" the fisherman exclaimed.

Stephen was uncomfortable but tried to hide his reaction for as long as possible, feeling good to be welcomed by men with whom he felt increasing rapport.

"Tell us," Matthew asked.

"Tell you what?"

"Some of what happened to you during the past year. We had stories brought to us by travelers but it would mean so much to learn from you directly."

"I thought I might not return to be with you," Stephen admitted, his throat constricting a bit.

"Where would you have gone?" asked Thomas.

"To our heavenly Father."

As a unit they gasped.

"What is that you say?" Peter asked, his large body trembling.

"Please sit down," Stephen spoke, "for you will be startled by what I have to tell you about something so recent that..."

And so the young missionary told them as they sat outdoors in a little alcove to one side of the Via Dolorosa. All paled as the details unfolded, and some wept.

As they made preparations for the simple dinner that was to be held that evening, comprised of unleavened bread and a few chunks of fish caught earlier that day, they managed to secure the upper room where the original twelve had had their last supper with Jesus.

"The only space left in all of Jerusalem," big Peter spoke grandly. "The last night we had with Jesus, the first night with our first deacon."

"Who is that?" Stephen asked innocently.

That brought laughter from the others.

"You, dear man," Peter told you, "you have been chosen. Others will be picked in the morning. But you are the first."

"Me?" the young man exclaimed. "Surely I am not worthy."

"It is not our choice, though we agree that it is a righteous one."

Stephen was perplexed. He honestly felt unworthy, yet he did not want to offend these men whose motives were unimpeachable.

"Who decided then?" he asked, no hostility or irritation in his voice.

Peter smiled broadly.

"The risen One," he said simply.

Stephen nearly choked, and his left cheek betrayed an uncommon twitch as he said, "Jesus?"

"Yes, it was He," Peter answered immediately, the other apostles remaining silent as the dialogue between the two men continued.

"Jesus spoke to you?" Stephen repeated, thinking that perhaps he had somehow misunderstood.

"As clearly as you are doing now."

But still the young man was unable to fully comprehend this revelation, and asked, "He said that He wanted *me?*"

Peter completely understood Stephen's reaction; he had felt the same way when it had become clear that he had been chosen to lead the new church.

"Why do you act so surprised?" Peter asked, judging that Stephen needed to work out his feelings before the other men.

"I have accomplished so little."

Peter glanced from Stephen to the rest of the apostles and then back again.

"You have no idea what you have accomplished, do you?"

Stephen shook his head.

"I suppose I do not," he acknowledged.

Peter's excitement was rising as he considered the acts of this remarkable young man during just a single year.

"Hundreds of converts!" he remarked.

"You *must* be mistaken."

"I am not."

"I did *meet* many, scores of people, I imagine, but I cannot believe that all of them were converted. Some surely must have gone on their way, turning their backs on the message I brought, and the salvation that was offered."

"Some surely did," Peter agreed.

"Then how can you say hundreds were redeemed?"

"Because that is how many we were told."

Stephen did not know what to say.

"Your expression shows your surprise," Peter told him. "But you must accept as real what we were told that you had accomplished."

Stephen had fought the temptation to glory in his successes on the mission field, assuming that this was a device of Satan's to get him off-track, to take the credit for himself and not give it to his Father.

"I have tried so hard to—" he started to add.

"To be meek," Peter spoke for him, "I am sure that that was what you were going to say, Stephen."

The young man nodded.

"You also need to be aware of what you have done so that you will not be tempted in another direction," Peter said.

"What do you mean?" Stephen asked.

"So that you will not fall into despair and melancholy, which would only sap your energy, making you less effective than you *have* been."

The big fisherman's wisdom was compelling. And it tapped deeply into Stephen's soul, for the young missionary had encountered a persistent battle while he was on the road, a battle that he understood must have come from Satan but into which he found himself propelled just the same.

"You do not give yourself *enough* credit," Peter continued.

"But self is—" Stephen started to say.

"Self is a battleground, yes, I know. I have fought that battle since our Lord was crucified, and I have lost it as often as I have won. But the struggle continues, my dear young man, and it will continue for the rest of our lives."

*… for the rest of our lives.*

Stephen felt a chill then.

"Is something wrong?" asked Peter.

Stephen was reluctant to say anything to contradict a man such as this one but he knew that he had to tell the truth.

"You spoke about the rest of our lives?"

"I did," Peter confirmed.

"I shall be dead soon."

An uproar came from the rest of the apostles. None of them was able to accept his statement.

"It is true, I think," Stephen reluctantly assured them.

"You are the youngest one here," Thomas remarked with stress in his voice. "You have the most to offer."

"I do not know why, but what I told you is the conviction of my heart."

The tone of the rest of the evening changed from how it had started. There was friendliness and unity and some meaningful prayer but, also, a collective melancholy over the possibility that Stephen, so young, would be so soon taken from them.

*nd the word of God increased; and the number of the disciples multiplied in Jerusalem greatly; and a great company of the priests were obedient to the faith.*

*And Stephen, full of faith and power, did great wonders and miracles among the people....*

This was not a long period of time, but the activity was great. Stephen's record of accomplishments grew but his humility never wavered, for he would not allow self to enter into anything he did.

He healed the blind and the lame; so many were made whole that there was some speculation that he might be Jesus come back in the flesh again. But the apostles, and Stephen himself, took great pains to dampen any such idle talk.

And it was Stephen who was responsible for the "great company of priests" who became Christians, a miracle in itself.

The sheer volume of this young man's successes doomed him. Saul could no longer stand by despite the many supporters of Christianity who were now circulating throughout Jerusalem and the surrounding countryside.

He had a powerful ally.

Caiaphas.

The high priest's hatred of the followers of the One he continually called the Nazarene never dissipated, and there was talk, in hushed tones, that he had been inhabited by Satan for a long time, for no mere man, on his own, could be so loathsome, so venomous in his thoughts, his conduct.

Despite the number of priests converted, the rest joined with Caiaphas and Saul in a confrontation with Stephen that was a repeat of what had happened at Tarsus. But Stephen was even more eloquent, brushing aside the specious statements of a small army of false witnesses.

Many left that place in front of the temple, shaking their heads in awe. Others stayed but fell silent.

Sensing an impending change in the mood of the crowd, Caiaphas hastily demanded Stephen's death, his paid lackeys stirring up the people, and Stephen was dragged from the temple grounds all the way through the main gate of the city and flung on the ground outside, where dozens of duped men and not a few women picked up stones.

And so it was, first one stone, another, a third, and a fourth, again-and-again-and-again, some missing their target but others finding it.

Stephen's left shoulder was fractured, then his right arm broken.

"Lord, do not charge them with this sin," he prayed, "for they are under the control of Satan and do not know what they are doing."

That infuriated all the more a group, which became a crazed, blood-lusting mob. More stones were found. One hit his jaw, breaking it in an instant. A particularly large stone that may have been a chip off a boulder hit his hip, cracking it on impact. In seconds his skull was caved in, and still the crowd kept throwing their deadly weapons, using far more of these than David had done with Goliath, until Stephen's body had caved in along the entire length of it, and then they left, muttering derisively until they were gone.

A man named Yaddua, one of the converted priests, arrived too late to help and rushed to what was left of Stephen's barely recognizable form, kneeling down beside it.

*"My God, my God!"* he sobbed.

"You take God's name in vain," a woman nearby spoke.

"You stupid creature!" Yaddua shouted back at her. "I was praying to Him, begging for forgiveness."

"Other men threw those stones, not you," she said.

"But I did not stop them. I could have been here to save him."

Trembling, his hand splotched with blood, Yaddua closed Stephen's eyelids as gently as he knew how, and got to his feet.

Saul ... the man responsible for Stephen's death ... was muttering, "Did you see his face at the last? Did you see what he was doing? He was smiling. I *saw* him smile. How could he do that? How could he smile? He was nearly dead. How could he—?"

Yaddua interrupted him.

"That was why, Saul. Stephen was smiling because he was so close to the end. The agony he endured must have begun to fade as he looked up toward the heavenly Father. That was why you saw this precious young man smiling. He was being beckoned to where pain would no longer touch him."

"You believe him!" Saul said, losing whatever grip he might have had left on his self-control. "You should have told me."

"I did not then, Saul, I did not believe him. How could I? I am a Jew. I await the Messiah. I do not accept—"

He looked up toward the sky.

"But I wonder now," he said. "If Stephen was actually being *welcomed* by Yahweh, as he spoke, then who am I to say that everything that young man believed, everything he preached was delusion or fraud? But then how can I know the truth?"

Saul was shouting at him.

"You are so stupid as to fall prey to such delusion!" he ranted. "What he *says* he saw proves nothing. Are you so blind to this?"

Yaddua, a much bigger man, grabbed Saul's neck.

"The tragedy, you ass, is that I do not know *what* to believe," he said, his contempt for the other man so strong that it was fearsome in itself.

Tears started to flow as he added, "And I shall carry that uncertainty to my grave."

Yaddua let go and started to leave that spot. But something made him turn just in time to witness Saul, shoulders slumped, standing over the body of Stephen. It lasted only a moment; then Saul straightened himself and, head held high, he spat on that heap of crumpled, battered flesh.

"May Almighty God have mercy on you," Yaddua whispered from his great sorrow, and walked haltingly back to where he knew the apostles and other Christians had gathered to tell them it was all over. Then he slowly returned to his modest quarters where he climbed into bed, consumed by grief that was too much of a burden on his erratic heart, and closed his eyes for the last time.

## — Epilogue —

*A*nd devout men carried Stephen to his burial. And made earnest lamentation over him.

As soon as Huram ben Sira learned of his son's stoning, he hurried from his home only to find that the body had been moved.

"My son! My beloved son!" Huram spoke in shock as he saw the grisly puddles of blood.

He could stand it not one moment longer, turning away and losing whatever food he had managed to consume that day.

"My God! My God!" he cried out. "Why have You forsaken us?"

The older of the servants who had accompanied Huram knelt beside him.

"That body is nothing, sir," he said.

Anger causing the veins on his forehead to become pronounced, Huram jerked around and faced the man.

"How *dare* you speak in such a manner!" he said not much below a shout, and raised his hand to strike someone whom he had hired a quarter of a century before.

The servant cringed but added, "Sir, I loved your son, not as much as you did, nor as much as his mother, but he was precious to me though. To see what has become of him is so very hard on me, you know, sir. I remember only a vibrant young man, a fine-looking one, a young man who could have served this world so well."

"How can we survive without him?" Huram pleaded, dropping his hand. "How can you and Hannah and I ever go on, seeing this, *knowing* this?"

"That body, sir, it was but a coat, however a fine coat, yes, but it served only to surround your son's soul. The time came when his Lord removed it, and said, 'This is what you truly are, My good and faithful young man. I am proud of you. And I am taking you home with Me.'"

"Jesus was proud of Johanan?" Huram muttered.

"Could He feel less so than you?"

"All these years ... and now he is gone."

"Until that time when you and his mother shed your own coats and Jesus takes you by the hand—"

Huram winced and held up his hand.

"Stop, please," he pleaded. "I can hear no more."

As soon as he was standing, he glanced one more time at that spot, then whispered, "Good-bye, dear son, good-bye, my precious lad, you were my reason for living. I never wanted to let you go, I—"

Tears which had remained trapped inside him suddenly began in earnest, and the three of them, master and servants, stayed where they were for the better part of an hour, passersby largely ignoring them.

"Where are all the people?" Huram said after a bit. "Does no one here care apart from the three of us? What about those he witnessed to? Where are—"

Any other words choked in his throat.

"I am sure many do," his wise servant assured him, "this day and beyond. Only eternity will show how many have escaped hell because of Johanan."

If only Huram ben Sira could have heard the exultant sound of ten thousand upon ten thousand angels as that very same young man he loved stepped past the gates of a resplendent heaven into the presence of the blessed Lamb for Whom he had died only to live again.

*End*